FIREPLAY

OTHER BOOKS BY SUZANNE CHAZIN

The Fourth Angel
Flashover

G. P. PUTNAM'S SONS

New York

FIREPLAY

SUZANNE CHAZIN

This is a work of fiction. Names, characters, places, and incidents either are the product of the author's imagination or are used fictitiously, and any resemblance to actual persons, living or dead, business establishments, events, or locales is entirely coincidental.

G. P. Putnam's Sons
Publishers Since 1838
a member of
Penguin Group (USA) Inc.
375 Hudson Street
New York, NY 10014

Library of Congress Cataloging-in-Publication Data

Chazin, Suzanne.
    Fireplay / by Suzanne Chazin.
      p.   cm.
    ISBN 0-399-15053-6 (acid-free paper)
     1. Women fire fighters—Fiction.   2. New York (NY)—Fiction.
  I. Title.

PS3553.H3468F45   2003   2002037102
813'.6—dc21

Printed in the United States of America
10 9 8 7 6 5 4 3 2 1

This book is printed on acid-free paper. ♾

BOOK DESIGN BY VICTORIA KUSKOWSKI

TO TOM

MY HUSBAND, MY PARTNER, MY BEST FRIEND

ACKNOWLEDGMENTS

This book would not exist without an amazing group of people.

First and foremost, I am deeply indebted to Gene West, retired FDNY fire marshal and storyteller extraordinaire. His expertise as an arson investigator is surpassed only by his fine eye for character and detail. I keep waiting for Hollywood to steal him.

I would also like to thank microbiologist and environmental scientist Michael Blizzard for his amazingly lucid discussions of the Venturi effect—especially its impact on coffee creamer. Thanks also to retired FDNY Bureau of Fire Investigation members Denis Guardiano and Don Vastola for figuring out how to get the most mileage out of the idea.

I'm enormously grateful to my agent, Wendy Sherman, and her associate, Jessica Lichtenstein, for all their hand-holding and manuscript coaxing. I couldn't ask for a more dedicated and enthusiastic team. Finally, I'd like to extend my appreciation, as always, to my editor at Putnam, David Highfill, my paperback editor, Tom Colgan, and my publicist, Michael Barson, who have been with Georgia and me from the beginning. Thanks for going the distance.

Half of the results of a good intention are evil;
Half of the results of an evil intention are good.

MARK TWAIN

FIREPLAY

"HEY, KID, LOOSEN UP." Jack O'Dwyer gave Douglas Hanlon a chuck on the shoulder. "Your first kick-ass fire's always scary."

Hanlon stared out the window as the truck turned onto West Thirteenth Street in lower Manhattan. A brick warehouse, two stories high, stood in the shadows of an abandoned railway bridge. Gray smoke pulsed out of the seams of a cellar hatch. There were no flames, but it didn't matter. Even a firefighter as green as Hanlon knew that something big was going on below.

" 'Bout time you stopped being a white cloud," Tony Fuentes ribbed good-naturedly over the squeal of the siren. A "white cloud" was firehouse slang for a firefighter who never saw much action. In the three months since Hanlon had been assigned to Ladder Seventeen, he'd handled nothing bigger than a couple of car fires and food-on-the-stoves. "I've pissed out bigger jobs," O'Dwyer liked to say.

Fuentes gathered up his ax and halligan, a firefighter's prying tool. Hanlon slipped on the shoulder straps of his grimy yellow air tank and grabbed his six-foot hook. He could feel the throaty bray of the air horn through the soles of his boots. The truck was pulling up to what had once been a meatpacker's loading dock. Strands of silver garland wreathed the corrugated-tin awning, glowing peach in the early morning sun. Christmas decorations. On a squat, nearly windowless building where bloody carcasses used to dangle from rusty hooks. A copper sign above the front doors wafted in and out of the smoke. *Café Treize* it read.

"What the hell is Café Trees?" asked O'Dwyer.

"Not *Trees—Treize*. Rhymes with 'says,' " Fuentes corrected. "French for thirteen, as in Thirteenth Street. Don't you read the papers, man? This restaurant's so hot, *Mick Jagger* has to wait for reservations."

"Maybe he can't pronounce that French shit neither," O'Dwyer grunted. After twenty-three years of fighting fires, there wasn't much that impressed Jack O'Dwyer.

"At least it'll be empty at six-thirty in the morning," Hanlon offered.

"Kid," said O'Dwyer, running two meaty hands down his broad, grizzled face. "First thing you gotta learn about fighting fires in New York: there ain't no such thing as a bona fide vacant building."

The air brakes hissed as the truck rumbled to a halt on the cobblestoned street. In the cab, Captain Joseph Russo cut the siren. Fuentes jabbed a finger at Hanlon's bulky black turnout coat with its horizontal stripes of fluorescent yellow and reflective gray. It wasn't until he took his hand away that Hanlon realized Fuentes had snapped up the coat's top metal clasp.

"Don't know what we'll find down there, Dougie," said Fuentes with a wink. "You ain't toastin' that lily-white Irish skin on *my* shift."

Hanlon nodded. He didn't trust himself to speak. Adrenaline flowed freely through his veins and he both loved and feared the sensation. Ever since he was a little boy, sliding the pole at his dad's firehouse, he'd hungered for this sense of belonging and purpose. It was a feeling he never could quite put into words. Sometimes he tried to, late at night when he and Kerry were snuggled in bed, his arm wrapped around her widening belly, gently thumping as the baby kicked inside. He told Kerry it was excitement, which it was in a way. A heart pounding rush that made him feel like Rambo in turnout gear.

Made him love every firefighter he worked beside, even if he'd just told them to go screw themselves ten minutes earlier. The blood in his veins, the breath in his lungs never felt quite so pure, so focused, so above reproach as that moment when he and his brothers beat back the fire. He felt—for one shining moment—like a hero.

But as Doug Hanlon looked over at the billowing smoke—so thick that it blotted out the faded, hand-lettered sign on the railway trestle advertising oxtails and lamb shanks—he knew there was another emotion inside of him, too. And this one felt just as powerful as the excitement. Maybe more so. It churned his stomach, parched his throat and brought a tingling to his limbs. It made him feel small and brittle. He never admitted these feelings to Kerry or his dad; it would worry them too much. But he couldn't hide them from Jenna. The little girl seemed to grasp them with the intuitive purity that only a four-year-old can.

"Everybody's afraid of something, right, Daddy?" she asked him one night after a bad dream. "Even monsters. They're afraid of bigger monsters. Even you. You're scared sometimes, right, Daddy?"

Even you.

Fuentes and O'Dwyer jumped off the rig while the chauffeur, Dave Jansky, was still maneuvering it into position. O'Dwyer headed to the roof to break open the skylights and vent the heat. Fuentes and Captain Russo hustled over to the cellar hatch. Hanlon stumbled to a compartment on the outside of the truck and grabbed the portable fire extinguisher—the men's only source of water until the engine's hose could be put into operation. As the junior man, Hanlon had to lug the twenty-five-pound extinguisher. Already, it was slowing him down and he pushed himself to keep up. His thirty-pound air tank shifted uncomfortably on his shoulders. He remembered too late that he'd forgotten to buckle the tank's waist strap, which would have distributed some of the weight to his hips. He cursed his ineptness. He couldn't put down his tools to buckle it now.

Fuentes used his halligan to pry off the padlock on the cellar doors. Then he swung them open. A torrent of hot, dark gray smoke flew at their faces. Hanlon coughed violently, embarrassed and panicked by how easily he had succumbed to the fumes while Russo and Fuentes barely coughed at all.

"Catch your breath, son," Russo told him. The captain had a calm, clear baritone that always sounded gentle and patient, even in the worst emergencies. It's what Hanlon liked about him. Russo surveyed the basement interior from the top of the stairs, then got on his handy talkie to the chief.

"I need a firefighter from Ladder Two-Nine to stand at the base of the stairs with a flashlight," he told the chief. Then the captain turned to Fuentes. "Get the life rope."

Fuentes pulled a face. "It's a warehouse, Cap. The basement's gonna be wide open. Eighty feet, front-to-back, tops. We can search it without a life rope."

"We got a probie with us, Fuentes," said Russo. "Don't try to be a cowboy."

Fuentes fetched the rope. A firefighter from Ladder Twenty-nine hustled over with a flashlight. Captain Russo handed him the rope and told him to remain at the foot of the stairs and feed them the line. "Masks on," the captain ordered.

Hanlon put on his mask, then secured it in place with his fire retardant hood. The mask smelled of smoke and plastic. The whoosh of his breathing sounded mechanical and rigid—a good imitation of Darth Vader in *Star Wars*.

It was twelve long steps into the cellar. The light faded quickly. The heat slammed up against them with almost physical force. Sounds took on a detached quality—magnified in some cases, muffled in others. The clink of their air tanks seemed to echo off the dank walls while the crunch of their boots across wooden pallets had the soft, dreamlike quality of tree branches snapping under heavy snow.

Hanlon kept his right hand on the life rope as he followed the captain. Fifteen feet inside the cellar, the smoke billowed at them in a black mushroom cloud of gases. The darkness was absolute. Even the men's flashlights couldn't penetrate it. The beams just shone back on them like headlights in heavy fog. They moved forward, single file, Captain Russo rolling out the life rope and leading the way. Hanlon's eyes were useless, his sense of touch diminished by heavy gloves. There were so many noises—from the whoosh of his mask to the crackle of voices over the captain's handy talkie—that his ears felt overwhelmed. Yet over the din, Hanlon felt certain he could hear a far-off roar punctuated by the occasional pop and hiss of what sounded like exploding cans. Above him, he could hear a faint sound of air rushing through the ceiling.

Yet he still hadn't seen a single flame. Hanlon recalled the movies his dad used to take him to when he was little. The flames would dance about on the screen like butane torches. There was never a wisp of smoke in sight.

"Is that what fighting a fire's like?" Hanlon once asked his father.

"Not even close," the old man laughed. "You take a camera into a *real* fire, all you'll come back with is a lot of black film and an X-rated sound track."

"But what about all those flames the actors are running through?"

Hanlon could still remember his father's solemn reply: "In a real fire, Dougie, no one who runs through that much flame *ever* gets to tell about it."

They were maybe forty feet inside the warehouse basement when the heat began to rise sharply. Hanlon could clearly hear a rumbling and crackling in the distance. His fire extinguisher was useless. Two and a half gallons of water wasn't going to be any help in this situation. The excitement he'd felt earlier had turned into something that seemed to burn white-hot inside of him. His breathing accelerated. His heart pounded in his chest. Fear seized hold of his muscles and made them quake against his will. He tried to take a deep breath. He was relieved that he was nearly invisible to the captain and Fuentes. He didn't want them to see how frightened he was.

"We're turning around," Captain Russo shouted through his mask. This time, Fuentes didn't argue. They reversed direction with Fuentes now in front, and felt their way backward along the life rope. Russo yelled into his handy talkie to relay his decision to the deputy chief now on the scene. The chief brooked no argument. Hanlon felt relieved—that is, until Fuentes stopped in his tracks. Hanlon could hear him poking around.

"Cap," Fuentes shouted through his mask. "Some kind of shelving's fallen on the rope. I can't lift it off."

Hanlon and the captain crawled forward and crouched beside Fuentes. They tried to maneuver their gloves underneath the heavy brackets of shelves. Hanlon was certain he could do it. He was only twenty-six years old, and at six-feet-three and two hundred and twenty pounds, there was very little he couldn't lift. It felt good to put his twitching muscles and panicked thoughts to something concrete. But in the darkness, it was impossible even to get a handhold on the shelving, never mind move it off the rope. None of them had any idea how big the unit was or whether the rope underneath would even be intact. After several tries, the captain tapped his shoulder.

"No way we're gonna move this. We'll have to try to pick up the rope beyond the shelves."

They moved cautiously forward, trying to feel their way back to the line. Overhead in the ceiling, Hanlon noted a wisp of orange through a crack in the tiles. It wasn't air above them in those ceiling ducts. It was fire.

Fuentes stopped again. "There's a wall here, Cap. We're gonna have to turn around."

We're trapped. Hanlon's breathing, already rapid and shallow, began to accelerate. He knew he was gulping too much air. Fuentes seemed to sense his panic. He put a hand on the probie's shoulder. "Relax, Dougie," he yelled through his mask. "Slow down your breathing. You're with the best—okay? Ain't nothing gonna happen to you."

They reversed direction. They moved left, then right. Each turn brought them to another dead end. The captain felt for the speaker of his handy talkie. It was clipped to his shoulder strap. He lifted it to his face. "Mayday, mayday," he said calmly. "Ladder One-Seven. We've lost our rope. Need assistance." His voice bore no hint of fear but his words were unmistakable. A mayday was always serious business. Instantly, the chief came on the line.

"Russo—we're sending in other companies. How far inside the building are you?"

"Fifty feet maybe, Chief."

"There's a back entrance to the cellar. O'Dwyer's holding a flashlight at it. Can you see him?"

Russo tried to stand, but Hanlon could tell that he saw nothing. And now, they had a new worry. In the darkness, they could hear a high-pitched whirring sound. It was coming from the air tank on Hanlon's back. He had about six minutes of air left in his tank—maybe less, given how fast he was breathing.

"Just relax, son," shouted the captain. "We'll get you out of here."

Above them, the ceiling was cooking. Some of the acoustical tiles had already burned away, revealing sinews of orange that pulsated like a living organism. The heat radiated down on them, pressing them into a tight crouch, their bellies almost touching the floor. Hanlon crawled behind the captain, amazed that the heat could turn his hulking body into a meek and tentative shadow of its former self.

Captain Russo told the chief he couldn't see O'Dwyer. There were companies scrambling to find them. Hanlon could hear them picking their way through the debris behind them, the water from their hoses turning to steam on the falling debris. But he couldn't see any of those men. And now the captain's and Fuentes' low-air alarms began to go off, too. Hanlon didn't have to be told that they were in deep trouble. It seemed as if they were crawling between little cubicles like rats in a maze. They no longer knew whether they were nearer the front of the building or the back.

Then suddenly, Hanlon saw it—a firefighter's flashlight, cutting in and out of the smoke. The firefighter was maybe forty feet away. He couldn't see them, but they saw him. The three men crawled toward the beam. But something yanked Hanlon back by the straps of his air tank. He called out. Russo and Fuentes scrambled to his side. Fuentes examined Hanlon's back. "Shit," said Fuentes. "He's tangled up on a goddamned bicycle."

Hanlon's low-air alarm rang wildly now. Sucking on his mouthpiece felt like trying to breathe inside a plastic bag. In panic, he ripped off his mask. His nose and cheeks began to burn. His airways felt like he'd inhaled pepper. He thrashed about, coughing violently. But he was still tangled in his straps, still joined to the bicycle. Fuentes pushed his own mask on the probie's face.

"Breathe, Dougie. C'mon, man. You're gonna make it."

Hanlon took a couple of breaths until his coughing died down, then pushed the mouthpiece from his lips. "No. I can't take your mask—"

"Shut up," Fuentes told him between hacking coughs. "Just fuckin' breathe, okay?"

The flames above them were an open river now. The heat was unbearable. They would all die if they stayed here much longer. Hanlon knew that. Survival was in reach for Fuentes and Captain Russo. They were still inside because of him.

Hanlon shared Fuentes' mask while the captain tried to cut Hanlon from his tank straps.

"Got it," Captain Russo shouted. "Now run."

Run. Hanlon heard the word in a part of his brain so instinctive he didn't question it. And so he ran. Toward the flashlight beam. Toward air. Toward life. When the ceiling collapsed behind him, when the burning debris tumbled down, he kept on running until he felt the reassurance of two strong hands yank him out by his collar and drag him up the basement stairs.

"Relax, kid. I gotcha. You're gonna be okay." It was Jack O'Dwyer. His gravel-choked voice seemed to move in and out of frequency. "Where's the Cap? Where's Fuentes?" O'Dwyer asked.

The probie's blistered lips moved but no sound came out. He blinked back tears as he glanced behind him at the flaming pile of debris. And the realization hit him.

Doug Hanlon thought he'd finished running. Now with a jolt, he understood: the running had just begun.

2

". . . BATTALION TWO to dispatch. Alert EMS. We've got firefighters down. . . ."

The words stopped Fire Marshal Georgia Skeehan cold. She leaned over the department radio that straddled the space between the Chevy Caprice's two front seats. The battalion aide's voice was flat and emotionless, colored only by a heavy New York accent. He gave no specifics over the public airwaves about the nature of the injuries. Then again, when it came to firefighters, no one ever did.

Georgia flipped the light-bar switch and turned on the siren. "Can't you drive any faster?" she snapped at her partner, Randy Carter. Normally, she chided him for speeding.

Carter stepped on the accelerator and zoomed through a light on Hudson Street that had just turned red. Georgia shivered, not sure if it was the bitter early December air seeping through the Caprice's vents that brought on her chill or the sound of those bleak words across the airwaves. Carter's lean, dark face seemed to pale at the wheel. She could tell he was thinking the same thing: *Not again. Dear God, not so soon.*

"I wish I'd stayed on vacation," Georgia mumbled, tossing an empty Styrofoam coffee cup in back. Not that it was much of a vacation. The weather stank. Richie was in school. Mac couldn't finagle any time off. The most Georgia had managed was a long weekend out in Montauk, on the eastern tip of Long Island, but it had rained most of the time they were there. Richie ended up glued to his GameBoy. Georgia ended up glued to a VCR, watching movies she'd had the good sense not to pay nine bucks for when they were first released.

Carter's vacation, on the other hand, appeared to have been quite good. Three weeks in sunny Florida had caused his skin to take on a rich chocolate color. His face had filled out from good food and regular sleep. And, up until the radio transmission a few minutes earlier, he'd begun to smile again. He hadn't done much of that lately. No one had.

"A couple of our guys probably took too much smoke—that's all," said Carter, laying on his soft southern drawl the way he always did in stressful situations. "I reckon we're just imagining the worst. Like the time Sal Giordano forgot to take his car off the Staten Island Ferry."

Georgia allowed a faint smile at the memory of Giordano lumbering into Manhattan base one evening while the Coast Guard was out dredging the waters for his body. Everyone worried that he'd slipped or jumped. For months after that, Giordano couldn't come to work without finding tuna fish on his desk or in his drawers. Sometimes the marshals were even nice enough to leave it in the can.

The battalion aide's voice came over the radio again, jarring Georgia back to the present. "Battalion Two to dispatch, I need the mixer off."

Mixer off meant the conversation would not be broadcast over the airwaves. It was private—between the chief and the dispatcher—and private conversations were always bad news. A cold wad of bile gathered in Georgia's stomach.

"It feels like my father all over again," she said softly.

"Maybe it's not as bad as all that," said Carter, but he took the corner sharply. The Caprice's wheels squealed on the pavement.

"One hell of a Christmas present for the family if it is," said Georgia.

"Your dad died in the autumn, right?"

"October twenty-fifth," said Georgia. "The kid who set the fire didn't even miss Halloween."

"They ever punish him?"

"I don't know. Counseling, I guess. He was only six at the time—too young to charge. I don't think he even spoke English."

Carter turned onto a wide, V-shaped swath of cobblestoned streets that formed the southeastern end of the meatpacking district. In a storefront window once used as a butcher's shop, several garishly bright oil colors competed for space. Carter took them in and shook his head.

"I remember when there was nothing down here but gay bars, cross-dressing prostitutes and guys in bloody aprons with meat cleavers. Some of my best informants came from this neighborhood."

"Things sure have changed," said Georgia, taking in two art galleries, a dance club and a couple of upscale restaurants all within a block of one another. The graffiti on the rolldown security gates had largely disappeared, as had the piles of trash and rusted oil drums that the homeless once used for outdoor fires.

They turned onto West Thirteenth Street. Fire trucks, ambulances and police cruisers were lined up beside a two-story red brick warehouse. Smoke the color of spoiled milk rose from an open cellar hatch. The fire was out, and it didn't look like it had extended beyond the basement. Silver garlands fluttered from a canopy above a former loading dock, and the mullioned window that had replaced a garage door still sported sheer white curtains.

"Café Treize," Carter mumbled, reading the sign. "This place used to be Weingarten's Wholesale Meats. And then it was a gay bar called the Meat Market."

"It's a really hot French restaurant now," said Georgia. "Madonna eats here. So does Julia Roberts. I read it in *People* magazine."

Carter gave Georgia a bored look. Celebrity talk never impressed him.

"They should've been here when it was a gay bar," he said. "Down in the basement, they used to have all these little cubicles where the guys used to, um . . ." Carter shrugged and looked away, embarrassed. At fifty-nine, he was old enough to be Georgia's father. Still, she loved to break his chops.

"And how would *you* know about that?" she teased.

"I hear stories," he said indignantly. "Y'all didn't have to ever go down there to know about it. The Meat Market's owner secretly wired up all these cameras in the cubicles. Sleazeball used to sell the videos to private collectors."

Carter parked the car down the street from the building so as not to block the rescue vehicles. A cold wind whipped off the choppy waters of the Hudson River as they got out of the car. They grabbed their turnout coats, helmets and toolbox from the trunk.

"How bad do you think it is?" Georgia asked. Carter didn't answer, but all the Florida sunshine had left his face. Georgia followed his line of vision to a dark blue van marked *Medical Examiner.* Somebody was dead, and judging from the somber looks on firefighters' faces, Georgia had a sinking feeling it was one of their own.

They found the deputy chief at the back of the warehouse, in an alleyway littered with broken bottles that glittered in the sharp morning sun. Broward was his name. He'd been a high-ranking chief longer than Georgia had been on the job. He gave them the faintest nod of his head as they walked over. He knew they had a job to do, but his men were hurting and that was all he cared about right now. Georgia would have felt the same way.

"Two of our guys from Ladder Seventeen didn't make it," he said through lips that barely moved. He squinted down a set of concrete steps to the warehouse's back door. "The probie got out. He's being treated by EMS for minor burns and smoke inhalation."

"What happened?" asked Georgia. She and Carter took turns leading investigations. This fire was hers. *Oh, joy.*

"Rubbish fire in the basement," said Broward. "Captain and two firefighters got separated from their life rope and couldn't find their way out. The basement's heavily partitioned. No one could find them."

"Any evidence of a break-in?" asked Georgia.

"The back door had been forced before we got here. The lock was broken."

Georgia frowned in the direction of the cellar. There was still a lot of smoke. She could only see a short way, but even in that distance, she noted the unmistakable oxidized heads of sprinklers in the ceiling.

"The sprinklers weren't working?"

"We had a busted water main in the neighborhood two weeks ago," grunted Broward. "City turned the water off. The landlord may never have turned the sprinkler line back on." The chief shook his head in disgust. He knew as well as Georgia did that a working sprinkler probably would have been able to put out that fire in minutes.

"Surely there was a valve in the basement somewhere," said Georgia. "The landlord would've known the sprinkler wasn't operational."

Broward gave Georgia an irritated look. Carter stepped in.

"A lot of these owners, they're afraid that the water damage from a nuisance fire will end up being more expensive to repair than the fire itself, so if the city forgets to tell them to turn their sprinkler system back on, they don't argue."

Broward nodded. "Owner probably figured that the most he'd lose would be a few crates of vegetables." He shook his head sadly. "Instead, we lost two of our finest men."

The chief's words sounded more resigned than enraged. It was the way all the men were now—even the ones who hadn't experienced that terrible September day. They had all borne too much for too long.

"The men who died," said Georgia. "Are they still in the basement?"

"I've got companies digging them out."

Georgia peered down the open basement door into the dim, soggy interior. The smoke had cleared. Firefighters were everywhere. They all had a downcast tilt to their eyes and a grayness to their faces. No one was smoking or conversing. An aide came over to ask the chief a question and he excused himself. Georgia went to descend the stairs. Carter put a hand on her shoulder.

"Go easy, Skeehan," he warned her. "Give the men space, okay? Emotions are running high down there. You know as well as I do that no one here gives a hoot and a holler about our investigation. Far as they're concerned, nothing we do is gonna bring their brothers back."

3

THEY LOOKED LIKE they were sleeping. True, their faces were slightly swollen from the heat and black with soot. The backs of their turnout coats had a ragged coarseness to them from the burning debris. But otherwise, Captain Joseph Russo and Firefighter Tony Fuentes looked like they should have been able to get up, dust off their gear and walk out of the basement of the Café Treize. There was still the glow of life in those grimy, handsome faces, a glow that made it impossible to comprehend that they would never go home to their families again. It was a hell of a piece of news to have to deliver three weeks before Christmas.

Georgia heard some of the firefighters speak about Russo and Fuentes in traded whispers as they gently scooped debris off them. Both were husbands and fathers. Both were veterans of the Gulf War. Russo's son had just received a football scholarship to Notre Dame. Fuentes' oldest daughter was dancing in a school production of *The Nutcracker* this weekend. His wife was expecting their fourth child in May. He had three girls. He had been hoping for a boy.

Georgia kept her distance, as Carter had cautioned. Like every fire marshal in New York City, she had once been a firefighter. But the dividing line between investigator and rescuer was keenly felt at a time like this, especially when the investigator was a woman.

The men had nearly finished unearthing Russo and Fuentes when Carter exchanged nods with a hulking figure in a helmet and turnout coat. He had a thick mustache and a broad, grizzled face smeared with grime. The dirty white leather patch on the front of his black helmet had a "17" on it. He was either the truck's roof man or the rig's chauffeur.

"O'Dwyer," Carter mumbled softly, inching toward him. "How y'all holding up?"

"Three hundred and forty-three men die in one fucking day," said the old veteran, "and you think you can't grieve for two more. But if it's one man or a hundred—a year or ten years later—it feels just the same."

"I know," said Carter. They shared a look that Georgia had seen before in firefighters who had lived through the day the World Trade Towers collapsed. No matter how much time went by, some part of them could never heal.

O'Dwyer ran a hand down his face and tried to shrug off the memory. "Anyway, it's not me I'm worried about," he said. "It's the kid—the probie."

"Where is he?" Georgia asked, joining the conversation carefully. She was heartened when O'Dwyer made eye contact with her. Carter, with thirty-one years in the FDNY, knew everyone on this job. He could go places that Georgia, a woman and a relative rookie with only eight years in the fire department, could not.

"With EMS," O'Dwyer told her. Then he leaned in close and lowered his voice. "Already there's a chill in the air, if you know what I'm sayin'."

Georgia frowned. "Why is that?"

"It was the kid's first real fire. Russo and Fuentes were pros. There's a feeling that maybe the kid . . . maybe he held 'em back." O'Dwyer massaged the back of his bull neck. His eyes locked on Carter's. Georgia sensed that the old veteran might have worked with Carter when he was a firefighter. He trusted Carter not to traumatize the young firefighter further.

"We'll go easy on him, Jack," Carter promised.

"What's his name?" asked Georgia.

"Hanlon. Douglas Hanlon. His father's a fire captain in Queens."

"Seamus." Georgia whispered the name. The lining of her gut felt like someone had just carved a set of initials in it. The last shred of Florida sunshine left Randy Carter's face.

"You know him?" asked O'Dwyer, bouncing a look from Georgia to Carter.

"A family friend," Georgia replied. She wished she knew Captain Seamus Hanlon less well—wished she hadn't walked around his empty kitchen only this past summer, and felt the palpable loneliness of a man who had lost his wife and his best friend, Jimmy Gallagher, in the space of a year. She was glad he hadn't lost his son as well, though it was too soon to know whether the young man who came out of that building would ever be the same as the young man who went into it.

The firefighters were getting ready to carry their brothers out. Carter touched O'Dwyer's sleeve.

"Do me a favor, Jack? Tell them we just need to take a quick look at Russo and Fuentes before you move 'em."

"No pictures," O'Dwyer growled. Georgia looked at Carter. They always took pictures of fire victims. It was an essential part of reconstructing an arson scene. But Carter simply nodded. This was not the time to push.

"No pictures, Jack. Of course," he said.

Georgia and Carter didn't speak again until Russo and Fuentes had been carried out of the basement. They were by themselves in a storage cubicle ten feet from the back door, surrounded by charred shelves and exploded canned goods. They'd been in about a dozen identical cubicles in the space of ten minutes. Café Treize's owner had obviously never taken down the partitions from the days when the warehouse was a gay bar. In the smoke and heat, those flimsy sheetrock dividers had become a fatal maze of dead ends.

"Did you notice that neither Russo nor Fuentes was wearing his mask?" asked Georgia.

Carter shined his flashlight at a soggy, blackened piece of cardboard on the concrete floor. It was the bottom of a carton of paper towels.

"Their air tanks were empty," said Carter. "Burning debris blocked their escape. They had a choice: Die from the heat and flames banking down on them, or take a couple of quick breaths of smoke and get it over with. I'd have done the same thing."

Georgia moved her flashlight beam up the charred paneling and across the concrete subflooring from the main floor above. The dropped ceiling that hid the ductwork had burned away entirely.

"This place was like a pizza oven," said Carter. "Concrete on the bottom. Concrete on top. Brick walls all around. You won't see any fire damage upstairs. The concrete contained it. But it killed our brothers. Baked them alive."

Georgia peered into the ductwork. "There's a lot of wiring up there for a warehouse basement. Maybe a circuit got overloaded."

Carter examined the wires. They were burned at multiple points along a continuous cable, rather than in one spot. "The blowouts are more consistent with fire damage," he said. "I don't think an electrical overload was the cause of the fire."

Georgia studied the burned cardboard box of paper towels. She shone her flashlight on the concrete ceiling directly above. A section of the ceiling about the size of a manhole cover had turned flaky and white—a condition known as "spalling," which occurs at prolonged high temperatures. "The fire seems to have been at its most intense in this room," said Georgia. "In fact, right above this box of paper towels."

Carter took in the box, then slammed a gloved hand against the wall. "Dang," he said. "This wasn't supposed to happen."

"These things never are." Georgia thought he was talking about Russo and Fuentes.

"No," he said. "I mean literally. Look at this place. There's nothing in this room that would spontaneously ignite. No shorted-out wires. No solvents. No evidence of a smoking accident. The back door was forced. Everything points to an arson."

"I agree," said Georgia.

"Yeah, but you saw those cubicles back there, Skeehan. There were cleaning solvents and cooking oils and linens stacked a foot high. Anybody looking to torch this place had his pick of highly combustible materials not ten feet from where we're standing. Yet he didn't use it—why?"

" 'Cause this was fast," said Georgia. "Force the back door, drop a match in the paper towels and leave."

"But if the sprinklers had been working, what would that have accomplished? Heck, the fire would've probably gone out before it had even finished consuming the box of paper towels."

Georgia nodded. "Then the torch knew the sprinklers had been shut down. It's an inside job."

"Yeah, but if it *was* an inside job, then the torch also would have known about the solvents ten feet in. He could've taken the whole place out with just a few more minutes of effort."

"You think maybe he just wanted to send a message?" asked Georgia.

"It makes sense," said Carter. "The torch forces his way in, drops a match into the paper towels, then splits," said Carter. "Only he doesn't know the sprinklers have been shut down."

"And a misdemeanor nuisance fire turns into a double homicide," said Georgia. "The press is going to be all over this one. We've got to get to Seamus's son before those vultures do."

THEY FOUND DOUG HANLON in a corner of the back alley. He looked impossibly young, even with the blisters and soot that marked his sad-eyed face. For most of the last half hour, Jack O'Dwyer had been hovering over him protectively, but he'd been called away to help on the roof, so Hanlon was alone. Georgia caught some of the fire-fighters giving him quick, curious glances. Innocent looks, most likely. But she knew how accusatory they must've felt to Doug Hanlon. God, how she knew.

"I think you should handle this one alone," said Carter.

"You do, huh?" Her tone was defensive. Carter stumbled about for a reply.

"You know his dad better than I do. . . . And . . . you're a woman. Hanlon will be more likely to open up to you than to me. If I'm there, he might feel like we're ganging up on him."

Georgia gave Carter a long, penetrating stare. "Those aren't the only reasons you want me to talk to him."

His face betrayed him. "I think maybe . . . you sort of know what he's going through," he said softly. "You can talk to him. Tell him what it's like—"

"This is a police interview, Randy. Not a therapy session."

Carter placed a hand on her arm. "Okay. Calm down. Forget I asked. Just get his statement, okay?"

"Where will you be?"

"Trying to get hold of Café Treize's owner." Carter gave her a reassuring nod. "Go easy on him, all right? Yourself, too."

They split up and Georgia walked over to the young firefighter. He was a big man, well built, with soft, pale gray eyes that seemed too young to be set in such a grief-stricken face. His nose and cheeks were red and speckled with heat blisters—second-degree burns. The burns had to be painful, but he seemed unaware of them.

"Doug?" Georgia forced a smile and extended a hand.

He blinked at her as if she'd woken him up from a deep sleep. His grasp was tentative. He didn't seem to want anyone to touch him.

"I'm Georgia Skeehan. I'm a fire marshal. I know your dad, Seamus. My dad used to serve in the same firehouse in Queens where your dad's a captain." Connections were important in the FDNY. To a firefighter, everyone was either family or an outsider. Georgia wanted to offer up as many connections as she could going in.

"Sure," he muttered in a way that suggested he hadn't really heard.

"You have some facial burns. Do you want to go to the hospital for treatment?"

"No. I'm fine."

"I need to ask you what happened in the basement, Doug. Can you tell me what went on down there?"

He turned away from her and hung his head. Georgia thought he was trying to compose his thoughts. But then she saw him put a hand up to his eyes. His shoulders started to quake. Georgia's stomach dropped into her shoes. She'd had people break down on her before in interviews. But she'd never had to do this with a firefighter. She loathed herself for having to put him through this.

"Doug," she said softly.

He wiped his nose along the sleeve of his turnout coat. What came out was black. He'd taken quite a feed of smoke down there. It was a wonder any of them came back alive. She sensed the other firefighters eavesdropping. She shot them murderous looks. They dropped their gazes.

"Doug," she said again. The site was crawling with firefighters—inside *and* outside the building. She couldn't get him into her department car, either. That would've meant walking the gauntlet of reporters in the street. The most private place they were going to find to talk was a corner of the alley. She beckoned him there now. They leaned against a rusted chain-link fence, surrounded by crushed cigarette packs and empty condom wrappers. He kicked a broken bottle at his feet to avoid her scrutiny. Green glass sparkled in the sun. The bright cold morning mocked their mood.

"All you have to do is tell me what happened down there as honestly and thoroughly as you can," Georgia coaxed. "This isn't an interrogation. No one's blaming you."

He turned away from her and grabbed the chain-link fence. He seemed too ashamed even to meet her gaze. Georgia realized in an instant why: the word "blame." She had given voice to his deepest fear. Georgia opened her mouth to try to tell him she understood, but nothing came out. She could not comfort him. After all this time, she still couldn't comfort herself.

"I don't know what happened," Hanlon said softly into the fence. His voice was raspy from the smoke. "We went in with the life rope, got turned around and couldn't find our way out."

Georgia eased a notebook from the pocket of her turnout coat. "Tell me what you remember from the moment you got down there until the time you came out."

In a hoarse and halting voice, Hanlon poured out his twenty-two minutes of hell in the cellar of Café Treize. Georgia interrupted only to prompt him to the next memory. But she noticed there was one thing he omitted.

"It's okay, you know, that you were sharing masks," she told him.

Hanlon stared at her with bloodshot eyes, but said nothing.

"Look, Doug, I understand. You ran out of air. You had no choice."

"But the rules," Hanlon stammered. "The rules say you're not supposed to—"

"The rules were written by a bunch of pencil-pushing staff chiefs sitting on their fat asses down at headquarters, Doug. You're a probie, for chrissakes. You'd never gotten turned around in smoke like that before. You were breathing hard, you used up your air and somebody gave you some of theirs." She nodded to his face. "You didn't do anything wrong. It's just that—I can see the burns on your face and I need to know."

Hanlon touched his face. He was in such deep shock, he probably didn't even feel them. He gave her a defeated nod.

"I panicked," he said softly. "And Tony, he . . . he gave me his mask. I told him he wasn't supposed to do that." Hanlon shook his head. "Tony and the Cap . . . they saved my life. That should've been *me* down there. Not them."

"It's not your fault," Georgia tried to reassure him. "It's the nature of firefighting. You never know what fate is going to bring you."

Two firefighters hefted a black body bag from the basement. Everyone stood at attention. A shudder traveled through Hanlon's large frame and he hung his head.

"Yeah, well, fate took the wrong guy."

Georgia waited until O'Dwyer returned to stay with him before she went to find Carter. She didn't see Randy outside, so she entered the restaurant through a fire exit that had been propped open. The cement ceiling of the basement that had baked Russo and Fuentes had also stopped the fire from spreading upward. The result, Georgia realized, was that the restaurant looked remarkably intact. The exposed brick walls showed no signs of soot damage, nor did the modern oil paintings that hung on them. There was no oily residue on the colorful hand-blown glass vases or the white linens on the tables. About the only damage Georgia could see was some broken glass scattered across the wide-board oak floors. It came from the skylights that the firefighters had broken on the roof two stories above.

With a guilty glance, Georgia picked up a menu at the maître d's station and scanned the offerings, all in French, though, thankfully, there were descriptions following each dish. This being a former beef wholesaler, they were heavy on French-style meat selections: sweetbreads and calf's liver and pâtés. But there were also dishes Georgia wouldn't have minded trying: andouille sausage with dried cherries, truffles and sage, escargot in a garlic cream sauce with vermouth, steak tartare on Parmesan-crusted bread with caramelized onions and capers. Georgia thought the prices were high, but not as bad as she'd expected. Then she realized with a jolt that she was reading off the appetizers.

She put the menu down and walked up the open-air metal staircase to the second floor. She followed the sound of voices to a thick oak door that was heavily scarred—probably one of the original doors in the building. She could hear two men's voices behind the door. One was Carter's. The other belonged to a man with a nasal, singsong way of speaking. He sounded agitated.

"I'm telling you, officer—"

"Marshal," Carter corrected.

"Whatever," said the man. "The facts are the same. Business couldn't be better. I'm booked solid for the next five months. Overbooked, as a matter of fact. I don't know how I'm going to find tables for all these people. I've got no enemies. You should be out canvassing the neighborhood for the crazy person who fell asleep in my doorway and almost cost me my business. That's who you should be looking for."

Georgia knocked and called out to Carter. He opened the door to a plush office done in sleek black leather. The walls were lined with photographs of celebrities wrapping their arms around a short, balding man with hungry eyes and a pinched smile. That man was in a chair behind a messy desk, rocking back and forth nervously and checking his watch. He wore dark gray slacks and a thick knit sweater with a geometric design on the front. Casual clothes, but they looked expensive. He narrowed his gaze at Georgia as she walked in, but made no move to shake her hand, so she didn't offer it.

"Barry Glickstein, this is Fire Marshal Georgia Skeehan," said Carter. "Georgia, Mr. Glickstein is the owner of Café Treize."

Glickstein held his hands parallel to his face and waved them back and forth rapidly in a slicing motion. Georgia had the sense he used this same gesture on recalcitrant employees and suppliers.

"I'm trying to tell your partner here that I don't have any enemies. This fire . . . it's some lunatic homeless person's doing. I've got the personal cell phone numbers of nearly every A-list celebrity in Manhattan. Does that sound like a man with enemies to you?"

"I'm asking Mr. Glickstein to open his books and show us his profit margin. I just want to see if his profits are in line with our perceptions."

"You think I'd burn my own restaurant? Kill the goose that lays the golden eggs? You're the crazy one, detective—"

"Marshal," Carter said through clenched teeth.

"Same thing." Glickstein shrugged. He turned to Georgia. He would play one off the other if he had to. "Darling, you look like a smart girl to me. Look around this place. It's a gold mine. Why would I burn it? I can fix that basement up in a matter of days. I won't even be out of commission for more than a day or two. Does that sound like someone trying to get out from under a business to you?"

"Then open your books, Mr. Glickstein," said Georgia.

"Not without a court order."

"Fair enough." Georgia rose from her chair.

"Where are you going?" Glickstein demanded.

"I have subpoena forms in the car. You want a court order, it can be arranged. Right here. Right now."

"Whoa." Glickstein put his palms on his desk. "You can do that?"

"We're fire marshals, Mr. Glickstein, not police detectives. We don't have to get a judge's permission to subpoena your documents. We have the power to do that ourselves." Georgia neglected to mention that Glickstein had a forty-eight-hour grace period to produce those records—even with her subpoena. She was banking on panic over reason. Cops do it all the time.

"Sweetheart, what are you doing to me? I'm no criminal. I'm a law-abiding citizen. Last year, I gave five thousand dollars to the Firefighters' Widows and Orphans Fund."

Carter's handy talkie began to crackle. It was Chief Broward's aide. "Is the owner in there with you?" the aide asked Carter.

"Affirmative," said Carter in a cool, collected voice. Somehow he always managed to remain calm, even in the most trying situations. "Does the chief need him?"

"Negative," said the aide. "But we've got an angry liquor supplier out here. The cops are restraining him now. He says Glickstein owes him eighty-five grand on his account, it's overdue and he's afraid that with the fire, he'll try to skip."

Glickstein got up from his chair, cursed and paced the floor. Carter bit back a smile.

"Tell him to stay cool," said Carter. "We'll be out in a moment."

He slipped the handy talkie back onto his duty holster, and they both stared at Barry Glickstein like two jackals moving in for the kill. "Care to explain that one?" asked Carter.

"It's not eighty-five thousand," said Glickstein. "It's sixty-eight thousand—"

"It's a lot of money," said Georgia. "You're booked solid for months, but you can't pay your liquor bill? I saw your menu, Mr. Glickstein. A dinner for two people without alcohol must run three hundred easily here. What's going on?"

"Nothing's going on. You don't think this happens twenty times a day in New York? I've got hundreds of suppliers, and they're always kvetching about not getting paid. *Always.* Whether I pay them or not."

Glickstein turned on his telephone answering machine. The red light was flashing. He had messages on his tape. "You don't believe me? Listen up."

He pushed Play. An oily voice came on.

Hey . . . Barry. It's Jeff. Listen, Mariah's absolutely got to have a table for eight this Saturday. Do me this favor, amigo, okay? Ciao, baby. I owe you . . .

"Mariah Carey's publicist," said Glickstein, rolling his eyes. "Man thinks I'm a table fairy. What does he want me to do? Book her on the ceiling?" There was a beep, then the next message started.

Barry . . . I'm sending Fred down today. Pay something on that cleaning bill. Five Gs . . . ten. You're going to get a lot of people very pissed off if Fred comes back empty-handed.

Georgia frowned. "Who's Fred?"

"He's with my linen-cleaning service," Glickstein explained. "It's like I told you, darling. Everybody wants money."

"Seems like you owe a lot of people a lot of money," said Carter.

"And they don't want me out of business because then they don't get paid," Glickstein shot back. "None of these jokers set any fires."

There was a pause on the next message, as if the caller wanted an uncomfortable silence before he spoke.

Barry, my boy . . . You should really clear out that rear stockroom, ya know? All those paper towels and shit—they're sooo combustible . . . I'd really hate to see a fire take down my favorite watering hole. . . .

Glickstein reached out to erase the message, but Carter was faster. He grabbed Glickstein's hand in midair. "Erase that sucker, and I'll lock you up right now for tampering with evidence." Glickstein withdrew his hand. The message continued.

So . . . how 'bout I come by for the money you owe me Friday night? Just put me in the reservation book—say eight-thirty? Freezer's the name, but you knew that already, didn't you?

There were no more messages. Carter popped the tape out of the answering machine. "We'll take this." He paused. "Unless you feel the *need* for a formal subpoena."

"No," said Glickstein sullenly. "Just take it. You're going to anyway."

"Who's Freezer?" Georgia asked Glickstein.

"How should I know?" said Glickstein. "I didn't even listen to that message until just now."

Carter leaned forward and held Glickstein's gaze. "How much is

McLaughlin shaking you down for?" Glickstein said nothing, so he continued. "That's why you can't meet your bills no matter how much y'all rake in, isn't it? Big Mike's putting the squeeze on you."

Glickstein dropped his head into his hands. He was sweating across his bald spot.

"Come on, Glickstein," said Carter. "I used to work this neighborhood back when men in pink hot pants and blond wigs walked these streets. Freezer's been in this racket so long, he could collect a pension by now."

"I want to talk to my attorney." Glickstein reached for the phone.

Carter turned to Georgia. "What do you think, Marshal? Should we read him his rights?"

Georgia could see the bluff in Carter's eyes, but Glickstein couldn't. She pulled a set of handcuffs off her duty holster and jingled them. "You have the right to remain silent—" she began. Glickstein cut her off.

"You can't take me out of here in handcuffs," he pleaded.

Georgia pretended not to hear as she discussed the evidence with Carter. "The grand jury case should be a piece of cake," she said. "We've got a taped confession from a man who set a fire that killed two firefighters. And he's calling Mr. Glickstein for money. Sounds like an arson-for-profit scheme to me." She turned to Glickstein. "You'll be a real hero to your A-list friends now when they find out you've been charged with the murders of two of New York's Bravest. They're going to *love* you."

"Please," he begged. "I had nothing to do with this fire. Why would I burn my own restaurant? It was McLaughlin. Michael McLaughlin. He did it because I'm behind in my payments." Glickstein turned to Carter. "You *know* Freezer. You know how ruthless he can be. This guy . . . when I owned my burger joint uptown? He chopped the pinky finger off one of my suppliers because the man was two weeks late with the money he owed."

Glickstein couldn't read Carter's passive expression, so he turned to Georgia. "I was scared. Wouldn't you be? I tried to make the payments, I admit it. But I'm no murderer."

"Seems to me, Mr. Glickstein, it's either him or you," said Georgia. "You talk. You walk. What's it gonna be?"

"All right, all right." Glickstein sighed. "I'll give you a formal statement. Whatever you want to know. But you're the fools if you think anyone can put the finger on Mike McLaughlin. On the streets, they say Freezer is Teflon-coated. Nothing sticks to him."

"It will this time," said Georgia.

5

"SO, WHO'S MICHAEL MCLAUGHLIN?" Georgia asked Carter. They were back in their car, heading north on the West Side Drive. The Hudson River rippled with the stark, clear light of a bright winter day as barges and tugboats plowed the waters. Carter was wearing a small, satisfied grin that hadn't left his face since pocketing the answering machine tape from Barry Glickstein's office.

"McLaughlin's Teflon, all right," said Carter. "But this time, he's stepped in it. I'll bet he had no idea the sprinklers at Café Treize had been turned off. If we get to him quickly, he may not realize what's happened. Once he knows, he'll lawyer up—maybe split town."

"You sound like you know a lot about him," said Georgia.

"He's an extortionist from way back," said Carter. "He used to run with the Westies. Y'all remember the Westies, don't you?"

"The Irish street gang based in Hell's Kitchen," said Georgia.

"*Based* in Hell's Kitchen, yes. But they operated all over the city. They were subcontractors—they offered muscle to just about anybody who was paying—the Mafia, the Colombians, the Tong down in Chinatown. And they were ruthless. You found an abandoned refrigerator in Hell's Kitchen, the contents were always the same: body parts, courtesy of Big Mike. That's why they call him Freezer. That's where his victims always ended up."

"But I thought the Westies were finished," said Georgia. "Aren't most of those guys dead or in prison?"

"Uh-huh," said Carter. "I put a couple of them there myself—ruthless brutes, all of 'em. But Freezer was different. Smarter. Calmer. More polished. The only time he ever did in the joint was for a nickel-and-dime robbery when he was, maybe, nineteen. Man was like a polecat in the woods. You could smell him, but you couldn't catch him."

Georgia smiled. The guys at Manhattan base were always razzing Carter for his down-home expressions. Georgia thought they were charming, and a whole lot more creative than the steady diet of four-letter words she heard the rest of the time.

"Do you know where to find him?"

"I know where to look," said Carter. "These Irish guys never go far from the neighborhood."

Traffic crawled north along the West Side Drive as it followed the contours of the Hudson River. At West Eighteenth Street, Georgia noticed a group of about fifty protesters in front of a chain-link fence by one of the piers. They were holding up posters with skulls and crossbones on them. *Stop the Dalcor Plant* read one poster. Another read *Butadiene will kill our children*. Georgia squinted past them to a spanking new two-story glass building with some kind of storage tank in front.

"I haven't been following the papers on this one," she admitted. "What are they protesting? The building looks a hell of a lot better than that abandoned marine terminal it replaced."

"It's not the building, it's what's in it," said Carter. "Dalcor is a big chemical manufacturer. The city paid a lot of money to lure them here. With all that's happened in New York over the past few years, a lot of businesses have pulled out—especially the last of the firms that relied on unskilled labor. Dalcor agreed to come in and set up a manufacturing plant."

"I would think people would be in favor of jobs and some development on the waterfront."

"Problem is," said Carter, "Dalcor uses some pretty toxic chemicals. The one those posters are referring to, butadiene, is not only flammable, it's supposed to be cancerous. This stuff gets into the air or the water, it could stick around for a long time."

Georgia looked around at the neighborhood. A new fifteen-story apartment building had just gone up across the street. Down the block, she could see the long, flat roof of a three-story public elementary school.

"I wouldn't want this so close to my home or Richie's school, either," said Georgia. "But I guess these people don't have a choice. It's here now."

Carter nodded to the protesters. "I guess no one told them the battle's over."

At Fiftieth Street, Carter turned off the West Side Drive into an area of mid-Manhattan formally known as "Clinton," but better known as "Hell's Kitchen." Though Times Square, to the southeast, had undergone a major facelift over the last decade, Hell's Kitchen was still primarily a drab stretch of tenements, laundromats, garages and convenience stores. Georgia had gotten to know the neighborhood well over the past eight months.

"Mac lives two blocks north of here," she said brightly.

"It's a dump," said Carter. Georgia gave him a sharp look but he didn't back down. "I worked 'round here when our old fire marshal's base was in the neighborhood. Believe me, I know. It's a dump."

"Would you like Mac any better if he lived on Park Avenue?"

"Did I say anything about Mac?" he shot back. "I'm talking about the neighborhood."

Georgia gave him a sour look and stared out the window. Though Carter never came right out and said it, he didn't like Supervising Fire Marshal Mac Marenko—and he especially didn't like him dating Georgia. Most days, she consoled herself that Carter's fatherly disapproval of Mac was sort of touching, given that her own father had never lived to see her to womanhood. But not today. Today, he was hitting a little too close to the bone.

"The man's technically our boss," Carter continued. "He earns maybe twenty grand more than we do a year. He could do better."

"Mac's got child support to pay," said Georgia. "And a mortgage on Long Island. He's working two jobs right now just to have a little spare cash for the holidays."

"Exactly," said Carter. He turned his face from the wheel and looked at her. "So where do you figure into all of this?"

Georgia hunkered down in her seat without looking at him. "I figure in just fine."

Carter turned onto Ninth Avenue and parked in front of a narrow, three-story building with a fire escape running down the front and a bar named *Kelly's* on the first floor. There was a shamrock between the *y* and the *s* instead of an apostrophe. The windows were dark and the door looked scuffed and unwelcoming. Georgia put a hand on Carter's arm.

"Randy, maybe you shouldn't go in there. I mean, I know you worked in the area, but these places—they're very rough and shanty Irish, and you're . . . well . . ."

He smiled. "I'm black. And they don't take to black folk—is that what you're saying?"

"Yeah."

"Relax, girl. Bobby and I go way back. I used to buy lunch here every day when I worked around the corner. I even broke up a fight in here once." He nodded to the windows. "I know it doesn't look like much, but they've got the best corned beef and cabbage in the city. And talk about cheap? I think the whole plate with coffee and home fries set me back maybe three-fifty."

It was only ten-thirty in the morning, and from the looks of it, Kelly's hadn't yet officially opened up. Even inside, the place wasn't much to look at: a faded oak bar, a few booths with ripped red PVC cushions, an aging pool table in the back long overdue to be refelted. On the wall over the bar were black-and-white photos of men with prizefighters' faces—all broken noses and scars. Some of the pictures had silver frames. Most had black.

"Those guys don't look like celebrities," said Georgia.

"They're celebrities, all right—inside the neighborhood," said Carter. "All those guys are Westies. The ones in the black frames are dead."

An enormous woman in a dirty white apron came out of the kitchen. Her hard, lined face broke into a smile when she saw Carter.

"I don't believe my eyes," she said in a thick Irish brogue. When she smiled, one of her front teeth gleamed with gold. "They can't kill us old-timers off, can they, Carter? We just keep going till the good Lord tell us it's time."

"Ah, maybe you, Bobby, but I'm getting a creak in these old bones."

Georgia shot Carter a dirty look. She didn't like it when he talked about retiring, however obliquely.

"This here's Roberta Kelly," said Carter. "Best cook in all of New York, and that includes all those high-falutin' joints downtown."

"Ach . . ." The woman punched Carter playfully in the arm, and he beamed. Georgia frowned. Two years she'd worked with the man, and she wouldn't have felt comfortable chucking him like that.

"I know why you're sweet-talkin' me, Randy Carter. 'Cause you want me to fix you my famous shepherd's pie even though it ain't on the menu. My old fingers can't do the crust no more."

"We'll eat anything you care to make us, Roberta."

"How 'bout two corned beef sandwiches?"

"My favorite."

Bobby brought out two white bread rolls and butter. The rolls looked soft and doughy—too doughy for corned beef. Bobby went to slap some butter on Georgia's roll. Georgia stopped her.

"No butter on mine, please. Mustard's all I need." Corned beef, to Georgia's way of thinking, should be served up in a kosher deli on Jewish rye bread with plenty of mustard. She might have been born Irish, but somewhere along the line her stomach converted.

Bobby frowned at Georgia. She had a smoker's face—deep lines and leathery skin. Her hair, gray at the roots, was the color of red cedar mulch at the tips. She'd probably been a redhead when she was young.

"What did you say your name was again?"

"Georgia. Georgia Skeehan."

"Skeehan, eh?" Bobby narrowed her gaze at Georgia. It was not a friendly look at all. "Unusual Irish name."

"People always mistake it for 'Sheehan,' " Georgia told her, trying to be friendly. *I should've kept my friggin' mouth shut and lived with the butter*, she thought. "When my dad joined the FDNY, there was a Sheehan in his probie class and—"

"Your father was a firefighter?"

"Uh-huh." Georgia shot a puzzled look at Carter. He seemed equally perplexed. Firefighting was often a family calling. It wasn't uncommon for firefighters to have had fathers—even grandfathers—on the job. Bobby turned her scrutiny to Carter.

"You ever talk to Sully these days?" she asked him.

"Not since he retired," said Carter. "How's he doing?"

"Still lives in the neighborhood. Comes in for a pint at least twice a week," said Bobby. "You should talk to him."

"Who's Sully?" asked Georgia.

"Jamie Sullivan," said Carter. "Luckiest sonofagun ever to walk the face of the earth. Went to Vietnam and took a thimbleful of buckshot, so they sent him home. Rest of his platoon got wiped out. Joined the fire department, learned to drive the engine and took a wrong turn one night on his way to a gas leak at an empty warehouse. The captain was ready to give him charges. Turns out those five extra minutes spared the entire company. The warehouse blew up before they arrived."

"Was he ever a fire marshal?" asked Georgia.

"For a couple of years," said Carter. "Out in Queens with my old partner, Paul Brophy, before Broph transferred to Manhattan. But Sully went back to firefighting after that. He didn't like wearing a tie and carrying a gun."

"Where is he now?"

"Retired," said Bobby. She laughed, the earlier incident seemingly forgotten. "Bought his first lottery ticket the day he retired and hit the jackpot. A cool million. I don't know what he did with the money 'cause he still lives on West Forty-eighth off Eleventh Avenue. But he goes to Florida every January. I'm always telling Sully to rub some of that luck off on me."

"How y'all holding up here?" Carter asked her.

"Ach, can't complain," said Bobby. "Terry, my son, helps out now and then, but I been thinkin' of selling the place, truth be told. Marty's been gone three years now, God rest his soul."

"Seems like only yesterday," said Carter.

"No truer words were spoke," said Bobby. "It's not the same 'round here no more. Too many ghosts. More than a body can take."

"Most of the old gang are dead now, I guess," said Carter.

"Aye," said Bobby. "And the yuppies don't come by except on Saint Patrick's. And they can't hold their liquor like the regulars."

"But the back room—y'all still use it, right? I mean, some of the old gang's still around."

Bobby sliced the corned beef sandwiches in half without answering. Georgia thought perhaps she hadn't heard the question. Then she noticed that the woman's hands seemed a little less steady with the knife.

"I won't have 'em no more," she said finally. "Not since Cullen . . ." Her voice trailed off.

"I understand," said Carter. "But you know where we can find 'em, right? None of them could live long without your corned beef."

Bobby stopped cutting and wagged her knife at him. "You're a charmer, Carter. You've got blarney somewhere inside that black skin of yours. But you can't play me like a fiddle. I've been in business as long as I have because I know when to keep my mouth shut."

"Roberta, please—help us." Carter's voice was soft and serious now. Even Bobby recognized the difference. "We've got a bad situation here and we need to talk to Freezer—"

"Don't say that name." She wiped her knife on her dirty apron without meeting his gaze. "The last time I heard that name was the day Cullen died."

Carter leaned across the counter as if to comfort her. His hand hovered in midair, then dropped to the scarred oak countertop. Bobby lifted her gaze now and a look passed between them. Georgia could see something intensely painful in that look.

"I'm sorry," Carter said softly. "I've got no right . . ." He nodded to Georgia. "I think we should go."

They slid off their stools. The only sound in the empty bar was the rip of two sheets of waxed paper being torn from a roll. Bobby wrapped up the sandwiches, then slapped them on the bar counter.

"He keeps a place near your old stomping ground—"

"The old Manhattan base?" asked Carter. "On Fifty-second Street, off the West Side Drive? I thought the city converted it into a stable for carriage horses."

"They did. Freezer's got a place right next door. Owns the whole building. Not much to look at from the outside, but I hear it's right fancy on the in."

Bobby stuffed the sandwiches in a paper bag and handed them to Carter. "No charge."

He took out his wallet and slapped a twenty-dollar bill on the counter anyway. "Now y'all stop that, Bobby, or my partner's gonna think you've been bribing me all these years."

Bobby smiled, but it was a sad smile this time—the lips never parted. "Take care of yourself, Carter. There ain't a lot of us old bodies around anymore."

6

MCLAUGHLIN LIVED in a three-story brick warehouse that looked quite ordinary from the street. All the windows were small and dark and covered over in heavy blinds. The front door was brown-painted steel. A small driveway sloped down to a garage door. It shared a common wall with the old Manhattan fire investigation base, which was now a stable. The smell of horse manure lingered in the air. Not the best place to wolf down Bobby Kelly's sandwiches, but then again, Georgia would have preferred a kosher deli anyway.

"What was all that stuff back there about some guy named Cullen?" Georgia asked Carter.

"Long story," Carter replied.

"Start now, finish later."

Carter flopped down the last quarter of his sandwich in the waxed paper and stuffed it into the brown paper bag. "Cullen Thomas was Bobby's kid brother. He was a little worm of a guy—and pretty timid when he was sober. Problem was, he wasn't sober much. All his offenses were petty offenses, but they started piling up. By the time he got into a drunken knife fight two years ago, he was looking at hard time. Bobby asked me what I could do to keep him out of prison. He would've fared badly in prison."

"I don't remember any of this," said Georgia.

"You wouldn't," said Carter. "It all happened right before we teamed up. Anyway, Cullen was looking to bargain. He told me if I could get the fight knocked down to a misdemeanor, he'd give me eyewitness details about a fatal fire that had been labeled an accident but wasn't."

"He asked you to *bargain* with the district attorney? On a case that wasn't even FDNY jurisdiction? I'll bet the D.A. wouldn't even speak to you," said Georgia.

"Oh, he spoke to me, all right," said Carter. " 'Cause the torch Cullen Thomas was willing to dime was somebody we *all* wanted to take down—Michael McLaughlin."

"What happened?"

"The D.A.'s office sent an investigator to talk to Cullen. I never learned the details—*that* the police did claim jurisdiction on. But soon afterward, the charges against Cullen were bargained down and he walked. I kept waiting for the PD to slap the cuffs on Freezer. But a couple of months went by and nothing happened. Bobby said Cullen started flashing a lot of cash. I didn't think Freezer would pay him off, but you never know. It sure looked like somebody did. Then one day, Bobby called me in a panic. She said Cullen had come into the bar, very drunk, talking about how it was cheaper to kill him than to pay him off. The police found him early the next morning in back of an SRO. The medical examiner's office labeled it a jump suicide."

"The cops must have taken another look at McLaughlin, then," said Georgia.

"I pressed them to—even asked a couple of my friends in the PD to find the interview Cullen gave to the D.A. and send me a copy. Nobody could ever find it. With Cullen gone, the case died. Bobby was devastated. I've always blamed myself. If I hadn't set the thing in motion, Cullen would probably be alive today."

"You couldn't have known," said Georgia. "I'm sure Bobby realizes that."

Carter twisted his brown paper lunch bag until it looked like a corkscrew. There was an edge to his eyes.

"I want to nail Michael McLaughlin, girl. I've never wanted to nail anyone as much in my life."

"What makes you think he'll speak to us?"

"Ego, for one thing," said Carter. "He thinks all us fire marshals are one step removed from meter maids. We're not real cops to him."

Georgia and Carter got out of the car and walked across the street. Georgia rang the buzzer. She noticed a closed circuit camera pointed at the stoop. A husky voice grunted from inside.

"What's your business?"

Georgia held her shield to the camera. "Fire Department, Mr. McLaughlin." *Fire Department* sounded less threatening than *fire marshals*. She and Carter always used "Department" around skittish witnesses and suspects. "We'd like to come in and talk to you."

The metal door buzzed and Georgia opened it. The small room they stepped into had a bare concrete floor, a tile ceiling and a large mirror running along one wall. Georgia sucked in her stomach before the mirror, only to catch Carter grinning behind her.

"That's a one-way mirror, you know. Don't pick your nose or I'll never live it down."

Georgia stepped back, feeling suddenly foolish. "How can you tell?"

"Been in enough interrogation rooms to know. I suspect Freezer wants to see his guests before they see him."

"And hear 'em, too," boomed a jovial voice on the other side of the door. It opened. The man standing before Georgia was tall—maybe six-feet-three— with a lumberjack's swagger and a chest like a Kevlar vest. He had a broad, clean-shaven face that would've fit in well in the fire department. A band of freckles rode up the bridge of his slightly flattened nose when he smiled. His hair, the color of honey in weak tea, rolled like ocean waves across his head, as if he hadn't had a chance to run a comb through it yet this morning. He was dressed in sweatpants and a sweatshirt, and his feet were bare, as if he'd just gotten up. He didn't look like a killer. He looked like an off-duty firefighter.

"My lucky day," he said, extending a hand. "If it isn't Randall Carter come back to the old neighborhood." His brogue sounded impossibly thick—much thicker than the voice on Glickstein's answering machine tape. "You see your old offices?" he asked Carter, nodding in the direction of the stable next door. "You know they put horses where you used to work?"

"Guess y'all get used to the stink after a while," said Carter. "Or maybe that's nothing new for you, Freezer."

McLaughlin feigned a hurt look. "Freezer? I don't know any Freezer. I'm just plain old Mike McLaughlin. I'm in the Irish import business these days. Crystal, linens, china . . ."

"Refrigerators?" Carter prodded. McLaughlin didn't take the bait. He turned and extended a hand to Georgia. He seemed too relaxed to have seen anything on the news about the fire.

"What's a nice lass like you doing with this old geezer? I'm surprised they even let him carry a gun at his age—or do they?" Before she could answer, McLaughlin turned to Carter. "Guess they don't pay marshals enough to retire."

"Some of us like to stick around until we've settled our scores."

McLaughlin grinned as if Carter had just told a good joke. "Come in and tell me what your business is."

They followed the big man through a carved oak door, peaked in the center. It looked like it had come from a church. On the other side was a magnificent home that would rival any old-money haunt on Park Avenue. The ceiling had been rebuilt to resemble a timber-frame lodge with exposed log trusses. The floors were covered in wide cherry boards. Crystal gleamed from the mantel of an enormous, reconstructed fieldstone fireplace. On the walls were fine oil paintings and high-quality photographs of lush green valleys, moss-covered cottages and four-masted schooners at sea. Georgia stepped closer to a small, framed picture of fishermen hauling in a catch.

"I took that one in Ireland," said McLaughlin. "It's a hobby of mine."

"So the photographs are yours?"

"Not all of them." He gestured to a black-and-white print of a waifish girl staring at her mottled reflection in a subway car. The lighting was so stark and eerie, Georgia could almost feel the buildup of grit along the mosaic tiles that spelled out *Times Square* in the background. The girl in the picture was perhaps seventeen, maybe a runaway. She was hauntingly beautiful, with round, dark sad eyes. "I bought this one off an artist I know. Pretty good, eh?"

Georgia didn't answer. She walked over to a large oil painting over the fireplace. It showed a gorgeous green valley beneath a cloud-speckled sky that looked so real, it made Georgia forget the December gray outside.

"Did someone you know paint this one, too?"

"Hardly," said McLaughlin. "That's a John Constable original. Painted in eighteen thirty-seven. Cost me half a mil three years ago, but I could get three times that today."

Georgia felt her breath catch in her chest. She didn't know which scared her more—the idea that a former gang member and murder suspect could have such an eye for beauty, or that he could casually toss about millions on things most people could only glimpse in museums.

"As you can see," said McLaughlin, "I only buy the good stuff." McLaughlin shot a glance at Carter. "None of this tribal mask jungle shit."

Georgia blinked her surprise—not at the racism, which she half-expected from a man like McLaughlin, but at the pointedness. The walls of Carter's Brooklyn brownstone were filled with African art. Perhaps McLaughlin was just fishing. Or maybe—just maybe—there was more history between the men than Carter had let on.

McLaughlin took a seat in a Queen Anne–style chair. Georgia and Carter sank into a buttery soft leather couch. McLaughlin pulled a remote out of a drawer and flicked on a large-screen high-definition television in a far corner of the room. Georgia avoided Carter's eyes. She was afraid of exchanging any look with him that might tip McLaughlin off.

"Mr. McLaughlin, can we leave the television off until later?" asked Georgia.

"I like it on, Miss . . . what did you say your name was?"

She hadn't. "Marshal Skeehan."

"Skeehan?" He gave her a quizzical look. "You got relatives in the department?"

"Why? Do you know any Skeehans?"

He shrugged. "Whatever you need to ask me, you can ask as well with the television on as off." He got up from the chair and walked to the fireplace mantel. A pack of Lucky Strikes lay beside a crystal decanter. He pulled one out and lit it. His lips curled slightly as he watched Carter shift on the couch. Carter hated cigarette smoke. McLaughlin seemed to know that.

"We need to ask you some questions, Mr. McLaughlin," said Georgia.

"About?"

"Your whereabouts since midnight." She and Carter had decided in advance that Georgia would take the lead interrogator position. She had no history with McLaughlin and so could remain more neutral.

"I've been here. Sleeping. Just got up before you arrived."

"You get up at noon?" asked Georgia.

"It's eleven-thirty, lass—"

"Marshal," Georgia corrected.

"Either way, the import business doesn't run on civil service hours."

"You have anyone who can corroborate your whereabouts?" Georgia asked him.

"Sometimes? Yes." He winked at her. "But this time? No."

Georgia pretended she hadn't seen the wink. He seemed to regard this whole interview as a joke.

"So you were by yourself. You didn't leave your apartment."

"That's right. I'm a homebody these days." He flopped back in the Queen Anne chair, his long legs spread out before him, and took another hit off his cigarette. He held it like a joint, and yet he was almost dainty about making sure all the ash fell in his porcelain ashtray. Come to think of it, the house looked impeccable. No dust. No cushions out of place. He was the neatest man she'd ever met.

"Tell us about Barry Glickstein." She cast the query in the broadest possible terms. You never knew what you could get a subject to admit to when the question was wide open.

McLaughlin put his cigarette on the corner of his ashtray and let the smoke curl around the room. "Don't know anyone by the name of Glickstein, I'm afraid."

"Think harder," Carter urged.

"Glickstein, Glickstein . . . Ah yes. Now I remember. He's that little Jew who owns the Café Treize down in the meatpacking district. They've got a nice cherry-and-hazelnut stuffed capon. You should try it sometime." McLaughlin smiled wickedly at Carter. He knew as well as they did that Georgia and Carter lacked the money and clout to get into the bar at Café Treize, never mind get a table.

"Ah, the life of a civil servant," said McLaughlin. "Guess it's mostly McDonald's for you. Next time you visit, maybe I'll take you to Café Treize—show you how the other half lives."

Georgia glared at him. She kept seeing Doug Hanlon's sooty, blistered face in that alleyway. She kept thinking about the baby Tony Fuentes would never get to know, and the son's football games that Joe Russo would miss.

"How do *you* get into Café Treize, Mr. McLaughlin?" she asked.

He shrugged. "Gotta know the right people."

"I was referring to this morning."

"This *morning*?" He clasped his hands behind his head. "They don't serve breakfast—unless you count brunch on Sundays."

The television blared behind them. There was a teletype sound, then the words, "Eyewitness News." A female announcer spoke in somber tones of the early morning restaurant fire in lower Manhattan that killed two firefighters. McLaughlin barely shifted in his chair, but Georgia could see it had registered.

"Why don't you two quit bullshitting me and tell me what you want?"

"How many Barry Glicksteins in this city are you shaking down, Mr. McLaughlin?" asked Gerogia.

"I'm not shaking anyone down. If Glickstein's got problems, they're *his* problems. I barely know the little twerp."

It looked as if Carter had been waiting for this moment. He pulled out a tape recorder from the pocket of his black overcoat and pushed Play. He'd already cued Glickstein's answering machine tape to McLaughlin's entry.

Barry, my boy . . . You should really clear out that rear stockroom, ya know? All those paper towels and shit—they're sooo combustible . . . I'd really hate to see a fire take down my favorite watering hole. So . . . how 'bout I come by for the money you owe me Friday night? Just put me in the reservation book—say eight-thirty? Freezer's the name, but you knew that already, didn't you?

Carter stopped the tape. Now it was his turn to smile. "Care to explain that?"

"You've been waiting for this for a long time, haven't you?" The question hung in the air. McLaughlin sighed. "Doesn't matter. That's not me."

"It's you," said Carter. "But don't take *my* word for it. There are scientists at our police lab in Queens who'd like nothing better than to run a voice analysis on it and testify about their findings."

"Perhaps if you gave us a statement," said Georgia,"—voluntarily, of course, Mr. McLaughlin—you could explain your side of the story."

She tossed off the comment in a light and breezy manner—just as they had rehearsed in the car. The answering machine tape and Barry Glickstein's sworn statement were enough to arrest McLaughlin right now. But then they'd have to take him to central booking. He'd call his lawyer, and that would be the end of any face-to-face talks. On the other hand, if McLaughlin came in voluntarily, he didn't need a lawyer, and they had a shot at wangling a confession. A confession could turn a good case into an airtight one.

"You want a statement?" McLaughlin shrugged. "I'll be glad to give you one." If he was worried, he wasn't showing it. He put a hand over his heart. "I'm a good citizen, Marshals. I *always* cooperate with the law." He rose from his chair. "Mind if I make a quick phone call upstairs first?"

Georgia and Carter shared an unspoken look of concern. *His lawyer. He's calling his lawyer.* Still, they really couldn't stop him—not without arresting him. And the arrest would mean he'd call his lawyer anyway.

"All right," said Carter. "Five minutes."

"Where are you taking me?"

"Manhattan base. The one we use now. On Lafayette Street," said Georgia.

McLaughlin disappeared up a circular staircase. A Persian runner on the stairs made his footsteps nearly inaudible. Georgia raised an eyebrow at Carter once he had gone.

"He seems so cool," she whispered. "Does he understand he's facing a double-homicide rap?"

"I'm not gonna be the one to break the news." Carter frowned in the direction of the stairs. "The sonofagun's got something up his sleeve. I can feel it. It's like Cullen Thomas all over again."

"What do we do?"

"We watch our step. Freezer is a very successful criminal—you know why? 'Cause he's patient. He waits for the other guy to make a mistake."

"But we've got the evidence," said Georgia. "I mean, even if he doesn't confess, he's not going to walk away from this one."

"You think, huh?" Carter kept his eyes on the stairs. "That's your first mistake."

7

MCLAUGHLIN TREATED THE TRIP to Manhattan base like a cab ride
to a social gathering. He exchanged his sweats for a sleek gray designer
shirt, wool pants and a black leather Armani jacket. He jovially agreed
to let Carter frisk him for a weapon, reminding the marshals face-
tiously that as an ex-con, it would be illegal for him to carry a gun.
Then, to top it off, McLaughlin offered to drive *them* to Manhattan
base in the Porsche he kept garaged below his house.

"You own a Porsche," said Georgia, shooting Carter a look. Somehow, it figured.

"Lemon yellow," replied McLaughlin. "But I have a black Nissan
Pathfinder, too, if you'd prefer it."

Georgia and Carter escorted McLaughlin to the back of their
Caprice. They didn't handcuff him. He wasn't under arrest. But their
manner was cool and professional. McLaughlin spied a copy of the
Daily News on Georgia's seat. He asked to read it. Georgia declined.
Although there was nothing in the paper yet about the fire, Georgia
had a sense that the wheels were always spinning in McLaughlin's
brain. Somehow, he'd find a way to make that paper useful.

"Ah," said McLaughlin, shrugging off the request. "Nothing in the paper I want to read anyway, you know? All those sad stories. You must see enough of 'em every day."

Georgia didn't answer. They were inching back down the West Side in heavy traffic. It was going to be a long trip.

"I'd think a nice lass like you—you'd rather be married, looking after little ones, not doing a job like this," McLaughlin prodded.

"I like my job," said Georgia.

"Really? I bet you're a firefighter's daughter."

Georgia said nothing, so he continued. "C'mon, lass. It's handed down through the generations, like flat feet or an obsession with seniority."

"Shut up, McLaughlin," barked Carter. He turned up the volume on the department radio. There was nothing much coming over the airwaves right now, just time checks and routine information.

"Course, neither Carter nor you would have your jobs without affirmative action," McLaughlin continued. "Carter'd be back in some hayseed town down south doing squirrel patrol. And you'd be working on your fifth baby."

He waited for the backlash. Georgia was a hairsbreadth away from giving him one. But Carter, as always, kept his cool.

"You're a doozy, McLaughlin. A real humdinger," said Carter. "You want to export something? Export yourself back to Ireland."

"Ah, well, that's the great thing about this fair country, Carter. I'm an American citizen, just like you. Been one since the age of seven. So this is my home. And I say, God bless America."

Carter nearly rear-ended the car in front of him. McLaughlin casually cracked his knuckles.

"So your dad was a firefighter, am I right?" McLaughlin asked Georgia again. Georgia didn't answer.

"Tell me, does he like you risking your neck for chump change?"

"Dang it, man—shut *up*," Carter said again. His voice had taken on the timbre of an army drill sergeant—not surprising, since that's what he was in his twenties.

"It's an innocent question," McLaughlin fired back. "What's wrong with an innocent question?"

"It's *not* an innocent question," said Georgia. "My father died in the line of duty, just like . . ." *Just like the two men you killed this morning,* Georgia almost sputtered. Carter shot Georgia a warning glance and she caught herself just in time. There was still a chance McLaughlin didn't know the extent to which he was implicated in the deaths of Russo and Fuentes. Georgia could've ruined everything by telling him. She suddenly understood how easily a man like Michael McLaughlin could draw people into places they didn't want to go. Perhaps it wasn't an accident he talked about African art to Carter. Perhaps Carter, more than anyone, understood just how dangerous McLaughlin could be. Georgia hunkered down in her seat and said nothing after that.

The Manhattan office of the Bureau of Fire Investigation was located above Ladder Company Twenty, a boxy, beige garage with none of the charm of the city's older firehouses. Up and down the street were discount stores with names like Chung-Lee Dresses and Hadjik Imports. The Bowery, with its snoozing drunks and panhandlers, was just a short walk away.

Georgia had called ahead to alert the marshals that they were bringing a suspect in for questioning. But as they neared the firehouse's garage door, Georgia noticed several official-looking cars parked along the sidewalk. One was a black Crown Victoria with a fire marshal from Brooklyn at the wheel.

"We've got company, today," Georgia mumbled to Carter. He nodded like he knew what she meant: Arthur Brennan, Chief Fire Marshal of the FDNY, head of the Bureau of Fire Investigation—and every marshal's ultimate boss. He must have come over from headquarters in Brooklyn when he heard the news. She understood why Brennan would want to be here. But still, she wished he had stayed away. The more routine and low-key she and Carter could make this chat session, the less likely McLaughlin would be to call his lawyer—that is, if he hadn't called him already.

Georgia noticed another vehicle parked in front of the Crown Victoria. It was a black Ford Explorer SUV with tinted windows. It looked like an official car, but it wasn't a make or model she'd seen in the Bureau of Fire Investigation before. A short, slight man in a dark jacket exited the firehouse with a soda in his hand and slid behind the wheel of the car. *Definitely not FDNY,* she decided. Not even a cop. He was in his midtwenties, with wispy brown hair that looked as if it might recede in a year or two, and thick, round, gold-rimmed glasses. His chest seemed almost concave inside his jacket, like he'd borrowed his father's clothes.

"I hope everyone hangs back upstairs," Georgia muttered.

"They won't." Carter had been a marshal for sixteen years. He knew how these things worked.

They hustled McLaughlin through the door and up an elevator to the fourth floor. The elevator let them off in a narrow passageway with a small kitchen on one side and the bathroom and bunk room on the other. Beyond the passageway was a large, open squad room with desks scattered across the beige linoleum floors and file cabinets lined up against the whitewashed cinder-block walls.

A tight knot of fire marshals in sport coats and ties was clustered around two well-dressed, serious-looking men. One of the men was in his midfifties, with a shaved head and the kind of rugged, lean build that suggested hours on a treadmill each day, followed by vigorous, ultra-competitive sessions of squash. His silk tie sported a gold tie clip with an American flag on it. When he moved his arm, Georgia could see the fluttering outline of a pistol in a shoulder holster beneath his jacket.

The other man, in his midthirties, had the blow-dried hair and stiff posture of a Jehovah's Witness making house calls. Georgia happened to glance at his feet. He was wearing cowboy boots. Fire Marshal Sal Giordano waddled over and handed the two men coffee.

"What gives?" Georgia asked Carter, nodding to the two lean, unfamiliar faces in a sea of jowly, familiar ones.

"Don't know," said Carter, but his eyes betrayed a certain wariness. He seemed to be running through the possibilities, and none of them pleased him.

The door to the men's room opened and Mac Marenko stepped out.

There was a moment of awkward hesitation for both him and Georgia—a re-calibration of their postures, a stiffness borne not of coldness but of embar-rassment. Although she never talked about it, all the marshals at Manhattan base knew they were dating. Marenko hated having his private life on display. And Georgia, aware of his discomfort, tried her best not to do anything to make it worse.

"Take Mr. McLaughlin into the conference room," Marenko said brusquely. "Get him coffee or a soda if he wants it, and then see me over by our guests." He said the word "guests" like he'd just swallowed paint thinner.

"Thank you, Mr. Fire Marshal," said McLaughlin with a mock salute. "That's right kind of you."

"You." Marenko pointed a finger at McLaughlin. "You don't talk to me—got that?" Marenko turned on his heel and stomped off across the squad room.

"He seemed a might peeved, wouldn't you say?" asked McLaughlin.

Georgia and Carter shot each other worried looks as they led McLaughlin into the conference room. Its outer walls were solid cinder block. The wall facing the squad room was glass and covered with smudge marks. There was a cheap, veneered conference table in the center of the room surrounded by half a dozen metal folding chairs. A portable blackboard sat in the corner with fresh erasure marks on it. Georgia could see the words beneath: *Giants . . . Jets . . . Patriots . . . Steelers.* The guys had been keeping tabs on their football betting pool.

They left McLaughlin with a soda and an ashtray, then went to see Marenko. He was perched on the edge of Georgia's desk, gesturing with ex-asperation at the Jehovah's Witness in cowboy boots. Boot man sipped his coffee, unfazed and unmoved by whatever points Marenko was trying to make. Sal Giordano and the other marshals crowded around, gazing starry-eyed at the stranger. Georgia wondered why this discussion was taking place by her desk. Marenko, as a supervising fire marshal, had his own office—just off the squad room. The door to that office was closed right now. Georgia also noticed that the stranger with the shaved head was missing.

"Go on, clear out," Marenko told the other marshals as Georgia and Carter approached. The men skulked away, muttering. Boot man put his coffee down and extended a hand.

"Agent Scott Nelson, FBI."

Georgia blankly shook Nelson's hand.

"McLaughlin," murmured Carter in disbelief. It took a moment for the connection to sink in. When it did, Georgia gave Nelson a panicked look.

"Oh, no," she said, stepping backward. "Tell me he didn't call you."

"Ma'am." Nelson pretended to tip a hat that wasn't there. He had a western twang to his voice. She could almost sense him clicking the heels of his cowboy boots. "By order of Charles Krause, special agent in charge of the New York office, I'm going to have to ask you to cease and desist all investigative activity pertaining to Mr. McLaughlin."

"You're not serious?" Georgia looked at Marenko. Marenko looked at the floor. It appeared he'd already had this discussion and it had gotten him nowhere. She could feel her blood pressure rising. "Where's Chief Brennan?"

"In my office. With Krause," said Marenko. *So that was the suit with the shaved head*, thought Georgia. *The FBI's number one boy in New York.* They were sunk.

"My SAC knows your chief," Nelson explained. *SAC—special agent in charge.* Already they were degenerating into FBI jargon. "He came along today as a personal courtesy." Nelson poured out the words like he expected a hearty expression of gratitude.

"You can't do this," Georgia sputtered. "We've got solid evidence that McLaughlin was responsible for the deaths of two firefigh—"

"Ma'am?" Nelson cut her off. "The FBI doesn't have to explain its position to you, your boss or *his* boss. You know the protocol. Federal jurisdiction supersedes all other police authorities. As far as the FBI is concerned, this discussion with Mr. McLaughlin never took place."

"We have a tape of McLaughlin all but admitting he set the fire," she argued. "We have an affidavit from the restaurant owner stating that McLaughlin was shaking him down."

"Mr. McLaughlin's name is never mentioned on that tape," Nelson countered.

Georgia gave him a stunned look. The only way he could've known that was if McLaughlin had tipped him off. "But he calls himself Freezer—"

"So you *claim*. And your affidavit from Mr. Goldstein is worthless—"

"Glickstein," Georgia corrected.

"Goldstein or Glickstein, the facts are the same," said Nelson. "The man would say anything to save himself—not to mention the A-list celebrity status of his business." Nelson stretched out his left arm, then crooked it at a ninety-degree angle and checked his watch. It was one of those wristwatches with more dials on it than a Nautilus sub. "Now if you'll just fetch Mr. McLaughlin, when Agent Krause is ready, we'll be going, ma'am."

"It's not *ma'am*, you prick, it's *marshal*—"

"Skeehan," Marenko cautioned, "don't make this ugly."

Georgia ignored him. "Two of our brothers died today, and you waltz in here talking about federal jurisdiction? You're lucky those boots are still on your feet, *cowboy*. 'Cause if you keep this up, you may have to get them surgically removed from certain orifices of your body—"

"Skeehan!" yelled Marenko.

Nelson turned to him. "You're a supervisor, yes? Then supervise. The FBI doesn't have to take this horseshit from the ATF, never mind some schmuck fire marshal just a few years out of hose patrol."

Georgia could see the veins throbbing in Marenko's neck. He wanted to belt the guy as badly as she did. But common sense told him that it wouldn't do any of them any good.

"Get McLaughlin," Nelson snarled at Georgia. "Now."

"Just a moment," growled a familiar voice from the doorway of Marenko's office. They all turned to see a beefy man in his early sixties filling up the frame. He had pitted skin, thinning silver hair and tiny features that looked as if they'd been crushed together in a vise. Chief Arthur Brennan was a bully and a tyrant with a long memory and a short fuse. But if there was one thing he hated, it was seeing anyone mess with his marshals.

"What the hell is going on here?" Brennan demanded.

"This . . . this *woman* was threatening me," said Nelson.

Marenko and Carter bit back grins and looked at the floor. At five-feet-four, Georgia was half a foot to a foot shorter than everyone else in the room. "Threatening" was not a word that came to mind when people described her.

"All of you, in my office. Now," barked Brennan. Actually, it was Mac's office, but this was not the time for any of them to point that out.

Georgia and Nelson steered clear of each other as they filed into the office along with Carter and Marenko. The office had a swivel chair behind the desk and two stiff-backed visitor's chairs. Brennan, as the ranking officer, took Marenko's seat behind his desk. The man with the shaved head got up from the other chair and extended a hand.

"I'm Chuck Krause, special agent in charge of the FBI's New York office," he said genially. Georgia noticed he referred to himself as "Chuck," whereas Nelson had called him "Charles." He was either sincerely trying to make up for his underling's pomposity, or he was pulling a typical cop interrogation tactic, downplaying his authority in order to lull his subjects into a false sense that they were all on the same side. For Georgia at least, the jury was out. She gave him a limp handshake, then retreated to the other side of the room.

Nelson gestured for Georgia to take one of the visitor's chairs. She glared at him.

"I'll stand."

Marenko and Carter seemed to feel the same way, so Krause and Nelson took the chairs.

"First off," said Krause. "I want to tell you all how deeply pained I am, personally and professionally, over the deaths of your men this morning." He leaned forward as he spoke, his palms on the knees of his dark blue suit pants. He affected a sincere demeanor. But that only meant that he was a better, more experienced cop than Scott Nelson. Krause seemed to know what Nelson didn't—that sympathy was a cheap bargaining tool.

"Chief Brennan and I have known each other many years," Krause continued. "And Arthur knows I speak from the heart when I tell you how difficult this decision is for me."

"Then cut us a break—please, sir," said Georgia. "This is one of the strongest cases my partner and I have seen in a long while."

"I understand your frustration, Marshal," said Krause. "I would feel the same way. I can only assure you that there are larger issues at stake."

At this, Carter spoke up. "Y'all been using Freezer as some kinda confidential informant, I reckon." He was laying the southern accent on thick, Georgia noticed.

"I'm afraid I'm not at liberty to share Mr. McLaughlin's status," said Krause. Georgia noticed that Krause never expressed any confusion over the use of McLaughlin's street moniker. Score one for Carter. He'd just proved, at least to the people in this room, that everyone—including the FBI—knew Michael McLaughlin as Freezer.

"That so?" asked Carter, pretending surprise. "The FBI been hanging out at Freezer's house lately?"

"I believe you're referring to Mr. McLaughlin," said Krause a little belatedly. He broke eye contact with Carter and looked at Brennan. "Arthur, I'm not going to stand here and justify myself to your people."

"Of course, Chuck. Absolutely. You shouldn't have to justify yourself to my people. Allow me." Brennan was Krause's equal at feigning cooperation while being totally uncooperative. For once, it was to their benefit. "What's your point, Carter?"

"McLaughlin's got a mighty fine place there, Chief. High definition, wide-screen television, million-dollar oil paintings, a Porsche in his garage. Not to mention the building itself—three stories of mid-Manhattan real estate. He's living pretty high on the hog for a criminal-turned-informant." Carter shot a pointed look at Scott Nelson. "Maybe not better than an agent with the FBI, but certainly a lot better than us *schmuck* fire marshals."

Brennan's face betrayed just a hint of a smile. "You've had some dealings with McLaughlin in the past, haven't you, Carter?" Georgia was sure the chief knew the answer to this question. They were simply doing a little dance for the benefit of Krause and Nelson.

"Yessir. Some of it *way* in the past. And he wasn't living quite so fine back then. Seems to me, being under the protection of the FBI has been *real* good for business."

"Mr. McLaughlin runs a legitimate import concern," Nelson sputtered. Krause flinched. Unlike Nelson, he seemed to know what they were being set up for.

"Y'all wouldn't mind then," said Carter, oozing southern charm, "if we local yokels took a peek at his tax returns."

Krause's jawline hardened. He turned to Brennan. He was through with Carter. "McLaughlin is FBI property, Arthur. That makes his tax returns FBI jurisdiction. You know the procedures as well as I do. I'm sorry, but there's nothing you or your people can do about it."

"You'd never sell that line of reasoning to the man in the street," said Georgia. "If the public only knew . . ."

She caught herself, but it was too late. The room went silent. The only sounds Georgia could hear were the high-pitched beeps of the fire truck below backing into quarters and a ringing phone on one of the marshals' desks. Everyone inside the room gaped at her in disbelief. She had just committed career suicide in front of not one, but two law enforcement agencies. It was desperation talking, but it was bad judgment nonetheless. Brennan was already turning a hypertensive shade of red. She wanted to rewind the last two minutes and start over. Better yet, she wanted to rewind the whole morning.

Scott Nelson was the first to break the silence. He wagged a finger at Georgia and bounced a look from Krause to Brennan. "Did she just say what I think she said? Did she threaten to take this to the press?"

Krause patted the air. "No threats were made here. Am I correct, Marshal?"

"Yessir. Sorry, sir."

"I'm assuming," said Krause, glancing around the room, "that Miss Skeehan simply got a little emotional. Because a leak like that could ruin somebody's career."

Brennan leaned back in his chair and pressed his fleshy palms to his forehead without speaking. Had they just been among fire marshals, he would've torn her to pieces for a stupid comment like that. But he was protective around outsiders—even of her. Right now, that was her one saving grace. "Carter, Skeehan," he grunted. "Go get some air."

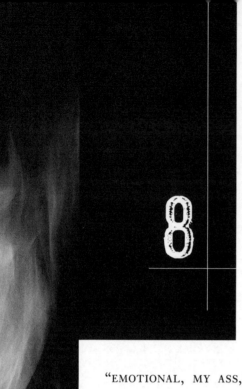

8

"EMOTIONAL, MY ASS," Georgia muttered, pacing the concrete stairwell outside the squad room. "Where does he get off with a comment like that? Because I'm a woman, I'm 'emotional'?"

"Because you shoot from the hip," said Carter. "You did a stupid thing back there, Skeehan. A thing that could cost you your job. Do you realize that now, if there are *any* leaks in this case, they're going to blame you? Even if you're not the source?"

Georgia opened her mouth to argue, but closed it again. She should have thought about that. She hadn't.

"And if there is a leak, do you *know* what the Feds will do to you? What Brennan will do to you? They won't even let you go back to being a firefighter after that. You'll be drummed out of the department."

Georgia sank onto one of the gray-painted steps and put her head in her hands. "Two of our men are dead, Randy. And the bastard who did it is sitting right there in our conference room, calmly smoking a cigarette. How can we just let him walk away?"

Carter slumped against the pipe-iron banister. "We've got no choice."

"Care to explain that one to Doug Hanlon? Or the families of Joe Russo and Tony Fuentes?"

"I *can't* explain it. And neither can you. You're a cop, Skeehan. Start acting like one."

A two-tone electronic chime floated up the stairwell, quickly followed by men's voices, the rumble of the garage door opening and the peal of the truck siren. Ladder Twenty had a run. The marshals worked right above firefighters just like Joe Russo and Tony Fuentes. It felt like the ultimate betrayal not to be able to do more.

"You know what Freezer has that you haven't?" Carter asked her. "Patience. He waits things out. He doesn't go shooting his mouth off in front of people who can only do him harm. You don't even know how big their Federal case is. Heck, maybe a lot more than two firefighters' lives are at stake here."

"I'm sorry," said Georgia. "You're right. I made a mistake back there. I'll see to it that it doesn't reflect on you."

"You think I give a hoot and a holler about that?" asked Carter. "I've got thirty-one years in this department. I'll retire before I take their sass. But you?" He sat down on the riser beside her. "You're a good investigator, Skeehan. I've been through a lot of partners in sixteen years as a marshal. You're the brightest, most passionate one I've ever had. You've got so much potential. But you're going to throw it all away if you don't pull back once in a while. I don't want to see that happen."

Georgia saw Marenko's face through the wire-mesh window in the door. He looked pale and nervous as he opened it. He couldn't meet Georgia's gaze.

"The Chief wants to see you both in my office."

Georgia and Carter followed Marenko through the squad room. She could feel the gazes of some of the other marshals on them as they passed.

Brennan was rocking back and forth nervously in Marenko's chair when they entered. Nelson stood stiffly by a small, grimy window in the office that overlooked an alleyway. Krause was gone.

"All right," said Brennan, clapping his fleshy palms together. "Here's the way it's going to be. The FBI has jurisdiction. They want McLaughlin. So we're going to give him to them."

Georgia kept her mouth shut and looked at the floor. Carter was right. She couldn't change whatever happened here. And maybe she didn't have any business trying.

"Agent Krause had to leave, but he assured me that if there is an arson arrest in this case, the FBI will let the Bureau of Fire Investigation make the collar."

"*If?*" asked Carter.

"That's right," said Brennan. "If." The Chief's stare made it clear he would brook no argument.

"In the meantime," Brennan continued. "The FDNY will cease and desist all investigative activity pertaining to Mr. McLaughlin." Brennan gave a pointed glance at Georgia. "Any leak about Mr. McLaughlin—to the press, other firefighters or civilians—will have serious repercussions for this department, and will result in termination of the individual suspected of initiating such a leak. Are we clear on this?"

Everyone nodded.

"Now." Brennan looked at Georgia and Carter. "Where's Glickstein's answering machine tape?"

Carter looked stricken. "But, Chief, that tape's our only evidence."

"Are there copies?"

"We can make 'em, if you give us a couple of hours."

"No dice," said Nelson. "That tape compromises the status of our investigation."

"Not if I lock it up," Marenko offered. "I can do that right now. I can even give the Chief the only key. No one at Manhattan base will have access. Not even me."

"Marenko." Brennan frowned and shook his head. Clearly, he wasn't happy about this arrangement either, but it looked as if he didn't have a choice. "We've been through this. Now, I'm ordering Carter to hand it over— as a show of good faith. And that's what he's going to do."

Carter sullenly pulled the recorder out of his suit jacket and ejected the tape. Nelson held out a hand to receive it. Carter ignored him and threw the tape on Marenko's desk. It clattered across some papers and came to rest in front of Brennan.

"You're going to give us a receipt for that tape I hope, Agent Nelson," said Georgia.

Nelson casually pocketed the tape. "No receipt. You'll get it back if the FBI determines that an arson charge will be filed."

Georgia and Carter exchanged worried looks. They were turning over the only piece of solid evidence they had against McLaughlin—to an FBI underling who'd stuffed it in his pocket without offering so much as a slip of paper to prove he'd received it. Georgia wondered if that's why Charles Krause had left early—so he could disavow any knowledge of the exchange.

"Now," said Brennan. "In return for the Bureau of Fire Investigation's good-faith cooperation—and a promise to keep everything confidential— Special Agent Krause has agreed to allow one fire marshal to be included in the Federal investigation. The role will be strictly as an observer, and the marshal cannot take any police action against Mr. McLaughlin or any other parties involved in the investigation."

Georgia turned to Carter. He knew McLaughlin. He was an experienced marshal. He had kept his temper in check and hadn't threatened to leak the investigation. He was the logical choice.

Agent Scott Nelson's cowboy boots clicked across the linoleum floor and came to rest where Georgia and Carter were standing. He smirked at both of them, hesitated, then held out his hand.

"Congratulations, Marshal, on your temporary appointment to the FBI."

Georgia was so busy watching Carter, it took her a moment to realize the outstretched hand was for her. She stared at Nelson's hand without shaking it and frowned.

"You want *me?* Why *me?*"

Nelson laughed. "Well, it's not for your charm, that's for sure."

9

MIKE MCLAUGHLIN STRETCHED OUT in the backseat of the FBI's black Ford Explorer. He was glad to be out of that grimy shit hole of a firehouse on Lafayette Street. Glad to be rid of that sad sack, Randy Carter, even if his little partner did have a nice ass.

"You can let me off anywhere," McLaughlin said cheerily to the agent driving the Explorer, a scrawny young man named Nathan Reese. Scott Nelson answered from the front passenger seat.

"Nothing doing, Mike. Agent Krause wants to speak to you—now."

"Where?"

"Where we tell you."

Reese headed the SUV south down Centre Street, in the direction of the FBI's headquarters at Federal Plaza. A block from the building, he nosed the car into an underground public parking garage. McLaughlin grinned when the Explorer pulled up next to a dark blue Buick with tinted windows. The FBI loved cloak-and-dagger shit. He could play along if he had to. He got out of the Explorer and gave Nelson and Reese a mock salute. "Gentlemen. It's been a pleasure."

Reese kept his eyes on the wheel without answering. Nelson was more direct.

"Don't pretend we're in your fan club, Mike. We did what we had to back there for the Bureau, not for you."

"And for your careers," said McLaughlin with a wink. He put a hand over his heart. "Your country will thank you for it."

He watched the Explorer speed away, then opened the front passenger door of the Buick. Charles Krause was at the wheel.

"Get in," muttered Krause without looking at him.

McLaughlin narrowed his eyes. The FBI's haughty attitude was beginning to tick him off. He decided to play it cool.

"I'm much obliged for your help back there," said McLaughlin.

Krause turned to him now. The top of his bald head was sweaty. "You've dragged the Bureau into some serious shit here, Mike. Very serious. We didn't take you on to have something like this blow up in our faces."

"It's not going to blow up. It's going to blow over."

Krause shook his head. "Do you *know* what the director of the FBI would do if he found out about this? You were supposed to keep your nose clean."

"I was *supposed* to help the Bureau. And I did. You got your money's worth. So don't hand me any of this holier-than-thou shit now." McLaughlin could see that Krause wasn't buying it. The guy was pale and shaky. "Look, would you just keep your shirt on? So a couple of firefighters died—so what? You think this is the first time an accusation like this has been leveled against me? This is Mike McLaughlin you're talking to. Not some street hoodlum. Trust me on this. In a week or two, no one will remember their fuckin' names. They're just a couple of nobodies, anyway."

McLaughlin could feel himself losing his temper. Control was the essence of his being. It's what had kept him out of jail when every other killer and con artist he'd ever known had gone down. Lose control and you make mistakes. He pulled out a pack of Lucky Strikes and unsealed the wrapper. It was the one vice he'd ever allowed himself—the one thing he hadn't tried to control.

"May I?" he asked Krause, holding up the cigarettes.

Krause powered open a window in response. McLaughlin took his time lighting up. "Did you get that answering machine tape back?" he asked casually.

Krause nodded. "It's FBI property now. But don't think you're off the hook, Mike. To get it, I had to put one of their marshals on our case."

McLaughlin froze. "Not Carter?"

"No. I argued for the gal."

McLaughlin's pale green eyes took on a steely glint. "If you think you're going to turn me over to the FDNY when you're through with me, think again, my friend. If I go down, I'll take the FBI with me."

"Don't threaten me," said Krause.

"Then don't give me reason to," said McLaughlin. "Get her off the case."

"I can't. The FDNY would be all over my people."

McLaughlin thought a moment. "Not if she takes herself off the case."

"She's not going to—"

McLaughlin cut him off. "I want you to find out every single thing you can about this girl fire marshal—what's her name?" He asked the question, though he already knew the answer. It rubbed at him like a splinter he could feel but not see.

"Skeehan. Georgia Skeehan," said Krause.

"Use your contacts and all those fancy databases Nathan Reese is always snooping in, you hear? I want to know everything about her. Everything."

"She's a fire marshal," said Krause. "A cop. You screw with her, that's serious business. I'm not protecting you—do you understand?"

"Would you just relax? Who said anything about anybody getting hurt?"

"Famous last words. Tell me, Mike—were they the same ones you used before you went to Café Treize this morning?"

10

BY LATE THURSDAY AFTERNOON, the sky had turned the color of slate and a light snow had begun to fall. Georgia looked out the window of Marenko's office. Her motorcycle was parked in the alley. The black vinyl cover sported a light gray frosting of snow. Not white. Snow was never truly white in New York City. If she'd been smart, she would have gotten her nine-year-old Ford Escort out of the mechanic's shop instead of taking her bike to work. Then again, if she'd been smart, she would have put the money she'd spent on her Harley Davidson a year ago toward a new car.

"No one said anything about *snow*," Georgia grumbled.

"They're flurries, Nanook," said Marenko. "Leave your bike at base. I'll drive you home."

"I don't want to drag you all the way out to Queens."

He shrugged. "I'm working on Long Island tomorrow anyway. I was planning to crash at my parents' house tonight."

"You're working again?" asked Georgia. For the past couple of months, Marenko had been snagging some extra cash moonlighting for his brother and uncle in their construction business. "I don't see why you need a second job so badly," she said. "You make more money than I do."

"Uh-huh. And you live with your mother in a house she paid off decades ago. I'm paying Manhattan rent, child support *and* part of a mortgage."

"Do you at least want to stay for dinner?"

"You cooking?"

"No. It's my mom's turn tonight. She's making lasagne."

He grinned. "Then I'm staying."

The flurries turned to rain by the time they crawled over the Fifty-ninth Street Bridge into Queens. Marenko's wiper blades squeaked across the Honda Accord's windshield. His car was also on its last legs, but it was mostly the interior that showed it. There were the telltale signs that his kids, Michael and Beth, had been there recently—a candy bar wrapper shoved between the seats, crushed Lifesavers under the floor mats. Marenko's tool belt and yellow hard hat were tossed on the seat in back, along with a scuffed pair of steel-toed workboots.

"It seems like you're always working lately," said Georgia. "This schedule is going to kill you."

Marenko stifled a yawn and rubbed his eyes. "I'm managing."

"Like hell you are." Georgia had begun to notice shadows beneath those fierce blue eyes. His hands carried the cuts and bruises of long days nailing up plyboard. He was a strong man in good physical shape, but he was also nearly forty. Hauling lumber all day made his back ache. Some nights, he could barely keep his eyes open to watch the ten o'clock news, never mind make love.

"I'd just like to be able to buy my kids a new pair of skates or take 'em to the movies without always worrying about where the money's coming from, that's all," said Marenko.

"Divorced father's guilt." Georgia regretted the words the moment they left her mouth.

"It's *not* divorced father's guilt," he bristled. "I take my responsibilities seriously. Not like . . ." He caught himself and shook his head. They both knew what he was going to say: not like Richie's dad, who didn't even bother to marry Georgia, never mind divorce her. It had been eight years since Rick DeAngelo had seen his son. In all that time, the child hadn't gotten so much as a card or visit, forget child support.

"C'mon, Scout," said Marenko, using the nickname he'd coined for her when they first started dating. He reached over a callused hand and patted her thigh. "It's just for a little while. Things won't stay like this. I promise." He reached behind her seat and extracted a dog-eared folder.

"While I'm driving, you'd better look at this," he said, handing her the folder. "Carter showed it to me this afternoon."

"What is it?"

"An old case of his. Carter wanted Brennan to take you off the FBI investigation. And for once, I agree with him."

"What?" asked Georgia, straightening. "Randy went behind my back to the chief? I don't believe it. What would make him—?"

"I think you'll feel differently when you look inside."

Georgia opened the folder to a creased fashion-photo spread of a glamorous-looking young black woman in a slinky red cocktail dress. The woman had big brown eyes and a flowing mane of raven hair that curled past her bare, taffy-colored shoulders. Her bronze lips were full and pouty, and her figure had just enough curves to fill out the dress. Georgia held up the picture to Marenko and gave him a quizzical look.

"Her name was Rachel Cross," said Marenko. "She was twenty-two in that photo shoot for Versace. It was taken twelve years ago. Six months later, Miss Cross had the misfortune to break up with a very rich banker's son named Alan Welty. Welty had a jealous streak. Keep digging in the folder, I think you'll see what happened."

Georgia rummaged through old police reports and medical records until she came to another photo. Those same two brown eyes were staring at the camera, but that was all that was recognizable about the face. Ropy scars and rough mottled brown skin covered the woman's once smooth cheeks. She wore a black wig on her head, and painted eyebrows where hair could no longer grow. She had no eyelashes and her lips were just crease marks now, her nose a lumpy bit of flesh. The face had a frozen quality to it, the result of muscle damage beneath the scar tissue. Sorrow and joy were no longer possible on a face like that, not that there was likely to be much joy again anyway.

"That's what Rachel Cross looked like after fourteen surgeries," said Marenko. "She stepped in front of a train a year after that picture was taken. She left a note telling her parents she didn't want them to have anything resembling a body to bury. She couldn't bear for anyone to look at her anymore—not even in death."

Georgia put the pictures back in the folder. It did nothing to erase the hideous image etched in her mind. "What's this got to do with the FBI investigation?"

Marenko turned to her. "McLaughlin," he said softly. "Alan Welty hired him to douse Rachel Cross's face with gasoline—not kill her, you understand. Just maim her. Carter could never get him on the assault. Rachel had no memory of it. And Welty lawyered up. Best lawyers in town. They managed to get every piece of incriminating evidence thrown out of court on one technicality or another."

"So this is about ego and revenge—is that it?" asked Georgia. "Randy wants his pound of flesh?"

"He's afraid of what Freezer will do to you," said Marenko. "I am, too."

"C'mon, Mac. You know as well as I do that the Feds are just going to have me shuffling papers anyway. They're not going to let me within ten feet of their investigation."

"Maybe." Marenko said nothing while they inched past a fender-bender on the side of Northern Boulevard. Georgia sensed he was deep in thought.

"What?" she asked. "Are you trying to tell me that Chief Brennan's already yanked me off the case?"

"No. Brennan turned Carter down. If the chief pulls you off the case, the Feds won't let him bring in a substitute. So it's you or nobody."

"Gee," said Georgia. "Thank you all for your vote of confidence."

"It's not that," said Marenko. "Look, Randy Carter is the most stubborn, difficult SOB I think I've ever worked with. But I'll say this about him: he's never been an opportunist—or an alarmist. So I don't buy him being jealous of you going over to the Feds. And I don't believe he brought up Rachel Cross just to scare you. He doesn't want you over there. And I don't think he's told us all his reasons."

"What makes you say that?"

"He signed out this afternoon to go to Metrotech."

Headquarters. In Brooklyn. "So? He went to plead with Brennan to put him on the Federal case instead of me."

"Nah. Brennan was in Manhattan all day. Carter handled that one by phone. I called down to Metrotech. Carter signed in at the records division."

"He was looking up Rachel Cross's file."

"Not Carter. He keeps copies of all his cases. He wouldn't need to go to the records division unless it was about a case he had nothing to do with."

"Did he say anything?"

"Nope. You know how secretive he is," said Marenko. "I ask him a question, he acts like he's doing me a favor to answer it. And I'm his supervisor, though God knows, he acts like it's the other way around most of the time."

"If Randy had a concern, why didn't he just come to me?"

"I don't know."

The rain had turned to drizzle by the time they reached Woodside, Queens. Marenko turned off his wiper blades and hung a left onto a side street of modest brick and stucco homes. Some of the tiny front yards sported life-sized plastic snowmen and Santas. Here and there, Georgia saw a crèche, but not as many as she used to when she was growing up. Back then, Woodside was defined by good Irish pubs and a strong parish church. Every car had a union sticker on the bumper, and about the only non-Irish thing in the neighborhood was Mario's pizza parlor. Now, the cars were Japanese, Mario's competed with a take-out Indian joint two doors down, the pub served frozen margaritas and the church held Masses in both Spanish and English.

Marenko found a parking spot along the street, then walked her back to her house. It was her mother's house, really. Georgia had simply been living here since she was seven. At least, that's how she'd always felt. In the bay window, her mother's Hummel figurines were lined up in front of sheer curtains and satin drapes. The figurines were of impossibly jolly, rosy-cheeked children—the kind Georgia and her brother never were. The front door had three little rectangular windows running diagonally down the front. She'd been staring out those windows since she could only see out the bottom one.

"Man, that smells good," said Marenko as Georgia opened the door and they inhaled the aroma of garlic. Margaret Skeehan emerged from the kitchen. At fifty-six, she was still a beauty—more feminine and graceful than Georgia could ever hope to be. Although age had made her more stocky, she still had curves in all the right places. Georgia's body never seemed to develop past adolescence.

Marenko kissed Georgia's mother on the cheek and Margaret beamed. Yet the smile stopped short of her eyes. Georgia had a sense she knew why.

"You saw the news, didn't you?" she asked. Margaret slowly nodded. She had buried two firefighters in her own life—Georgia's father nineteen years ago, and, less than a year ago, her lover, Jimmy Gallagher. Every firefighter's death seemed to bring it all back.

"Did you know those men?" Margaret whispered. Richie was still upstairs.

"No," said Georgia. "But there was a third firefighter with them—a probie, Ma. It was Seamus Hanlon's son, Doug." Jimmy and Seamus had been best friends.

"Oh my Lord." She brought a hand up to cover her mouth—one of those little gestures that defined her, along with her Nina Ricci cologne and her impeccably manicured nails. Georgia's were always ragged and bitten. "Is he all right?"

"Physically? Yes. Emotionally? He's a wreck."

"Have you spoken to Seamus?"

"Not yet. He's got a lot on his mind right now. And we've got nothing concrete to offer him about the case." Georgia and Marenko exchanged glances. They both knew that was the understatement of all time.

Richie's footsteps thudded down the stairs. At ten, he was all arms and legs and feet as big as snowshoes. He had his father's face—the perfectly bowed lips, the tiny dimple in the center of his chin. He had Rick's mannerisms, too—a kind of hyperkinetic energy that always seemed to make some part of him jiggle. If it wasn't a bouncing leg, then it was a swaying foot or a set of fingers drumming. He was into the homeboy look these days, so his jeans and sweatshirt were about four sizes too big, and a Mets baseball cap sat backwards atop his dark, shaggy hair. You could've probably fit his entire body into one leg of his trousers.

"Hey, Sport," said Marenko. He held up a fist for Richie to knock against. It was part of their secret handshake—a complicated set of moves Richie had seen between two rap performers on MTV. He'd taught the moves to Marenko last fall, and they'd done it so many times since then, both of them could do it in their sleep. But tonight the boy kept his hands in the pockets of his jeans.

"What? No handshake?" asked Marenko.

"I don't feel like it."

"Oh." Marenko gave the child a questioning glance then shrugged. "Hey, that's cool."

"I hope you like my lasagne." Margaret called out as she headed back into the kitchen. "It's probably not as authentic as your mother's." Marenko was of Italian descent on his mother's side, Polish on his father's.

"You kidding? My mom had to learn how to cook all over again when she married my dad. Growing up, I thought everybody ate knockwurst with spaghetti."

Marenko helped Georgia make a salad and set the kitchen table. Normally, Richie followed Mac around like a puppy when he was in the house. But tonight, he stayed upstairs, doing homework.

"Richie seems sort of quiet tonight," said Marenko as he sliced up the garlic bread. "Everything okay?"

"I guess he's a little disappointed."

"About what?"

"Well . . ." Georgia dished the salad into bowls. ". . . you *did* promise a month ago that you'd help him with his Scout project."

"Aw, jeez." Marenko slapped his forehead. "He wanted me to build that model race car with him. I forgot all about it."

"I know." Georgia took a minute to let that sink in.

"When's the derby again?"

"The Friday night before Christmas vacation," she said. "In two weeks. You promised you'd be a judge, too."

"Aw, man. I think I'm on duty that night."

"You can't switch it?"

"I'm busy all that week. Christ, I don't even know when I'm gonna visit my *own* kids."

"I see," said Georgia.

"Don't give me that 'I see' tone. I'm working, Scout. It's not like I'm hanging out at a bar or something."

"If it was Michael . . . or Beth—"

"What? I'd do it? Damn straight, I would. They're my kids, Scout. You want me to be Richie's father. And I can't. I barely have time to be a dad to my own two. So don't go putting that guilt on me."

"He's very fond of you."

"And I'm fond of him, too. But another man let him down—not me. I can only fill up so much of that hole in his life." Marenko wiped down a counter-top and tossed the napkin angrily into the garbage. He muttered under his breath.

"You made your point," said Georgia. "What are you so angry about?"

"I didn't mean to let him down. I just forgot."

"All right, you forgot."

"Tell him I'll make it up to him."

"*You* made the promise. *You* tell him," said Georgia. "I didn't ask you to build that race car with Richie. You offered."

Over dinner, Georgia told her mother and Richie about her new, tempo-rary appointment to the FBI. She told them the appointment was for "training," a lie Marenko wholeheartedly backed up. He did the same kind of spin doctoring with his family.

Richie said little at dinner and picked at his food. Mac sheepishly tried to coax him into conversations about everything from the best basketball players in the NBA to his favorite television shows, but Richie offered only one- or two-word answers while tapping his fork and jiggling his legs. He tipped his chair on its back legs and spoke with his eyes focused on the ceiling—both annoying habits his father used to have when he was restless and wanted to disengage. Georgia wondered where he'd learned them. Rick hadn't been around long enough to impart anything—not even a last name.

As soon as the boy finished dinner, he got up from his seat and announced that he still had homework to do. He waved off Marenko's offer of an arm wrestle. Normally, Richie spent half the meal pleading with Mac to wrestle him.

"I let him down bad, didn't I?" Marenko asked Georgia when they were clearing the dishes. "Why didn't you say something before now?"

"How could I? You're always so tired and busy. It would've sounded like nagging."

"You're handy enough," said Marenko. "Why don't you build it with him?"

"I offered. But he doesn't want my help. It's a 'guy' thing, he says." Georgia began rinsing the dishes and stacking them in the dishwasher. "Maybe it's just as well this happened now. Richie was getting too dependent on you. It's like you said—you have your own family. They come first."

"Now you're making it sound like some kind of betrayal. It's not." Marenko sank into one of the kitchen chairs and rubbed his eyes. "Look, I shouldn't have promised something I couldn't deliver on. And I'm sorry. But you expect too much from me, Scout. You expect me to take the place of Richie's father. And I can't. It's Rick you're frustrated with. I just keep getting to pay for his mistakes."

"Fine," said Georgia.

Marenko laughed. "Why is it when a woman says 'fine,' it's anything but?"

Georgia allowed a small smile. "Why is it when a man says 'sure thing,' it never is?"

Marenko grinned sheepishly. "Okay, point taken. What do you want me to do about it now?"

"At least tell him you're sorry."

Marenko looked at the kitchen door like he expected monsters on the other side. "I'm not good at that stuff." Georgia said nothing. "All right—I'll go upstairs and speak to him."

11

MICHAEL MCLAUGHLIN LOOKED at the thick dossier of computer printouts and government records before him, then slowly dialed a number he knew by heart. Charles Krause picked up groggily.

"How the hell did you get my home phone number?" the agent demanded. "It's unlisted."

"*You* have ways of getting things," said McLaughlin. "And so do I. I'm just reading through those files you obtained."

"It's midnight, Mike. This isn't the time. Or the place."

McLaughlin ignored him. "She is, as you predicted, squeaky clean. No departmental misconduct. No drinking or drug problems. Not even a traffic ticket. She pays her taxes on time and doesn't beat her kid."

"I told you this going in. She's the daughter of a decorated firefighter who died in the line of duty, for chrissakes. You can't get much cleaner than that."

McLaughlin paused on the line. "About the kid—"

"No. Absolutely not, Mike. Touch that boy, and I'll go after you myself."

"Keep your shirt on. I'm not going to mess with the kid. I just want to know about her love life."

"Do I run a dating service?"

"There's no record of marriage or divorce here, but there's a father's name listed on the kid's birth certificate."

"Marriage isn't a prerequisite for having babies."

"Her tax returns don't list any child support from this deadbeat. Is he in jail or something?"

"No. No criminal record," said Krause. "He's an electrical contractor in Toms River, New Jersey. He's carrying some heavy debt, but there's no evidence he ever paid support. I don't think they have any contact—financial or otherwise."

"Any other men in her life?"

"I don't know. Look, Mike, I've done all I'm going to do here. We're looking at a dead end. The best I can do is keep her on the sidelines, so you won't have to deal with each other."

"On the contrary, my friend," McLaughlin chuckled. "I think I'm going to be needing a lot of help from Marshal Skeehan. A *lot* of help."

12

GEORGIA ARRIVED AT FBI headquarters on Friday morning wearing her most conservative blue wool pants suit. Much as she hated to admit it, she was excited by her first day at Twenty-six Federal Plaza. There was a glamour to the FBI that the New York City Fire Department lacked. And besides that, she was still angry with Carter for trying to get her thrown off the investigation. She wanted to prove her worthiness to both the Feds and her own people.

Georgia handed a security guard her I.D. and shield. "An agent will escort you upstairs," the guard told her.

A few minutes later, a short, slight man in his midtwenties with thick glasses emerged from an elevator and called her name.

"Marshal Skeehan? I'm Agent Reese. Nathan Reese. You can call me Nathan, if you'd like. I saw you and your partner yesterday when I was driving my boss to the meeting." He extended a hand and Georgia shook it. His fingers were childlike and soft. Georgia couldn't hide her shock. He looked nothing like her image of an FBI agent.

"Pleased to meet you," said Georgia belatedly. She squinted at his dark suit jacket that hung limply across his slightly stooped shoulders.

Beneath it, she noticed the bulge of a shoulder holster. He had a gun, all right. But in all her dealings—with the NYPD, Federal marshals, agents from the ATF and DEA—she had never met a man who looked less like law enforcement.

"Go ahead, say it," said Reese.

"Say what?"

"My grandmother looks more like a cop."

She laughed. "Now that you mention it." She wondered if she had offended him, so she tried to recover. "I just expected to see Agent Nelson, that's all."

"Hopalong Cassidy?" asked Reese. "He's polishing his spurs."

Georgia laughed again. Obviously, she wasn't the only one who thought Nelson's cowboy boots looked ridiculous.

"You're not at all my image of the FBI," she admitted.

"And you're not at all my image of a New York City firefighter." He paused a beat and grinned. "I thought they all had mustaches."

"Give me twenty years, I probably will."

"Come on," said Reese. "I'll show you around, get you settled."

Reese ushered Georgia into an elevator and pushed the button for the twentieth floor. He was about the same height as Georgia in stocking feet, but with her inch-and-a-half heels, she came off as taller. It was the only time in her work life she could ever remember looking down at a colleague.

"Where are you from?" she asked him.

"New Yawwk—can't you tell?"

"No, really."

"Really—New York. The Big Apple," said Reese. "I was born in Queens, but my family left when I was small. I grew up in Bakersfield, California. But I can still put on a 'be-you-tee-ful' New York accent when I want to."

"Not bad," said Georgia. "But a native like myself can tell."

"Yeah?"

"Fuggedabowdit," said Georgia.

The elevator stopped at the twentieth floor. On the wall was a huge brass insignia: *Department of Justice, Federal Bureau of Investigation*. Beneath the scales and laurels were etched the words *fidelity, bravery and integrity*. Beyond the plaque was a set of security doors. Reese took an electronic key card from his suit then paused.

"I know we were joking around before," he said. "But really—I want to tell you how sorry I am about those two firefighters' deaths and this whole situation. I mean that, Marshal."

"Georgia," she said. "Please call me, Georgia."

"Okay, Georgia. I know the FDNY is between a rock and a hard place on this. There are plenty of agents who like to throw their weight around. But . . ." He looked down at himself. "As you can see, I don't have a lot of weight to throw around."

He swiped the card through a security device and held the door open for her. At a large front desk, he asked the receptionist to buzz Scott Nelson.

"Scott's really in charge of this operation. I'm just your bodyguard," he said dryly.

"Seriously, what do you do?"

"You didn't buy the bodyguard line—huh?" He shrugged. "I'm a computer hacker. One of the best in the country, actually. The FBI pays me to do what I could go to jail for doing any other way."

"How did you get into that?" asked Georgia.

"Almost went to jail."

Scott Nelson came out of a hallway and walked toward Georgia now. The heels of his cowboy boots clicked across the polished floor. She suppressed a grin thinking about Reese's "Hopalong Cassidy" line.

"Ma'am," said Nelson. "Good to see you again."

"Call me, Georgia." She extended a hand and he shook it too firmly—a little power play in the making.

"I hope there are no hard feelings about the other day," he said. "Special Agent Krause and I were just doing our jobs. Once he briefs you, I think you'll see things differently."

"Thank you," said Georgia. "The FDNY appreciates being included in your investigation." It was bullshit talk—they both knew it. But Georgia also recognized the harsh realities of her situation. She was on FBI turf—their guest. It wouldn't do to make enemies with the only people who could hand over McLaughlin.

Nelson nodded to Reese's security card. "We'll get you one of those and some I.D. right after we deputize you."

"Deputize me?"

"That's right. You don't have any federal law enforcement authority right now. We can't make you an FBI agent, but we've submitted the paperwork to the U.S. Attorney's office, so that we can deputize you as a U.S. Marshal."

"Really?" A *U.S. Marshal.* It sounded sort of exciting.

Nelson grinned. "Welcome to the major leagues, Georgia."

He wasn't kidding. The FBI's offices were large and well equipped. Everyone had a Palm Pilot. Everyone had a notebook PC. None of the chairs were covered over in duct tape and none of the desks looked like hand-me-downs from other city agencies. No one smoked or downed greasy doughnuts at their desks. And ten whole minutes had gone by without her hearing a four-letter word. She could get used to this.

Nelson walked Georgia over to an empty cubicle with modular furniture, a phone, computer, filing cabinet and coat tree. There were no soot marks or sticky stains on the computer keyboard, no cigarette burns in the chair, no raunchy calendars pinned to the wall.

"This will be your space while you're with us," said Nelson. "I'll be down the hall. Agent Reese's office is directly across from you." Georgia peeked into Reese's open door. He looked like he ran a computer repair shop, he had so much hardware jammed in there. "We've got a meeting with Krause in ten minutes. Would you like some coffee before then?"

"Thanks. That would be great," said Georgia.

Nelson disappeared and Reese went to get coffee. Georgia took off her coat and hung it on the coat tree. There was nothing exciting to look at in her cubicle, so she wandered over to Reese's office. He had two video monitors, two keyboards and a host of electronic equipment she couldn't even identify. The most ominous-looking was a black box the size and shape of a carton of laundry detergent. It hummed softly atop one of the video monitors. She jumped when Reese came up behind her, bearing two steaming cups of coffee.

"You're looking at spy central," he joked, handing her her coffee. "I told you I'm a hacker."

"I guess I can't ask what you're doing."

"I can't tell you the details, but I can give you an overview." He gestured to a shelf away from the computer equipment. "Put your coffee there. You spill anything on these babies and six months of work could be lost."

Georgia put her coffee down and nodded to the black box. "What does that do?"

"It's called a keystroke bug. It intercepts email. Anything the subject types, even if it's encrypted, I can read it."

"Wow," said Georgia. "I thought that was illegal."

"The legal limits are being explored by the U.S. Attorney's office as we speak. In the meantime"—he shrugged—"it's fun to read what people don't want you to. I used to do it with my older sister's diary when we were growing up."

"If my kid brother had ever read my diary," said Georgia, "he would've remained a kid permanently."

Georgia walked over to the shelf and took a gulp of coffee. "Nathan, were you joking before when you said that you almost went to jail?"

"For once, no," said Reese. "When I was fourteen, I hacked into the National Crime Information Center's computers. Found the names and Social Security numbers of a bunch of big-shot California politicians who'd been arrested for everything from DUI and wife battery to exposing themselves. I floated it all over the Internet. It was pretty juicy stuff. Some of it made the *Los Angeles Times*."

"How long did it take the Feds to catch you?"

"Four days. I wasn't as savvy back then. Anyway, they locked me up for a night, put the fear of God into me. But they were also really nice guys. They showed me all their equipment and told me stories about what it was like to be an agent. I was hooked. And I guess I had something to offer them, too, in the way of technical expertise, because they recruited me while I was still in grad school and accelerated me through the academy."

"You were a computer major?"

"Mechanical engineering and physics, actually. But computers are my life. I got transferred to New York mostly to handle computer surveillance for the organized crime task force. But right now, I'm working with Nelson in the domestic terrorism unit. Pretty much anything that goes through this agency electronically goes through me."

Nelson reappeared to escort Georgia to Krause's office. Reese remained behind. Charles Krause worked one flight up. They took a spiral staircase to reach the twenty-first floor—saving them a trip back through security.

As the special agent in charge, or SAC, Charles Krause had a corner office with overstuffed leather furniture and a commanding view of lower Manhattan. A wall of certificates, plaques and photos showed him shaking hands with presidents, the pope and two New York mayors.

"Welcome, Marshal Skeehan," said Krause. "I'm delighted to have you on board."

"Thank you," said Georgia.

"I trust agents Nelson and Reese have helped you settle in?"

"They have, sir."

"Good. Let's take care of the basics first." Krause walked over to his bookshelf crammed with leather-bound legal volumes and FBI procedures. He moved aside a picture of two very attractive dark-haired women—one in her late forties and the other in her early twenties—Krause's wife and daughter, no doubt. Then he pulled down a Bible and held it out to Georgia.

"Sir?" she asked confused.

"Agent Nelson explained that you need to be deputized, yes? The U.S. Attorney's office has completed the paperwork. This is merely a formality. Please put your hand on the Bible."

Georgia did as she was told and Krause rattled off an oath of allegiance to the United States government, which ended in Georgia saying, "I do." It was almost like getting married. Except there was no death-do-us-part stuff. At least not yet.

"Agent Nelson will help you with the paperwork later." He motioned for her to have a seat across from Nelson but didn't sit himself. "What I'm going to divulge to you now is highly classified FBI information. All of it falls under Rule Six-E. Are you familiar with Rule Six-E, Marshal?"

"It's a Federal statute regarding confidentiality, right?"

"Correct. That means you cannot share any fact or circumstance that I disclose to you with your family, your friends, your fellow fire marshals— even your chief. To do so would constitute a breach of Federal law. And it would put a lot of lives in danger. Are we clear on this?"

"Yes, sir," said Georgia.

"Good." Krause perched himself on the edge of his desk and stared down at her, fixing her in his gaze like a judge. "Marshal, are you familiar with an organization that calls itself the Green Warriors?"

"Weren't they the people who claimed credit for that ski resort fire in Utah a couple of years ago?"

"And a lot more besides," said Krause. "The Green Warriors started out about ten years ago as an offshoot of some of the mainstream environmental groups. Their membership is small, but fanatical. They'll do whatever they have to—arson, sabotage, even murder—to get their message across."

"Have you been following them from the start?"

"Our West Coast offices have. So has the ATF. There have been numerous attempts to infiltrate the Green Warriors, without much success. Our intelligence sources tell us, however, that there has been a struggle within the ranks over the past couple of years. One faction of the Green Warriors wants to abandon violent acts and gain the mainstream respectability of such groups as Greenpeace and the Sierra Club, especially now that the word 'terrorism' has such intensely negative connotations. But another part of the organization is committed to continued acts of violence."

"Why is this a New York issue?" asked Georgia.

"Because, Marshal, we have reason to believe that the leader of the violent faction—a figure we know only as Coyote—is based in the New York area and is formulating plans for a series of new attacks. And we want to take Coyote out and stop the attacks before they start."

"When you say 'attacks,' do you mean like putting spikes in trees?"

"I can tell by the way you asked that that you don't think of eco-terrorists as 'real' criminals."

"I'm sorry sir. I didn't mean to imply anything," said Georgia. "It's just that . . . compared to the types of criminals we see in the FDNY, they seem more like a costly nuisance than a danger."

"What if I told you," said Krause, "that eighteen months ago the Green Warriors blew up a generating plant in Tucson, Arizona? Thousands of homes lost power during a heat wave in which average daily temperatures soared to over a hundred degrees. Seven people died when their dialysis machines and respirators failed because of the power outage."

"You want to talk about dangerous?" Nelson added. "Six months ago in Michigan, Green Warrior operatives set off incendiary devices in a meatpacking plant. The devices were set to blow at four a.m., because—the operatives later claimed—no one would be *in* the plant at that hour. Just one problem: four a.m. is clock-in time. It was only by the grace of God that everyone managed to escape."

"What about in the New York area?" asked Georgia. "Have there been any incidents?"

"Two," said Krause. "Both fires at new housing developments on Long Island. At one of those fires, a volunteer firefighter fell off a collapsing roof. He's paralyzed from the waist down."

"For a fringe group, they sure get around," said Georgia.

"They have money," Krause explained. "Some of it is channeled through front organizations. The rest comes from sympathetic mainstream environmentalists and people in Hollywood, though that seems to be drying up since terrorism took on new meaning in this country." He leaned forward. "The problem, as we see it, is the splintering of the group and the rise to power of Coyote. If the Green Warriors become mainstream, it'll drive the militant element deeper underground. We've got to get their leader before that happens. That's why we've had to depend so much on our confidential informant." Krause paused and waited for the realization to sink in.

"McLaughlin?" Georgia straightened. "Michael McLaughlin is your confidential informant? An ex-Westie who drives a lemon yellow Porsche?"

"He's not *in* the Green Warriors," said Krause. "But he's got a reputation as a good, reliable 'events planner,' as they call it. A lot of the Warriors' early assaults were very amateurish. In one case, an alleged member blew *himself* up. So the Green Warriors started contracting out the jobs."

"But to a guy like Freezer? The man's entire social conscience wouldn't fill up a Tic Tac."

"The Green Warriors needed a professional torch, and McLaughlin wanted the work," said Krause.

"How did the FBI hook up with him?"

"A few years ago, we busted up some of his interstate operations in stolen goods," said Krause. "He was looking at maybe ten years. A guy like McLaughlin could pretty much handle that. But when he found out we were in a position to put a lock on his assets, he asked to deal. He said criminals made sense to him, but the radicals pissed him off. He was happy to hand them over, tidy up his affairs and retire."

"Do you believe him?"

Krause shuffled about uncomfortably. "Marshal, you need to understand something. Fighting terrorism is this country's top priority right now, and domestic terrorism is part of that mission. The Bureau is doing everything in its power to cultivate contacts among terrorism networks. We cannot question the motives of our informants too deeply when the information they give us gets results."

"Yet McLaughlin can't tell you who Coyote is?"

"It's a very secretive group," explained Nelson. "Everything is handled by email and passwords. We've got Nathan Reese working on that end of things almost around the clock."

"McLaughlin has assured us he's on the brink of making contact with

Coyote," said Krause. His face grew positively radiant when he said this. Georgia felt a hollow thud in her stomach. The Feds had so much invested in McLaughlin, there was no way they were going to just hand him over to the FDNY when they were through.

"Do you know what the exact nature of Coyote's plans are?"

Krause didn't reply. Instead, he slid off the edge of his desk and walked over to the window. He stood there for several long, uncomfortable minutes studying the skyline of lower Manhattan. The morning sun glinted off the suspension cables of the Brooklyn Bridge and gave the high-rises a coppery glow. He turned to her. "Marshal, have you ever done any undercover work for the FDNY?"

"Not unless you count the time I tried to deliver a bogus payment to an arsonist in the South Bronx."

"Did you succeed?"

"No. It's kind of hard to pass yourself off as the Latino girlfriend of a drug dealer when you've got reddish-brown hair and freckles."

"I'm sure you and your superiors believed that we would stick you in a corner, shuffling papers, while the real work of this investigation went on elsewhere." He paused a moment to make sure she understood that that had been precisely his intention.

"Instead, I'm in a position to present you with a unique opportunity. Michael McLaughlin is supposed to meet some high-level members of the Green Warriors late tomorrow afternoon to discuss Coyote's New York plans. We need an agent to pose as his girlfriend—someone who looks nonthreatening and yet believable. We'd like you to be that undercover operative."

Georgia bounced a look from Krause to Nelson. She was sure she'd misunderstood. "You want *me* to go undercover?"

"You don't have to *do* anything, Marshal," said Krause. "You just have to be present. You'll wear a wire. Agent Nelson and I will be in a backup car, trailing you. We have no reason to believe that you'll be harmed in any way— by McLaughlin or the Green Warriors."

Georgia swallowed hard and tried to collect her thoughts. "May I ask why you're not using one of your own agents?"

"We have four senior female operatives in the New York office. One is a rather large black woman with a Mississippi accent. Another is Asian. The last two are in their fifties. I doubt sincerely that the Green Warriors will buy any of them as McLaughlin's girlfriend."

Georgia's chest tightened. She closed her eyes. The only image she could see before her was the hideously scarred face of Rachel Cross.

"It's not that I'm not honored—" Georgia stammered out, but Krause cut her off.

"Look, Marshal, surely you must have been wondering why we chose you over any number of more experienced FDNY marshals. This is the reason. We need a law enforcement operative at this meeting. *You* can provide that vital service. There's nothing else you can contribute to this investigation. You walk away from this . . ." He held up his hands. "I can't promise we'll be in a position to give Mr. McLaughlin up for a long, long time. I'm counting on you not to let us down."

13

GEORGIA WALKED THROUGH the rest of the morning in a daze, filling out paperwork and getting security cards and I.D. as if she were going to prison instead of getting clearance to work with the FBI. Here she was, expecting to have to fight to be included in the case, and suddenly, Krause wanted to turn her into their star undercover operative.

At noon, Nathan Reese strolled by her desk. "I hear you're going to be working undercover."

"I don't know. I guess." Georgia didn't meet his gaze. He flopped down in a spare seat in her cubicle.

"Nervous?"

"A little."

"How about we grab some lunch? The FBI has a nice cafeteria."

"I don't feel much like eating," said Georgia.

"It's because you're going under with McLaughlin, isn't it?" asked Reese. "He's a scary guy. Did you know on the street, they call him Freezer?"

"Yeah. And I know why, too."

"Can you get out of the assignment?"

"If I turn it down, there's no way the Bureau will hand McLaughlin over for prosecution. The only piece of evidence we had tying him to the fire at Café Treize was an answering machine tape that Nelson confiscated. Now, we've got nothing."

Reese frowned. "An answering machine tape?"

"Yeah. With McLaughlin's voice on it. Why?"

"Because I'm in charge of the evidence log, and I've never heard of that tape."

"But my partner gave it to Nelson," Georgia insisted. "In my chief's office. Yesterday. I saw him do it."

Reese beckoned Georgia across the hall to his office and logged into his computer. He pulled up a file and scrolled down it. "I'd remember the tape, but maybe Nelson logged it in himself." He ran through a list of reference numbers then shook his head. "There's no tape here, Georgia."

"That bastard." She kicked a shoe at the trash bin. In the FDNY, it would be army surplus metal and make a lot of noise. Here, it was PVC and barely thudded. "I knew it. The FBI has no intention of handing McLaughlin over. The tape is gone. Maybe even destroyed."

"Do you want me to ask Nelson?"

"I bet you he denies the existence of the tape."

"You think?"

"Try it sometime when I'm not around. See for yourself."

Reese massaged his forehead. "This is bad, Georgia. I don't know what to suggest. I love the FBI. Being an agent—it's everything to me. But sometimes I really hate the way my people treat other agencies."

"Your SAC wants to look good with the boys in Washington," said Georgia. "And all those guys seem to care about is fighting terrorists. I don't think a couple of dead firefighters are going to be much of a priority to them."

"Then the only way the FDNY is going to get McLaughlin is if my people no longer need him," said Reese. "Which means going undercover may be your only option."

"I feel like I'm going into this blind," said Georgia. "I know almost nothing about Michael McLaughlin." Then an idea came to her. "Say, Nathan, you have access to the FBI's data files. Can you find a file on McLaughlin?"

"Probably." He hunched over his keyboard and began typing. His face suddenly lit up. "Let's check our career criminal database."

"Isn't that just going to show his rap sheet?" Georgia could get that herself through the FDNY. Reese shook his head.

"Your files will only show his arrests and convictions in the State of New York. The Bureau's CCD is more like a Who's Who of career criminals. It will list every crime McLaughlin's alleged to have been involved in nationwide, even if he was only a suspect and never arrested or convicted. And, get this—it will list crimes where he might have been the victim instead of the perpetrator, too."

"I don't know why the Bureau would care about that," said Georgia.

"With organized crime figures, it's very important. If you know an attempted hit was made on their lives, you can figure out where there's a power struggle brewing."

"I know McLaughlin did five years upstate for robbery when he was very young," said Georgia. "But that's all I think will show up."

Reese typed in a series of codes and commands, then pressed Enter. A few seconds later, some print popped up on Reese's screen and he scrolled through it, a confused look on his face.

"Nothing, right?" said Georgia.

"Actually, plenty, but almost none of it in New York," said Reese. Georgia peered over his shoulder. "In New York, all I've got is that robbery when he was nineteen. But I've got a dropped assault charge in Virginia four years ago. And last year, he was questioned about some illegal dumping activity in South Jersey. He was picked up along with an associate of Louis Buscanti's."

"Louis Buscanti, the mobster?"

"One and the same," said Reese. "McLaughlin's got friends everywhere, it seems."

"What about this?" asked Georgia, pointing to something on the screen.

"This won't help you because McLaughlin isn't accused of a crime. He's the one doing the accusing."

"*McLaughlin* went to the police?"

"It looks more like the police came to him," said Reese. "He and a bodyguard were ambushed by a guy with a baseball bat when they walked out of a Midtown restaurant. Doesn't sound like a mob hit, though. Those guys use bullets, not bats."

"Freezer probably tried to shake down the wrong guy," said Georgia. "Did he press charges?"

"Apparently not."

"When did it happen?"

"Two years ago." Reese shrugged. "Knowing McLaughlin, the dude's probably fish food by now."

He went to scroll down further when Georgia stopped him. "Scroll back for a moment. I want to take a look at that name."

"What name?"

"The name of the guy who assaulted him."

Georgia leaned over Reese's chair until their bodies were almost touching and stared at the screen. "He's not fish food," Georgia muttered.

"McLaughlin's attacker? How do you figure?"

"I know him. Well, I don't actually *know* him. My partner, Randy Carter does, however. Paul Brophy is his ex-partner."

"Could be a different Paul Brophy," said Reese.

"No, look," said Georgia. "On the arrest report, under 'occupation,' he wrote, 'retired firefighter.' And he's the right age, too. Does the arrest sheet give any details of the attack?"

"Let's see," said Reese. "Not much. It looks like a pretty unprovoked attack. McLaughlin stepped out of a restaurant on West Forty-fourth Street, and Brophy came at him and the bodyguard with a baseball bat. Looks like Brophy got the worse end of the deal. Two cracked ribs, a busted collarbone and a broken wrist. McLaughlin never got a scratch on him, and the body-guard had only minor bruises. But even the witnesses to the complaint say Brophy came out of the blue and just started whacking away."

"I wonder if Randy knows. He must know."

Reese looked down. Georgia suddenly realized he was blushing. "I guess this means you won't have time to have lunch with me today."

"Another day, I promise." She touched him on the sleeve of his jacket. "Thanks, Nathan. You're the best."

"That's what all the New York women say."

14

RANDY CARTER HAD JUST returned to Manhattan base when Georgia arrived. His hangdog expression told her where he'd been even before he uttered the words: Ladder Seventeen. Russo and Fuentes' firehouse. She couldn't be angry at him when she saw him looking so heartbroken.

"They've still got all the names on the riding board for Thursday morning," he told her. "Nobody's got the stomach to erase it."

"They're going to be hurting for a long time."

"I know that." Carter sighed. "I just can't go there anymore. I've done it so often these last few years, I feel all used up inside."

"That's because you're not Irish," said Georgia. "The Irish have an infinite capacity for suffering. Who else would parade around every year in the middle of March when it's absolutely guaranteed to be rainy and cold?"

He gave a small chuckle. He knew she was trying to cheer him up. "So, what are you doing back at Manhattan base? Slumming?"

"Taking you to lunch."

Carter stroked his mustache and regarded her through narrowed eyes. "What's up?"

"Come to lunch with me, and I'll tell you."

They caught a cab over to their favorite bagel shop on West Fourteenth Street. It was sandwiched between a Third-World marketplace of discount stores and stalls that sold everything from *I Love NY* T-shirts to cheap suitcases. Georgia didn't talk much on the way over and Carter didn't push. It wasn't until they got their bagels that she spoke.

"There's something I wanted to run by you. Mac says you know stuff about McLaughlin that you're not sharing."

Carter looked surprised—even a little impressed. Georgia waited for him to elaborate, but he seemed to be weighing something in his mind. "Can you get off the case?" he asked her finally.

"If I do, we'll lose Freezer forever."

"We may anyway."

"Randy—" She searched for the right words. Carter's ex-partner was always a delicate subject. "Did you know that Paul Brophy tried to assault Michael McLaughlin with a baseball bat two years ago?"

Carter didn't answer. He didn't have to. Georgia could tell from his eyes that he knew. "Do you know why Broph attacked him?" she pressed.

"Where did you hear this?"

"Never mind where I heard it. Is it true?"

Carter swirled his coffee without meeting her gaze. "Yeah. It's true. He told me he was upset about the Rachel Cross case."

"But that case was ten years old by then," said Georgia. "And Rachel had been dead for at least seven."

Carter shrugged. "Broph was a fire marshal when Rachel killed herself. An assault would've cost him his job. He was a civilian when he took a swing at Freezer. And the FDNY couldn't do any more to him than *I* already had." Carter winced as he spoke. Georgia knew why. Paul Brophy didn't retire from the FDNY—he was fired. And Carter was the one who got him fired after Brophy accepted a bribe to label an arson fire as accidental. Carter did the right thing, to Georgia's way of thinking. But it dogged him for the rest of his career. No one wanted a rat for a partner. Then again, no one wanted a woman, either. That's how they ended up together.

"Why didn't Freezer kill him?" asked Georgia. "He's killed men for less."

"Well, he beat him up pretty good. Besides, if Broph had died, it would've brought a lot of heat on McLaughlin. I guess he thought busting him up was good enough."

"So where is Paul Brophy these days?"

Carter shook his head. "Don't talk to him, Skeehan. That's not a good idea."

"Why? I won't tell him I'm your partner."

"That's not why I'm telling you this." He leaned back in his chair and wiped two long, bony sets of fingers down his tired face. The deli was packed with customers yelling out orders and employees slapping together sandwiches. It was hard to concentrate over the noise and commotion. Yet Georgia knew she had to. She sensed Carter was struggling to tell her something.

"I found out something yesterday," he said slowly, toying with a packet of sugar. "Something I should've figured out sooner. Girl," he leaned forward. "You trust me, don't you?"

"Of course I trust you—even after you pulled that stunt yesterday going behind my back to Brennan."

"I did that for your own good. And this is for your own good, too," he said. "I don't want you to see Paul Brophy."

"Why?"

"I can't tell you."

"So I'm just supposed to obey you—is that it?"

"It's for your own good."

"I'm not a rookie anymore, Randy. You can't treat me like one."

"Two years as a marshal, eight in the FDNY, doesn't qualify anyone as a veteran."

"I'm not saying it does," said Georgia. "But you haven't even apologized for going behind my back yesterday."

"If I'd discussed it with you, would you have backed off?"

"No."

"So? You left me no option."

She frowned. "What's gotten into you? Did you lose respect for me because I mouthed off in front of the Feds yesterday?"

"That's got nothing to do with this," said Carter. "I know what I'm doing here, Skeehan. And I'm telling you to stay away from Broph."

Georgia rose from the table. "And I'm my own person, Randy. I'm not that rookie anymore. I know a lot more than you give me credit for. Maybe not everything. Certainly not as much as you. But a lot. So if you want me to follow your lead, you'll have to give me a reason. Otherwise, get out of my way."

"He won't talk to you, you know," said Carter. "As soon as he knows who you are, he'll slam the door."

"Because I'm your partner? He hates you that much?"

He didn't answer. Instead, he threw the sugar packet across the table in disgust. The past was something very much alive in Randy Carter. And judging from his reaction, Georgia guessed it was very much alive in Paul Brophy, too.

15

NATHAN REESE FOUND Paul Brophy's address for Georgia through the Division of Motor Vehicles computers. He lived in College Point, a working-class neighborhood of row houses and small apartment buildings on a northern peninsula in Queens, just east of La Guardia Airport. And Reese found out something else, too. Broph had a limousine driver's license. That's how he was earning his keep these days. The FDNY had stripped him of his pension.

She changed into jeans and a leather jacket and retrieved her motorcycle from Manhattan base without heading up to the squad room on the fourth floor. She couldn't face Randy right now. This was something she had to work out on her own, the way she always worked things out: straddled across the leather seat of her fire-engine red Harley Davidson. Thirteen hundred and forty cubic centimeters of twin-mounted evolution engine with a hand-painted rose on the gas tank. Plenty of torque. Plenty of chrome. One year old and no major encounters with asphalt—at least, not yet.

She headed out of Manhattan, north on the Brooklyn-Queens Expressway, toward College Point. She didn't call Paul Brophy in advance. She didn't want to give him a chance to turn her down.

Rush hour traffic was at a near standstill on the BQE, so Georgia snaked her bike down the lane marker between the cars. Her mother would have had a coronary watching her, but Georgia had gained confidence over the last year. And besides, she was freezing. The December wind bit right through her heavy jeans, stinging her like a swarm of fire ants. She tucked her legs close to the engine, luxuriating in that small bit of warmth. One of these days, when she had the money, she'd get an all-weather, insulated jumpsuit. The kind that would make her look so cool, it wouldn't matter that the only place she ever rode besides work was to PTA meetings.

She exchanged one highway for another until she was finally on the Whitestone Expressway, heading into College Point. Paul Brophy lived in a pale green aluminum-sided row house on a street of similar houses anchored on one end of the block by an auto parts store and on the other by a liquor distributor. The trees were all small and scrubby and the cars looked like they had some mileage on them.

She walked up a concrete flight of stairs to a front door identical to the one on her mother's house. Three small rectangular windows on a diagonal slant. The two houses were probably built during the same time period— early sixties, if she had to guess. She rang the buzzer.

A bald, thickset man with an enormous reddish blond handlebar mustache opened the front door. He was wearing dark, dressy-looking pants and a white dress shirt, but the shirt was open to an undershirt beneath. He must have either just gotten off duty or he was just going on.

"Mr. Brophy?"

"Yes?"

"*Paul* Brophy?"

"Only Brophy here, sweetheart."

"I was wondering if I could talk to you a moment. I'm an investigator and I'd like to ask you some questions about Michael McLaughlin."

"An investigator?" He frowned. "What *kind* of investigator?"

Georgia didn't want to use her name, Carter's name, or mention the FDNY unless she had to. Since she was here finding out information for an FBI case, she didn't see anything wrong with keeping her fire department credentials a secret. She pulled out her newly issued U.S. Marshal I.D., complete with photo, then whipped it away before he could read her name or begin to make an association.

He folded his hands across his belly and stared at her. He did not invite her in. "I gotta go to work in a minute. What do you want?"

"Can you tell me anything about your relationship with Michael McLaughlin?"

"Relationship? I don't have one. I was a fire marshal and his name came up in some cases I was involved in."

"Rachel Cross, right?"

"That was one of 'em."

"What were the others?"

The muscles beneath his eyes twitched. He wasn't buying her story. "Who are you?"

"I told you, an investigator."

"What is it you're investigating?"

"Why did you assault Mr. McLaughlin outside a restaurant two years ago?"

A spark of something registered across his face. The anger faded. He leaned closer. "Are you Georgia Skeehan?"

"I am," she admitted. "Look, Mr. Brophy, I know you and my partner, Randy Carter, aren't exactly on the best of terms, but I'd really—"

"Does Carter know you're here?"

"I didn't get your address from him. He has nothing to do with—"

"I don't think I should be talking to you, Georgia. Not like this. It's not a good idea."

"But why?"

He shook his head without meeting her gaze. He seemed suddenly embarrassed. "I should've killed the bastard when I had the chance. I wish I'd had the guts. I'm sorry."

"Sorry?" Georgia asked.

"Sorry I didn't kill him. Sorry I didn't come clean about everything sooner. At the time, we really thought it was an accident. Sully and me . . . we just figured it didn't make sense to stir up shit we couldn't do anything about."

"Sully? You mean . . ." She recalled the named tossed about by Bobby Kelly and Carter in the bar. ". . . Jamie Sullivan?"

Brophy lifted his head and gave Georgia a sad-eyed look. "I'm really sorry, Georgia. That's all I can say. I've got to go." Then he closed the door.

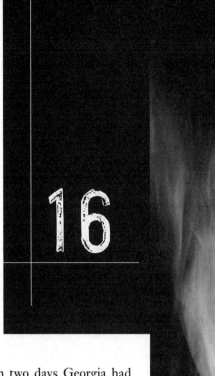

16

JAMIE SULLIVAN. It was the second time in two days Georgia had heard that name. She found his address on West Forty-eighth Street in a Manhattan phone book. She left a vague message on his answering machine explaining that she wanted to talk to him about an old case, along with her name and phone number. She waited for a return call as she went about her evening, helping Richie with his homework, fixing dinner and getting ready to drive to Joe Russo's wake. She could feel the weight of something pressing on her, telling her not to allow herself to be swept any deeper into McLaughlin's schemes than she already was. Maybe Sully felt the same thing. He never called back.

She drove out to Belle Harbor, Queens, a spit of land bordering the Atlantic Ocean. She had been to so many firefighters' wakes and funerals these past few years that the parlors and churches had all begun to look the same. And yet, for Georgia at least, the process never got any easier. She felt it when she looked at Joe Russo's open casket. The life she had seen in that grimy handsome face Thursday morning was now gone. What was left was just a shell. His skin had a pale white gleam. His features were expressionless. His dark hair was slicked back. His hands were crossed over his chest, clutching a crucifix. In that placid imitation of a face, she saw the brief, fleeting vision of her own father when he was laid out. Her mother had kissed him goodbye. Georgia, then twelve, had refused to touch his cold, dead body. She stole one more glance at Joe Russo and something hard thudded in her chest. She wished she'd given her father that last goodbye.

Georgia paid her respects to the family, then heard someone call her name. It was Seamus Hanlon. Doug's father. He was a stout man with silver crew-cut hair, a broad, walrus face and a droopy mustache. There were always bags beneath his watery blue eyes, but this evening, they looked particularly pronounced as he tugged on the sleeves of his dark blue suit jacket.

"I tell you," said Seamus, giving her a hug, "you're one face this body's glad to see."

"Where's Doug?" Georgia knew from Seamus that Doug lived with his in-laws, only fifteen minutes away in Rockaway Park.

The brightness left him. He wiped a hand down his mustache. "He's, uh . . . he's got some breathing problems, Georgia. He's going to try to come later. Right now, he's lying down."

"Is he going to be all right?"

Hanlon didn't meet her gaze. "I'm not sure. Listen, I need to grab a cigarette outside. Can I talk to you a moment?"

Georgia followed him out of the funeral home. A bitter wind gusted off the ocean. She wrapped her coat around her and stamped her feet to keep warm.

"My mother and I tried to call you today," Georgia told him. "Your line was always busy."

"I know," said Hanlon, cupping his hands over the lighter for his cigarette. "The phone was ringing off the hook. But thank you anyway, lass. And your mother, too."

Hanlon squinted into the middle distance, past a row of double-parked cars and bare trees. "Dougie's not sick. He can't bring himself to come to the wake." He took a long drag on his cigarette. "He won't talk to me. Won't talk to anybody. He's been lying on his bed, watching cartoons with Jenna, his daughter, since he got home." Hanlon exhaled a long, slow cloud of smoke, as if the image of his son on that bed was like a punch to the gut. "Georgia, he won't even look me in the face."

"He's ashamed," she said softly.

"Of surviving?"

"He feels he let Russo and Fuentes down. And you're his father. You're a fire captain with a fistful of medals. Seamus, he feels he let *you* down."

"Ach," Hanlon threw up his hands in annoyance. Yet his eyes looked watery and confused. "Why should he feel he let me down? He's my boy. I thank God he's alive."

"And if that had been you down there? With Russo and Fuentes? What then?"

He shrugged. "That's different. I've got twenty-eight years on the job. I should know what I'm doing. But Dougie—he's just a kid. *My* kid. I don't care if he ran out of that building kicking and screaming. I don't care."

"But he does," said Georgia. "Have you called the counseling unit?"

"He won't talk to them. And I can't say as I blame him there. I tried the counseling unit fifteen years ago when I was trying to get sober. The fellow I met with told me every firefighter he was treating for alcohol abuse. He might as well have put the names in the union newsletter. I don't want those quacks seeing my kid. I want someone who understands what he's going through."

Hanlon threw his cigarette down and stamped it out. He shoved his hands in his pockets and turned his back to the fierce ocean wind. "Georgia? I, uh . . . Before Jimmy Gallagher died he, uh . . . he told me about what happened to you when you were a firefighter."

Georgia closed her eyes. She didn't answer.

"I wouldn't bring it up, lass. It's none of my business—"

"It isn't," said Georgia sharply. "And it wasn't Jimmy's, either."

"He didn't tell me 'cause he thought you'd done anything wrong. He just . . . we were just . . ." Hanlon's voice trailed off. He sighed. "Doug refuses to talk to anybody, Georgia. I figured maybe he'd talk to you."

"I'm not a shrink."

"And I'm not looking for one. But my son is losing it. He's got a little girl, and Kerry's expecting another baby in April. I don't think he's going to pull himself out of this without someone showing him the way."

"And I'm the poster girl for the gutless—is that it?"

"I never said that. I never *thought* that. And Jimmy didn't, either. I just never faced what you faced that day—what Doug's facing now. Please, Georgia—a half hour just telling him what you went through—that's all I ask."

17

DOUGLAS HANLON LIVED two blocks from the beach, in the basement apartment of a white, stucco-sided raised ranch that his wife's family owned. Ray Connelly, Doug's father-in-law, was a retired New York City police detective. Kerry and Doug met when Doug was on a leave from the army, sunbathing one day at nearby Jacob Riis Beach. They married when Kerry was five months pregnant with Jenna, who was now four. Doug's appointment to the FDNY four and a half months ago had been the promise of a better life to come.

But now the dream had shattered. Georgia could see it on Kerry Hanlon's face as she opened her parents' front door. There was shock and suspicion in her eyes until she caught sight of Seamus. She opened the door a little wider. Hanlon introduced Georgia.

"She's a fire marshal, Kerry. And a family friend. Doug spoke to her right after the fire. I think he should talk to her again." Georgia was thankful that Hanlon didn't elaborate on why Georgia was the designated "talker."

"Have you found the arsonist?" asked the young woman. There was a note of desperation in her voice as she pulled at the seams of her oversized denim shirt. It was probably Doug's. The sleeves were rolled up, the shoulder seams hung halfway down her arms, but her belly, five months pregnant, was straining at the buttons. She looked too tired for a woman in her midtwenties.

"I'm afraid the investigation is still ongoing," said Georgia. "But I'd like to talk to Doug anyway." From the living room beyond, voices quieted. There was only the canned laugh track of a sitcom coming from a television.

"Is Doug downstairs?" Hanlon asked her.

Kerry nodded. A little girl with wispy blond hair scampered over in feet pajamas, dragging a large, floppy-eared stuffed rabbit.

"Poppa!" the child cried, running up to Seamus Hanlon and wrapping her arms around his knees. "Can you play with me? Daddy won't play with me!"

"Your old granddad's always up for a game, lass. Let me just take care of business first."

Hanlon introduced Georgia to Kerry's family: her ex-cop father, mother, two brothers, two sisters, a couple of spouses and one baby. For such a large gathering in such a small house, it was surprisingly quiet. Everyone was in a somber mood tonight. Kerry led Georgia down the stairs to the basement. Seamus stayed behind to play with his granddaughter.

The back of the basement was above ground, so it had a door that opened onto the backyard with full-sized windows on either side. Still, it was a claustrophobic space. The ceiling was low and set with acoustical tiles. And the furniture had the look of a couple just starting out. The kitchen table was surrounded by mismatched chairs. Framed wedding photos were hung prominently over the sagging floral couch. Toys were scattered all over the worn rug. A small bathroom had been built off the kitchen area and two flimsy doors had been set into Sheetrock walls that cordoned off two bedrooms. One door was open to a child's bed. The other was closed. Georgia could hear the chatter of a television set on the other side. Kerry knocked on the hollow-core door.

"Doug? Baby? There's a fire marshal here to see you. You spoke to her at the fire."

Kerry opened the door. The room was dark except for the bluish flickering light of the television. The bed took up nearly the entire floor space. There was room only for a small night table and a portable closet. The items had the flat, assembly-required look of warehouse imports.

Doug Hanlon blinked at the shaft of light coming into the bedroom. He was wearing a light blue T-shirt that said *Virginia Beach* on the front, and black sweatpants. His blisters looked less raw, the fluid had abated, but he hadn't shaved since the fire. He had part of the chenille bedspread between his fingers and he was twisting it violently while a game show host told a screaming contestant that she was a winner. Bells and a horn sounded at the news. Hanlon flinched as if they belonged to a fire truck instead of a TV show.

"Doug? Remember me?" asked Georgia.

"Uh-huh," he answered in a hoarse, distracted voice.

"Your dad's worried about you. He says you won't talk to him."

Hanlon shrugged. "There's nothing to talk about." He returned his gaze to the television.

"He wants you to come with him to Captain Russo's wake."

"No." Hanlon twisted the bedspread some more between his fingers.

"You think it's going to be easier a day from now? Or a week? Or a month?" asked Georgia.

"Nobody's mad at you, honey," said Kerry. Georgia said nothing. Civilians didn't understand the firehouse code. Rightly or wrongly, Doug felt he had broken faith. And deep down, so would they. No one would say a word out of line to him, but the awkwardness would be there. The sideways looks and conversations that would fall away as he walked over.

"Please, Dougie," Kerry begged. "Please just come upstairs. The whole family's upstairs. No one wants you to be alone down here."

"I *want* to be alone, all right?"

Georgia could hear the tension building in his voice. The whole house seemed tense.

"I can't live this way," said Kerry, her voice beginning to choke up. If Georgia could recall anything about her own mood swings when she was five months pregnant, it was that she was always on the verge of tears. "You've got to talk to somebody. If not me, then your dad. If not him, then this marshal here. We can't go on like this."

Hanlon turned on her. "We can't go on like this because *I* should've died in that basement yesterday. *Me*, Kerry. Not Captain Russo. Not Tony. *Me.* You want me to be happy about that? Just because you're not a widow? You'd have been better off a widow."

Kerry started to cry. Georgia wanted to disappear into the Sheetrock. She didn't know what to say to either of them. She could see what was happening. Making his wife cry was a far easier guilt for Doug Hanlon to bear than feeling responsible for the deaths of two firefighters. He could make up to Kerry. He could never make up to Russo and Fuentes.

"Why are you doing this?" Kerry sobbed. "Why are you pushing everyone who loves you away?"

Georgia didn't even know she was answering until the words left her mouth. "Because you hate yourself, don't you, Doug? You wish to God they were burying you instead. And everyone's well-intended sympathy—it just sounds like pity to you. Pity for a coward. A loser . . ."

Kerry stopped crying. Her face got hard. "How *dare* you talk about my husband that way? Who the hell do you think—"

"She's right." Hanlon flopped back on the bed and looked at the ceiling. "That's how I feel. I don't want anyone's sympathy. I just want to die." He brought a forearm up to shield his eyes. Now they were both crying. *Oh, this is going very well—very well, indeed,* thought Georgia. *Bring on the Mid-East conflict.*

Kerry pushed past Georgia and sat next to Doug on their bed. "Don't talk that way," she said to him. She gave Georgia a sharp look. "Don't let this woman mess with your head. She doesn't know a thing about what you're going through."

"Unfortunately," said Georgia, "I do."

Hanlon palmed his eyes and sat up.

"I've been there, Doug," said Georgia softly. "I know the pain. The guilt.

The self-hatred and what-ifs. I know what it's like to be scared to death to see the firefighters you used to work beside every day. I know about those sleepless three a.m.s, those bargains with God. I know about feeling like every comment from a brother has a double meaning, every look from an officer casts a shadow of doubt."

In the flickering light of the room, Hanlon's eyes met Georgia's. They were no longer blank and glazed. They held the pleading look of a drowning man.

"Let's take a walk to the beach," she offered.

He swung his feet off the bed. Kerry touched his elbow and gave Georgia a wary look. "I thought you were here to talk to Doug about the investigation. Now you're filling his head with all sorts of—"

"Kerry," Hanlon said hoarsely, putting a hand on his wife's shoulder. "I've got to do this, okay? I *need* to do this."

THEY BUNDLED UP and walked the two blocks to the boardwalk that fronted Rockaway Beach. It used to be made out of wood. Now the weathered boards were gradually being replaced by ones constructed from gray recycled plastic—a blessing, Georgia decided, since she was still wearing black pumps and the plastic didn't have bent nails and splinters and knots that could swallow a heel.

The stores along the promenade—ice cream stands, an arcade, a five-and-dime—were all shuttered tight on this December night. The streetlights cast a cold, yellow glare on their shoulders. To her right, Georgia saw the infinite blackness of the Atlantic, broken only by the roaring crash and spray of white surf. She wrapped her black wool coat tightly around her. Hanlon, by contrast, seemed oblivious to the bitter wind. His down jacket was open to only a T-shirt beneath. It was as if nothing could touch him anymore. Georgia recalled the feeling. After Petie Ferraro died, just putting food in her mouth felt like an unnatural act.

"Are you eating?" Georgia asked him, breaking the silence. He shook his head.

"Not really. Not sleeping, either."

"Staying away from the booze?"

"I don't think you can get through this *without* drinking."

"Be careful, Doug. You, especially."

"I'm trying," he said. "I know it would break my dad's heart if I . . ." He swallowed the thought, embarrassed. They both knew that Seamus had conquered his own demons in that department years ago.

Hanlon sighed. "I just wish I could go back to the hour before everything happened. Jesus, you know how many guys my house lost on nine-eleven? Six. Six fathers and husbands and sons. And now, I just put two more names on the wall."

"I understand you feel that way," said Georgia. "But I can assure you that in time, others will forget you were there. People move on. I know it's hard to believe, but things *will* get better."

"I look in the mirror, and I hate the man looking back at me. That's never going to change." Hanlon stopped in midstride and braced his hands on the rails of the boardwalk. He stared out at the surf. In the shadow of streetlight, Georgia could see his glassy eyes. She took a deep breath of sea air. The cold rush of it in her lungs felt good.

"Tell me about the men—Captain Russo and Tony Fuentes," she said, hoping to divert his thoughts to something he could feel positive about. "What were they like?"

"Captain Russo was a firefighter's firefighter," said Hanlon. "A real standup officer. Calm. Fair. Nobody ever saw that man get rattled. All the guys told me I was lucky to be a probie under him. He never made you feel like an idiot, even when you were."

"And Tony Fuentes?"

"My best friend on the job." He smiled sadly. "Tony grew up in the Bronx, in a tough Puerto Rican neighborhood. He said all us Irish and Italian kids from the suburbs were nothing more than rednecks who couldn't parallel park."

"Sounds like he had a sense of humor," said Georgia.

"The best. He was never mean about it, but he hated pretense of any kind.

Every time someone boasted a little too much about what they did at a job, Tony used to bring in a toilet plunger from home and knight the guy, 'Sir Full-of-Shit.' I heard that after he got a medal two years ago, he even knighted himself." Hanlon shook his head. "He had three girls and he was dying for a son to play stickball with. He kept telling me that baby number four was gonna be named Tony Junior, even if it was a girl." Hanlon's voice caught in his throat and he looked out at the surf. "I can't believe he's dead. I keep expecting to see him."

"It's like that," said Georgia. "You talk a lot to shadows."

"Tell me what happened," Hanlon said thickly. "To you, I mean. When you, uh . . ."

"I was assigned to Queens Engine Company Two-Fifty-two, but I was doing an overtime tour in Ladder One-Eighteen across the floor."

Georgia never talked about that horrible day anymore—not to anyone. She'd done her best to make peace with her past. Now, every word felt like it weighed a hundred pounds.

"We got a run to a fire in a row frame. I was doing a search, got turned around and started running out of air. And like you, I got rescued by someone more experienced—a firefighter named Petie Ferraro. He threw me out of a room as it flashed over. Then the floor collapsed beneath him."

Georgia closed her eyes. She could still feel the heat melting her face piece and the strong, secure grip of Ferraro grabbing her turnout coat and flinging her like a rag doll out of that room.

"I thought Ferraro was right behind me, but he'd fallen through the floor. I ran to a window and gulped some air. By the time I understood what had happened and went back, it was too late. He never regained consciousness and died the next day."

"But you went back for him, at least," said Hanlon. "*I* didn't."

"You *couldn't*, Doug. Nobody could. They were trapped behind falling debris. If you'd gone back, you would've died, too."

"That's not what the other men think—I know it. They think I ditched them."

"Has anyone said anything to you?"

"Nah. Jack O'Dwyer—he keeps telling me I did fine. But he never looks me in the eye when he says it. And everybody else—they just kinda slide away from me. I *know* what they feel, Georgia. I feel it myself. I don't belong on this job."

"Then by your definition, *I* don't belong on this job either."

He wiped a hand across the stubble on his cheeks and stared out at the waves without answering.

"Listen to me, Doug. Since that day, I've been awarded two class-one medals. I've crawled through a burning apartment to rescue a downed fire marshal. I've helped evacuate civilians from a New York City landmark on the brink of a major explosion. And I've risked my life to save a cop and a fire marshal from certain death by drowning. I've spent my career and my life trying to make something good out of the bad that happened that day. I didn't quit. Nothing good can come of quitting."

"I can't hurt anyone else if I quit," said Hanlon.

"And you can't *help* anyone else, either. That's why you joined the fire department, isn't it? To help people?"

Georgia leaned her back against the boardwalk railing and listened to the steady pounding of the surf. It rumbled like a joist giving way in a burning building. It sounded like the nightmare that each of them would relive for the rest of their lives.

"Doug, listen to me. You have every right to grieve. But at some point, if that's all you do, then Russo and Fuentes will have wasted their lives to give you yours."

"I don't know what else to do."

"If you really want to honor them, then you've got to be brave and keep doing the work they would've done if they were here. Find a way to honor them, Doug. They have enough people to grieve over them."

18

GEORGIA DIDN'T SLEEP that night. Her dreams were filled with the memory of Petie Ferraro, his sly grin beneath his black mustache, the nonsense Italian words he sang in the firehouse kitchen, the care he lavished on the firehouse rigs as if they were his personal vehicles.

In her dreams, he would always be making spaghetti sauce. And then the smoke would come. Dark gray smoke. It would billow out of nowhere, and suddenly they'd be back in that row house in Queens again. And Georgia would be gulping air out of a shattered window, looking down at shards of glass and a rusted red tricycle on a patch of dirt. When she had this dream, she always woke up gasping for air. And she always woke up thinking—not of Petie, for she guessed on some level that she couldn't bring herself to think of Petie. She woke up thinking about her father.

Ferraro's death haunted her in the details and the guilt they inspired. But her father's death, ironically, had a more subtle power over her. It was the power that came from not knowing. What were George Skeehan's last moments like? Did he suffer? Was he afraid? Was there a firefighter who could've pulled him out? Was there a chief who shouldn't have let him go in the first place? His death had robbed her of a future with him. But it had also robbed her of a way to make sense of the loss. Her father had not died saving anyone. Like Petie, he had been the hero in a drama for which there were no villains or victims. Where was the villain in a child playing with matches? Or an untended cigarette? Or an overloaded electrical circuit? Where was the closure? Georgia's family had never gotten any, nor had Petie Ferraro's. And that's what often plagued her most on those sleepless three a.m.s.

I can give closure to the families of Joe Russo and Tony Fuentes, Georgia reminded herself. *I can bring their killer to justice—if I go undercover for the FBI.*

On Saturday morning, Georgia called Krause. "You've got your deal," she told him. "I'll pose as McLaughlin's girlfriend if it means getting a shot at him when the FBI is finished."

"Excellent," said Krause. "Come into the office as soon as you can. Agent Nelson and I will be here. We'll set everything up."

Georgia begged her mother to watch Richie for the day, then slipped into her most conservative clean clothes—a white turtleneck sweater, a black wool pants suit and some low-heeled pumps. She was heading out the door when the phone rang. She hoped it might be Jamie Sullivan. She was surprised to hear Nathan Reese's voice on the other end.

"I'm sorry to call you at home, Georgia. But I have something I know you'll want to hear."

Her heart leaped. "You've found the Barry Glickstein tape?"

"Something even better." Reese paused. "Look—don't take this the wrong way, but the safest place to meet is my apartment in Manhattan. Do you think you might be able to come in?"

"I'm headed over to the FBI right now," said Georgia. "Are you in the vicinity?"

"Sort of." He gave her an address in the West Twenties.

"All right. I'll swing by first."

NATHAN REESE'S CHELSEA studio apartment was decidedly spartan: a bed, a large bookshelf, a couple of chests of drawers, a bike hanging in a corner and, of course, a computer. He had just collected his mail, and Georgia noticed that he had several overdue notices from credit card companies in a pile on his tiny kitchen table. He was much neater than Mac, but he appeared to be no less strapped.

Reese noticed her looking at his bills. "I'm, uh . . . not normally so delinquent in my debts," he said with some embarrassment.

"Hey," said Georgia. "It's none of my business."

Reese nodded. "Can I get you a soda?"

"Sure thing," said Georgia. He pulled two diet Cokes out of the tiny refrigerator and searched for a glass. Georgia could see he was nervous. She wondered if he had many women to his apartment. "The can is fine," she said.

He swept the bills off the table and placed them in an even bigger stack of creditor's letters Georgia hadn't noticed before on the kitchen counter.

Georgia eyeballed the stack. "I thought the FBI paid pretty well. I mean, you guys get a twenty-five percent cost of living adjustment just for working in New York."

"I guess there are some debts even an FBI salary can't seem to get rid of." Reese slapped the can of soda down on the table as if to close the conversation. "By the way, did that address I gave you on Paul Brophy ever pan out?"

"It did," said Georgia. "I spoke to him, but as soon as he figured out who I was, he shut down. I can't put my finger on it, but there's something no one's telling me about Freezer—not my partner, Randy, and certainly not Paul Brophy. I've been trying to reach an old partner of Brophy's—a guy named Jamie Sullivan. His name keeps coming up over and over. I called him, but he never returns my calls."

"Maybe he's out of town," said Reese. "Want me to check him out on any databases?"

"No. That's okay," said Georgia. "You've got enough to do. He lives in Hell's Kitchen. Sometime when I have time, I'll just take a ride over there and speak to him in person." Georgia took a sip of soda and leaned back in her chair. "So, what did you want to show me?"

Reese walked over to a briefcase by the front door and extracted a small tape recorder. "The Glickstein tape, I'm sorry to say, is probably a goner," he explained. "I think Krause had it destroyed. But you might find this an interesting substitute." He placed the recorder on the table and pushed Play.

. . . So a couple of firefighters died—so what? You think this is the first time an accusation like this has been leveled against me? This is Mike McLaughlin you're talking to. Not some street hoodlum. Trust me on this. In a week or two, no one will remember their fuckin' names. They're just a couple of nobodies, anyway. . . .

Georgia stared at Reese with wide-eyed fascination. "Where did you get this?"

"Never mind where I got it. I'm not supposed to have it. No one is. It's not part of the evidence log. It's a duplicate tape from an illegal wire I was asked to install."

"By whom?"

"I can't say."

"Can anyone trace this to you?"

"Only one person, and he's as guilty of ordering the illegal wire as I am of installing it," said Reese. "So I don't think it's going to be a problem. Still, if it came back to me, I'd have to deny it."

"I understand," said Georgia. "Can I keep this copy?"

"I figured you would. I'll leave it to your judgment who you share it with in your department."

Georgia listened to the tape again. "You know, McLaughlin never actually admits on tape to killing those firefighters."

"Wouldn't matter if he did," said Reese. "The tape's inadmissible in court anyway. There are sections missing, and you can't divulge where you got it. That pretty much renders it useless as evidence."

"Then why are you sharing it with me?"

"Because if all else fails, maybe it will help the FDNY jump-start an investigation on Freezer one day."

Georgia popped the tape out of the recorder and slipped it into her handbag. "I'm going to be working tonight, so I don't want it on me. I'll hide it in a desk drawer at work and retrieve it tonight when I go home."

Reese's face clouded over. He knew what "working tonight" meant. "You're going undercover with McLaughlin?"

"I have to."

"Be careful, Georgia. Believe me, I know a thing or two about how ruthless he can be. That tape is all the ammunition I can give you."

Georgia spent the afternoon getting briefed on the basics of undercover work. Scott Nelson told her things she would've figured out through common sense—not to volunteer information and to always stay in character. He showed her what a J-bird body wire looks like and how it would be concealed. She was used to the older and more bulky NAGRA wires. He took her down to security and got a fake driver's license made up with a different last name—*Stevens*—and a different address. He even had some credit cards issued in her new name.

"Ooh, time for a shopping spree," Georgia joked. But Nelson didn't laugh. Apparently, Reese was the only Federal agent to be issued a sense of humor.

In a special room downstairs, Georgia unholstered her weapon, emptied it of ammunition and handed over both for vouchering. This step terrified her most of all. Once she gave up her gun, she didn't stand a chance against a man as powerful and cunning as McLaughlin.

A female agent helped her attach a microphone and transmitter to the inside of a specially designed bra.

"Won't they frisk me?" Georgia asked Nelson after she was wired up.

"They're not likely to chance pissing Mike off by asking to feel inside his girlfriend's bra."

Nelson and Georgia met up with Krause, who went over the details of the operation. Georgia would take a cab to McLaughlin's house. From there, McLaughlin would drive them to the meeting in his Nissan Pathfinder. The FBI had installed a tracking device under the bumper. Krause and Nelson would follow in a separate car.

"Don't worry, Marshal," Krause assured her. "Every word of conversation you have in that car or out of it will be broadcast to us. We can follow the car. We can follow you. McLaughlin knows that. You're in no danger."

By the time the cab let Georgia off in front of Michael McLaughlin's home, she felt sick to her stomach. She was sweating so much, she was certain she'd already shorted out the wires.

McLaughlin buzzed her into the hall with the one-way mirror again, then opened the interior door. Georgia could barely bring herself to step inside. She froze by the doorway and stared up at the man. He was dressed in gray wool slacks and a striped, button-down shirt of pale gray and seafoam green. He was clean-shaven, and his tea-and-honey-colored hair had just been razor cut. He seemed amused by her hesitance. He pulled a cigarette from a pack in the pocket of his trousers and offered her one. She declined.

"You're gonna have to loosen up, love, or they'll peg you as a cop from the get-go." He allowed his eyes to travel slowly down her black blazer and white turtleneck sweater and frowned. "Then again, they might figure it out anyway."

Georgia felt her chest. McLaughlin grinned.

"It's not the wires in your bra, love. They're fine. It's just that . . . you dress like a cop."

"What's *that* supposed to mean?"

"Well . . . you know. Sort of frumpy. Tomboyish. No style."

"I have plenty of style."

He shrugged. "No need to get offended. I'm just saying you've got a nice figure. Why not show it off?"

"This is what I came in. I'm afraid you're going to have to live with it."

McLaughlin did a one-eighty around Georgia, eyeing her from head to toe. "You're a size eight, maybe? Size eight petite?"

Georgia hesitated. "So?"

"I've got a closetful of designer clothes upstairs. My girlfriend's. You'd look great in a Badgley Mischka chiffon blouse, some Marc Jacobs black hip-hugger jeans and a pair of Manolo Blahnik boots."

"You want me to *borrow* your girlfriend's clothes?"

"Why not? I bought 'em. She can't take them home." He winked at her. "Her husband's likely to wonder where she got 'em."

"She's married?"

"Best kind of woman to have, I always say." McLaughlin chuckled. "They never pester a man for commitment."

"Forget it, McLaughlin. I'm not changing." A cell phone rang inside Georgia's bag. She frowned. She'd had to give up her own cell phone along with her gun and the contents of her handbag for security purposes. This one belonged to the FBI. The only person who could be calling her was Krause. She picked up.

"Marshal, Mike is right," said Krause. *At least the wires haven't shorted out,* thought Georgia. Krause apparently had heard their entire conversation. "Everything you say and do that's different from what they expect will stand out. You don't have to look like a streetwalker. But you don't want to look like a cop, either."

McLaughlin seemed to guess the nature of the conversation. "Look, love," he interrupted. "It's no skin off my back how you dress. But we both want this meeting to go smoothly. It'll succeed a lot better if you don't fight me all the way." His eyes traveled to her hips and a slight gleam came into his eyes. "Then again, maybe you won't be able to fit into my girlfriend's clothes anyway. She's taller than you, with a little more on top and a little less across the hips."

"My hips are fine."

"Of course," he said, then clucked his tongue. "Some people think big hips look good on a woman."

That did it. "Where do I change?"

19

GEORGIA HAD TO ADMIT, the clothes looked good. Sexy. Expensive. And unlike anything she'd ever worn before or would ever again.

McLaughlin gave her a quick once-over as they stepped into his black Nissan Pathfinder.

"Very nice. Very nice, indeed." He nodded. "A beautiful woman should always wear beautiful clothes."

Georgia gave him a warning look, but she couldn't hide the blush in her cheeks. Mike McLaughlin knew how to play a woman. She'd have to be very careful not to get taken in.

He nosed the car onto the West Side Drive, heading north. He was a conservative driver, which surprised Georgia. He didn't speed and he always signaled.

"Can I ask where we're heading?"

"Fort Lee, New Jersey," said McLaughlin. "I'm supposed to meet my contacts at a diner on the other side of the George Washington Bridge."

"Not in some dark bar somewhere?"

"I don't drink," he said flatly.

"Ever?"

"I saw enough drinking to last a lifetime when I was a kid." He shook his head. "It was not a pretty sight."

"You're the only teetotaling Westie I've ever heard of."

"There are no Westies anymore. They're all dead or in prison. Me? I don't drink. I keep my head screwed on right, and here I am, out riding with a pretty young woman." He winked at her and she pretended to ignore it. "You see? A rough life doesn't always equal a rough mind." He pulled a pack of Lucky Strikes out of his pants pocket. "May I? It's the one vice I could never shake."

"If you wish."

He lit one and rolled down the window. "So your dad died in the line of duty, eh?"

Georgia turned her face away from him and stared out the window. They were cruising up the West Side of Manhattan. Across the narrow stretch of Riverside Park, brownstones and apartment buildings sprouted above the bare branches of trees, already illuminated by streetlights.

"I can tell you were very fond of him."

"I don't want to talk about my father."

"C'mon, love. I'm just making conversation here."

"Please don't call me that," said Georgia.

"Call you what?"

"Love. I'm not your 'love.' "

"Figure of speech. I can't exactly call you 'Marshal' when we're undercover, now can I?"

Georgia grinned in spite of herself. "Call me Georgia, okay?"

"Okay, Georgia." He took a hit off his cigarette. "You got a boyfriend, Georgia?"

"That's none of your business."

"I told you about my girlfriend."

"You only tell me what you want to."

"Okay. So what do you want to know?"

She gave him a sour look. "You know what I want to know."

"You want me to confess to the fire at Café Treize, is that it?" He laughed. "You cops—you're all so one-track-minded. You know, the funny thing is, I get accused of doing things I never did. And the stuff I've done, nobody ever gets me on."

"Are you saying you *didn't* set the fire at Café Treize?"

McLaughlin winked at her. "See? That's what I mean. A good con man would wonder what I *hadn't* been nabbed on. You—you're still beating a dead horse."

"You didn't answer my question."

"You're wrong, lass. You just didn't *hear* the answer." He flicked his cigarette butt out the window. "Besides, I love firefighters. And police, too. I gave a check for five hundred dollars to the Widows' and Orphans' Fund last year."

"All right, here's a question for you," said Georgia. "How come Paul Brophy assaulted you outside a Manhattan restaurant two years ago?"

"Who?"

"Paul Brophy. An ex-fire marshal. You never pressed charges."

"The gambler. Yeah, I remember him. He took a kickback on an arson case to label it accidental."

"He was fired for that, you know," she reminded him. "No one covered it up."

"So I heard," said McLaughlin. "In fact, your partner, Randy Carter, dimed him out." He chuckled. "You know how the old-timers spell Carter, don't you, lass? Take away the C, the E and the R, and all you're left with is R-A-T."

He was getting to her. She'd sworn she wouldn't let him do it, but he was doing it just the same. "You haven't answered my question: why did Paul Brophy assault you?"

"You'd have to ask him."

"I did. He wouldn't talk. And his former partner, Jamie Sullivan, hasn't returned my phone calls."

"Can you blame them? You're the partner of a rat."

"Oh, that's really insightful coming from a confidential informant out to save his own skin."

"Least I'm honest about it." McLaughlin shrugged. "I don't pretend it's anything else."

They headed west across the George Washington Bridge. McLaughlin made several sharp turns until they were in the parking lot of a large silver diner. Highways crisscrossed all around them, and tall apartment buildings with balconies grew shadowy under darkening skies. A cell phone rang. Georgia realized it was his. He mumbled into the receiver, scribbled something on a piece of paper, then dialed his cell phone.

"What's wrong?" asked Georgia.

"Change of plans. Happens all the time," said McLaughlin. Then he spoke to Krause and relayed the information to him. The new meeting place was a construction site off the New Jersey Turnpike. It was in an area known as the Meadowlands, a bucolic name for a marsh filled with industrial runoff from the surrounding factories and landfills. Georgia felt sick all over again. She'd been willing to go undercover because she'd assumed she'd be someplace public, surrounded by Federal agents who could help her out if things went wrong. Out there, at an empty construction site surrounded by marsh, Nelson and Krause wouldn't even be able to find her, much less see her.

McLaughlin seemed relaxed about the change. Relaxed about everything, in fact. *He's got something up his sleeve.* She could feel it from the moment she stepped inside his house this afternoon and he convinced her to change clothes. She stared down at her high-heeled Manolo Blahnik boots. Then she looked across at his shoes. Crepe soles. With tie-up laces. Great for trampling about in the brush. With her boots, she didn't stand a chance of keeping up with him.

"You knew the Green Warriors weren't going to hold the meeting in the diner, didn't you?" she asked when he hung up with Krause.

"Why would I know that? I told you, this stuff happens all the time." He pulled the car out of the parking lot and onto an on-ramp for the Turnpike.

"What's your game? You've got one, I know it," said Georgia.

McLaughlin's smile chilled her. *Is he running a scam on me?* She asked herself. *Or is a scam the least of it?*

20

IT WAS A MOONLESS NIGHT and very dark by the time McLaughlin turned the car into a dirt service road that wound through a thick section of marsh. There were no streetlights out here, only a ring of security lamps attached to a chain-link fence. Beyond the fence, Georgia could see an excavation site surrounded by heavy construction equipment. A trailer sat off to one side, half-buried in shadows. They were about a mile from the bright stadium lights of the Meadowlands sports complex, but between it and them there was only a vast, dark emptiness, covered over in tall grass that shot up like cornstalks. She activated her recorder and tested it, as she'd been instructed to do. Everything they said from this moment on would be part of the FBI's investigation file.

The entrance to the construction site was open. Georgia saw a padlock dangling from the gate, but it didn't appear to have been cut.

"The Green Warriors have access to this construction site?" asked Georgia. "I would think the only way they could get in would be to break in."

"Maybe they've got a sympathizer," said McLaughlin. He drove the SUV through the gates and parked about twenty feet from the trailer. On the other side sat a battered pickup truck with a cap on the trunk bed and Jersey plates. Only the denseness of a shadow in the driver's seat told her someone was sitting in the cab. She wondered if the driver had a gun trained on both of them.

McLaughlin stepped out of the car and walked around to open Georgia's door. Before he could get there, she flung the door open herself and stepped out. The ground was uneven and her high-heeled boots sank into the half-frozen muck. She stumbled. McLaughlin grabbed her just before she fell and tried to steady her, but she pushed him away.

"For chrissakes, Georgia," he growled. "You think it's gonna kill you to touch me? Now would be a good time to start acting like you're my girl, you know."

He was right, much as she hated to admit it. She grabbed his arm and forced a smile.

"That's better," he said, slipping an arm around her waist. He winked at her. "You could get to like this."

Next time I hold your arm, it'll be to cuff it, she thought, but kept it to herself.

They walked up to the trailer door and McLaughlin knocked. A tall, gaunt man with long hair, a beard and glasses opened the door and ushered them into a dark room with desks and computer equipment scattered about. At first, Georgia thought he was black, because his hair was in dreadlocks. But as her eyes adjusted, she could see that he was young and white, though trying desperately to look like a much older, more culturally hip Rastafarian.

A short, stocky figure in the corner turned on a small desk lamp, casting a dim light through the interior. Georgia saw now that she was a woman. She wore a cape over a peasant dress and had long brown frizzy hair that seemed to fan out in a perfect triangle from the center parting on her head. She reminded Georgia of a sphinx.

"Hey there," said McLaughlin, giving a mock salute to the young couple. "How many of your people are here tonight?"

"Just the two of us," said the Sphinx. She had a nasal voice and a sharp-edged manner that suggested that she, not Dreadlocks, was in command. "And our driver."

McLaughlin nodded in the direction of the front gate. "Somebody had a key to this place, I see. Are we going to encounter any trespass issues?"

"We shouldn't," said Sphinx. "Our driver will lock up when we're through."

Georgia had to hand it to McLaughlin. He had managed very deftly to uncover the fact that one of the Green Warriors had legal access to this construction site. She couldn't have finessed the information any better.

McLaughlin rubbed his hands together. It was cold in the trailer, cold enough to see their breath. "So . . . you got my assignment?"

"It's a big one," said Dreadlocks. Georgia could see the white of his teeth set in a grin. Good, straight teeth—the product of thousands of dollars of orthodontic work, she'd guess. It was in total contrast to what Georgia could see of his clothes: baggy denims and a frayed sweatshirt, which looked as if it had come from the Salvation Army. Georgia wondered what he would have made of McLaughlin's lemon yellow Porsche or his John Constable oil painting. Then again, with teeth like that he didn't exactly grow up in a soup kitchen.

Sphinx pulled her cape around her and regarded Georgia suspiciously. "Before we go any further, we're going to have to check you for wires."

McLaughlin held up his arms. "Be my guest."

"Not a frisk," said Sphinx. "A strip search. Both of you."

Georgia froze. She shot a quick glance toward McLaughlin. A frisk probably wouldn't undercover the wires in her bra. But a strip search would. It would blow the entire investigation. Not to mention that she could easily wind up dead before the Feds could find them. Maybe this was what McLaughlin had in mind all along.

McLaughlin put an arm around Georgia's shoulder. It felt strangely reassuring. "You want to strip search me? No problem. But no one—and I mean no one—sees my girl naked but me. You touch her, I'll walk and you'll have to explain it to Coyote. And you *know* Coyote won't be pleased."

Sphinx frowned. "Then she waits in the car."

McLaughlin walked over to one of the trailer windows. "You want me to send my girl away when you got a driver in that truck out there, and I can't even see him? How do I know he hasn't got a gun pointed at me?"

Sphinx and Dreadlocks looked at each other. "He's not part of the negotiations," said Sphinx.

"Fair enough," said McLaughlin. "Order him to get out of the truck and stand near the trailer door where I can keep an eye on him. Then I'll send my girl back to the car."

Sphinx pulled a handy talkie out of the pocket of her cape and relayed McLaughlin's instructions to the driver. A few seconds later, Georgia heard the truck door open and shut and the crunch of what sounded like work boots on gravel. She felt a sigh of relief. She was going back to their car. It would all be over soon. As much as she hated Michael McLaughlin, she had to admit that, in this instance, he had helped save her life.

McLaughlin kept his eye on the trailer window. When he was satisfied he could see the driver near the foot of the stairs, he gave Georgia the okay to leave.

She opened the door and stepped out. It took a minute for her eyes to adjust to the darkness outside. In that moment, as she started down the stairs, McLaughlin grabbed her rear end and gave it a squeeze, in full view of the two radicals inside and the man from the truck at the bottom of the stairs. Georgia kept her head down, clenched her teeth and said nothing. She didn't want to chance tripping again in her stiletto-heeled boots. She just wanted to get to the car and have this meeting be over.

Yet even with her head down, she sensed the man from the truck staring at her. She could see his thick-soled work boots and the baggy legs of his jeans. She lifted her head and looked at his face. A stalled breath escaped her lips, misting in the cold night air. Her brain reacted slowly—at first recognizing the face, then arguing against it.

He was wearing a baseball cap, the brim pulled low enough to cast shadows that could play tricks on the mind. And yet, judging from his startled reaction, this was no trick of the mind. Their eyes met. She took a step backward. A breeze rustled through the tall brush. It was the only sound Georgia could hear besides the distant whoosh of cars along the Turnpike and the thumping in her chest. Eight years had changed a lot of things—had made his face fill out, had made his shoulders widen. Eight years had made that dimple in his chin more pronounced, as Richie's would be more pronounced one day. The man in the baseball cap looked just like her boy. And that was only natural. Rick DeAngelo was Richie's father.

He took his hands out of the pockets of his insulated denim jacket and made a move toward her. He was going to speak. He was going to blow everything—maybe for both of them. She was wired. Every word would be recorded. She had to cut him off. She shot him a pleading look, but kept her words cool.

"Hey, buddy, if *I* have to leave the warmth of the trailer," said Georgia, "I'm sure as hell not gonna stand out here and kill time smoking cigarettes with you."

He flinched like he'd been punched in the shoulder. His dark hooded eyes were glassy and full of that hurt puppy look he always knew how to give. For a moment she was almost taken in by it. Then the realization hit her like an Atlantic breaker. Rick wasn't a cop. He was an electrician. He'd let the Green Warriors into this construction site. He was the one with the key. He was here of his own free will. She gave him a cold look back. She didn't even know which she was madder about—the fact that he was working with terrorists, or the fact that he hadn't had any communication with their son in eight years. Before he could try to speak again, she turned on her heel and headed to McLaughlin's SUV.

Georgia didn't look back until she was inside. *What am I going to do?* she wondered. If she told Nelson and Krause that she knew Rick, they would include him in their sting. He would be arrested. She would have to testify. Her testimony could send the father of her son to prison. *God, how will I ever explain that to Richie?* Yet to withhold that kind of information would mean compromising the FBI's case. Her career would be ruined. The Feds would never turn McLaughlin over to the FDNY after a fiasco like that. *McLaughlin's counting on me to withhold what I know about Rick to the Feds. That's his game. That's why I'm here. He knows.*

Georgia watched Rick standing by the trailer, hands in his pockets, shooting occasional glances in her direction. He didn't walk over to talk to her. And just as thankfully, he made no moves to alert Dreadlocks and Sphinx, either. After what seemed like an eternity, McLaughlin emerged from the trailer and walked back to the car.

"Are you okay?" he asked as he stepped inside.

"Fine," she said tightly.

"You owe me a thank-you. The wire may be a bust, but I saved your ass in there."

"I seem to recall you grabbed it more than saved it."

"Just keeping in character, lass." McLaughlin started up the engine. "You seemed a might nervous when you walked by their driver outside. I think you spoke to him. You know each other or something?"

"I didn't really see his face," Georgia lied. "The light was bad."

A small grin spread across McLaughlin's freckled features. "Funny, I thought the light was just perfect. Maybe we only see what we want to see, eh?"

21

KRAUSE AND NELSON refused to tell Georgia anything about the
Green Warriors' plans. "The less you know, the safer you are," Krause
explained.

"I'm not so sure about that," said Georgia.

The agents interrogated McLaughlin privately in the back of their
Chrysler at a remote spot off the New Jersey Turnpike, while Georgia
changed back into her own clothes and waited in McLaughlin's SUV.
There, her thoughts bounced from one extreme to the other. She
knew what she was supposed to do: tell the Feds about Rick, then ask
to be taken off the case. But if she did, she'd be responsible for sending her son's father to prison.

If I don't tell, how can they prove I recognized him? But Georgia understood the folly in that reasoning. Rick might already be telling the
Green Warriors about her. It wasn't only a question of ethics, but
safety as well. *And what if the whole thing was a set-up? What if the Feds
know I saw Rick?* Her integrity could be riding on whether she came
forward.

And yet she couldn't. Not tonight. Not this way. *I need to sleep on this*, Georgia decided. Tomorrow, she'd tell the Feds. Georgia felt certain McLaughlin was somehow behind this. He seemed to know so much about her. Yet after three hours with him, she knew almost as little as when she started. All she had on him was that tape Nathan Reese had given her—and she couldn't even make that public. Randy wouldn't tell her anything more about McLaughlin. Neither would Paul Brophy. She had only one option left.

At Federal Plaza, Georgia retrieved her gun, cell phone and belongings, including Reese's tape from her desk drawer. Krause offered to have an agent drive her home, but Georgia declined. Instead, she took a subway north to an address on West Forty-eighth Street that she had written down. The building was a chocolate brown turn-of-the-century tenement that had seen better days.

Georgia walked up the front stoop and into a small, tiled vestibule where mailboxes were set into the wall. The entrance door beyond the vestibule was locked. She scanned the mailboxes until she found one marked *J. Sullivan, 3B*. Georgia smiled. Jamie Sullivan was a lottery millionaire and a retired fire-fighter with a pension. He could have afforded a nice beachfront condo in Florida or a co-op on the Upper East Side. Instead, he lived in a dilapidated building that Georgia suspected he'd been living in for easily thirty years. It was the way of so many firefighters, especially the older ones. They took incredible physical risks every day. Yet emotionally and socially, they seldom ventured far from the familiar. When they were comfortable with something, they stuck with it.

She hit the buzzer and waited. A dog barked somewhere inside the building. There was no response from 3B, so she searched for the superintendent's buzzer and rang it.

A gray-haired, barrel-chested old man hobbled to the front door and squinted at her. Georgia produced her FDNY shield. She sensed it would carry more weight here than any Federal I.D. He unlocked the inside door.

"I'm looking for a Mr. James Sullivan."

"Nope, sorry," said the super. "We don't need any paint or wallcovering."

Georgia suddenly noticed the hearing aid in the man's right ear. She wondered if he had it turned on.

"I'm not selling paint," she said loudly. "I'm looking for Mr. Sullivan."

"Who?"

"Sullivan" she shouted. "A retired firefighter. He lives in—"

"I know where he lives," growled the super, switching his hearing aid on. "Man owns the whole building. Don't you think I know where he lives?"

"Sully owns the building?" asked Georgia.

"Yeah. After he won the lottery." The super allowed a faint smile. His teeth were so full of gaps they reminded Georgia of clothes pegs on a laundry line. "The owner was gonna tear this place down for condos, kick all the old people out. Sully didn't want to leave. So he bought the building."

"Do you know where he is this evening?"

"I know where he isn't—on my doorstep with the twenty bucks he owes me from poker last night. I've been banging on his door since early this afternoon and he won't answer."

"Could he be away?"

"Away where?" asked the super. "Everybody he knows lives within five blocks of here."

"Would you mind if I looked around—made sure he's all right?" asked Georgia.

"You think he's sick?"

"I don't know. But I'd like to check it out."

The super nodded and fished out a huge ring of keys from the front pocket of his faded work pants. Then he led Georgia up two flights of narrow stairs. The beige carpet was brand-new and had a cheap plastic smell to it. It did nothing to make the walls, painted the color of yellowing newspapers, look any less dingy.

"Sully really saved the building, I tell you," said the super. "See this carpet? Sully put it in. And the front security door, too. Next year, he's gonna replace all the broken mailboxes. It makes all the old people feel safe again, you know?"

Georgia nodded politely. In truth, the building still looked shabby, but it was possible the old-timers were comfortable with things the way they were.

When they reached the third floor, a cold breeze flew at their faces. The super walked over to a window at the end of the hallway. It was wide open. "Who opens a window in December, tell me that?"

He tried to close it, but it wouldn't budge. Finally, he waved a disgusted arm at it. "I'll fix it later. Next thing we should do is get new windows around here, if you ask me."

At a steel door marked 3B, the super made a fist and thumped loudly. "Sully, open up." The only sound on the other side was the mewing of a cat. The cat sounded hungry. Even the super suddenly looked concerned.

"He wouldn't go away and leave Cinders without food."

"Cinders? That's his cat?"

"Saved her from a fire. Damn thing's fourteen and blind now, but he treats her like his baby."

"Does the fire escape run by any of his windows?" asked Georgia.

"The living room window," said the super. Georgia climbed out the open window at the front of the building and onto the fire escape. Sully's window was locked, with a heavy drape across it. She returned to the hallway.

"Do you have a key to his door?"

"Of course," said the super. "Just because Sully owns the building doesn't mean *everything's* changed."

The old man sorted through his ring of keys until he came to the right one. "I hope you're decent, Sully," he yelled at the door. " 'Cause I ain't looking at no floor show." He slipped the key into the lock and Georgia heard the mechanism give way. She pushed the door open. The light from the hallway flooded the room. She couldn't find a light switch.

"Mr. Sullivan? This is Fire Marshal Georgia Skeehan. May I come in?"

No answer. The living room looked undisturbed. All the drapes were closed. It was a simple room, but neat. A big plaid recliner. A plaid couch. A couple of tables and lamps. The same new beige wall-to-wall carpet that had been laid on the stairs. No beer cans, laundry or pizza boxes on the floor. No signs of a scuffle. Or a robbery. Sully owned a 36-inch Panasonic television and a top-of-the-line VCR. Both sat placidly facing the couch. He didn't live like a Lotto millionaire, but then, thirty years in the FDNY could do that to a person.

A light but steady breeze drifted over Georgia's shoulder. It was coming from the open window in the hallway outside the apartment. It went through her like ice, then seemed to pass down a dark, windowless hallway that Georgia guessed led to a bedroom in the back. She called out again. Still no answer. The cat mewed at Georgia's feet. She could smell a faint ammonia odor from the litter box. She couldn't tell if it was faint because it had recently been changed or because the breeze through the apartment was sucking out the odor. She glanced at a small open kitchen off the living area. No dishes in the sink. She opened the refrigerator. Not a lot of food—a half-open can of cat food, a six-pack of beer, the remains of some Chinese takeout. Still, none of it smelled like it had been in here more than a couple of days.

Georgia wished she'd had her latex gloves with her. She didn't want to touch anything without them. She slipped on a wool glove from her coat pocket and peered down the hallway. There was a square, chest-high opening on the left that Georgia guessed was an old dumbwaiter. The door to the dumbwaiter had been pushed up. The breeze picked up in this direction. Sully had to have left a window open in the bedroom. *But in winter?*

She had a sudden, stabbing realization at what might await her at the other end of the hallway. People who live alone often aren't discovered dead until their bodies begin putrefying enough to alert neighbors. An open window in winter could dissipate the odor and delay that process for weeks. With her gloved hand, she flicked on the hallway light switch.

And then she heard it. At the end of the hallway. A click, followed by a whoosh, like a gas stove igniting. The wind over her shoulder suddenly intensified. The cat raced past her, out of the apartment. When she looked back at Jamie Sullivan's bedroom, flames were mushrooming across the ceiling. The bed crackled like it had been hit with napalm.

"Get out of the apartment!" she yelled to the super. "Call nine-one-one."

Georgia had never seen a fire move so fast. Within seconds, flames were shooting up the bedroom curtains. The wind, too, had intensified. It howled through the apartment and gusted over her shoulder like a train barreling through a subway station at top speed. And yet, perhaps because of that god-awful wind, there was very little smoke. She could see everything as if she were watching a Hollywood movie. She looked back one last time at the bedroom, now completely engulfed. She saw no body. Heard no cries. She prayed Jamie Sullivan wasn't home. Without turnout gear and a hose line, she couldn't save him. Then again, she had no illusions that anyone in that bedroom would be alive now anyway.

She raced out of Sullivan's apartment, then slammed the front door shut to stop the spread of fire to the rest of the building. The super had said there were a lot of elderly people living here. If the fire expanded beyond Sully's place, some of them might not make it out. Already, the super was knocking on other apartment doors, trying to evacuate tenants. Georgia joined him. In the street, a pumper was turning the corner.

Georgia didn't leave the building until she had rounded up all the tenants she could. Many of them had canes. Some didn't hear especially well. She helped them make their way down the stairs while firefighters filed up. By the time she got to the street, dark gray clouds of smoke were puffing out the back of the building, blotting out the halogen-lit sky. Now that the flames had been contained, the smoke had intensified. It looked more like the fires Georgia normally rolled up on. Deadly, yes. But recognizable. She shuddered as she recalled the sudden fury of the flames in Sully's bedroom. The room had to have been doused in accelerant. But why didn't she smell anything?

An EMS technician walked over to Georgia. "Do you need medical attention?"

"No, thanks." Georgia squinted over at a dark blue Chevy Caprice pulling up across the street. She closed her eyes and cursed softly as a tall, lean black man got out of the driver's seat.

"Besides, I think I'm going to be stuck here awhile."

22

RANDY CARTER gave Georgia a dark look as he approached.

"Girl, don't even try to tell me you had nothing to do with this."

"All I wanted to do was talk to Jamie Sullivan," she sputtered. "He wouldn't return my phone calls."

"Well, for sure, he ain't gonna return them now."

Georgia paled. "Firefighters found a body?"

"The ten-forty-five came in over dispatch as we pulled up," said Carter.

"Oh, God." She collapsed against the side of a fire engine. "I killed him."

"Can't tell that until Suarez and I get inside." Carter shot a look over his shoulder at his temporary partner, just getting out of the car. Eddie Suarez was a squat marshal with a weight-lifter's physique and a broad, black mustache like Pancho Villa. He had hung back on purpose, Georgia suspected. He knew better than to get between two partners. It was like refereeing a fight between a husband and wife. Suarez, twice divorced, had had enough battle scars in that department. He approached them gingerly, making eye contact only with Carter.

"I'm going to talk to the super, check out the fire scene," Suarez offered.

"Be there in a minute," Carter grunted. Then he turned back to Georgia and wagged a bony finger at her. "You and I have to talk. Now."

Georgia meekly followed Carter over to the Caprice. She felt naked being at a fire scene without a length of hose, a halligan or a tool kit in her hand. Worse still, she was on the wrong end of the questioning. Carter was barely inside the car when he tore into her.

"I want to know everything that happened tonight. And don't give me some jive story about how you were just in the neighborhood. Broph is missing, Skeehan. He never showed up for work last night. I *know* you saw him after I asked you not to. And now he's missing and Sully's dead."

"But I don't get it," said Georgia. "Broph didn't tell me anything."

"Well he told you about Sully or you wouldn't be here."

"Randy, what's going on?"

"You tell me." He opened up his notebook and clicked on a tape recorder.

"You're doing a formal interview?"

"You entered a man's apartment without his permission and cremated him. You think I'm just going to shrug it off?"

"No. But you're being pretty hostile."

"You did something I asked you not to do. Who's the hostile one?"

A voice crackled over Carter's handy talkie. It was Suarez.

"Is Skeehan still with you?"

"Affirmative."

"Tell her I'm up in Sully's apartment and I just checked out the body," said Suarez. "I think he was dead before the fire started. He's on his back, not his stomach. He wasn't anywhere near the window. The area beneath him is protected, so he wasn't moved. And there's no evidence of cherry red lividity."

Georgia felt a small twinge of relief. She knew that blood settles in the body after death—a condition known as "lividity." A cherry red coloring would suggest the victim had inhaled carbon monoxide from the fire. The absence of it suggested that the victim hadn't inhaled any fumes because he was dead before the fire started.

Carter didn't seem the least bit mollified by the news. "Any gunshot wounds? Strangulation marks?" he asked Suarez.

"None that I can see," Suarez answered. "But I figured Skeehan would be relieved to hear that maybe she didn't roast the poor bastard."

"All right, thanks," said Carter. "I'll be up there soon." He clicked off his handy talkie and turned to Georgia. "Don't get all comfortable yet, Skeehan. The medical examiner's still got to check his windpipe for soot and do a toxicology screen for carbon monoxide in his blood."

"I know that," she shot back. "I'm just relieved there's a chance I didn't kill him."

"The moment you decided to talk to him, you killed him. I told you to stay away." He looked down at the running tape recorder and pushed Stop, then Rewind. "I don't want that on tape," he explained. "That's between you and me."

Georgia opened her bag and pulled out the tape Reese had given her earlier. "Here's something else you probably shouldn't have on the record." She handed the tape to Carter.

"What's this?" he asked suspiciously.

"Play it," said Georgia.

"Is it the Glickstein tape?"

"That, I fear, may already be in that big blank-tape heaven in the sky. But this is almost as good. Listen for yourself."

He did, and his face worked through all the same emotions Georgia had had when she first heard it: shock, rage, determination and, finally, a little bit of disappointment. While it seemed painfully clear to them that Michael McLaughlin had set the fire at Café Treize and didn't care that two firefighters had died as a result, it would be useless as evidence in a courtroom.

"Where did you get this?"

"I can't say," Georgia told him. "And you can't do anything with it right now except share it with Mac and Chief Brennan and then lock it up. I guess you could call it our emergency backup plan. If all else fails, at least we have an 'almost' admission from McLaughlin. Maybe we can't present it to a jury, but it's better than nothing."

Carter pocketed the tape. His mood brightened a little and Georgia felt more at ease as she slowly poured out what had happened tonight from the time she entered Sully's building until she saw Carter on the street. After she'd finished, Carter shut down the recorder and turned to her.

"Now do you believe me when I tell you you've got to get off this case with McLaughlin?"

Georgia thought about Rick standing outside that construction trailer in the semi-darkness. "Believe me, Randy. I'm going to be kicked off this case soon, anyway."

"Why?"

"Conflict of interest. That's all I can tell you right now."

"Whatever the reason, far as I'm concerned the sooner the better," said Carter.

"When I get off, will you tell me what's going on?"

"No."

"I won't tell anyone," Georgia promised.

"It's not *anyone* I'm concerned about," said Carter. "It's you. I can't tell *you*."

"Why?"

"Because once I tell you, I can't *un*-tell you. And this is something I don't think you are ever going to want to know."

"Broph was mixed up in some gambling trouble with Freezer, is that it?" she asked. "You always said he was a big gambler and that he owed a lot of money to underworld types. And Sully was involved somehow, too."

Carter gave her a sad smile and shook his head. "Skeehan, you are so far from the truth." He sighed. "Sully had no enemies. McLaughlin killed him. Or he had someone do it for him. Those are the only two possibilities. Believe me, I know."

Georgia stared up at the third floor. A gaping black hole, wreathed in soot, was all that remained of Jamie Sullivan's life. Now that he was gone, the building he'd tried so hard to save might be sold off for condos anyway. The old-timers would be scattered to relatives and nursing homes. Only a few people in the neighborhood like Bobby Kelly would even recall his name. Maybe he wasn't as lucky as everybody claimed after all.

"I guess I have to let the Feds know I was here tonight," said Georgia. "That alone is probably enough to get me drummed out of the FBI."

Carter agreed. "Call them. Then come upstairs and walk me through what happened, step by step, okay? This may be the fire that allows us to finally put the screws to McLaughlin. I don't want anything overlooked."

23

GEORGIA COULDN'T REACH KRAUSE on his cell phone or beeper. She felt relieved that all she had to do was leave a brief message. She didn't feel like going through everything tonight.

Upstairs, in Sully's apartment, Georgia picked her way across the inky slush that had once passed for wall-to-wall carpet. The air was acrid with fumes from the burning of foam rubber and plastics in the carpeting, draperies and furniture. If there was any accelerant in the apartment, Georgia's nose was too overloaded with odors to distinguish it.

She spotted Suarez in the living room, hunched over a section of carpet, taking samples. He was dressed in navy blue fire department coveralls, his latex gloves filthy from handling debris.

"What have you found so far?" she asked him. He straightened and glanced down the hallway to where Carter was measuring something. He seemed unsure whether to answer. There was a dividing line between them now. Georgia was working for the FBI. Suarez and Carter were fire marshals. On top of that, Georgia was, at the very least, a witness to the crime. Carter frowned in her direction.

"You've been invited up here to walk us through what happened," he said. "Not participate in the investigation."

"Well, then here's something you should know," said Georgia. "The fire lit up in Sully's bedroom like there was gasoline in there. But I never smelled any accelerant in the apartment."

Two technicians came out of the bedroom now with what looked like a black garment bag. Carter asked them to stop a moment and unzip the bag. He made sure Georgia had a long look at Jamie Sullivan's charred face, burned like a marshmallow left too long over a campfire. Only a very intense fire could've done that much damage to him. Only a fire started by an accelerant like gasoline could've done it so quickly.

Georgia turned away, feeling ashamed and guilty that her desire to talk to him had in any way contributed to his death. When the zipper again closed, she flinched. There was a finality to that sound that all the priests with their talk of God and heaven couldn't erase. She'd heard that zipper close too many times on this job, and in her experience, there was very little afterlife in it.

"You've made your point," she muttered to Carter when the technicians had left. "I'm sorry I went against your wishes the other day. That doesn't mean I know who murdered Jamie Sullivan and doused his bedroom with gasoline."

"There aren't any pour patterns in that bedroom," said Carter. "No pour patterns or evidence of gasoline in the entire apartment, as a matter of fact."

"But the fire looked just like something started with a lot of gasoline," said Georgia. "It was the most intense blaze I've ever seen. Like something from the movies: fast-moving flames, no real smoke, tremendous heat. The only way to describe it was—"

"A fireball," Carter offered.

"Yeah," said Georgia. "Was there a bomb back there?"

"No bomb," said Suarez. "Somebody rerouted the bedroom light to the hallway junction box, then clipped them so they'd short when you threw the light switch."

"That was your spark, your ignition source," said Carter. "You had plenty of oxygen from the open window in the front hallway."

That was two-thirds of the fire triangle, thought Georgia. Heat and oxygen. But where was the third prong—the readily combustible fuel? "Was there a natural gas leak?"

"Negative," said Carter. "We checked. The only odor of fuel so far came from the roof, when firefighters vented one of the scuttles during the blaze. They smelled gasoline."

"On the roof?" asked Georgia. It didn't make sense. The fire never reached the roof. And besides, gasoline vapors are heavier than air. They don't rise, they settle.

Georgia stood at the entrance to the bedroom hallway. The carpet squished beneath her feet. The walls were blistered and blackened. She tried to picture it before the fire, when she stood here, feeling for the light switch. It was dark. She noticed nothing but the breeze over her shoulder, and the . . .

"The dumbwaiter," said Georgia, walking over to the shaft in the wall. It was still open. She checked the upper rim beneath the soot and saw a fresh tool mark imprinted upon the many blistered layers of paint.

"Eddie, pass me a screwdriver."

Suarez retrieved one from his toolbox and handed it to her. She matched it against the marks on the metal. "This was pried open recently, and it was open when I entered the apartment." Georgia stuck her head into the shaft and looked up. She could see the night sky above. She could smell gasoline vapors below.

"I'll bet you anything this was the shaft firefighters vented when they reported an odor of gasoline on the roof."

Carter and Suarez exchanged glances. "I'll check it out from the basement," said Suarez. He left the apartment. Carter gave Georgia a long appraising look—part impressed, part annoyed. None of this, in his opinion, would have been necessary if she hadn't talked to Broph.

"That still doesn't explain how vapors as heavy as those in gasoline would end up concentrating in Sully's bedroom," he reminded her. "It takes a pretty sophisticated torch to manage that feat."

"You think Freezer did it," she said.

"Or someone who works for him." Carter led her over to the soot-smeared kitchen table. Evidence—in the form of samples from rugs, bedspreads, paint chips and floorboards—lay sealed and labeled inside plastic bags and silver coffee-can-sized containers.

"Sully had an appointment this morning," said Carter. "He wrote it on his phone pad."

Carter picked up a sealed evidence bag and handed it to her. Inside the clear plastic, Georgia saw a day calendar. The top page was blackened with soot and shriveled at the corners from the heat. The second sheet, tomorrow's date, had pencil rubbings on it—an old trick Georgia had learned as a child to make impressions in paper legible. There was a telephone number on the sheet. In the 732 area code. New Jersey. The number must have been written on the top sheet—today—before it was damaged in the fire. Beneath the phone number was some scribble, presumably Sully's: *R @ 10:30 a.m.*

"Where did you find this?" Georgia asked.

"By the telephone in the kitchen. The fire never really got that hot except in the bedroom. By the time it started making its way in this direction, our guys were here to put it out." Stacked paper, Georgia knew, never burns particularly well anyway. She had only to look at the pile of old newspapers Sully had by the front door to see that. Despite the intense, napalm destruction in the bedroom and the heat damage to the living room ceiling, the papers were only soggy and surface-burned.

"Do you think this 'R' person had anything to do with Sully's death?"

"All we've got to go on is the phone number," said Carter. "And I can't tell if the number is related to the appointment or not, but we'll check it out."

Suarez bounded back into the apartment carrying a five-gallon container of gasoline, a broad smile beneath his Pancho Villa mustache. "Look what I found inside the dumbwaiter in the basement. Here's your gasoline."

"That still doesn't explain how those vapors got from the basement to the third floor," said Carter.

"Or why the whole dumbwaiter shaft didn't burn when the fire took off," Georgia added.

"Maybe all the vapors were concentrated in Sully's bedroom by that point," said Suarez. "Even so, that's a pretty neat trick."

Carter's eyes canvassed the blackened hallway. "I'm too old for tricks."

IT WAS NEARLY 10:30 P.M. before Georgia caught the Number Seven train to Woodside. As the train lurched along the subway tracks, she tried to reconcile the man in the baseball cap she had seen earlier tonight with the boy she had fallen in love with more than a decade ago. Rick DeAngelo had always been a bit of a dreamer. He once sank his savings into buying a bunch of condemned bungalows in Rockaway on the rumor that the city was going to sanction gambling on the waterfront. It never happened. He not only lost all his money, the city sued him for back taxes.

About the only practical dream he'd ever shared with her was his lifelong desire to become a New York City firefighter. When she met him—at Mike Flynn's bar in Woodside, where she waitressed part-time—he was already running five miles a day after putting in long hours as an apprentice electrician. He was twenty-two. She was nineteen and in college, but already itching to quit. She liked his dimpled chin and his Cheshire-cat smile. But more than that, she liked his wicked sense of humor. No one had made her laugh that much since her dad.

They trained together for the firefighter's physical endurance test. To Georgia, it was just a lark—a chance to spend time with the young man she adored. To Rick, it was an obsession. He worked harder to get that job than any man she had seen. And he lost his chance on a technicality—he fell off a training wall on the day of the test and hurt his ankle. Georgia had always wondered whether their lives would have been different if he had passed and she had failed, instead of the other way around. She wondered with a sickening thud whether she finally had her answer.

"Sixty-first Street and Roosevelt Avenue, Woodside," the conductor mumbled over the intercom. Georgia disembarked the train and walked up the steps of the subway station. A bitter wind stung her face and made her eyes water. Holiday lights flashed in the plate-glass display window of a Duane Reade drugstore. A plastic menorah had another yellow bulb glowing for the fourth night of Hanukkah. Outside the Blockbuster Video, a bored-looking fat man in a Santa suit and glasses rang a bell for the Salvation Army. All around her, people were hurrying with shopping bags and packages, even at this late hour. Christmas, as the television ads kept reminding her, was only a few weeks away.

She turned off the main thoroughfare and walked down side streets she had known her whole life. It was the kind of neighborhood her firefighter dad had felt right at home in: a good Irish bar, a strong parish church, rows of tidy, cookie-cutter houses filled with people who put their Virgin Mary grottos on display and kept their problems under lock and key.

Georgia pulled up the collar of her coat and walked beneath the yellow glaze of streetlights. Cars were sandwiched end-to-end along the curbs. Television lights flickered behind heavy drawn curtains. Only the occasional dog-walker still braved the bitter cold. Her house was in sight. She could see the chain-link fence and the bay window with the velvet drapes and her mother's Hummel figures on the windowsill.

She went to cross the street. She never saw the door of the dark blue pickup truck open until it blocked her path. Georgia's heart tightened like a fist as a man in a baseball cap and denim jacket stepped out of the truck. For eight years, she'd longed to see him back on her mother's street. And now that he was finally here, she wished more than anything that he'd just go away.

"Gee Gee—what the *hell* are you doing? Do you realize how close you came to getting killed tonight?"

She had forgotten he used to call her that. Long ago, it had seemed endearing. Now, the sound of it on his tongue chilled her. She fumbled inside her coat for the reassuring outline of her Glock 9-millimeter on her hip.

"Did you get yourself in some kind of trouble?" he asked.

"You shouldn't be here," she answered weakly.

"*I* shouldn't be *here? You* shouldn't have been *there.* The fire department finds out about this and your *boyfriend,* Mr. Lucky Charms, the Irish Mafioso, you could lose your job."

"That's my business," she said.

"Well your *business* is gonna get you killed."

Georgia frowned. "Is that a threat? Is that what you've become? Some kind of bag man for a bunch of political extremists?"

He winced as if she'd just punched him. He took off his baseball cap. A Yankees cap. He had always been a die-hard Yankees fan, while Georgia preferred the Mets. His dark hair was full and almost curly—just like when they were together. The face had filled out, though. It wasn't a boy's face anymore. It was a man's. He smacked the side of his truck with his baseball cap and cursed. But he didn't deny her accusations.

"Gee Gee," he said softly. "Stay away from these people. For your own good. I could've told them tonight that you're a New York City firefighter. And it would have gone down badly—very, very badly."

"I'm supposed to thank you?"

"I'm trying to help you here."

"*Help* me?" Georgia couldn't stem the bitterness in her voice. She could feel eight years of anger and heartache boiling inside of her. A hundred painful moments of being a single mother. There was the time Richie fell off a seesaw and Georgia had to rush her bloody, screaming son to the emergency room for stitches. There was the time he caught head lice from a borrowed baseball helmet. Georgia spent two weeks on her hands and knees, scrubbing and boiling everything in the house, then picking nits out of his hair every night. There were the hundred-and-four fevers, the stomach flus, the nightmares. And the smaller things, too. The times her boy watched some man teach his son to bat a ball or reel in a fish or hammer a nail—things Richie would never get to do with a dad. Hell, Rick hadn't even bothered to answer a simple letter Richie had written him last spring. And now, he claimed to want to help?

Georgia wanted to shoot him. She wanted to shout at him. She wanted to beat her fists into his chest. And she couldn't do anything because it would compromise an investigation. It was the very thing she was certain McLaughlin wanted.

Georgia took a deep breath. "It's too late," was all she managed to choke out. She started to walk past him.

"Don't say that. C'mon, Gee Gee. I need to know what's going on here. Please."

Rick grabbed her arm. She shook him off. His hand slipped toward her hip and he recoiled at the touch of something hard and metallic beneath.

"Whoa." He stepped back, his hands in the air. "Holy shit. You've got a gun?"

Georgia pulled back her coat, revealing her holster. "I suggest you not lay another hand on me."

"So you shoot people now? Man, it's a good thing we never got married. You'd be hell in a divorce court."

"Then consider yourself lucky."

Rick dropped his hands. He fingered his baseball cap and examined her now. She had time to do the same with him. He didn't look like a terrorist. He looked like someone Mac might work with on his side job. Beneath his denim jacket he wore a flannel shirt. His work boots looked like he actually worked in them. On his left hand, a wedding ring glistened. She knew he was married, but the glint of gold felt like a knife to her heart.

"How is he?" Rick asked softly. The question took her by surprise. She didn't answer.

"Does he hate me?" Rick pressed.

"This is not the time to talk about that."

"No sweat." A favorite expression of Rick's. And fitting too, since he'd never sweated anything in his life. He closed his eyes and spoke very slowly. "Put your coat down," he said, his breath misting in the cold night air. "I don't need to see the gun anymore. I got the message." He shook his head. "You didn't even like when I used to go hunting. Now you own a gun? I can't believe you've changed that much."

"You did."

Rick leaned against the capped bed of his pickup truck. He drummed his fingers nervously against it. He had Richie's fidgetiness—or rather, Richie had his.

"Forget about me for a moment. I'm a lost cause. But you? You're a firefighter, Gee Gee. FDNY. Goddamn it, that's the best job in the world. What are you risking it for?"

After all these years, Georgia could still hear the ache in his voice when he talked about being a firefighter. She didn't know what to say.

"I've got to go." She turned and forced herself to begin walking away from him. They were the hardest steps she'd ever taken.

"You're working undercover." It wasn't even a question. He knew. "Shit," he said, punching his thigh. "Shit, shit, shit." Georgia flinched. Then she forced herself to keep walking. He ran in front of her. "I'm gonna get busted, aren't I?"

"Please don't ask me any more questions."

He looked confused. "But you're a firefighter. How did a firefighter get . . . ? Wait a minute, are you a fire marshal now?"

It's worse than that, Georgia wanted to say, but didn't. He went to reach out a hand to her then caught himself. He had no wish to have a gun trained on him. "All right. No more questions. Will you just hear me out then?" He caught her gazing at her mother's house. He suddenly looked embarrassed. "I won't ask to come inside. I know I'm not welcome there. Just sit with me in my truck. I'll turn the heater on. Please, Gee Gee, for old time's sake."

25

"SO THE GUN'S LEGIT, HUH?" asked Rick DeAngelo. "You don't just keep it on you for when old boyfriends drop by?"

"It's crossed my mind," said Georgia. They were sitting in the cab of his Ford F-10 pickup with the engine and heater turned on. Georgia hadn't frisked him, but it occurred to her now, belatedly, that she probably should have. At the very least, she should know if he had a gun in his glove compartment. She moved her knee up to the glove compartment button and pushed against it. It fell open. There was no gun. Instead, a child's crayoned picture of a house with flowers tumbled out. Georgia glanced at it and noticed Rick shifting in his seat and tapping the steering wheel to a rhythm only he could hear.

"That's, uh . . . that's . . ."

"Your daughter's. I know," said Georgia.

"You do?"

"What? You think you live in the Himalayan Mountains? South Jersey's not Tibet, Rick. I get news of your life whether I want it or not."

He gave her a confused look so she elaborated. "Your cousin, Robbie."

"Oh, yeah. His wife, Stacy—she's the sister of your old friend . . ." He snapped his fingers. He was always bad with names.

· "Mary Beth," said Georgia. "You went to her wedding, remember?"

"I remember that you threw champagne at me."

"I remember that when I caught the bridal bouquet, you said it should've been a shotgun, 'cause that's the only way you were ever getting married."

She waited for him to come back with a one-liner. He was always good with those. But instead, he just sank lower in his seat and shoved his hands in his pockets. He didn't seem to want to talk about the past. "Can you get out of this assignment?"

"Why? Do you think that's going to save your tail? They're going to nail you whether I'm involved or not."

"That's not why I'm asking. I'm asking because these are dangerous people. More dangerous than you realize."

"Are *you* dangerous?"

He pulled a face. "I'm an electrician, Gee Gee, not a terrorist. About the only thing I've ever destroyed is my credit rating."

"Then what are you doing with these people? Why did you let them into that construction site? *You* had the key."

He looked surprised that she knew that. "Aw, Christ," he sighed. "This is so embarrassing. I don't even know where to begin. Do I talk to you as a fire marshal? As my ex-girlfriend? As the mother of my child?" He allowed his famous Cheshire-cat grin to creep across his clean-shaven face. "As my cousin's wife's sister's girlfriend?"

"I'll take it any way I can get it."

"You never used to say that," he teased.

"You never used to give it. At least not after Richie, in any case."

He took a deep breath and tried to distill eight years of separation into something logical and understandable. She knew the first part—or figured she knew. The rift between them started the day Georgia found out she'd scored high enough on the firefighter's physical endurance test to have a decent shot at landing the job. Rick knew he'd failed the moment he fell off that wall. Georgia had tried to reassure him. She didn't want the job, she kept telling him. She'd gladly turn it down if it made him happier. She cringed now thinking about her girlish impulsiveness, her willingness to throw everything away for a man. She was glad it had never come to that. It was the one thing he'd had the decency *not* to take from her.

The pregnancy came out of nowhere soon afterward. Rick hung around, but the bonds had already begun to loosen. Guilt kept him in the picture maybe a year and a half longer. By the time Richie was two and Georgia was a probationary firefighter, he was gone entirely from her life. He had an uncle in Toms River, New Jersey, who was a building contractor. Rick, who had always loved the ocean, drifted down there and found work as an electrician. Somewhere along the line he married and had at least one daughter—maybe more. Georgia never wanted to know too many specifics.

"I got that letter, you know," Rick suddenly blurted out. "The one Richie sent me last spring."

"Then why didn't you write back?"

He shook his head and looked down at his hands. "Guilt, I guess. That was part of it. I figured, how could I have a relationship with Richie without helping to support him?"

"Why should that stop you? You never supported him before." She couldn't erase the anger from her voice.

"I gave you *some* money." The justification died in his throat. He became contrite again. "It wasn't enough, I know that. And I feel bad about it. Don't you think I carry that around with me all the time?"

"You didn't feel bad enough to do anything about it."

"My work is cyclical, Gee Gee. When I make money, I make good money. But there are a lot of dry times, believe me. When we split up, I didn't even have a job. And you? You'd just become a firefighter."

"I was a *probationary* firefighter, Rick. That first year, I earned under thirty thousand, and I worked my tail off for every bit of it. I didn't win the lottery. So don't use my job as an excuse for ditching your responsibilities."

"Look, if it was that important to you, how come you didn't take me to court for child support? You could have, you know."

"And spend my life chasing you? You never had any money anyway. You weren't worth my time."

He gave her a hurt look. Georgia turned away from him and caught her reflection in the truck's rearview mirror. She didn't like the face looking back at her—all pinched and bitter. They had regressed right back to where they were eight years ago. She wanted to let the past go, but it kept getting the better of her.

"You're right," Rick said softly. "I'm not arguing that you're right. But that's exactly why I didn't write Richie back. I couldn't without offering you some bread. And I haven't got any. I'm broke. Facing bankruptcy, in fact."

"What?"

Rick turned off the car engine and wiped the condensation that had formed on the inside of the windshield. "I started my own electrical contracting firm four years ago. Got overextended on a couple of jobs, and things just snowballed from there. I maxed out on every credit card and all my loans and still couldn't meet the debts. Then I got a call from a guy named Louie Buscanti—ever heard that name?"

"You're working for Buscanti? The South Jersey mobster?" asked Georgia.

"I work for myself," said Rick indignantly. "But Buscanti controls the construction trade in South Jersey. Nothing happens in Ocean County without his say-so. So when he offered me the electrical contract on a hotel renovation in Seaside Heights, I couldn't turn it down. The job was big enough to wipe out all my debts. And if I kicked back his fifteen percent on time and did a good job, there would be others. I'd be in the clear."

"So you took it."

"So I took it. Then yesterday, Buscanti pays me a visit at the job site. Tells me he needs a favor. All I've got to do is pick up two people at a service station on the Turnpike and drive them to a construction site in the Meadowlands where my firm laid some cable about a month ago. I tell him 'no drugs'—

'cause I figure that's what it's about. Buscanti promises me they're not drug couriers. It's just a one-shot deal—'For a friend of his,' he says. Believe me, Gee Gee, you don't say no to Louie Buscanti."

Georgia frowned at him. "What do you know about the two people you drove?"

"Not much. At first, it was like picking up two college kids. Radical clothes, radical talk, but for the most part, they seemed pretty amateurish. I was just a driver to them. They didn't talk to me, I didn't talk to them. I just wanted the night to be over. Then they started talking about some dude named Coyote and his green army. That's when I got really nervous."

"Green army," said Georgia. "Do you mean Green Warriors?"

"Yeah, that's right. What are they?"

Georgia didn't answer and Rick immediately caught her drift. "Oh, yeah, I'm the criminal. You're the law. Pardon me."

"Don't make this personal, Rick."

"Speaking of personal, that Irish guy who grabbed your ass—is he a cop?"

"No."

Rick's face paled. "He's not really your boyfriend, is he?"

"God, no. And that's all I'm going to say." She paused a beat to make sure it sank in. "Did they mention any plans? Any places the Green Warriors might hit?"

"You kidding? They didn't talk to me. I'm nobody to them."

"Did Buscanti tell you why he wanted you, of all people, to drive these people to this meeting?"

"All he told me was that he was doing a favor for a friend and he knew I had access to that construction site. He didn't tell me anything else and I didn't ask. You don't question Louie Buscanti."

Georgia stared at him now. She was trying to reconcile the boy she knew with the man sitting before her spewing out this improbable tale. "Can anyone else verify your story?"

"Yeah . . . Corinne." Then, more sheepishly, he added. "My wife."

Georgia tried to keep her face impassive at the mention of the name, but she could feel a burning in her cheeks she was sure he noticed. *Corinne. Corinne DeAngelo.* The name conjured up long, shapely legs, a musical laugh, a flowing mane of dark hair. Corinne sounded like a name for a ballet dancer. An artist. An earth mother. Not a firefighter who crawled around in burning buildings and didn't even get home in time to tuck her child into bed.

"If you're telling the truth, I can hook you up with people who can maybe help you."

"Help me how?"

She reached into her bag and scribbled her cell phone number on a slip of paper, then handed it to him. "Wire you."

"Those two sixties leftovers aren't going to tell me anything."

"I'm not talking about them, Rick. I'm talking about Buscanti." *And his relationship to Michael McLaughlin,* Georgia wanted to add but didn't.

"Oh no." He waved his hands in front of his face. "No way. I don't know what Buscanti's game is here. But I'm absolutely not going against the most powerful mobster in New Jersey. That would be suicide. For me *and* my family. You've heard of *The Sopranos?* Hell, these guys make the Sopranos look like choir boys."

He draped his arms over the wheel, dropped his head forward and cursed softly. "This can't be happening. I swear, I'm not running with terrorists. I'm just trying to get out of debt."

"I'm sorry, Rick, but that's the best I can offer." She went to get out of the car. He put a hand on her wrist.

"Please, Gee Gee. Please don't do this. Buscanti comes after me, I'm either gonna have to tell him you're a cop or get killed myself."

"You'd rat me out to a mobster? The mother of your son?"

"You're not giving me any options."

"You got yourself into this mess," she reminded him, then sighed. "Look, let me think about how to handle this, all right?"

"No sweat."

"If you're feeding me any crap—"

"I swear, Gee Gee, I'm telling the truth."

26

THE HOUSE WAS DARK by the time Georgia got in from her session with Rick. She crept down to the basement, stripped off her clothes and threw them in the gentle cycle of the washing machine. On her father's old workbench, she noticed two fresh-cut panels of wood surrounded by sawdust. Above the panels sat a taped picture of a red sports car with some pencil markings she recognized as Marenko's. He must have been over this evening to start building the race car with Richie. Georgia ran her hand along one of the sanded panels. She was touched by his efforts.

I've moved on with my life, Richie's moved on with his life. And now, Rick DeAngelo has to come back? Like this? She had thought that the worst that could happen to Richie was to never hear from his father again. Now, she knew there was something far worse—to find out that his father was a criminal, and his mother had helped send him to prison. She didn't know how she could ever explain that one.

She fished a clean sweatshirt out of the dryer, slipped into it, then quietly made her way upstairs to take a shower. Stepping out of the tub, Georgia suddenly realized that she had given Rick her cell phone number tonight, but he'd offered her no number to contact him. *I probably have his number in my address book*, she decided. She toweled herself off, checked in on her sleeping son, then rummaged in her bedroom drawers until she unearthed her address book. Rick's home address and phone number were there, but Georgia had no idea whether he had a cell phone, a beeper number or a business number. All she had was a number that Corinne was sure to pick up. And if there was one thing she didn't want to do, it was speak to Corinne.

Georgia stared at the entry for Rick. The phone number was in the 732 area code. She closed her eyes, recalling that note in Sully's apartment Carter had shown her: *R @ 10:30,* with a phone number starting with 732. She recalled that the three digits after 732 were 245—just like the number here. She couldn't sleep until she knew. She dialed Manhattan base. After two rings, Carter grunted his name into the receiver. She could tell he was having a tough night. She was about to make it tougher.

"Randy? It's Georgia. Listen, I know this sounds crazy, but did you try calling that phone number you found in Sully's apartment yet?"

"Skeehan . . ." He drew out her name with annoyance. "This isn't your case."

"I know. But please indulge me. It's important."

He sighed. "Suarez called the number. He got an answering machine and left a message."

"Did the machine identify whose number it was?"

"It wasn't a private number. It was a business. Some kind of electrical contracting firm. I don't remember the name. We'll check it out tomorrow."

Georgia's stomach tightened. "Was the name 'DeAngelo,' by chance?"

"Maybe. Why?"

She sank onto her bed. She hardly had the energy to speak. "Because the 'R' Sully may have been meeting was my old boyfriend, Rick DeAngelo—Richie's father."

Dead air passed on the line between them. "What would he want with Sully?"

"I'm afraid to ask. New Yorkers don't normally import electricians all the way from Toms River, New Jersey, to rewire their apartments."

"You don't think he's . . . he's involved in Sully's death, do you?"

"I don't know anymore," said Georgia. "Remember I told you I've got a conflict of interest working the FBI case?"

"*He's* the conflict? Sonofa . . . This has got to be Freezer's doing."

"I think we need to talk," said Georgia. "In person. Can you meet me to-morrow when you get off work?"

"I'll be in Queens tomorrow morning, over at the crime lab," said Carter. "I talked Ajay Singh into coming in and giving me his thoughts on what hap-pened inside Sully's apartment. You want to meet me there?"

"Yeah. I think I'd better."

"Have you told the Feds any of this yet?"

"Not yet. I was going to in the morning."

"Let's meet first. This is a humdinger of a situation. You're gonna want to be careful how you lay it all out."

27

THE NYPD CRIME LAB was a four-story concrete slab of a building in Jamaica, Queens, about twenty minutes southeast of Woodside, but a world away. It was in a poorer neighborhood where factories and brick housing projects loomed over storefront churches, check-cashing services and bodegas selling lottery tickets. The street that housed the lab sat across from an auto body mechanic. The adjoining parking lot had a chain-link fence with razor ribbon on top. Georgia parked the car by the curb under a *No Parking* sign.

"You can't park here," said Richie in the know-it-all tone of a ten-year-old. Georgia rolled her eyes. She hadn't planned on taking her son with her this Sunday morning, but she'd had no choice. Margaret was going Christmas shopping after church with her sister and some friends. Richie had been invited to a birthday party, but it wasn't until this afternoon.

"I can park here until I get you inside," said Georgia.

Richie clucked his tongue in disgust. He knew he was being dragged around like baggage, and he intended to get as much resentment mileage as possible out of it.

Two unmarked steel doors and a buzzer fronted the building. Georgia held up her shield for the security cameras and waited for the door to unlock automatically. Inside, in what passed for a lobby, a receptionist sat behind a high, Band-Aid colored counter. She was a heavyset black woman with bifocals and Bo-Derek-blond braids. She did a double take when she saw Georgia walk in with a child in tow.

"We're not open for school projects," said the receptionist.

"I'm not here for my son," said Georgia. "I'm here on a case and I had to bring him along. He'll sit out in the lobby and he won't bother anyone." Richie gave his mother a sour look and stuck a pair of earphones in his ears.

"Did a fire marshal named Randy Carter arrive yet?" asked Georgia. "I'm supposed to meet him here."

"No."

"How about Dr. Singh? Marshal Carter has an appointment with him."

The receptionist scanned a list of names on a pad at her desk. "He's here. But if he's in on a Sunday, honey, it means he's *way* too busy to talk to you. I need the case number."

"I don't know the case number," Georgia admitted. She would if it were her case, but it wasn't. Still, she wanted to understand everything she could about Sully's fire—if only to figure out in her own mind whether Rick could have been involved. "Can you tell him Fire Marshal Georgia Skeehan is here?"

"I can try."

While the receptionist waited to get through to Dr. Singh in the lab, Georgia parked her car in the lot. As she started to close the gate, she saw Randy Carter pulling up. She beckoned him through. He rolled down his window.

"I've got to go over the case with Singh first, then we'll talk, okay?"

"I'd like to hear what Singh has to say as well," said Georgia. "After all, I'm the one who told you to look in the dumbwaiter."

Carter pulled a face. "Skeehan, you know I can't do that. Forget the fact that it's not your case for a moment. You're a witness."

"Not to mention a suspect, right?"

"You're in the clear for killing him at least," said Carter. "The ME estimates time of death about four hours before the fire. I spoke to Nelson this morning and he backed up your story that you were working then."

"So let me hear Singh out."

"No can do. You're still the ex-girlfriend of a potential suspect—"

"Who you only know about because I told you," Georgia reminded him. "Look, Randy, we're both breaking the rules here. I'm not supposed to divulge anything about the FBI's case to you, and you're not supposed to let me in on the Sully investigation. I gave you that tape of Freezer virtually confessing to the Café Treize fire—that's FBI property. So we're both stepping over the line. But what choice do we have? We've been played from the very beginning on this one. Let me just hear Singh out, okay? Maybe I can help."

"Famous last words." He frowned at her. "All right. But only if you promise me you'll keep your mouth shut in there, is that a deal?"

"I promise."

By the time Georgia and Carter returned to the lobby, there was a brown-skinned man with a black beard and mustache sitting next to Georgia's son, doing coin tricks. He wore a loud red-and-yellow flowered shirt and a turban the color of port wine. She wondered if all Sikhs had Ajay Singh's odd sense of color. He rose when Georgia walked over.

"Your partners seem to be getting younger and younger, Marshal."

"I see you've met my son."

Singh smiled and flipped Richie the coin. "He says he has no interest in science."

"Do you have children, Dr. Singh?"

"Two, but the oldest—my son—is only five."

"When he's ten, he'll most likely tell you he has no interest in anything that doesn't involve a ball, a video game or a skateboard."

"You are probably right." He pressed his palms together and gestured to Georgia and Carter with the slightest bow.

"You are here about the Sullivan fire, yes? The reports won't be ready until next Tuesday or Wednesday, I'm afraid."

"I know that," said Carter. "But I was wondering if you could explain something that's puzzling me . . . us," Carter corrected, shooting a quick glance at Georgia. Neither of them wanted to make issue of the fact that Georgia didn't belong here. "Sullivan was burned very badly, yet there was no accelerant pour pattern in the apartment. The nearest evidence of accelerant we could find was a five-gallon can of gasoline at the bottom of a dumbwaiter shaft three stories below."

"Yes, I noticed that from your report."

"But given the nature of gasoline vapors, we're at a loss as to how it got up that dumbwaiter shaft and then didn't burn the shaft when the vapors ignited," said Carter. "Do you have any idea how this could happen?"

"There was a constant current of air blowing through the apartment, am I correct?" asked Singh.

"That's right. Entering from a window in the front hallway and exiting in the back, out of the bedroom."

"Are you aware of a scientific principle called the Venturi effect?"

Carter nodded. "I know it has to do with air-pressure differentials." Georgia gave Carter a blank look. "Did you forget your probie manual, Skeehan?"

"I remember the term in relation to how certain pumps and siphoning operations work, but I've never heard it used to describe a fire," said Georgia.

"It is named after the eighteenth-century Italian physicist, Giovanni Battista Venturi," Singh added.

"Sounds like roll call at my old firehouse," joked Georgia.

Singh laughed. "It does. Do you understand the principle?"

"Not exactly," Georgia admitted.

"Venturi discovered that when air enters a tube or narrowed opening, its velocity increases and its pressure drops," said Singh. "At the point where the drop in pressure occurs, other substances—because of the unequal air pressure—can be sucked in. These can be fluids, gases—even smoke. Firefighters do this when they aim a fog nozzle out a window."

"The fog nozzle creates a column of low-pressure air traveling at high speed," Carter explained. "It's the same principle as when someone's smoking in a car and you open the window. The smoke gets sucked out because the air pressure inside the car is greater than the pressure outside it."

"Oh."

"Conversely," said Singh, "when the air or liquid leaves the narrowed opening, it expands rapidly. Atomizes, in other words. That can make some substances introduced into the restricted column of low-pressure air more flammable—even substances that were not flammable before."

"Could that narrowed opening apply to a dumbwaiter shaft as well as a tube?" asked Georgia.

"Absolutely. A hallway. A pipe. An air duct. Any constriction," said Singh. "The Venturi effect explains a lot of basic science we take for granted, from automobile carburetors to spray bottles." He furrowed his brow, then gave them a satisfied smile. "I think the Venturi effect might explain why that gas traveled upward instead of settling at the bottom of the dumbwaiter shaft." Singh checked his watch. "I am waiting for some solvents to run through a dye process. I can spare about twenty minutes. Would you like to see what the Venturi effect looks like in action?"

Georgia looked at Richie, who was slumped in a chair, thumbing through a book with a bored look on his face. "I won't be long," she told him.

Singh looked thoughtfully at the boy. "I may be able to sneak him back there if he promises not to touch anything," Singh told Georgia. "All the rules can be bent a little on Sundays."

"That's okay," Richie answered. "I'll wait here."

"I am going to take ordinary nondairy creamer—the kind people put in their coffee—and turn it into a raging fireball," said Singh. Richie's eyes lit up.

"Really?"

"Really."

Richie shut off his CD and looked at his mother, who shrugged. "Cool. I'm in."

They followed Singh through a set of steel doors and down a long, drab corridor. At a bend in the hallway, Singh led Carter, Georgia and Richie through a glass door and into a tiled room with stainless-steel counters, microscopes and machines that whirred and hummed.

"Stand right here. Do not touch anything and I will find what we need to demonstrate the Venturi effect," said Singh. He went into an adjoining supply room and came back a few moments later with three lengths of black rubber tubing, each a different diameter in size, some duct tape and a large brown jar of nondairy creamer.

"I swiped the creamer from our stash of coffee and sugar," said Singh. "The secretaries will hate me tomorrow morning." He handed the largest-diameter tubing to Richie. "This is half-inch-diameter rubber tubing. I'm going to join the quarter-inch tubing to it, then attach the eighth-inch tubing to the quarter-inch."

"So the tube gets skinnier and skinnier," said the boy.

"Correct. Only it is in reverse. We will start with the constricted end and work our way up to the big tube."

"I don't want him involved in anything dangerous," said Georgia.

"This is perfectly safe," said Singh. He finished taping the ends of the tubes together, then knocked on a large, stainless-steel box, four feet high and four feet wide with a viewing window on top and several sets of gloves on the side. "We will do the whole experiment under this hood. But even if I did not, you would not have to worry. Do you know who uses coffee creamer and the Venturi effect to make fireballs?"

"Who?" asked Richie, clearly riveted.

"Disney World. When you see fire shooting out of a dragon's mouth there, it is nothing more than coffee creamer blown out by compressed air and ignited electrically. Do you know why they use it?" he asked.

"Uh-uh," said the boy.

Singh unscrewed the lid of the coffee creamer jar and poured about half a cup of the white powder into a glass beaker. He rummaged through a drawer, pulled out a book of matches and struck one of them. He threw the match into the creamer. It went out instantly.

"You see? Under normal conditions, coffee creamer will not burn." Then he smiled wickedly at Richie. "But we will make it burn."

Singh opened up the hood and stuck the tubing inside. He flexed the smallest end at a forty-five degree angle and placed a small petri dish full of coffee creamer underneath it. At the largest end, he rigged the tube up to a Bunsen burner. "Now," he said. "We need a current of air. In this case, we'll use compressed air." He reached for a half-inch diameter rubber hose on the wall and turned it on, then snaked it through an entry valve in the hood.

"Richie, I want you to come over to this end and hold the compressed air hose. When I say go, you will point the hose at the entrance of the tube, just above the dish of coffee creamer."

"Okay."

Singh lit the Bunsen burner. A small blue flame shimmered in the base.

"Ready. Set. Go."

Richie aimed the compressed air at the narrowest opening of the tube. The coffee creamer disappeared at once into the tube. A second later, at the wide end of the tube, the Bunsen burner's blue flame exploded into an orange mass of fire as large as a soccer ball. Georgia was glad Singh had done the experiment under the hood. Had she been holding the fiery end, the shock might have made her let go. It was like turning on a hair dryer and getting a blowtorch instead.

Richie strung out his favorite word until it became three syllables long. "Co-oo-ol."

After a couple of seconds, the creamer burned away, the flame died down and Singh turned off the air compressor.

"You have just created the Venturi effect," he told them.

Georgia wagged a finger at Richie. "Don't get any stupid ideas about doing this with your friends," she said.

"Mom," he whined, "you don't even like nondairy creamer."

"I still don't get how this works," said Georgia.

"When airflow is constricted, its velocity increases and its pressure drops. If you introduce a substance at the point where the drop in pressure occurs, it will be absorbed rapidly into the air stream and atomized at the other end. In essence, the lower air pressure can make things that aren't normally flammable—like grain or flour or nondairy coffee creamer—flammable because it disperses them into a fine dust. And it can maximize the flammability of things that are, like kerosene and gasoline. Most importantly, for your purposes, it creates a suctionlike effect, so that something that might not normally rise or disperse, will do so under these conditions."

"So the dumbwaiter shaft leading to Sullivan's apartment was like this tube," said Carter, gesturing to the black tubing on the counter. "And the five-gallon can of gasoline at the base of the shaft was like this coffee creamer."

"Correct."

"You saw what a little coffee creamer can do," said Singh. "Now you understand what a little accelerant, placed in the proper location, can accomplish."

"A fireball," said Georgia.

"A fireball," Singh agreed.

"This was a pretty sophisticated torch—don't you think?" asked Carter.

Singh shrugged. "Not necessarily. Many old-law tenements in New York have dumbwaiters. The rest is simply a matter of knowing the laws of physics. The torch had to create an air current moving over the exit of a tube or shaft, then place the accelerant at the beginning of the shaft and the ignition source at the end. He could have found out how to do this over the Internet, if he really wanted to. In fact," Singh added, "rewiring the junction box in the hallway to short out the wires in the bedroom was probably the only part of the process that required any ability at all."

Georgia recoiled without meaning to. Singh didn't know it, but he'd just told her that the most involved procedure in the entire operation was the one Rick DeAngelo was more than capable of handling.

28

"SUAREZ AND I HAVE TO question him—you understand that, right, girl?"

Georgia noticed Carter was careful not to say Rick's name in front of Richie.

"Honey, go wait in the car," Georgia told Richie. He rolled his eyes but obeyed.

Georgia turned back to Carter. "I understand," she said. "I'm going to call Krause as soon as I get home, tell him everything and get off this case."

"Good."

"I've told you what I could," she reminded him.

"I believe you have."

"So now it's your turn. Why is Broph missing and Sully dead?"

Carter paused a beat before answering. "I don't know," he said finally.

"But you know more than you're saying."

"When I've got something solid—"

"Goddamn it," she said. "Why are you keeping me out of this? I told you I'm quitting the investigation."

"This has nothing to do with the FBI."

"Then it's me you don't trust, is that it?"

Georgia's cell phone rang before Carter could answer. She fished it out of her bag. It was Krause. She turned her back to Carter and mumbled into the phone, requesting a meeting as soon as possible.

"I understand you went to a fire scene last night you had no business being involved in," said Krause.

"Sir, I can explain—"

"I think you'd better," said Krause. "As of ten minutes ago, our office assumed jurisdiction over the Sullivan fire—"

"What?" Georgia stared wide-eyed at Carter. Clearly, no one had told him. "But Jamie Sullivan was an ex-marshal. It's a local case."

"It's a local case if the FBI *says* it's a local case, Marshal. In the future, you will limit the scope of your investigating talents to those specifically sanctioned by the FBI, or you will find yourself *out* of the FBI—are we clear?"

"Yessir. That's what I want to talk to you about."

"I'll be at an art show at Columbia University this afternoon. My daughter's exhibiting some of her work. Meet me at the student center and we'll discuss the situation." He disconnected and Georgia gave Carter the bad news.

"Sonofagun," he said, slapping his thigh. "Somebody tipped the Feds off that DeAngelo's phone number was in Sully's apartment, and he's part of your FBI case. That's the only way to explain this."

"That, or the Feds know for a fact that Freezer had a hand in this fire, and they're covering for him."

"They don't need to cover for him," said Carter. "Nothing ties him to Sully's death. And best of all, *you* are his alibi at the time of Sully's murder."

Georgia gave him a shocked expression. She didn't know he knew that.

"I checked out Freezer's whereabouts last night, too," said Carter. "I don't know what y'all were doing, but I understand you were doing it together."

Georgia turned red under Carter's gaze. She felt bad keeping secrets from her partner. But there was nothing she could tell him, and thankfully, he didn't press. He banged the flat of his hand against the chain-link fence. "I can't believe the Feds have stolen our case. Bunch of computer geeks and desk jockeys," he hissed. "They're not interested in solving Sully's murder. They're using it for Lord knows what end. Heck, the Feds can't even scratch their own butts without a global positioning system and a silicon chip up their behinds."

Georgia left the crime lab and took Richie for lunch at McDonald's, then dropped him off at his friend's birthday party. Her mother had promised to pick him up. From there, she drove into Manhattan. She tried to piece together the Rick she once knew with the evidence before her now. She could picture him being stupid enough to ferry a couple of hippie radicals to a meeting. But she couldn't picture him as a murderer. Then again, she couldn't picture McLaughlin, with so much heat on him already, ordering the murder of another firefighter, either. Not unless his life was riding on it.

Maybe it is, thought Georgia. Sullivan was dead. Brophy was missing, possibly dead. The two had been partners. And Broph had been mad enough at McLaughlin over something to take a baseball bat to his head. Could everything be tied to one of Brophy and Sullivan's cases? Georgia could probably unearth copies of their files at the records division at headquarters. But the division was closed on Sundays. And even if they'd been open, she knew that cases going back more than a decade weren't on computer. She'd have to search them by hand. Besides, the cases were filed by defendant and case number, not by the marshals who handled them.

There had to be some other way of finding out. Georgia parked her car on a street near Columbia University, dialed Manhattan base and asked for Marenko. She knew he was working today.

"Where the hell are you?" he asked when he heard her voice. "I waited for you all yesterday evening at your house. And then this morning I heard about that fire at Sully's."

"I know. I'm sorry, Mac. Listen, I really appreciate all the work you did last night on that car with Richie. I know he's thrilled."

"Forget about it," he said, but Georgia could tell he was secretly pleased she'd mentioned it.

"I need some advice."

"Shoot."

"Is there any way to find out about the cases Jamie Sullivan worked on with Paul Brophy? I understand they weren't partners for very long."

He hesitated. "If the FBI, once again, wants to take over one of our cases, let 'em. But I'm not gonna help them do their jobs."

"Mac, this isn't for the FBI. It's for me. I need to know why someone's got a beef against Sully and Broph."

"Why do you need to know so bad?"

"I can't tell you all the reasons right now, but believe me, this isn't to brownnose the FBI."

"It's Sunday, Scout. Headquarters is closed."

"Wouldn't Manhattan base have those records?"

"Broph and Sully were partners in Queens, not Manhattan," said Marenko. "Queens might have them, but you'd have to search them by hand. It could take days. And Broph can't help you. He's still missing."

"No sign of him?"

"There's been activity on his bank account, but it isn't clear whether the figure the bank picked up on ATM surveillance is Brophy."

"I need to go through all the cases they handled jointly," said Georgia. "I really think the key to Sully's death and Broph's disappearance is in there. Any ideas?"

"Carter knew Broph. Why don't you ask him?"

"Because he won't tell me," said Georgia. "He's covering for somebody."

"Bullshit. He'd never cover up a crime. This is a man who dimed his own partner."

"He didn't dime him, Mac. Brophy got what he had coming."

"I'm not saying he didn't. I'm just talking about personality. Carter fills out his time sheets to the minute, for chrissakes. I don't even like the SOB and I'd vouch for his integrity."

"Mac, when I talked to Broph the other night, he kept telling me he was sorry. Like he'd done something wrong—but not intentionally wrong. A mistake. I remember his words went something like 'me and Sully thought it was an accident.' A few days ago, Randy told me about a guy named Cullen Thomas who came forward two years ago about a fire that had been labeled an accident and wasn't. Thomas said McLaughlin was behind it. Then *he* died before anyone could learn more. Don't you think there might be a connection?"

"That's a reach," said Marenko.

"That's a motive," said Georgia. "If it turns out to be true, we may be able to get McLaughlin even if the Feds refuse to hand him over for Café Treize or Sully's death. An arson that old would precede their hold on him. And there's no statute of limitations on murder."

Marenko thought a moment. "Broph went to jail for taking a bribe. That means the Manhattan district attorney's office would have a file on him. They'd have gone through all his cases with a fine-tooth comb after something like that. Every defense attorney with a client Broph sent to jail would've tried to claim their guy was set up."

"You think they'd have records of all his cases?"

"Not records. But maybe some kind of listing—like an abstract. In case the defense attorneys started making noise. I've got some good contacts in the D.A.'s office. They're much better at computerizing their stuff than we are. Let me see what I can dig up."

"You can narrow it to cases that Brophy and Sullivan handled together. I'm looking only for fatal fires that were labeled accidental."

"Gotcha. I'll call you later if I find anything."

"Thanks."

"So this isn't about sucking up to the Feds, huh?"

"No."

Marenko waited for Georgia to elaborate but she didn't. She couldn't bring herself to tell him the real reason she so desperately wanted to nail McLaughlin for Sully's death.

She couldn't admit—even to herself—that no matter how much she thought she hated Rick DeAngelo, she didn't hate him enough to help send him to jail.

29

GEORGIA HAD LIVED in New York all her life, and yet she had never set foot inside the quadrant of stone paths and manicured lawns of Columbia University. The Greco-Roman buildings had the look of greatness about them: Doric columns, broad steps and sweeping views of open plazas. It made Georgia wish she hadn't dropped out of college halfway through her sophomore year. Then again, it wasn't like she would have ever attended a school as lofty as Columbia anyway.

She approached a couple of students barely out of their teens and asked for the student center. It was a modern, low-lying steel-and-glass structure, just off the main plaza near Butler Library. Inside, there was a coffee bar and a cafeteria. There were bulletin boards crammed with offers of apartment shares, typing services and tutoring. There were posters encouraging students to join picket lines for at least a dozen causes, from legalizing gay marriages to closing down the Dalcor plant on the Hudson River.

Georgia asked around about the art show until she found the right room—a large, open space lit by skylights. It was crowded with young people with dyed-black ponytails, purple mohawks and rings in their noses. Paintings, photographs and collages adorned the walls, punctuated by sculptures in stone, metal and, in one case, recycled aluminum cans. Georgia's eye was drawn to a cluster of bold black-and-white photographs that looked strangely familiar. One showed children running through an open hydrant on a New York City street. Another was a portrait of a thuggish-looking teenager beside a rooftop pigeon coop. Each of these stark, simple photographs reminded Georgia of the girl in the subway station that Michael McLaughlin had hanging in his house.

"My daughter's."

"Hmmm?" Georgia turned. Charles Krause was standing behind her, nodding to the photographs. "My daughter took those."

"She did?" Georgia squinted at the initials: *LP.*

"Lauren uses her married name, Paley, these days. She thinks that being the struggling artist wife of a filthy rich investment banker is more glamorous than being the daughter of an FBI agent, I'm afraid. She's very good, isn't she? She does a lot of freelance photography for newspapers and magazines, but she also sells some of it directly to galleries."

"Those galleries have some interesting clients," said Georgia. "I think I saw one of your daughter's photographs in Michael McLaughlin's house."

Krause frowned. Clearly, this was news to him. *So I'm not the only head McLaughlin likes to play with,* thought Georgia.

"My daughter doesn't always know where her prints end up," said Krause. "My wife is pretty good at keeping track of the buyers for her, but"—he cast a quick glance in the direction of a young woman who looked surprisingly like the waif in McLaughlin's photograph—"art and money make strange bedfellows."

"I'm sure," said Georgia, staring at the woman now. She had long dark hair and wore a tight black scoop-necked shirt that barely skimmed the waistline of her faded hip-hugger jeans. The jeans had huge tears in each knee. When she lifted a plastic tumbler of soda, Georgia noticed a tattoo of red hearts encircling her wrist. She wondered what her FBI-father had to say about that—or, for that matter, her investment-banker husband.

"You had something urgent to discuss with me," said Krause. "Let's find a quiet place to talk." He led Georgia out of the room and down a long hallway to the cafeteria where they found a corner table. She could see that Krause was gearing himself up to lecture her about being at Sully's apartment last night. She decided to take the offensive.

"I'm here, sir, because I think you should know that I recognized one of the people at the Green Warriors meeting last night."

Krause leaned back in his chair. "Recognized? From where?"

Georgia closed her eyes and took a deep breath. As angry as she was at Rick, she took no pleasure in what she had to do now. "The man is my son's father."

"Your ex-husband?"

"We were never married." It always pained Georgia to say that. "I wasn't sure it was him at the meeting. Our encounter was brief. It was dark. And I haven't seen him in eight years. That's why I didn't say anything last night. But when I got back to my house, he was waiting for me."

"Did you break cover?"

"No," said Georgia. "But he knows I used to be a firefighter. It wasn't that hard for him to figure out that I'm a fire marshal and that I'm working undercover. I never mentioned the FBI, though," she added quickly.

"Has he ever shown any . . . proclivities . . . toward extremist groups or environmental causes?"

"Never." Georgia smiled to herself. The only proclivities Rick had shown when she knew him were the three Bs: beer, broads and bikes. Then again, people were always more complex than they appeared. "The closest Rick DeAngelo ever came to nature was the time he totaled his motorcycle when he hit a deer."

"Did you say Rick DeAngelo?" Krause couldn't hide his shock. "That's why you went to Jamie Sullivan's apartment." Clearly, he had already obtained Carter's initial case report with Rick's business phone number noted in the evidence log.

"No," said Georgia. "I had no idea Rick's number would be there. I didn't even know it was his number until after I saw him."

"Did he say why he's working with terrorists?"

"He claims he isn't," said Georgia. "He said he was just doing a favor for Louie Buscanti."

"DeAngelo works for Buscanti?"

"Rick says he doesn't work for Buscanti. He's an electrical contractor. He says Buscanti got him work wiring a hotel."

"Did he mention Sullivan?"

"No, sir." She felt Krause's scrutiny and it embarrassed her. He had to be wondering what kind of people she ran with in her youth. She was wondering the same thing. "Look, I don't want to compromise the FBI's case," said Georgia. "I think it makes sense for me to resign from the investigation."

Krause didn't respond. He steepled his fingers and stared out the window at a passing group of students. After a few moments, he turned to her.

"Do you think DeAngelo told the Green Warriors that you're a cop?"

"He didn't then. Now, I don't know," Georgia admitted.

"Interesting," said Krause. "He could have blown the entire operation right then and there last night. Three years of work—out the window."

"I think that's what Freez—Michael McLaughlin—was banking on," said Georgia. "That, or that I wouldn't come clean and tell you about Rick."

"Do you think DeAngelo will try to make contact with you again?"

"I don't know," said Georgia. "He knows he's in trouble."

"He could offer us some very valuable information."

"He says he doesn't know anything about the Green Warriors."

"He has a relationship with the kingpin of South Jersey mobsters. If we could tie Buscanti into the Green Warriors, we could take down two major public threats with one informant."

"I don't think he wants to become an informant, sir."

"Would he prefer spending a big chunk of his future in prison for the murder of Jamie Sullivan? Because if that's the threat the FBI has to hold over his head, then that's what we'll do." Krause's pager went off. He looked down at the number, then decided to ignore it. "Tying Louie Buscanti to the Green Warriors would be a major feather in your cap, Marshal. A major feather. I don't see how the FBI could stand in your way on acquiring McLaughlin if you succeeded in getting DeAngelo to work with us."

"If he testified against Buscanti, he'd have to go into the witness protection program, wouldn't he?" *Richie would lose any chance of having Rick in his life forever.*

"It's possible."

"That's a big step," said Georgia.

"I realize that," said Krause. "That's why I'm only asking you to meet with him. Tonight, if possible. Feel him out. I can arrange it so that I'm a short distance away if you need me."

"Is this the only way?" asked Georgia.

"Keep your priorities straight, Marshal. We both want to see the fire department get justice for those dead firefighters. You get Rick DeAngelo to cooperate with us, and I will do my damnedest to see that that happens."

30

GEORGIA CALLED Rick's business number—the same one that was scribbled on the pad in Sully's apartment. As soon as he heard her voice, he went ballistic.

"Gee Gee—what in hell's name are you trying to do to me here? Some guy from the FDNY called me this morning and told me I'm a suspect in a murder investigation. I don't even know who the bastard was I'm supposed to have murdered. All I did was give a ride last night to two punks. And now I'm supposed to be a terrorist and a killer?"

Georgia forced herself to remain calm, but inside, she was shaking. "I think we should meet and talk about the offer I made last night."

"That's no offer. That's a death sentence. Tell your bosses I'll take my chances with Buscanti before I take 'em with them. I didn't kill anybody. I didn't blow anything up. And I'm not gonna end up a cement slab under some parking garage just 'cause somebody thinks I did."

"You were at that Green Warriors meeting, Rick. And your phone number was scribbled on a pad in the dead man's apartment, beneath an appointment that looks like it was set up with you."

"Well, it wasn't."

"You want to tell that to a jury?"

He took a deep breath. "What am I supposed to do?"

"Meet with me," said Georgia. "Let me help you try to sort this out."

"What? You, me and twenty thousand listening devices? No way, Gee Gee."

"No wires, Rick. No listening devices. Just you and me."

He laughed. "Man, talk about a reunion that won't be warm and fuzzy."

GEORGIA SET UP the meeting with Rick for six p.m. at the diner right near the George Washington Bridge in Fort Lee. She called Krause with the details. Then she called her mother to plead with her to watch Richie for the evening.

"I can't do it," said Margaret. "I told you weeks ago that I was going to the Woodside Irish League's Christmas party tonight."

"I'll get home early."

"I don't care if you get home before you go." An Irish-ism, as Georgia called them—a nonsensical saying. Her mother had dozens of them from, "I'll kill you if you die in a motorcycle accident," to so-and-so was "the picture of health at his wake."

Georgia got off the phone and ran through the possibilities. In the end, there was only one. She felt guilty about asking him, given that he was working two jobs. And, especially, given whom she was meeting.

"Mac?" she said when he picked up the phone at Manhattan base. "Any luck with those case files from the D.A.'s office?"

"I've got the stack on loan in my car," he said. "I figured we could grab some dinner and maybe go through them later."

"I've got a big, big favor to ask you."

"What?"

"I know it's your only night off. I know you're seeing your own kids tomorrow." She took a deep breath. "But I've got to work."

"Oh." He sounded disappointed. "On a Sunday night?"

"I've got to meet someone connected to the FBI case—at a diner in New Jersey. I won't be late. Maybe we can see each other at my place afterward. My mother's not going to be home until very late."

"Where will Richie be?"

Georgia took a deep breath. "That was my big favor."

"You want *me* to baby-sit?"

"I'm in a bind, Mac. I wouldn't ask otherwise. I'll look at those files with you when I get home. Please? You guys can work on the race car."

"I'm exhausted, Scout."

"This is really important," said Georgia. "If tonight goes well, we may be one step closer to getting McLaughlin."

"Man," he sighed. "Sometimes I wish you *did* have an ex. At least he could baby-sit now and then."

Georgia decided not to answer that. "Ma will let you in. There's plenty of food in the house. And I won't be home late—I promise."

SHE WAS SUPPOSED TO meet Rick at six p.m. at the diner. It was 6:10 and dark already by the time she stepped out of her car—a dark blue Chrysler sedan with a busted antenna, on loan from the FBI. There was no sign of Rick's truck. Punctuality was not one of his strong suits. He rarely made the previews of a movie. He missed Richie's birth. In fact, the only time she'd seen him be early to anything was the morning they took the firefighter's physical.

She took a seat in a booth at the far end of a row. The short, gray-haired man who seated her grimaced. "Minimum two people in a booth," he said in heavily accented English.

"I'm waiting for someone."

"Wait at door."

Georgia opened her purse and slapped a twenty on the tabletop, still wet from being sponged down. "I'll take a coffee and a grilled cheese sandwich, and you can keep the rest if my friend doesn't show."

The man wrote down her order, pocketed the twenty and then disappeared. It was another thirty-five minutes before Rick showed up. By then, Georgia had picked at the sandwich, finished two cups of coffee and made a smiley face on her plate with the pickle and tomatoes.

She glared at Rick as he sauntered over, baseball cap pulled low across his face. He was wearing jeans and a sweatshirt beneath a down jacket. He looked like he needed a shave. He hadn't exactly dressed for the occasion. Georgia, on the other hand, had redone her makeup and slipped into her favorite pants suit—silky pants with a stripe of blue and gray and a matching jacket. He slid into the booth and picked up the menu like he was right on time.

"You haven't changed, have you?"

"I just sat down to order—you already got a problem?"

"You're forty-five minutes late."

He made a face. "I spent last night with terrorists, got accused of murder this morning and raced halfway up the state in rush-hour traffic to meet my pissed-off ex-girlfriend who'd like nothing better than to toss my ass in jail. I think I deserve credit for even being here."

"That's not the point. You could have called. . . . Oh, forget it." She sat back in the booth and folded her arms. They had reverted right back to their old habits. He had an answer for everything and she sulked over each of them.

He removed his baseball cap and did a quick scan of her makeup and clothes. He looked embarrassed as he rubbed a hand along his cheek. "I didn't have time to shave or change," he apologized. "I mean, if the FDNY is going to bust me, what's the difference?"

"I didn't need a meeting to arrest you, Rick. If that's what anybody wanted, it would already have happened."

"I figured maybe you wanted to have the pleasure."

"You think that's what this is? A pleasure?"

"No," he said. "I'm sorry. That was uncalled for." Rick, she noticed, hadn't removed his bulky down jacket.

"You're not carrying, are you?" she asked him.

"A gun? Of course not. I don't even hunt anymore." He removed his jacket, then his sweatshirt. Beneath them he wore a bright blue T-shirt tucked into his jeans. He still had a nice body—not as tall or broad as Mac's but lean and muscular just the same. She noticed him looking intently at her and basked a little bit in the attention. Beneath her jacket she was wearing a soft gray silk sweater—form fitting, with a scooped neckline, of course. She hoped Corinne was fat.

"You're not wearing a wire, are you?" he asked. *So that was the reason for his scrutiny.* Georgia felt herself deflating.

"No." She pulled at the neckline of her tight sweater. "See?"

Rick grinned. "I remember when I saw a little more."

"I'm sure you see enough at home."

"Are you . . . ?" He played with a fork in front of him.

"Am I what?"

"I know you're not married, Gee Gee. But are you—you know—involved with anyone?"

"That's none of your business."

"Hey, no sweat. I'm only asking because I really want your life and Richie's life to be happy."

"You're asking because you want to feel off the hook, Rick. And that can't happen. *I* can move on. I *have* moved on. But it's different for Richie. You're still his father."

Rick looked down at his place mat. There was a map of the turnpike on it. "You think I'm a monster, don't you?" he asked. He'd now started playing with his spoon as well. If the waiter didn't take his order soon, Georgia was sure the silverware would end up on the floor. And she thought only Richie could be this fidgety.

"I think you're irresponsible and selfish."

"I gave you that six thousand dollars—most of my inheritance from my grandmother—before I split. It's not like I left you with nothing."

"Six thousand dollars over eight years, hmmm," said Georgia. "That works out to about . . ." She did the calculations on a napkin. "Less than sixty-five dollars a month. I couldn't keep a dog on that."

"It's all about the money, isn't it? That's why I never came around after a while. You made me feel . . . worthless."

"Oh, blame me now."

"I'm not blaming you, Gee Gee. I'm embarrassed—can't you understand that? I want to offer Richie something he deserves—something I haven't got."

"I'm sure your family isn't starving."

"You want to see my tax returns? Want me to give you—or some lawyer—a blow-by-blow description of my finances?"

"Forget it," said Georgia. "Just forget it. It's not about the money anyway."

"It sure sounds like it is."

Georgia closed her eyes and fought for control. The hurt had nothing to do with money—or with her, for that matter. "What I wanted most from you," she said softly, "was for you to be a father to Richie. I can sort of forgive you the money, Rick. It's a lot harder for me to forgive you for not being there to help him grow up."

The waiter appeared at Rick's elbow, and he mumbled his order without looking up: a bowl of chili, no onions, black coffee and a side of coleslaw. Rick had always loved coleslaw.

"I don't know what to say," he said into the place mat after the waiter left. "I wasn't ready to get married, never mind be a father."

"Do you think I was?"

"No," he said. "But you and your mother were so mad at me, I couldn't imagine how I was going to visit a toddler around the two of you—especially when I was always out of work. I put it off, Gee Gee. And then I moved to Toms River and got married and Gracie came along and I was so busy with her. And then Becky and—"

"Whoa," said Georgia. "You have *two* daughters?"

He looked up. "Yeah. I thought you said Robbie told you everything."

"He didn't tell me about the second one."

"Gracie's five and Becky's two." He looked suddenly embarrassed. "I'm sorry. I thought you knew."

"It doesn't matter," Georgia said unconvincingly.

The waiter put coffee, chili and coleslaw down in front of Rick. "Look, Gee Gee—tell me what you want and I'll try to do it."

"Are we talking personally? Or professionally?"

"We'll get to the professional in a minute. Right now, I want to know what you'd like from me as a man. You want an apology? I'm sorry. No jokes. No bull-shit. I really, truly am sorry. I wish I could have been more mature. I wish I could erase everything and start over. You want me to leave you and Richie alone forever? No sweat—I'll respect your wishes. You want me to give you some bread? I'll try to scrounge up something, though it'll probably create World War Three with Corinne. Gee Gee—I'll do whatever you want. I'm hoping that maybe—just maybe—you might give me a second chance with Richie."

Georgia didn't say anything. She just fiddled with her coffee cup.

"I know what you're thinking," said Rick. "That I'll just ride in and play dad when I feel like it. That he's better off not seeing me at all."

"That's pretty close to it," Georgia admitted.

"Believe it or not, I'm a good dad to my girls."

"I'll make sure to send you a card next Father's Day."

"You're still angry at me." He made it sound like an unjust accusation.

"You're damn right I'm angry with you. Do you have any idea what it's like to raise a child by yourself? When you're not even twenty-one years old?"

"You had your mother."

"That's not the same, Rick. I've been through the three a.m. bouts of colic. The stomach flus and earaches. The time he broke his wrist. The two weeks I spent combing lice out of his hair."

"No one's taking any of that away from you."

"Oh, goody."

"Gee Gee—you're still his mother. You'll always be his mother. I could never be to him what you are."

His food was getting cold. Georgia nodded to it. "Just eat, okay? We'll talk about this stuff another time."

He stirred through the coleslaw, picking out the tiny shreds of carrots. "You still hate vegetables except for coleslaw and potatoes, huh?" she asked.

"Yep. Some things don't change, right?" He smiled and shook his head. "I'm still broke and you're still beautiful."

"You're still a bullshitter, too."

He ate about half his chili before he spoke again. "I can't do it, Gee Gee," he said finally.

"Do what?"

He put down his spoon. "I've been turning it over in my mind the whole drive up here. I can't go against Buscanti. I came here to tell you that. The guy's all-powerful in South Jersey. Anybody who went against him would wind up dead."

"I can get protection for you."

"The only kind of protection that would work is to relocate me and my family to some godforsaken hick town somewhere in another part of the country. And I'm not doing it. No way. Corinne has a big family. She could never be separated from them like that."

"You could've told me all this on the phone," said Georgia. "Saved me the trouble of coming out here."

"I was hoping to talk you into letting me see Richie."

Georgia changed the subject. "How about at least finding out from Buscanti who set you up?"

"Are you kidding?" asked Rick. "You want me to walk up to the most powerful man in the construction business in South Jersey and ask him who his underworld friends are? Come on, Gee Gee, get real."

"You only have to ask him one question."

"What's that?"

"Ask him if Mike McLaughlin called him to arrange your presence at that meeting."

"Who's Mike McLaughlin?"

"You met him at the construction site the other night. He was the man with me. And that's all I'm going to tell you about him. But I think he set you up."

He pushed his food aside and leaned in close across the table. "You never answered me about Richie."

"That was my answer."

"You don't want me to see him? Ever?"

"Not while you're in this mess. The 'ever' part will have to wait."

The waiter brought the check. Rick reached for his wallet. Georgia waved it away. "I'll get reimbursed," she said.

"So what's gonna happen now?"

"I'll take your decision back to my superiors and they'll decide how to handle this from there."

"Am I going to jail?"

"I don't know."

"Whatever happens, I just want you to know—I won't blame you, okay?" Rick grinned. "I might try to get myself on The Jenny Jones Show or something—'Men who Get Busted by Their Ex-Girlfriends.' But I won't blame you."

Georgia smiled and he seemed warmed by her amusement. "You could reenact it in front of a studio audience," he teased. "Women would love it."

"Believe it or not, I don't want to see that happen."

He gave her a quick kiss on the cheek. The gesture was so unexpected, Georgia had no time to react. "I'm sorry about a lot of stuff, Gee Gee. But I'm not sorry there was once a me and you."

31

OUTSIDE THE DINER, the air temperature hovered around freezing and rain had begun to fall, turning to ice the moment it hit the pavement and the cars.

"God, what a mess," Georgia remarked as she and Rick left the diner. The lot appeared murky after the intense brightness inside. For a moment, Georgia forgot what the car she was driving looked like.

"Where are you parked?" asked Rick. "I'll walk you to your car." Georgia slipped on the ice and he caught her. "Better yet, I'll walk— you skate."

Georgia squinted around the parking lot. She remembered parking out of the way, near the Dumpsters. Her dark blue Chrysler with the broken antenna looked too FBI for her to draw attention to it. No one drove a car like that unless they were government—or ready for Social Security. Rick made the same connection.

"That's not your car, is it? I thought you still had the Escort."

"I do. And a Harley Davidson, too."

His eyes widened. "Really? You ride motorcycles now? You never wanted to get on mine when I had it."

"Kind of hard to ride a motorcycle when you're eight months pregnant."

"Oh, yeah. I forgot." Georgia hadn't. A month shy of Richie's birth, and what did Rick blow his money on? An 883 cc Harley Sportster. He obviously didn't remember the argument, but she did.

A sheet of ice already covered the car. It seemed to weight it down on the passenger side. Rick noticed it too and walked around to examine it.

"Your front tire is flat. You ran over a two-by-four with nails in it."

"What?" She walked to the other side of the car and Rick pointed to the piece of wood, still lodged near the rear tire. One of the nails was stuck in the rear tire as well. When he dislodged it, the rear tire, too, began to deflate.

"Damn it. I didn't even feel the car go over it."

"I'd change it for you, but one spare won't do you any good with two flat tires."

"I suppose not," said Georgia. "If you can drop me off at the supermarket complex up the road, my boss is there. He'll call a garage and get it towed."

"Your boss? You mean you've got a fire marshal with you?"

"Sort of."

He looked stricken. "Did you think I was going to hurt you or something?"

"It's standard procedure, Rick. Don't take it personally. Anyway, I'm glad he's here. If you can give me a ride over to the supermarket parking lot, I'll tell him what happened and we can get it towed."

"Okay." He wrapped an arm around her and gently guided her across the icy parking lot. It felt odd to be in Rick DeAngelo's arms again. Odd, and not entirely unpleasant. Georgia tried to turn off those feelings. There was no place they could go—no place she even wanted them to go. She was with Mac now. Rick was with Corinne. Things were the way they should be. She told herself that, but she still got a rush of something being this close to the first man she had ever loved. Maybe it was just her youth she was pining for—a time when she was young and free and the world seemed full of possibilities.

The front windshield of Rick's pickup truck was thick with ice, and his wipers looked cemented in place.

"Do you have a scraper?" asked Georgia.

"Somewhere behind the seat." He shrugged. Knowing Rick, it was in there. Knowing Rick, it was buried beneath twenty pounds of junk. He unlocked the cab doors and they both climbed in. Several minutes of searching through jumper cables, duct tape, rolls of copper wiring and pieces of sandpaper produced nothing. From the cab's back window, Georgia noticed a big steel toolbox welded to the inside of the truck bed.

"Could it be in your toolbox outside?" she asked.

"Could be."

"Can't you find anything?"

He winked at her. "I found you after eight years, didn't I?"

"That was easy," said Georgia. "I was right where you left me."

"So's the scraper." He tossed her the keys. "Scoot over to the driver's side, turn on the engine and put the defroster on. I'll check the toolbox." He closed the door and went around to the back of the truck.

Georgia stuck the key in the ignition. That's when she noticed it—a great big ice scraper half-buried beneath a floor mat. She turned over the engine and reached under the mat.

She never got to do more. From underneath the truck came a sudden whoosh of air. Then a boom like an M-80. The hood flew off the car. The windows shattered into tiny pebbles of safety glass. The doors blew open. The front of the truck rose three feet off the ground. Georgia was thrown onto the pavement, dazed and bleeding. She scrambled back as the truck bounced up and down on its struts before finally settling back onto the asphalt. The tires were on fire. Flames were spreading quickly from the engine compartment to the cab. Not that it would have mattered had she stayed in the passenger seat. The explosion had pushed the seat to within four inches of the roof of the cab. Anybody sitting there would have been crushed to death.

"Gee Gee, are you all right?" asked Rick as he scooped her up and carried her away from the burning truck. Her ears rang. Her side hurt. She could taste something bitter and metallic in her mouth. Already, people were rushing out of the diner, dialing their cell phones. There was a lot of commotion, but it all sounded far off, drowned out by the ringing in Georgia's ears.

"Can you hear me, Gee Gee?" Rick asked again.

"My ears are ringing," said Georgia as she tried to ease herself onto her feet. Her side felt bruised. Her jaw ached, as if she'd been chewing for a long time. But thankfully, her only other injuries seemed to be a couple of minor cuts on her hands and arms. She followed Rick's gaze to his truck. Black smoke was pushing out of the open driver's side door of the cab and orange tendrils of flame were licking the roof. She could feel the heat from a hundred feet away.

"What in hell happened?" Rick wondered aloud in a dazed voice.

"A bomb," Georgia mumbled. "Set off by the car's ignition. I can't believe I got out."

"You didn't get out, you were thrown from the truck as it blew," said Rick.

"Still, I should be dead." She closed her eyes and shuddered.

"Buscanti," Rick mumbled. "He must've found out about our meeting." He wrapped his arms around her to warm them both. Then he suddenly stiffened. "I don't get it, Gee Gee. You're a New York City fire marshal. Bureau of Fire Investigation, right? I don't know enough about Buscanti's operations to really hurt him at this point. Why bomb my truck?"

"I'm working for the FBI."

Even in the shadows of the street lamps, Georgia could see Rick's face pale.

"Please tell me you're dyslexic and you mean the BFI."

"I mean the Feds, Rick. I'm on loan from the fire department. This is a Federal case."

"Then I'm a dead man." He loosened his grip and stepped back from her. "I've got to get out of here."

Sirens were wailing in the distance. The police and local fire department would be here any minute, with Krause no doubt on their tail.

"You can't go home."

"I know that."

"You've got to stay with me. I'm the only one who can protect you."

"Protect me? You call this protecting me? My truck just got blown up. My wife and daughters are alone in my house, two hours drive from here."

"The FBI can help you—"

"In return for ruining my life."

"You don't have a choice, Rick. I'm sorry. I never intended this to happen. But the way things stand, you don't have any options."

"I'm going to give myself up to Buscanti."

"He'll kill you. He probably just tried."

"Wake up, Gee Gee. He tried to kill *us. Us.* You think you just happened to have a two-by-four with nails under your tires? Somebody only made it look that way. They wanted you dead, too."

Georgia froze. In the shock of the moment, she'd forgotten about that.

"If I stay here, I've got no options but to wire up against Buscanti and the Green Warriors," said Rick. "The best I can hope for after that is to go into the witness protection program. Do you understand what that means? It means I'll never see you or Richie again—ever. And it means that you're still at risk."

Georgia closed her eyes. Her head throbbed as if she'd just spent six hours at an Aerosmith concert. She could see the logic of Rick's words. Once Krause got his hooks into Rick, he'd never let him go.

"That's why I've got to talk to Buscanti," Rick pleaded. "I've got to get my wife and kids someplace safe and then handle this my own way. Please—if you ever cared about me, please listen to what I'm saying."

"You can't get out of here," said Georgia. "Everyone will see you."

"Not if I leave right now before the cops secure the scene. I can just blend into the crowd."

She sighed. "Do what you have to do. I just hope you live through it."

The police cars were turning into the lot now. There was just enough darkness and confusion for Rick to slip away.

"I feel bad leaving you," he said.

"*Now* you feel bad." She smiled weakly. "How about eight years ago?"

He smiled. All he said was, "Later." And then he was gone.

32

BY THE TIME the Fort Lee Police walked over to speak to Georgia, Rick DeAngelo had melted into the crowd and disappeared. By every rule of police work, Georgia should have insisted he stay on the scene—held him at gunpoint, if necessary. And yet her gut told her to let Rick slip away until they could both figure out what had happened tonight.

"Ma'am," asked an officer as he approached her, "do you need medical attention?"

"I'm okay."

He nodded to the burning truck. Firefighters were dousing it with water. "Was that your vehicle?"

"No."

"Whose was it, then?"

"It belongs to Richard DeAngelo."

"And where is he?"

"I don't know," Georgia mumbled. "He was here a minute ago." She suddenly realized how vague she sounded. "I'm working on a case with the FBI. I'm sure my supervisor, Charles Krause, is en route." She slowly reached inside her bag and produced her U.S. Marshal's I.D., which the officer examined.

"Is this Mr. DeAngelo a law enforcement officer?"

"No. He's part of an undercover operation. I think you'll need to talk to Agent Krause for anything more."

"Go inside the diner and warm up," said the officer. "I'll direct Agent Krause to my supervisor when he arrives."

Georgia took two steps, then turned. She wasn't thinking clearly since the bomb blast. "There's a Chrysler Three Hundred in the corner by the Dumpster. It's mine, on loan from the FBI. It has two flat tires, which may be intentional. For all I know, it could be wired with a bomb, too. Please advise your people."

The officer nodded and reached for his radio. "Are you sure you don't need medical attention?"

"I just need some coffee."

Georgia went inside and collapsed in a booth. The diner was now empty of patrons and most of the staff. The owner was speaking on a phone in what sounded like Greek. From the tone of his voice, he didn't sound happy.

"We're closed," he yelled at her as she came in. Georgia flashed her shield. He didn't soften, but at least he got her a cup of coffee. She was grateful for small favors.

The brightness of the diner made it hard for her to follow what was going on outside. The local firefighters had the blaze under control. The officer she'd spoken to earlier asked for the keys to her Chrysler. Georgia squinted at the activity beyond the portable spotlights. A bomb squad unit appeared to be checking her car—inside and out. Nothing blew up, thank goodness. She couldn't decide if she was relieved or not. Someone had tampered with her tires after all. If Rick was going to get blown up, she was certainly intended as part of the deal.

Georgia could see Charles Krause out in the lot now. He was talking to a man in a fire helmet by the steps of the diner. There were several other men in trench coats swarming the area. She didn't recognize the faces, but they all looked like FBI. Maybe it was the New Jersey office. Georgia rose from her seat and headed to the door.

The sleet had turned to snow and the hose runoff from the fire trucks was turning the parking lot into a sheet of ice. She walked slowly toward Krause. As soon as he saw her, he excused himself and hustled over. He looked shaken.

"Marshal, are you all right? There are EMS people—"

"I'm okay," said Georgia. "Just a little ringing in my ears."

"Do you know how lucky you are? The fire investigators on the scene are telling me you should be dead. The only thing that saved you was a home-made skid plate welded to the underside of the truck. I guess DeAngelo put it in place to prevent damage to his undercarriage when he drove on unpaved construction sites. In any case, it absorbed some of the bomb's impact and probably saved your life. Where is DeAngelo, by the way?"

"He's not here, sir."

"I know he's not here," snapped Krause. "Where is he?"

"I don't know." Georgia sneaked a look at the burned hulk of his truck, the metal pitted and rust-colored from the fire. Fire investigators had re-moved the skid plate. It was convex in the center from the impact of the bomb. That could've been her. She shuddered at how close she'd come.

"You let him walk away?"

Georgia took a deep breath and felt the cold air slice through her lungs. Behind them, the smoke rising from the wreckage was white and translucent in the night air. The ringing in her ears was beginning to subside, but it was now replaced by a pounding in her head. She felt as spent as the fire.

"Marshal, I asked you a question. Did you let a man suspected of murder and conspiring with terrorists walk away tonight?"

"I was in shock, sir."

"And how is it that he's not hurt and you are?"

"He got out of the truck before it blew."

"You were in a suspect's truck after he exited the vehicle?"

"Yes. I guess so," said Georgia, feeling more foolish by the minute.

"So, in other words, he set you up."

"He was looking for an ice scraper in the truck bed." Even Georgia realized how stupid she sounded.

"So in other words, you got into a suspect's truck. You allowed him to exit it without you. You failed to maintain visual contact. And then you let him get away?"

"I'm sorry, sir." Georgia swallowed hard and fought back a sickening sensation in her stomach. She knew what was coming even before he said the words.

"You failed every single basic tenet of police work, Marshal. And for one reason only, as I see it. Because you have an emotional attachment to the suspect. I see no choice but to terminate your involvement with the FBI's task force, effective immediately."

"I understand," said Georgia, trying to remain calm. "I would just like to ask that the Bureau give consideration to handing McLaughlin over when the FBI is through with him."

"That's no longer your concern, Marshal. I'll take that up with your chief—after I explain exactly what you did and didn't do tonight."

33

IT WAS NINE-THIRTY on Sunday evening before an FBI agent delivered Georgia back to Woodside. By then, Chief Brennan had already been beeped at home and informed of Georgia's "grievous misjudgments" this evening, and Krause's subsequent decision to dismiss her from the case.

Georgia didn't speak to Brennan. She was told only that he had an all-day meeting on Monday, but expected her to report to him at headquarters on Tuesday morning. She knew there would be talk of charges. But that wasn't what was worrying her right now. Brennan, as both Marenko's supervisor and his "rabbi," or mentor, in the department, would have briefed him on the situation. Georgia had no idea how much Mac had been told. But considering he was at her house, watching her son while she was out with her ex, it promised to be a hell of an evening.

Marenko was waiting for Georgia as she walked in the front door. He hung back by the open doorway to the basement and wiped sawdust off his hands and onto his jeans. His blue eyes looked blank and distant. She understood why as soon as Richie scampered up the basement stairs. The child had Georgia by the arm before her coat was even off. She was thankful her cuts from the blast were small. Richie didn't even seem to notice.

"Mom, you gotta come downstairs and see it," said Richie excitedly. "The race car Mac and me are building. It's almost done. It's gonna be red and the wheels are huge—two on each axle."

Georgia followed her son down the basement stairs. Richie practically skipped across the floor to the workbench. The race car had been cut and assembled. Some of the pieces were freshly screwed and glued in place.

"Mac gave the back a spoiler," said Richie, pointing to a flat protrusion from the rear of the car. "He said it will break up air flow and make the car go faster."

"I'm sure it will," said Georgia. She turned to Marenko. "Thank you," she mouthed softly. Men usually came into her life and wrecked everything she'd tried to build. This was the first time one had ever tried to build anything. And now she was doing all the wrecking.

"We're gonna give it a white pinstripe," said the boy.

"Not tonight, though. Right, Sport?" said Marenko. His tone was overly bright. He was fighting to keep himself in check while Richie was awake. "Time for bed for you."

Upstairs, Georgia put Richie to bed. Then she ditched her clothes in favor of jeans and a sweatshirt. She looked in on the child one more time before she went downstairs. His eyes were closed, and he suddenly looked much younger than ten. It was hard to run her eyes along that dark wavy hair and the little dimple in his chin, and not see Rick—not the Rick of memory, but the flesh-and-blood man who had fathered her boy. She wished she could tell her son about his father. But she couldn't. It wouldn't do the boy any good. And yet it hurt to keep it inside, like a helium balloon you have to keep both hands on to hold down.

Mac was still in the basement cleaning up when she found him. She sat on the stairs and watched him a moment from behind. He was squinting at the tools, trying to figure out which ones were his and which ones were Georgia's. He tossed his in a gray metal toolbox on the floor. He was a big man, well built, with a head of thick blue-black hair and a nonchalant way of carrying himself that never ceased to make him attractive, even in old jeans, work boots and a denim shirt.

"Chief Brennan told you, didn't he?"

"Yep." He kept his back to her.

"About who I was meeting? And what happened?"

"Everything," he grunted. Georgia could hear the hurt in his voice. *Chalk up one more part of my life McLaughlin has ruined.*

"I'm sorry, Mac. I wanted to tell you, but Krause told me I had to keep the meeting in strict confidence. This wasn't a pleasure visit, believe me."

"He almost killed you."

"Someone almost killed us. I don't think Rick had anything to do with it."

"Convenient how he left the truck before it blew up, don't you think?" Marenko patted his shirt pocket for a piece of nicotine gum, unwrapped it noisily and popped it in his mouth.

"Rick wouldn't do that. I know him."

"Do you now?"

"C'mon Mac, don't be jealous."

"Hey, you do what you want. There are no chains on you."

"But I want you to understand—I didn't choose this."

He gave her his "cop" look—intense, distrusting and cold. "The Feds think you know where DeAngelo is. Do you?"

"No. He believes if he can see Louie Buscanti, he can straighten things out with him. I don't know where or when that will happen, or if he'll even survive the encounter."

"You're not hiding him?"

"No."

"Why did you let him run?"

Georgia closed her eyes and searched for an answer. "Because things aren't adding up."

"No, Scout. You don't *want* them to add up. You've still got feelings for this guy. And you're putting your career—your life—on the line for him."

"I met Rick for the first time in eight years at an undercover operation the other night—an operation McLaughlin set up. You don't think that's a big coincidence?"

"Even if McLaughlin set you up initially, that's got nothing to do with tonight."

"It's got *everything* to do with tonight," Georgia argued. "Nobody was supposed to know about tonight's meeting except Charles Krause, Rick and me. If Rick didn't rig that truck bomb, then Buscanti probably did. How did he find out about the meeting?"

"DeAngelo told him."

"Rick's frightened to death of Buscanti. No, Mac. Buscanti found out because he knows McLaughlin. The FBI's own data files say so. How do you know McLaughlin didn't tip him off?"

"Perhaps."

"The thing I don't get is, why?" asked Georgia. "I'm just a cop to him. If I get killed, some other marshal will take my place. It won't necessarily get him off the hook for the Café Treize fire."

"Maybe that's not what he's trying to get off the hook for."

"What do you mean?"

Marenko closed his toolbox. "Come upstairs. I think you'd better look at something."

On the dining table, Marenko had spread out stacks of old incident reports, each with a decaying rubber band around it and a summary sheet, yellowed with age, on top.

"You got hold of Brophy and Sullivan's old cases," said Georgia. She stepped closer and noticed something else. There were several nicotine gum wrappers balled up on the table. A half-pint of ice cream had been emptied and left on the side with the encrusted spoon still in it. Four toothpicks had been shredded. Marenko was fighting the urge to smoke in a bad way. Maybe it was just nicotine withdrawal. Or maybe it was something more.

"You asked me to come up with every fatal fire that Broph and Sully handled together and labeled accidental," said Marenko. "In eleven months, they handled twelve such fires."

"Twelve. That's more than I would have expected in such a short time," said Georgia.

"It was a busy period for fatal fires in Queens. Lots of immigrants were moving into the borough and subdividing single-family homes."

"Any sense whether any of those fires might have involved McLaughlin?"

"No way to tell. He's not mentioned. But there's something I *did* come across that I think you should know about. Could be just a creepy coincidence. Or it could explain why Sully's dead, Broph is missing and Carter never wanted you on this case." He spit out his nicotine gum into the empty ice cream container. "Georgia," he said hoarsely. He rarely called her Georgia and the sound of it always made her sit up and take notice. "One of the twelve fatal fires? It was your dad's."

"Brophy and Sullivan were the marshals who investigated my father's death?"

"Uh-huh."

"Are you saying maybe they blew it?"

"It's possible. Then again, it could've been some other fire that Cullen Thomas was referring to when he offered to testify against McLaughlin. We'll never know."

"Randy knows," said Georgia.

"No, he doesn't," said Marenko. "I spoke to him this evening. All he has are suspicions—the same ones we have now. That's why he pulled the incident report on your father's fire. That's what he was doing the other day at the records department at headquarters. But he doesn't know. None of us do. The only one who really knew was Cullen Thomas and he's dead."

Georgia felt a wave of anger like a hot poker across her skin. She wanted to hit something—hard. To feel it succumb like Silly Putty beneath her fist. She tried out the words in her head and refused to believe them. *My dad was murdered. My dad died by an arsonist's hand.* And not just any arsonist. Michael

McLaughlin. The man who killed Joe Russo and Tony Fuentes and turned Doug Hanlon's life into a living hell. A man so vile he'd burn a woman's face for the sake of a few dollars. *When would it end?*

"What am I going to do?" asked Georgia. She felt light-headed and nauseous. "You're telling me that Michael McLaughlin might have murdered my father, but all the people who can help me piece it together are dead or missing?" She thought about McLaughlin's words on the tape Nathan Reese had given her: *So a couple of firefighters died—so what? You think this is the first time an accusation like this has been leveled against me?*

"I want back on the FBI case," she said.

"No can do," said Marenko. "You heard Krause. You're off. And I agree. You're too close to this."

"I'm not sitting on my behind while that sonofabitch waltzes out of yet another murder rap."

Marenko tried to pull Georgia close. She resisted. "No, Mac. I want justice. If I don't get it from my department, then I'll go about it on my own."

He shook his head. "Look, I know what you're feeling, but you can't go there. You're a fire marshal. A cop. You can't take the law into your own hands."

"I want him dead. I want him to suffer. The way they all suffered."

Marenko tried again to pull her toward him. This time she didn't resist. "I swear to you, Scout, I'll do everything I can to nail this bastard."

34

DOUG HANLON WENT OUT for a late-night run. It was the only thing these last few days that seemed to make him feel any better. Inside the house, he felt claustrophobic, unable to breathe. Everyone was always looking at him, measuring him—wondering. Even tonight, he could hear his father and father-in-law talking in the kitchen. He noticed how their voices hushed when he walked over to the refrigerator to grab a beer. He caught the disappointment on his father's face. *You're a fine one to judge,* he felt like yelling at him. But he said nothing. And they said nothing. He was drowning and all anyone could do was stand and watch. And so he ran. It was the only thing he was good at anymore.

He ran along the boardwalk under the stars, the wind off the sea so cold that it felt like needles on his face—especially on the tender burns that were still healing. He welcomed the pain. It was the only sensation he could feel. The rest of him felt numb.

Tomorrow was Tony Fuentes' funeral. Hanlon knew he had to go, had to face Tony's widow, as pregnant as his own wife, Kerry. And the girls—one of them the exact same age as Jenna. His stomach churned with the thought. He had never been good with words. Tony was the funny one, the one who always had a sly remark at a drill, the practical joker who could spend half his day coming up with raunchy punch lines to deliver across the P.A. system. A chuck on the shoulder from Tony Fuentes along with a mumbled, "well done" was the best compliment Hanlon had ever received. He loved the man. He'd learned from the man. He wasn't ready to bury him.

And yet, the words that flew freely through his head when he was running got all tangled up inside of him when he thought about seeing Fuentes' widow tomorrow. He burned with shame, a shame so hot and fiery that he felt like he was watching himself from afar, making his hands and feet move like a marionette. Smiling felt like the oddest muscle spasm to him. Where before, he hadn't been able to keep his hands off Kerry, now he lay beside her at night, feeling cut off from her body. Inside of him was a great void that no one could fill up. Not Kerry. Not Jenna. Not his father.

His father. In some ways, facing his father was the toughest of all. The man had buried a lifetime's worth of friends after nine-eleven. Neither of them imagined Doug would be the reason he'd have to relive the nightmares all over again. Captain Seamus Hanlon embodied everything Doug wanted to be: a highly decorated officer in the FDNY. A combat veteran with a purple heart and a silver star. His father's only weakness had been alcohol, and he had even managed to conquer that—he'd been clean and sober for sixteen years. Doug hadn't fallen too far down that hole yet, but he had a sense that he might. So did his dad, and that seemed to pain each of them more than anything.

He was like his father in one respect—he solved his own problems. And he did it with his own two hands. But here was an unsolvable problem. He couldn't bring those men back. And he couldn't live with the guilt.

He stopped running and bent over, hands on the thighs of his sweatpants to catch his breath. His side hurt. He knew he'd run a long way. Sweat poured off his body and the wind raced past his ears. He pulled his black wool knit cap down over them and looked out at the deserted beach. He had run a long way—past Rockaway, past Seaside. He was in no-man's-land now—the bleak, barren ocean front that formed the dividing line between the high-rise projects in Arverne and the modest one-family homes in Hanlon's neighborhood. Out here, homeless people wandered. And packs of stray dogs fed on piles of garbage dumped from passing cars. He could walk into the ocean out here and no one would find him. He could disappear. Save his family the heartache and shame of living with a coward. He was slowly dying anyway. Why not just speed things along?

Doug Hanlon wasn't sure how long he'd been standing on the boardwalk, under the halogen lights, staring out at the blackness of the sea. But the sweat had chilled on his skin, and he could hear a car slowly spinning its wheels over bits of gritty sand and gravel as it came to a stop on the road that paralleled the boardwalk. Hanlon turned to see that the car was his own—a Dodge Neon. He crossed the street and saw that Kerry was at the wheel, tears streaming down her face. She unlocked the door and he climbed inside.

"What are you doing out here?" he asked her. "What's wrong?"

She started to speak, but her words were unintelligible. She cut the engine. Hanlon pulled her close and tried to calm her down. "Are you hurt? Are you having contractions? We've got to get you home."

"No. I'm fine," she managed to choke out. She reached down to her handbag and pulled out a tape recorder with a tape inside. "It's this."

Kerry handed the recorder to Hanlon. He frowned. He'd seen the tape recorder before. It belonged to his father-in-law, Ray Connelly. Connelly used to tape confessions on it when he was a city detective. Hanlon pushed Play and heard a scratchy sound, followed by a gruff voice with a slight brogue.

. . . So a couple of firefighters died—so what? You think this is the first time an accusation like this has been leveled against me? This is Mike McLaughlin you're talking to. Not some street hoodlum. Trust me on this. In a week or two, no one will remember their fuckin' names. They're just a couple of nobodies, anyway. . . .

Hanlon rewound the tape. He pushed Play and listened again. There was no sound before it or after it. There was nothing else on the tape. *Mike*

McLaughlin. Mike McLaughlin. He would never forget that name as long as he lived. He pounded a fist on the dashboard. The glove compartment flew open. Maps and FDNY parking placards flew out across the floor. Hanlon spewed out a string of expletives. Normally, he tried to curtail his language around Kerry.

"Where did you get this?" he asked her.

"My father and your father were talking in the kitchen tonight. I knew they were upset about something, but they wouldn't discuss it with me. They kept talking about a tape. When my dad walked your dad out to his car, I found the tape recorder in the kitchen and listened to the tape. As soon as I heard it, I knew I had to find you."

"Who the hell is Mike McLaughlin?" asked Hanlon. "He killed my friends and I don't even know who this bastard is." Hanlon ran a hand down his face and tried to get his emotions under control. "I've got to find him, Kerry."

"No, Doug. No. I'm sure that's why our dads didn't share this with us. I'm sure it's because they thought you were better off not knowing."

"Who else knows about this McLaughlin guy, huh?"

"I don't think anyone knows, Doug. I don't even know whether my dad got ahold of this tape—or your dad did. Certainly the widows don't know about this. I just spoke to Tony's wife, Rosa, today."

"I'll tell you who must know," said Hanlon bitterly. "The marshals. That Georgia Skeehan. She knew who killed Tony and Captain Russo. She *knew* goddamn it—and she never told me. All that bullshit talk about doing justice to their memory and finding a way to honor them. It was nothing but talk."

"Maybe you should speak to her."

"Maybe I should do more than that," said Hanlon.

"Doug, please. I don't like it when you talk that way."

"I can't help it, Kerry. Everyone's treating me like a child. And I'm a man. Or at least I was. I handled things. I didn't just sit around letting everyone else solve my problems." Hanlon reached up a hand and brushed away his wife's tears. "Can you drive home?"

"Where are you going?"

"I just want to run some more. I need to think."

"Will you be all right?" asked Kerry. "I'm worried about you."

"I'm fine," said Hanlon. "I'll be home in a little while." He picked up the maps and stuffed them back into the glove compartment without meeting her gaze.

"We'll talk to my father and yours tomorrow," Kerry assured him. "I know they want to see justice done just as much as you do. I'm sure the marshals do, too."

"Uh-huh. Okay," said Hanlon. He kissed his wife on the cheek and stepped out of the car. His breath clouded in the salty air as he watched Kerry do a U-turn and drive away. He walked across to the boardwalk rail. His legs seemed to lose all feeling and he collapsed against it. *Justice, my ass,* thought Hanlon. *Chump justice—that's all that was.* He'd allowed everyone to lie to him and coddle him long enough. It was time, Hanlon decided, to do the one thing he could really do for Captain Russo and Tony Fuentes—to hell with the consequences.

35

GEORGIA AWOKE EARLY on Monday morning after a restless night. She couldn't get her father's fire out of her mind. Richie was still asleep and so was her mother. The house was dark. It would be another forty-five minutes before she'd have to get her son up and ready for school. She didn't have to be at Tony Fuentes' funeral until noon. She pulled on an old pair of jeans and sweatshirt and walked into the upstairs hallway.

The cape-style brick house Georgia's parents bought when she was seven had a pull-down stairs in the hallway ceiling. The stairs were almost like a ladder—made of plank wood with a damp, musty smell that reminded Georgia of the passage of years. The attic was full of the castoffs of a life that seemed like somebody else's now—her father's helmet and dress uniform, her brother Dennis's old skateboard, Richie's playpen, a box of Georgia's old maternity clothes. Dusty clumps of cotton-candy–pink insulation clung to the rafters. Georgia shivered in the unheated space, lit by a single bare bulb. She didn't like being up here, surrounded by memories.

She had told herself she was up here to bring down the Christmas decorations. But instead, she brought down only one box about the size of a microwave, its corners dog-eared and dusty. It was the one marked *George Skeehan—newspaper articles.* The words, written in black Magic Marker, had begun to fade. It weighed very little and that saddened her right away. The only time her father had made the paper was when he died—the biggest loss in her life was a sound bite of news for little more than a day.

She had never been able to look at those clippings. A part of her wanted to, to make him come alive again. But another part felt that those brittle, yellowing sheets would only serve as a reminder of how much time had passed without him. If there was one trait Georgia had inherited from her mother, it was a discomfort at looking at the past. And yet, those files Marenko had brought her had called into question the most basic assumption of her childhood. Her father's death had been viewed by family and friends as an act of God—horrible, perhaps, but something natural and unalterable. Like a freak storm or a terrible illness. She had learned to accept her father's loss in those terms. George Skeehan had chosen the life of a firefighter. He had chosen to go into buildings to rescue people, knowing that some of the men who do that don't come out. It was the essence of the job—what separated the doers from the dreamers. She could accept that her father had gotten unlucky.

She could not accept that he'd been murdered. She could never accept that his murderer had gone free.

Georgia carted the box into the living room. The tape that secured it had yellowed from nineteen years of neglect. When Georgia cut through it, it crinkled like the wrapper on a hard candy. This box of newspapers wasn't her mother's doing. Margaret had been too distraught when Georgia's father died to think about newspaper clippings. This was the work of Aunt Dotty, her mother's older sister.

Aunt Dotty was very meticulous. She'd not only saved the clips. She'd saved entire newspapers. Seeing her father's death relegated to a couple of columns of type in the city section of the newspapers made Georgia realize how very little note anyone seemed to take of the death of a thirty-nine-year-old firefighter in an Astoria, Queens, convenience store. The papers instead were filled with headlines about President Reagan's summit with Russian leader Yuri Andropov and announcements that Democratic senator Walter Mondale had chosen Geraldine Ferraro as his running mate in the upcoming presidential election. Ads played on the popularity of the Rubik's cube.

Everything seemed hopelessly dated. There were no ads for cell phones or Palm Pilots or personal computers. Crime had a quaint, local quality to it. Bad guys were people in one's own backyard—not terrorists from halfway around the world. And the worst New Yorkers had to fear was getting mugged on a graffiti-choked subway.

Her father's death got different coverage in all the local papers. In *The Daily News* and *The New York Post*, it was front-page news, though the text was buried inside. In *The New York Times*, it was a metro story. In *Newsday*, it was referenced on the front page, but covered deep inside the paper. Georgia read every clipping her Aunt Dotty had assembled—from the day of the fire through the two months until the investigation was complete.

When she tried to think back to that time, it was like being a child in the backseat of her parents' old Pontiac, cruising the Long Island Expressway. Some things were too far away to see clearly or passed by too quickly to take note of—the details of her father's death, the funeral, the myriad of paperwork and insurance forms that her mother had to grapple with. And yet she herself was standing still, acutely aware of the small cocoon encasing her. Those images were still sharp in her mind: the downpour on the day they buried her father, the key chain he'd given her that she'd temporarily lost down a storm drain, his deathly white skin at the wake—and most of all, the darkness of her bedroom at night without him there to tuck her in. A part of her never recovered. She grew up, but deep inside she was still that little girl waiting for her daddy to tuck her in.

She stared at the black-and-white photographs of the fire-damaged convenience store in Astoria. It was an aluminum-sided corner building on a street of two- and three-story brick-front stores. Georgia could see an elevated subway line in the background. Although the fire had started in the basement, it had quickly taken the entire wood-frame structure. The windows—even on the second floor—were knocked out and the roof had partially collapsed. A sign above the front door still hung on its hinges, though it was charred on one corner. *Rysovsky's Deli*, it read. The newspapers said little about the family. They were Russian immigrants. That much Georgia knew. The father's name was given as Max; the mother's as Lara. There was a line about "fire department officials" still trying to determine the cause of the eight a.m. blaze, but nothing more. About the only mention she could find regarding the cause of the fire was a one-column piece two months after the fire in the *Daily News*. It said what she already knew: that the fire was attributed to the couple's six-year-old son playing with matches. The child wasn't charged, and because of his age, his name wasn't given.

If I can track down the Rysovskys, maybe I can find out what really happened, thought Georgia. The *Post* and *News* articles gave an exact address of the store, though Georgia was sure the family no longer owned it. She opened up a phone book, but found no listing in Queens for Rysovsky. There were three in Brooklyn, but none of them was for a Max or M. Rysovsky.

Richie found her in the living room, poring over the articles.

"What are you doing, Mom?"

Georgia shuffled the clippings and began to put them back in the box. She didn't want her mother to see them. Even after all this time, Georgia knew it would upset her. "Oh, just getting stuff down to decorate the tree."

Richie yawned. "That doesn't look like the tree."

"I've just started. You want to help me this afternoon?"

"I'm going to Jimmy's house after school." Jimmy DeLuca was Richie's best friend.

"Well, tomorrow then, after school."

The boy shrugged. "If it takes more than an hour to put up, I'm not helping." Richie loved to pretend the process bored him, but Georgia knew he would have been crushed if she didn't make the effort.

"Fair enough. Now, get dressed. I'll make breakfast."

36

GEORGIA HID THE BOX of her father's newspaper clippings until after Richie left for school and her mother for work. Then she went back to the attic, returned the box and fetched the artificial tree and Christmas decorations. Most of the decorations were her mother's. There were lots of kitschy-looking angels and bears in turnout coats and dalmatians beside fire hydrants. Georgia supposed the dalmatians and hydrants were supposed to be shorthand for firefighters, but all they made her think of was a dog with a bladder problem. Ironically, Georgia had never seen a firehouse tree yet with a firefighter ornament on it. Not unless you counted the time that Eddie Suarez and Sal Giordano decorated the squad tree in air filter masks and garlands of bright yellow *Fire Line: Do Not Cross* tape.

Tony Fuentes' funeral was at noon in the Bronx, but Georgia left much earlier than she needed to. She had another destination in mind first.

She drove west along Broadway, then north along Thirty-first Street, under the wide, dark trestles of the elevated N subway track. Even on this bright winter morning, the street beneath was shadowy and the wind blew fast-food wrappers and old newspapers across her path. To the north, Georgia could see the brick storefronts and hooded awnings of restaurants and stores with Greek names. In the summer, Astoria bustled with Manhattanites in search of good, cheap restaurants that served up Middle Eastern and Spanish food. But this time of year, the four- and five-story brick apartment buildings that shadowed the boulevards had a ghostly feel that was broken only by the occasional rumble of a train overhead. Georgia stared up at their fake peaked rooflines, small windows and heavy lintels. The buildings had that frumpy, sedate look of pre-World War II housing. She imagined the neighborhood looking pretty much the same when her father arrived here on that autumn morning nineteen years ago.

Georgia stared at the address she had scribbled off the newspapers. Rysovsky's Deli once stood at the corner of Thirty-second Street and Newtown Avenue, a block from the elevated tracks. The aluminum-sided frame house was gone. In fact, the entire row of stores looked as if they'd been replaced by one continuous two-story commercial building—a taxpayer, firefighters call them, because of their cheap construction. From the signs above the stores, Georgia noted a dry cleaner, a pharmacy, a Greek pastry shop and a Spanish grocery. The pastry shop now stood on the corner where Rysovsky's had been, its plate-glass windows filled with cakes and pans of flaky baklava.

Georgia looked in the window. People were lined up by the counter, placing orders. But even with his back turned to her, it was impossible not to recognize the tall, lean black man jotting some notes as he spoke to a plump Greek woman on the other side of the counter. Georgia waited for Carter as he exited the store, a small white box of bakery goods in one hand, a notepad in the other.

"Skeehan," he said stiffly, then froze. He seemed unable to say more.

Georgia eyed his clothes. He was wearing a black wool coat over a black suit, a white shirt and a black and burgundy silk tie. His shoes were polished to a military shine. She was sure he was decked out for Fuentes' funeral. But

Astoria, Queens, was not exactly on his way from his home in Brooklyn to the funeral in the Bronx.

"What are you doing here?" she demanded. "You suddenly get a jones for some phyllo dough and chopped walnuts?"

He sighed. "You know what I'm doing, 'cause you were just about to do it, too. I'm checking out where the Rysovskys have gone."

"And?"

"I've asked everyone on this block. All anyone knows is that they sold out and moved west after the fire. Nobody's even sure where they settled."

Georgia regarded him coldly. "You knew McLaughlin might have murdered my father. And you didn't tell me. Even now, you're carrying on your own little investigation behind my back." She began to walk to her car. Carter followed, the little white box in his big hand looking as ridiculous as a woman's handbag.

"I *didn't* know, girl. I *don't* know now."

She turned to face him. "This is my father you're talking about, Randy. I have a right to know what happened to him. If you still have Brophy and Sullivan's incident report on that fire, then you should let me see it. I'm your partner. Your equal. And you owe it to me to treat me like one."

Carter shook his head. "You're not my partner on this one, Skeehan. You're the daughter of a dead firefighter. You want me to pretend you can look at this stuff with a clinical eye? You can't. Heck, I didn't even know your dad and *I* can't."

"Shouldn't I be the one to make that choice?"

"You want to see that report? You want to look at the radio transmissions? Is that going to bring him back? Is that going to bring you peace?"

"I don't know what it will bring me."

"I'll tell you what it'll bring you: pain. You remember seeing Fuentes and Russo in that basement? I told you they took off their masks and inhaled the fire 'cause they figured they'd die quicker."

"I remember," said Georgia.

"Your father was one tough sonofagun, Georgia. He didn't make that choice. He hung on, gasping for air, trying to dig his way out of that cellar until the bitter end. Twenty minutes, girl. Twenty agonizing, horrible, choking minutes. Broph and Sully didn't pull any punches in their report. George Skeehan fought for his life. And he died anyway. And nothing in their report or my interviews gets me one bit closer to figuring out whether Freezer set that fire. I wanted to come to you when I had something definite I could offer you. Something that would put Freezer away. I don't have that. To tell you all this and not give you satisfaction—that seemed cruel."

Georgia felt rooted to the pavement, her arms leaden at her side.

"I know you're angry with me for keeping this stuff from you, girl. But I did it to spare you, not because I don't respect you."

"You think he did it, don't you?" she asked him softly.

"I'll tell you what I know. And I'll tell you what I think," said Carter. "Then you tell me what you want me to do."

They sat in Randy's immaculately clean, blue two-tone Cadillac Seville, parked around the corner from the Greek pastry shop. Georgia spied the incident report on her father's fire on Carter's backseat. He didn't protest when she asked to read it. He had warned her that the report would not be easy to stomach. She tried to remain detached and professional as she read the yellowed typewritten pages, splotched with Wite-Out. She tried to pretend that the dead firefighter wasn't her father. Because he was just a firefighter, he carried only a handy talkie—so none of his words were recorded. But the chief's words, bloodless and calm as they were, were on record with dispatch, and they were duly transcribed. Georgia looked at the interval and saw instantly that Carter was right. For at least twenty minutes, George Skeehan struggled to free himself from a fire-choked cellar that had become blocked with debris. He hadn't given up easily. And he died slowly while firefighters frantically tried to dig their way in.

Georgia had always assumed the end had been fast—that a chunk of ceiling had fallen on her dad and killed him. That's what she'd always been told. And maybe the ceiling did fall on him. But clearly, there had been a long and frightening interval before that. He had fought bravely, but it pained her to think of the man she loved in such a hopeless situation. Georgia blinked back tears and focused on the visor above the passenger seat to keep them from falling down her face.

"It's okay," said Carter softly. "No shame in crying, girl. Lord knows, you've seen me cry."

Georgia wiped her eyes and shook her head. "I'm okay," she said hoarsely.

Carter waited until she'd finished the report before he spoke again. "I didn't know any of this until Roberta Kelly called me Thursday afternoon—after we went over there—and told me about an argument her brother Cullen had once had with Jamie Sullivan at the bar. Sully started getting all melancholy one night about the fires that made him the saddest. Bobby said he mentioned your dad's fire. I think it was one of the reasons he went back to firefighting. He didn't feel like he was experienced enough to have been the lead investigator in such an important case. Anyway, Cullen was there—very drunk, according to Bobby—and he started telling Sully that maybe if he'd done his job better, he could've caught the guy responsible for that fire. Bobby said that was all she knew about the argument."

"Did they get in a fistfight?" asked Georgia.

"Sully supposedly took Cullen outside and sort of threw him to the sidewalk. Cullen was a little weasel—that probably would've been enough to get him to go home and sleep things off. Bobby said Cullen never mentioned it again. Then, two years ago, when Cullen got into trouble, he said he had information about a fire that Freezer set and never got caught on. It occurred to Bobby that maybe it was the same one, but Cullen never said, so she didn't either. And then you came in, and she figured, since you're my partner, she should tell me."

"Then you don't know for sure if McLaughlin set my father's fire."

"No. I don't think anybody even suspected it wasn't an accident until two years ago, when Cullen talked to the D.A. to cut a deal. Mac tried to get the transcripts of those meetings, but no one can find them. They found all that stuff on Broph and nothing on Cullen Thomas."

"Any word on Broph?"

"Nothing, but I'm still looking." Carter let out a long, defeated sigh. "My gut tells me that Freezer killed your father, girl. The Westies worked all over the white neighborhoods of the city in the collection rackets. I think he was trying to scare the Rysovskys into paying him protection money and things went bad—same as they did at Café Treize. But just like there, I think he might get off the hook."

"I want to kill him," said Georgia.

"So do I."

"No, I mean really," said Georgia. "Somebody's got to stop him."

Carter leaned closer to her and wrapped his big hands around hers. Her fingers were cold. His were warm. "Listen to me, girl. Freezer wins 'cause he's patient. Now you've got to be patient, too. Something's going to turn up eventually. You'll see."

Georgia bit her lip. "What do I do in the meantime? Just live with this?"

"I guess you're gonna have to." Carter looked at the clock on his dashboard. "You headed to Fuentes' funeral? I can give you a ride."

"I can't. I'm double-parked," Georgia lied. She didn't feel like company right now. "I'll meet you there."

37

GEORGIA NEVER KNEW Tony Fuentes, but walking through the crowds gathered at the steps of the huge granite Roman Catholic church, she caught snatches of conversations from men who did. Tony was a city kid, born and raised in the Castle Hill section of the Bronx, the child of Puerto Rican parents. He learned stickball as soon as he could walk, cooked a mean roast pork with *tostones*—fried green banana chips—and considered a day in the country to be a trip to the Bronx Zoo. Georgia thought about Doug Hanlon's stories of Tony bestowing a toilet plunger on a braggart. He had a firefighter's sensibilities. He would've probably been embarrassed by the outpouring of affection from all these "rednecks who can't parallel park," as Doug said he called them. And yet they were all here for him—so many, in fact, that the Latino neighborhood looked decidedly Anglo today. A sea of dark blue stretched out in every direction from beneath the pale, oatmeal-colored stone statue of Saint Cecilia. Each man looked as stony-faced as the saint. Each man looked worn out.

Georgia squinted into the wind to see if she could locate Carter, but she couldn't. He had somehow managed to disappear into this crowd of mostly white faces. Inside the packed church, family and close friends assembled, along with the Bronx Borough president, the mayor and a string of ever-revolving fire department brass. Beyond the profusion of blue, Georgia noted a smattering of reporters and satellite dishes. The press was here, though not in the numbers she would have expected. A firefighter's funeral was no longer the rare tragedy it had once been.

Then her eyes caught a familiar face across a crowd of men a head taller than Georgia. She recognized the walrus jowls and droopy, ash-colored mustache immediately: Captain Seamus Hanlon. He was in his dark blue dress uniform with a white cap on his head and white gloves on his hands. Across his left breast, a row of fire department medals gleamed. Georgia made eye contact with him and inched through the crowd. She was surprised he hadn't walked over and surprised still more when she hugged him and he stiffened under her touch. Maybe he was embarrassed.

"Is Doug here?"

"He's in the church, with the rest of the fellows from Ladder Seventeen," said Seamus. Georgia expected him to offer more, but he didn't.

"How's he doing?"

"How do you think he's doing?" Seamus snapped back.

"Seamus . . . Captain," Georgia stumbled. Maybe today wasn't the day to be informal. "Did I say something wrong to Doug the other night?"

Seamus stuffed his hands in his pockets and stared at the long, straight rows of sand-colored steps leading up to the huge double-paneled doors of the church. "It's what you didn't say, lass." His pale blue eyes fixed on hers. "You *know*," he whispered. "You know who set the fire. And you're not doing anything about it."

Georgia felt her breath stall in her lungs. She held Seamus's gaze, but could find no words to say. Inside the church, she could hear the sound of an organ, punctuated by the wail of bagpipes. In life, Fuentes probably never got within fifty feet of a bagpipe. But in death, even the non-Irish families tended to find comfort in the traditions. The sound cut right through her heart.

"Who told you this?" she asked finally.

"Is it true?"

"Seamus—Captain—please don't put me in this position. You don't even know if the information you have is correct."

"All right," he hissed. "*You* tell me if it's correct. Yesterday, Ray Connelly, Kerry's father, gets a tape in the mail. Some bastard named Michael McLaughlin is boasting about killing firefighters."

Georgia tried not to betray her shock. "Who sent it?"

"We don't know. There was a typed note inside, telling Ray that he and his buddies in the NYPD should know about this tape, but that he shouldn't share it with Doug. Whoever sent it seemed to know that Ray was a retired police detective and Doug's father-in-law."

"You didn't tell Doug about the tape, did you?"

"I went over to the Connellys' house last night and spoke to Ray. We agreed not to tell Doug. But when Ray walked me to my car, Kerry listened to the tape and showed it to him."

"Oh, Jesus." Georgia felt weak. She could hear the shuffling of bodies around her and the priest's delivery of the Twenty-third Psalm floating in the bitter December air. A few blocks over, traffic on the Bruckner Expressway had the steady whoosh of ocean waves, and a far-off siren cried out, as if on cue. Hanlon straightened. He was breathing hard, as if he'd just run from someplace. Yet he was standing absolutely still. He looked at Georgia. He could read it all over her face. She'd never been good at lying.

"It's all true, isn't it?" asked Hanlon.

"Is Doug . . . is he okay?"

"Where's Michael McLaughlin?"

"I can't talk to you about this."

"You can't *talk* to me about this?" Hanlon's voice rose above the murmuring inside and outside of the packed church. Firefighters craned their necks to see what the commotion was about. Hanlon, embarrassed, immediately lowered his voice. "For godsakes, lass," he muttered. "This isn't some staff chief or politician in pleats you're talking to here. This is me—Seamus Hanlon. I'm the captain of the engine company your father worked in, God rest his soul. I see his bronze plaque in my firehouse every day. And Dougie's my son. He's hurting, Georgia. They're all hurting. They deserve the truth."

"Don't you think I'd tell you if I could? I can't, Seamus. Don't put me in this position." Georgia tried to retreat through the mass of bodies. She needed air. Space. A chance to control the trembling in her limbs. *You are a police officer. You must uphold the law,* she told herself. And then she thought of Doug Hanlon. And Joe Russo and Tony Fuentes. And most of all, her father. She understood how Paul Brophy felt when he swung that baseball bat at McLaughlin, how Randy felt when he looked at those pictures of Rachel Cross. She wanted to pull the trigger on McLaughlin herself.

The men were ten deep by the church and they fanned out across the closed boulevard of stores and small shopping arcades. She felt the claustrophobia of this sweep of blue. She saw the men look at her as she walked past. Every one of them seemed to stare in judgment, as if they all knew the terrible secret she was keeping. She wondered, if her father were here now, would he have kept such a secret? Would he have wanted her to?

She crossed the street. Awnings creaked above a Laundromat. On the second floor, a law firm advertised injury claims in English and Spanish. She had lost her bearings. She couldn't even remember which direction her car was in. Hanlon caught up to her. For a heavy man, he was fast on his feet. Like most veteran firefighters, his survival had often depended on it.

"Don't run away from me, Georgia—please," he begged her. "I'm not trying to get you in trouble. I'm just trying to understand. Two firefighters are dead, love. Tony Fuentes' wife is expecting their fourth child. Joe Russo's wife is on three kinds of tranquilizers. Dougie's started drinking heavily. Everybody's a mess. What could be more important than giving these families a sense of closure? Of justice?"

"I could tell you everything about Michael McLaughlin and you still wouldn't have a sense of closure or justice. Do you understand what I'm saying?" asked Georgia. "*I* want to kill him. *Me.* Right now with my bare hands. I want to blow that motherfucker away. But I can't. And *you* can't. And I can't tell you why."

Hanlon looked shocked. Georgia wasn't sure if it was because she'd put things so bluntly or because she'd confirmed McLaughlin's name or simply because she expressed her own desire to kill him. Whatever the reason, he suddenly became very pale.

"Dougie wants to kill him, too," said Seamus softly. "I caught him this morning calling his brother Brendan's precinct trying to track down where this McLaughlin might live."

"Does he understand—do *you* understand—the implications of what he's doing?" asked Georgia. "If Doug takes the law into his own hands, everything this department stands for will be ground into dust. We're about saving lives—not taking them. You've got to make him understand that."

Seamus Hanlon slumped against the graffiti-covered roll-down gate of a shoe repair store. "I'm trying, Georgia. But it's like he can't hear me anymore. You should see him. He was so calm this morning. Almost dreamy. I thought his anger was bad, but this is worse. Before Doug went inside to Mass, he asked me to tell Brendan that he can have Doug's old baseball mitt signed by the Yankees. That's Doug's most prized possession."

"I'm no shrink, Seamus, but when a person gives away their most cherished belongings, it sounds like they're fixing to die."

"He wouldn't—"

"Yes, he would. I know the feeling, only I just wanted to die. Doug wants to take Michael McLaughlin with him. You have to get him help. Right away."

Across the street, the doors of the church opened and mourners began pouring out. Georgia could hear the wail of the bagpipes playing "Amazing Grace." She saw six strapping men in firefighters' uniforms bearing the flag-draped casket of Tony Fuentes. Behind, a small, caramel-colored woman in a black dress and veil with a swollen belly was helped down the steps, along with three dark-haired little girls. Georgia's throat began to close up and tears came to her eyes. She thought she couldn't cry for the dead in this job anymore. And maybe she couldn't. But she could cry for the living. She was crying for them now.

"Don't let Doug out of your sight today, Seamus—whatever you do. I will try to work out something. But please, please, get him some professional help. Make him see that he can't take the law into his own hands. Nothing good can come of that."

Hanlon turned and saluted as the casket was carried down the steps and into the hearse. Georgia did the same.

"What good can ever come of this?" he asked her hoarsely.

She pretended not to hear. She couldn't bear to tell him what she felt in her heart—that nothing good could ever come of this.

38

GEORGIA WATCHED the funeral procession until the bagpipes mingled with the fierce breeze and the Fuentes family had piled into dark cars, their doors thudding with the finality of a casket. Firefighters were standing about in tight-knit clusters. Many of them were smoking. The veterans had vacant stares. They had started out seeing men bury fathers on this job, and now they'd seen too many of them burying their sons.

She trudged down side streets of shadowy apartment buildings with ornate façades caked with years of grime. Here and there, in apartment windows, families had taped up signs: *God Bless the FDNY.* Georgia felt cheered by the words. A firefighter lives his life knowing that he may be called upon to lay it down for strangers. And when he dies, it seemed only fitting that strangers honor him.

Cars were double-parked for blocks in every direction. No one ticketed them. Every last one of them had either an FDNY sticker on the back window or one from another department. Georgia found her red Ford Escort and fished her keys from her purse. She stepped closer, then did a double take. The front passenger seat was tilted all the way back and a figure with a baseball cap over his face lay sprawled out, sleeping. At least she thought he was sleeping. She wanted to believe it wasn't her car. She wanted to believe it wasn't him. But as she checked the wheel base and saw the rust marks, and as she checked his unshaven chin and saw the dimple, she silently cursed under her breath and unlocked her door.

"What the hell are you doing in my car? You want me to arrest you? Is that it?"

Rick DeAngelo jumped up from what had obviously been a sound sleep. He blinked at her and fumbled in the front pocket of his jeans to produce a key. He was wearing the same clothes he'd worn last night. He obviously hadn't gone home. If he had, he would have been arrested. Georgia was sure the Feds were looking for him.

Rick tossed her the car key. "I helped you tie this spare behind the bumper when you bought the car, remember?"

"How could I forget?" said Georgia. "You borrowed my brand-new car and locked the keys inside—*remember?*"

"I knew you'd still have the key behind the bumper," he said, yawning and ignoring her dig. "If it was me, I'd have moved it by now."

"If it was you," said Georgia, "the car would've been *repossessed* by now."

He allowed a grin and tipped his baseball cap down low again as firefighters and cops passed by to their own cars.

"What are you doing here?" Georgia demanded. "And how did you even know I'd be here?"

" 'Cause I know *you.* Even before you were a firefighter, you were always very passionate about firefighters' funerals. I knew you'd never skip it. I can't go near your house. The cops are watching it. But I figured they wouldn't tail you to this. You always go for your dad, don't you?"

Georgia let the question brush past her. "You're a wanted man. Everyone thinks you tried to kill me."

"Tried to kill you? Gee Gee, my truck got blown up. If the windshield hadn't iced up, we'd probably both be dead."

"I got thrown off the FBI case because you ran last night. My boss is probably going to give me charges."

"I'm sorry. I didn't mean to get you in trouble."

"Your *being* here is getting me in trouble."

He depressed the lever on the side of his seat and it became upright again. "Do you want to arrest me?" he asked.

"Don't tempt me."

"No sweat." He held his wrists out. "Slap on the cuffs. Maybe you'll get a medal."

Georgia closed her eyes. She didn't want that. And he knew it. "Why are you here?" she asked sharply.

"I got ahold of Louie Buscanti, Gee Gee. He agreed to see me tonight."

"You mean kill you tonight."

He picked at a hangnail without answering right away. He seemed to be debating that himself. "Maybe. I don't know. Either way, I don't have a choice. I can't run from Buscanti."

"You can't run from the Feds, either."

"I'm not planning to," said Rick. "If I can straighten everything out with Buscanti—make him see I'm not fixing to go against him, I'll turn myself into the Feds willingly. There's nothing I can give 'em. I don't *know* anything and I didn't *do* anything. That'll come out in time."

He seemed pretty confident. Then again, Rick was never one to worry—even about things he should worry about.

"I can't approve something like this," said Georgia.

"I'm not asking for your permission."

"I can arrest you," Georgia said, not as forcefully as she would've liked.

"If you were going to, you already would've," said Rick. "And I would've run. So unless you're planning to shoot me, I suggest you drop the idea."

"In other words then, you just dropped by to get me into more trouble, is that it? Or am I supposed to feel guilty when they dredge your body from the Hudson River?"

Rick reached over to a key chain attached to Georgia's car keys. On the end of the chain was a brass cast of her father's old badge number—her badge number now. It was attached to a plastic photo insert of Richie. It was a candid shot of him, taken last summer at their above-ground swimming pool in the backyard. His dark hair was plastered around his face, his hazel eyes were bright. He had a band of freckles across his nose—just like Georgia. And a dimple in his chin—just like Rick. Rick fingered the photograph now.

"Does he know I've seen you?"

"No."

"I, uh . . . I wish I could see him."

"You think that's fair?" asked Georgia. "Walk out of your son's life for eight years and then waltz back in right before you're facing a truckload of legal trouble and a mobster's bullet?"

"No." He sighed. "You're right." He reached into the back pocket of his jeans and pulled out a crumpled napkin. "I didn't have any paper, but I, uh . . . I wrote him a note. You can read it, Gee Gee, if you like. Maybe you . . . can give it to him." He handed the crumpled napkin to Georgia. She read it.

Dear Richie,

I've kept the letter you wrote me last spring in a drawer by my bed. I know you think I've forgotten you, but I always look at the school picture you sent me and think about you. You are my only son. I don't deserve to call you that. If you hated me, I wouldn't blame you. I was young and stupid once, and I ran away when I shouldn't have. Now, I am a lot older and a little wiser. But it isn't so easy to come back. I am in some trouble now and I don't want you involved. But I swear to you, if I get out of this mess and your mother agrees, I will try to be a friend to you, even if I haven't earned the right to be your father.

Yours,

xxx

"I didn't sign it," said Rick. "I didn't know what to call myself." When Georgia didn't respond, he added with a grin, "I'm sure you've got a few suggestions."

Georgia swallowed. She didn't know what to say.

"That bad, huh?" he muttered. "It ain't Shakespeare, I know."

"It's fine."

"Hey, no sweat." He looked at her. "Will you give it to him?"

Georgia nodded. Rick leaned over and kissed her on the cheek.

"You know, Gee Gee, you're still a hell of a woman."

" 'Hell' was a word you used to use a lot to describe me."

He laughed. "Funny, too. You're still the only woman who could ever go head-to-head with me."

"I aim low."

He put his hand on the door and went to step out of the car.

"Will you at least call me?" asked Georgia. "Let me know how your meeting went?"

He smiled ruefully. "Let me put it this way, if I *don't* call, I think you'll know how it went." He looked back at her and mimed holding up a glass of champagne. "Here's looking at you, kid." Then he closed the door and began to walk up the street, hands in his pockets, a little bounce in his step. At this distance, it was as if no time had gone by between them. He still looked like the boy in his early twenties she had known in that lifetime before she became a firefighter. She had been softer and more trusting then—weaker, some might say. More dependent. But there was also something about the girl she had once been that she wanted to be again.

He wants to see his son. And I said no? a voice inside her asked. But of course she said no. Any mother would. It was basic common sense—something Rick sorely lacked. Could she really introduce Richie to a man who might get killed?

But what if he is killed? What if I stopped my boy from his only chance to ever meet his dad? She had never yet made the right decision when it came to Rick. She had no idea if she was making the right one now. She turned on her car's ignition and eased out of the tight parallel parking space. Rick had just turned the corner when she caught up with him and rolled down her window.

"Get in."

"Huh?" He tilted his Yankees cap back on his head.

"You heard me. Get in."

He walked over to the passenger side and slid into the seat.

"Ground rules," said Georgia as she pulled out into traffic. "No telling him about your legal problems or your meetings with wiseguys. No making promises you can't keep—"

"You're taking me to see Richie?" he asked in amazement.

"I *should* be taking you to see my boss at the FBI," snapped Georgia. "I *should* have my head examined. Richie's at his best friend's house. I'm supposed to pick him up. I don't want you in the car when I do. And I don't want you in our house. That's too much for him. It's got to be someplace neutral."

"How 'bout the playground on Woodside Avenue, near the Amtrak rail yard?" asked Rick. "You and me, we used to—"

"Never mind what we used to do there," said Georgia. "Yeah. That's a good place. It's only a couple of blocks from the house. I'll drop you there, then pick Richie up, give him your note and ask him what he wants to do. If he says no, Rick . . ."

He put a hand on her arm. "You don't have to explain it to me, Gee Gee. I'll do whatever you and he want."

39

JIMMY DELUCA HAD BEEN Richie's best friend since the boys were six. Georgia liked Jimmy and his family, but the comparisons were hard sometimes. Jimmy lived in a house not unlike Richie's. Both boys went to Saint Aloysius Catholic school. But there the similarities ended. Jimmy lived with a mom and dad, a sister and brother and a big golden retriever named Butch. Jimmy's mother hadn't worked since his older brother, Joey, was born. His father held some kind of office job with the Port Authority. Jimmy often told Richie he was lucky to be an only child and to have all his mother's attention and a grandmother to fuss over him all the time. But Georgia knew that Richie never felt like the lucky boy Jimmy DeLuca made him out to be.

Georgia picked Richie up just before 4:00 p.m., as promised. In the car, Richie extolled the virtues of Jimmy's new PlayStation—not something that was possible in the Skeehan family budget.

"There's this game, Mom. It's really cool," said the ten-year-old. "It's just like skateboarding. Only there are these dudes with guns, chasing you. And you have to skate over the canyon to beat them.

There are at least a hundred horrible things that can happen to you in the game."

"And this is good?"

"It's awesome. You can fall down the canyon. Or get attacked by animals. Or get shot at, of course."

Sounds like a description of my job, thought Georgia. She let Richie finish telling her about the game. She was relieved to hear him chatter away. She didn't know where to begin to tell him about Rick. Finally, while the car was idling at a light in heavy traffic, she took a deep breath and spoke.

"Richie, I have something to tell you."

"You're breaking up with Mac."

She gave him an astonished look. "No. Of course not. Who told you that?"

"Nobody," said Richie. "You've just got that tone."

"This isn't about Mac." She saw him beginning to form another statement and cut him off. "No one's sick, either. God, you're just like Grandma. You've got that good Irish sense of tragedy to you." She tried again. "Something very unexpected happened a few days ago, honey. I ran into your father."

"With a car?"

Georgia laughed, then realized he was serious. "No, of course not. I mean, I happened to meet him. By chance."

"Where?"

"On an assignment I've been doing. For the FBI—"

"My father's an FBI agent?"

"No," said Georgia. "He's an electrician, Richie. I can't tell you every-thing right now except to say he's got some problems that he's trying to work out. But he wrote this. He wanted me to give it to you." She handed him the napkin. He read it. Georgia tried to sneak a look at his face. She couldn't gauge his reaction.

"This is really him?" the boy asked.

"Yep. Rick DeAngelo. Your father."

"Where is he?"

"Do you want to see him?"

He took longer to answer than Georgia would have expected. He was growing up, she realized. He knew something about being let down. He was weighing that in his mind against the curiosity of seeing his father.

"What's he like?"

"I didn't spend that much time with him," she admitted. "But from what I can see, he's pretty much the same person he always was. He's . . . well, he's sort of a scatterbrain. Sort of immature. But he's not an evil man."

"I thought you were really angry with him, Mom."

"I am. But I'm trying very hard not to let that spill over to you. I don't want you to turn around when you're grown and say that I didn't let you see your father."

Richie was quiet for a moment. He reread the note. "He wrote this on a napkin?"

"Well, the circumstances weren't ideal." Georgia thought about it some more, then shook her head. "I guess, even if they were, he'd probably do something like that. He's not exactly the prepared type."

"Where is he?" Richie asked again.

"At the playground on Woodside Avenue," said Georgia. "Look, he and I discussed this, and you don't have to see him. You've got no obligation. We could postpone this meeting. Maybe try a few phone calls first. It's absolutely up to you."

"I'm a little nervous," said the child.

"I'm sure he is too. And he'd totally understand if you didn't feel ready."

Richie looked at her. Georgia kept her eyes on the road, afraid that he might be able to read the what-ifs in her eyes. *What if Rick doesn't show? What if Richie sees him this once and never again? What if Richie has built him up so much in his head that he's let down by the reality? Is it worse to be disappointed by what is? Or by what isn't?* It was the very question she sensed Randy Carter had been struggling with ever since he suspected Michael McLaughlin of setting the fire that killed her father. The truth, Georgia was beginning to understand, wasn't always better.

"I think I want to see him," said Richie.

"You're sure?"

The boy shrugged. Georgia sensed he was trying to invest himself as little as possible in the encounter so he'd have the least to lose.

"Okay. I'll take you to him."

THE PARK ON Woodside Avenue was about half an acre of asphalt paths and bare patches of dirt surrounded by a chain-link fence and some stubby gray leafless trees. On the other side of the park was the Amtrak rail yard, which ran like a wide-open scar from behind the old concrete recreation hut all the way down to the southwestern tip of Queens, across from Manhattan. By the time Georgia and Richie arrived, the bright sun had disappeared from the sky, leaving it the color of faded blue jeans. In an hour, it would be dark. At the far end of the park, a group of young men were playing a pickup game of basketball on a court with two backboards and no nets on the hoops. On the playground, the empty swings swayed and creaked in the breeze, the toddlers long gone at this hour. The evening chill had already begun to settle over the scenery.

Georgia parked the car. She and Richie walked the cracked sidewalk without saying a word. Just north of them, silver Amtrak trains rumbled through the rail yards, with commuters bound for Long Island. Richie's steps slowed instinctively as they neared the playground. Georgia thought it was because he'd caught sight of Rick, but when she looked around, she didn't see him. She wondered if he'd chickened out. Then she noticed him by the basketball court, fingers dug into the chain link, watching the game. He turned casually, then froze. Richie stood next to a park bench and followed his mother's gaze.

"Is that him?"

"Uh-huh."

Richie had a thick down jacket zipped around him, but he shivered just the same. Georgia instinctively wrapped her arms around him. Rick sauntered toward them, though Georgia sensed it was taking all his effort to maintain his relaxed stride. He took off his Yankees baseball cap. Two feet from the boy, he stopped and shoved his hands and his cap in the pockets of his own down jacket. It was black and made by North Face—just like Richie's. Father and son were wearing identical jackets.

"Hi, Richie," Rick said hoarsely. He ran a hand along the stubble on his cheek. Rick being Rick, it had obviously just occurred to him that he hadn't shaved, showered or changed his clothes since yesterday.

"Hi."

"Did you, um . . . get my note?"

"Yeah."

"I got yours, too. Thank you." Rick shot a quick, pleading look at Georgia. *I don't know what to say* was written all over his face. Georgia shrugged. She didn't know how to help him. What's more, she wasn't sure she wanted to. It had been crazy to undertake such a risky encounter—risky careerwise for her; risky emotionally for the child. And who knew whether anyone had tailed them? Georgia had a sudden, overwhelming urge to flee. But it was too late.

Rick caught the boy glancing over at the teenagers playing basketball. "You like basketball?" he asked. "I think you told me you did in your letter."

"Uh-huh," said the child. "But I'm not very good at it."

"Me neither," said Rick. "Only way I could make a three-pointer would be standing on Michael Jordan's shoulders. And he'd have to hold my hairy legs, and I don't think he'd like that."

The boy laughed and Rick looked pleased. "Mind you, when I played, they didn't wear all these shorts that come down to your knees. They look like you borrowed your grandmother's underwear." Richie grinned sheepishly and Rick suddenly realized what he'd said. "I mean, not *your* grandmother— Richie. Your grandmother—"

"Quit while you're ahead," Georgia told him.

"Right." Rick nodded to the basketball game. "So, you want to go over and watch 'em?"

Richie looked at his mother. "Is that okay, Mom?" They all understood the implication. She wasn't invited. Georgia swallowed back a sense of betrayal.

"For a little while," she said. Rick looked at his watch.

"I've got to go in fifteen minutes anyway, Gee Gee. I've got to get back and see . . ." His voice trailed off. He looked at the boy. "But if everything goes okay, I'll try to come back real soon."

She watched Rick and Richie walk over to the chain-link fence while she stayed behind near the old recreation hut. Long ago, park matrons used to hand out balls and sports equipment to children here, but those days were long gone. Now, the hut was in shambles. Graffiti covered the walls inside, and the back of the building had a giant hole in it that made for easy access to the rail yards beyond. Georgia and Rick used to make out here on summer nights. All the kids did. It seemed like a lifetime ago.

She stamped her feet to keep warm and watched the two of them from a distance. Rick said something and Richie tossed back his head in laughter. They had the same mannerisms, the same slouch when they stood. It was both comforting and frightening that after all this time, the boy and the man had so much in common. Still, she couldn't escape the nagging doubt that she had done something stupid here. She just hoped she wasn't setting her son up for a fall.

It was almost dark when Rick and Richie began to saunter back to her. The basketball game was over. Streetlights that dotted the perimeter of the park flicked on. Traffic thinned. When she squinted past father and son, she noticed a dark blue Chrysler 300 slowly circling the park. As it passed under a streetlight, she saw that its antenna was broken in half—exactly like the FBI undercover car she had used last night. A jolt of panic seized her. If the Feds found her with Rick, her career was over. Yet she couldn't leave. Richie was with him. She waited until the Chrysler made a turn that took it out of viewing range for a moment, then ran over to Rick and her son.

"Richie, honey," said Georgia. "I want you to walk straight home right now. Don't stop for anything. Tell Grandma I'll be home as soon as I can."

"But, Mom!"

"Don't argue. Don't say a word. And don't stop at the car. You're two blocks from home. Go. Right now. That's an order."

The boy gave her an angry look, then cut a pleading one to his father. Rick gave a small shrug. Then Richie stomped off toward home.

"You didn't have to be that rough, you know," said Rick. "You didn't even let me say goodbye."

"Hey, not for nothing, kiddo, but eight years ago you didn't even bother." She glanced over her shoulder. The FBI car had returned. She was sure they were calling for backup. The park would be crawling with agents in a matter of minutes. "The Feds must have tailed me here. They're about to close in."

"Shit. I've got to get out of here," he said. "If I stand Buscanti up, that's it. He'll assume I've turned informant."

"You run out now, my career is ruined. I've just been seen talking to a fugitive."

"What am I supposed to do, Gee Gee? Stand around and make like I've been holding you at gunpoint? They'll shoot me for sure."

A thought came to Georgia. "Remember the hole in the back of the rec hut? It's still there. And it still leads to the rail yards."

He grinned. "Nobody knows those yards like a kid from Woodside."

"But first," said Georgia, "you've got to do something."

"Okay," he said slowly.

"Hit me," she said. "Hard. Across the face."

"What? Are you crazy? I've never hit you in my life."

"If you care at all for my career, you'll do it now. It's the only way I'm going to walk out of this, Rick. You've got to do it. There's no time to lose."

He took a deep breath. "I don't want to."

"Hit me, goddamn it!" she shouted. He closed up his right fist and aimed it at the side of her face. Georgia felt the pain a second or two after impact. It radiated across her cheek and out her eardrums, exploding like a series of fire-crackers going off in her brain. Her legs gave out on her and she landed on the dirt. She wasn't unconscious, but she was dazed. And her left cheek hurt like hell.

Rick knelt down beside her. "I'm sorry, Gee Gee. I don't think I broke anything."

"Get out of here," she moaned at him. He hesitated. She picked up a rock on the ground and threw it at his legs. "Go."

For the second time in eight years, Rick DeAngelo was out of her life. He never left yet without causing her pain. At least this time, she had an outward scar to prove it.

Two cars pulled up within minutes of Rick's departure. Georgia was surprised to see Charles Krause step out of one of them. The yellow streetlights illuminated his shiny shaved head. Scott Nelson and Nathan Reese were with him.

Reese was the first to get to Georgia. He helped her to her feet. She felt woozy when she stood. She put a hand to her left cheek. The skin felt tight and very painful to the touch. It was probably swollen and bruised, but she didn't think there was any permanent damage at least.

"Georgia, are you all right? Which way did DeAngelo go?"

"He ran into that building," said Georgia, gesturing to the cement-block recreation hut about ten feet away. By this time, Nelson and Krause were on hand, their weapons drawn. They went into the hut. Georgia already knew what they'd find, but she feigned surprise when they came out. Krause spoke into his handy talkie.

"Suspect has escaped into the Amtrak rail yard. Alert our people on the other side of the rail yard to be on the lookout for him." Then he clicked off the button and eyed Georgia suspiciously. He knew as well as she did that the rail yard extended for miles. Rick was as good as gone.

"How badly are you hurt?" Krause asked Georgia. His question seemed more probing than sympathetic.

"I think I just need to go home, sir."

Krause eyed her face then asked Reese to find an instant cold pack in the trunk of their car. "Your cheekbone does not appear to be broken. Where is your gun?"

"I still have it."

"But you didn't attempt to defend yourself."

"I didn't expect to run into Rick DeAngelo today," said Georgia. *Not ex-*

actly a lie. "As soon as I saw him, I sent my son home and attempted to talk him into giving himself up."

"Really? And just like that, he hit you?"

"I tried to arrest him."

Reese came running over with a cold pack. She put it on her cheek. The cold felt worse than the punch.

"Where do you think DeAngelo is now?" asked Krause.

"I don't know, sir. Can I call home?"

"Give me your number. An agent will call for you."

"I can make the call myself," said Georgia.

"No hard feelings, Marshal. But I'm, shall we say, *concerned* that you might tip Rick DeAngelo off—inadvertently, of course."

"He's not at my house, if that's what you're implying," said Georgia.

"We checked."

"I'm calling my family," she said, whipping out her cell phone.

"Then you'll do it in my presence," Krause insisted.

Georgia's mother picked up on the second ring. "Ma?" She couldn't get another word out. Margaret Skeehan told Georgia about the men searching for Rick DeAngelo at their house. Thankfully, she didn't mention anything about Richie's meeting with Rick. Then again, maybe Richie, seeing the serious-looking men at their door, had chosen not to say anything. Richie might be only ten, but he probably understood what sort of trouble his father was in. And he probably already felt a desire to protect him.

"Is Richie watching television?" Georgia asked. She didn't care what her son was doing. But she wanted to make sure he was home. Margaret explained that they were just about to sit down to dinner. *He's safe. Thank God.*

"Why would anyone look for Rick DeAngelo here?" Margaret wanted to know. But Georgia cut her off.

"I'll explain later, Ma—okay? I've got to go." She pressed the Disconnect button while Krause studied her profile.

"You didn't tell your mother you met up with Rick DeAngelo the other night?" he asked her.

"No, Agent Krause. I was under confidentiality orders, as I think you may recall."

He nodded. "Yes, confidentiality is very important to the FBI. That's why I'd like to share something with you, Marshal."

Georgia followed Krause to the backseat of his black Ford Explorer. They were alone, the windows shut, sealed off from the commotion of agents on the sidewalk. Krause pulled a small Sony tape recorder from a black leather briefcase and pushed Play.

. . . So a couple of firefighters died—so what? You think this is the first time an accusation like this has been leveled against me? This is Mike McLaughlin you're talking to. Not some street hoodlum. Trust me on this. In a week or two, no one will remember their fuckin' names. They're just a couple of nobodies, any-way. . . .

Krause shut the tape off. "Ever heard this before?"

"Is that Michael McLaughlin?" asked Georgia, hoping to avoid Krause's scrutiny.

"You didn't answer my question."

"You didn't answer mine."

"Don't get smart with me, Marshal. You're in enough trouble already. This tape arrived in the mail yesterday at the home of a retired NYPD detective named Ray Connelly. Do you know who he is?"

"He's the father-in-law of Douglas Hanlon, the firefighter who survived the Café Treize fire," said Georgia.

"Doug Hanlon's father is a personal friend of yours, I believe."

"You don't think *I* sent that tape to Ray Connelly, do you?"

"You stood in your own squad office before the top agents in the Bureau of Fire Investigation and the FBI and threatened to publicize McLaughlin's status to the media. Now a confidential tape shows up in the hands of the father-in-law of one of the victims, and you want me to believe you *didn't* mastermind this?"

"I didn't," said Georgia.

"You've never heard the tape before in your life?"

Georgia closed her eyes. There was no way out of this. She couldn't tell Krause that Nathan Reese had given her a copy of that tape. And she didn't know how it had gotten into Connelly's hands. For all practical purposes, it certainly looked like she had done it.

Krause seemed to read her thoughts. "You've allowed your emotions to intrude one time too many into the FBI's case, I'm afraid, Marshal. Chief Brennan has requested a meeting with the U.S. Attorney at Manhattan base tonight to discuss some charges the FDNY is fixing to make against my people—unfounded charges, I might add. Maybe it's time *your* people found out just how thoroughly you have compromised *our* case. Because as far as I'm concerned, Marshal, your actions leave me no recourse but to keep Mr. McLaughlin under FBI jurisdiction for the forseeable future. The FBI will not be turning him over for state prosecution. Not now. And—as long as I'm head of the New York office—not ever."

40

IT ALWAYS AMUSED Michael McLaughlin the lengths that people and companies went to to ensure the security of their homes and businesses. Video surveillance. Electric fences. Metal and motion detectors. Keyless entry locks.

It made the average Joe on the street feel secure. It pacified the insurance companies and placated the citizenry. But it never kept a determined professional out. Real security, McLaughlin knew, was fairly simple. Three hungry pit bulls and an AK-47 pointed at the door. Every crack dealer in the city knew that. Problem was, real security couldn't take place in the genteel world of corporate boardrooms and legal procedures. Everything else was just a game. And Michael McLaughlin knew that the best way to beat the game was not to play at all. He wouldn't break into his target tonight. He'd walk in.

A bomb threat—called in by one of Coyote's stooges—was all it took to bring out the circus of emergency personnel. When it came to the Green Warriors, nobody in law enforcement took any chances. Within minutes, five fire companies were on hand, along with half a dozen police cruisers. Then a chief in a Chevy Suburban. Then a Haz-

Mat truck, followed by the NYPD's bomb squad and Emergency Services Units. Soon after, a suit from the Office of Emergency Management showed up and another from the Department of Environmental Protection. In New York City, there was no shortage of agencies available for any occasion.

Michael McLaughlin blended perfectly into the throng. He looked like a firefighter—tall, broad, with big hands and an open Irish face. His father's face, before drink took it away. It helped too, that he was wearing a turnout coat and helmet, one of many stolen uniforms he kept in storage over the years.

He walked up to the two-story building behind the gates. The bright lights had a sort of forced cheer at this hour. In fact the whole building looked out of place in New York. Too modern. Too suburban. Too much glass. He missed the days when the neighborhood wasn't quite so yuppified, when hookers and bums warmed themselves over fires in open trash cans. Those were people he understood. Not these radicals he worked for, with their lattes and credit cards and lofty notions of saving the world. McLaughlin knew that about the only thing you could ever save or destroy was yourself, and he'd done plenty of both.

But the New York of McLaughlin's youth was fading. He was forty-five now. A part of him never expected to live that long. So many of his contemporaries hadn't made it past thirty-five, and those who did had ended up old before their time behind cell block walls. He knew he'd been lucky. Smart, and lucky. He'd operated without partners and had kept a fairly low profile as he got older. He never killed—never even raised his hand—except for business. That's what picked off most of his friends: temper and drink. He'd kept an iron grip on both. But the older he got, the more he understood that the game can only be played so long. He had to get out. Even the rackets had changed. All the good cons were Internet-based these days. Credit-card scams. Stock manipulation. Insurance fraud. It was hard to muscle in on operations with no overhead and no labor force. It was hard to shake down an operation that could close up shop and move to El Paso or even overseas in twenty-four hours. McLaughlin felt like a dinosaur in a dying industry.

He lifted a handy talkie to his mouth and began to speak into it as he made his way through the open security gates. No one stopped him or even seemed to notice his presence, not even the two security guards, who appeared to be more interested in discussing pension plans and retirement benefits with a couple of bored firefighters.

He took the first fire stairs he came to. It opened onto a large room in the semi-basement, with two large storage tanks and catwalks above. Everything looked new. Everything looked meticulously clean. Along the catwalk were exposed galvanized steel pipes. He followed the pipes that fed storage tank one and storage tank two until he found the return line that would direct any refill back to the tank outside. Right next to the return line was a large spindle valve. They had big plans for the future here, McLaughlin could see. Though there was no third storage tank, already the firm had inserted a line to accommodate one.

No need to worry about that anymore, he thought with a smile. Two turns of the valve handle with a wrench was all it took to open. There was nothing in the return line right now. There would be.

The fire rigs were still parked at the entrance, their flashers beating out a staccato rhythm on the building as McLaughlin walked to the other end of the facility. There, he buried a small tube of white phosphorous powder and a timing device inside a carton of plastic pellets and computer casings. Pushing the numbers 1-2-3 on a cell phone would activate the device. Coyote's words echoed in McLaughlin's head now: *I don't want any bloodshed, Mike.*

It constantly amazed McLaughlin how squeamish all these radicals were about violence, except in the abstract. And so he'd promised: No bloodshed. He would keep that promise. He wouldn't shed any blood at all. Coyote would do it for him, without even meaning to. It wasn't personal—just good business. He couldn't afford anyone being able to tie him to this operation. And now, there wouldn't be.

41

GEORGIA WAS SHOCKED to walk into the meeting at Manhattan base and see Paul Brophy in the conference room, looking very alive and very uncomfortable in the presence of so many former colleagues who had helped send him to jail.

"You found him," Georgia murmured to Carter when he helped her into a seat. All eyes were on Georgia, with the shiner on her cheek the size of a plum.

"That's one of the reasons we're here," he said softly. "That, and you—your behavior with DeAngelo."

Georgia had thought the Feds were her biggest concern, but looking at the grim expressions on Chief Brennan, Mac Marenko and Carter, she realized that her own people were just as angry with her. It was hard even to look Mac in the eye. She wondered if he felt betrayed on a personal level as well.

A lawyer from the U.S. Attorney's office introduced herself coolly to Georgia as Arlene Steinberg. She was a stern-faced, heavyset woman and she took a seat next to Krause and Nelson. Georgia was placed on the end of the table so everyone had an equal shot at her. Her only potential ally—Nathan Reese—wasn't part of the meeting, having been ordered to wait in the car.

Everybody was trying hard to act professional, but the veneer was paper-thin. The marshals were convinced the Feds had given McLaughlin too long a leash, and he'd used it to commit crimes right under the FBI's nose. The Feds countercharged that Georgia was undermining their case from within— by helping her fugitive ex-boyfriend and publicizing a confidential tape. The Green Warriors didn't even seem to figure into the power struggle anymore. This was personal.

Krause went on the offensive, slamming his tape recorder on the table and replaying the voice of Michael McLaughlin.

"Anyone here care to dispute that your own fire marshal, a woman entrusted with the confidentiality of a Federal investigation, breached it in order to pass along this tape?"

It was a clever tactic, Georgia noted. By keeping the discussion on the tape's dissemination, Krause kept it away from the tape's content. But Carter wasn't going there.

"Are y'all even listening to what that man's saying?" he shot back. "He's practically admitting to the killing of Russo and Fuentes."

"He's admitting to being *accused*, Marshal Carter. That's all. The tape is inadmissible in court. You know that. And Marshal Skeehan knew that when she mailed it to that NYPD detective."

"I didn't mail anything to Ray Connelly," said Georgia.

"Of course. Just like you *didn't* let DeAngelo get away tonight," said Krause. "The point is, security was breached. Our good faith agreement has been broken."

"Good faith?" Marenko snarled. "What good faith? You sent a rookie cop undercover with absolutely no training. And you kept her there after she informed you of a conflict of interest. She almost got killed last night at that diner."

"Diner? What diner?" asked Arlene Steinberg. "I was under the impression that Marshal Skeehan's sole contact with Mr. DeAngelo was at an undercover meeting several nights ago."

Krause fumbled with some papers before him and slid them toward her. "It's all there in my report," he said.

"Do you mean to tell me that Marshal Skeehan made contact with Mr. DeAngelo at a separate meeting that was never authorized by my office?"

"We have the report."

"I don't care what you have now, Agent Krause. Your office appears to have made some mistakes on this case as well. It appears you put a marshal in a situation that was inadequately supervised after she'd already informed you of a conflict of interest."

Arthur Brennan had remained remarkably quiet until now. But at Arlene Steinberg's words, he placed his palms on the table and leaned his girth forward slightly. "I have a more serious charge I'd like to have an answer to, Chuck. Mr. Brophy here says that Jamie Sullivan had a meeting scheduled with your office before he died. Now, I want to know what that was about."

Krause spread his palms. "I know nothing about any meeting."

Brennan looked at Brophy, who shrugged. "That's what Sully told me," said Brophy. "He told me he thought Freezer—that is, McLaughlin—might be under Federal protection. He wanted to find out 'cause me and him, we always felt bad that maybe we made a mistake with the George Skeehan fire." Brophy's voice died out when he mentioned Georgia's father's name. He stared at his hands on the table then shot her a quick, pleading look.

"We didn't know, Georgia. Honest," said Brophy. "I had some problems later as an investigator, but me and Sully—we did the best we could. We didn't know until Cullen Thomas came forward two years ago that maybe Freezer set the fire that killed your father."

Georgia cut a look to Krause. "Is that true? Did McLaughlin set that fire?"

Krause shook his head. "I have nothing—nothing—to indicate that there is any truth to that rumor."

"It's not a rumor," said Brophy. "Sully told me he had an appointment with the FBI."

"Whom did he make the appointment with?" asked Krause.

"I don't know," Brophy admitted. Krause gave him a withering look and returned his gaze to Brennan.

"That's who you're going to listen to, Arthur? A convicted felon who was drummed out of your own department? That's what you brought me in here to discuss?" Krause rose from the table. Nelson rose as well.

"The FBI will notify this department if and when we pursue any litigation against Michael McLaughlin. If the FDNY wishes to have *any* claim against Mr. McLaughlin in the forseeable future, may I heartily suggest that you do your utmost to find and destroy all copies of the tape I played here tonight. Good evening."

Krause snatched up his tape recorder as he and Nelson left, profusely apologizing to Arlene Steinberg on the way out for not keeping her up to date on the investigation. Georgia couldn't help but smile. Even the FBI had asses to kiss. Brennan ordered Carter to take Brophy home. That left Georgia and Marenko. Brennan's benevolent dictatorship ended the moment everyone outside the FDNY had gone. He made that clear by ordering them into Marenko's office, then slamming a fist on the desk the moment Georgia closed the door.

"You," he pointed to Georgia. "The only reason I'm not giving you charges is because I'd have to explain what happened here. And I don't want any of this going beyond this room."

Georgia stared down at her shoes. She debated whether to take her drubbing in silence or make a stab at defending herself. Defense won out, though it had the feel of Custer's last stand. "Chief, I didn't give that tape to Ray Connelly."

"I know you didn't." That stopped her. Georgia bounced a look from Brennan to Marenko. Marenko rose in response and walked out of the room. A moment later, he came back with a sealed envelope that he tossed in front of her.

"There's the tape you handed to Carter." Obviously, Marenko and Brennan had made the decision during the meeting not to let Krause know they still had a copy—not only because it would have been a tacit admission of guilt, but because Krause would almost certainly have taken it. "It's been in an evidence locker since you turned it in."

"That proves I'm not to blame," said Georgia.

"But you *are* to blame," said Brennan. "The moment you opened your mouth in this office last Thursday and *threatened* a leak, you put the entire credibility of the Bureau of Fire Investigation up for grabs. Krause wouldn't even have been *in* here, assuming a breach, if you hadn't given him just cause."

Georgia's insides churned. Brennan was right. She could feel Marenko looking at her, but she made no attempt to make eye contact with him. She knew he was probably angry with her for getting herself into this mess. Marenko seemed to take the hint. He grabbed a stack of envelopes and papers in his "in" box at his desk and began thumbing through them to save her the shame of his scrutiny.

"As for this DeAngelo situation—" Brennan continued.

"Chief," Marenko interrupted, looking up from his papers with a pained expression. "She's hurt, for chrissakes. You can't fault her for getting beat up. The Feds put her in this situation."

"You," Brennan pointed a stubby finger now at Marenko, "are entirely too personally caught up in this to offer an opinion." The chief returned his gaze to Georgia. "Now I want a straight answer from Skeehan. Do you know where Rick DeAngelo is?"

"I know that he went to try to make his peace with Louie Buscanti," said Georgia. "But I don't know where either Rick or Buscanti are right now."

"Did he attack you tonight, Marshal?"

Marenko stopped opening his mail. Georgia could see that he wanted an answer to this one, too, but he kept his eyes on the envelopes before him. It was the only way he could maintain control.

"He hit me because I asked him to," Georgia admitted. "Some agents saw us in a park and I knew my career would be ruined if it looked like I was conspiring with a fugitive. I had to make it look like I'd been attacked."

"And why were you in that park with DeAngelo?"

Georgia cut a look to Marenko. He caught it, then pretended not to.

"He wanted to see my son. *His* son. I know it was a stupid thing to do, but I didn't know if I'd ever see him again." Georgia turned to Marenko. "I just wanted Richie to see his dad."

Georgia expected Brennan to yell at her. Instead, he leaned back in his chair and took a deep breath. He looked exhausted from tonight's encounter. "Both of you, go home. This discussion about DeAngelo never took place—understood? As far as I'm concerned, Skeehan, you were attacked by a fugitive."

"Yessir. Thank you, sir."

42

BRENNAN LEFT and Marenko walked Georgia outside a few minutes later. A light snow was falling, turning to rain as it hit the streets. Tires hissed on the wet pavement.

"You want me to call you a cab?" he asked woodenly.

"Mac, I know you're upset about tonight."

"I'm tired, Scout. I don't want to talk about it right now."

"I think we should."

"All right." He stuck his hands in his pockets. "You put everything on the line tonight for this guy—your job, your son, me. I think you still have feelings for him."

"He's Richie's father, Mac. No matter what else I feel, I can't deny that. Richie really needs a father. You're always telling me you can't be a dad to him."

"And you think this joker can? A man who crawls into your life 'cause he's on the lam?" He shook his head. "I thought you had more common sense. But this . . . I feel like I don't know you anymore."

"I made a mistake. A big mistake." She sighed. "And I'm sorry. Please believe me—it's got nothing to do with how I feel about you."

Marenko looked at her cheek under a streetlight. "I was going to beat the shit out of DeAngelo for what he did. I guess I'd better reconsider."

"I guess you'd better. Thank you for sticking up for me with Brennan tonight."

"You took a hell of a risk, Scout. It seems to me maybe he should've thought of that before he asked to see Richie under the circumstances."

Georgia didn't answer. She knew he was right. She'd spent most of her life taking stupid risks for men. She was hardwired at this point for such things.

"Have Richie and your ma seen you yet? With your shiner?"

"No."

"Maybe they shouldn't until it's gone down a little and you can come up with another reason why you got it," said Marenko.

"I'll tell them you proposed, and I was so shocked I fell down the stairs," said Georgia only half-jokingly.

Marenko rolled his eyes. "I'd be the one falling in that case."

"No, you'd be jumping."

He handed her his cell phone. "Call your ma. Stay at my place tonight. And think up a better line in the morning."

"I'm not very pretty to look at," said Georgia.

"I'll keep the lights low."

Georgia called her mother and assured her she was fine and just needed to stay in the city tonight—with Marenko. She asked if there had been any phone calls this evening for her. Her mother said no. She checked her cell phone. No phone calls on there, either. Marenko saw right away what she was doing.

"No message from DeAngelo, huh?" he asked her.

"You can call him 'Rick,' you know," said Georgia.

"I'd prefer to call him a lot of other things right now," said Marenko. "So you're figuring that if Buscanti doesn't kill him, he'll phone you and let you know what's going on."

"I guess," said Georgia. "He didn't call."

"He didn't call you for eight years. Why break old habits?"

"You think he's a bum, don't you?"

"I think any man who doesn't see his kid for eight years isn't exactly a great guy."

"I never criticize Patsy," Georgia reminded him.

"Patsy didn't abandon our kids for eight years, then show up with a murder rap hanging over her head."

They got into Marenko's car and headed up the West Side to his apartment. Georgia stared out the window. Marenko broke the silence. "Look, Scout, you do what you want with DeAngelo. If I said something I shouldn't have, I'm sorry. I'm only thinking of Richie."

"So am I."

"Then just remember, whatever you say, DeAngelo's number was on Sully's phone pad."

"Because McLaughlin put it there," said Georgia. "To get me into a compromising position on this case."

"It still doesn't add up," said Marenko. "I mean, why would Freezer kill Sully and not Paul Brophy? Two years ago, Broph took a bat to him and Freezer never took it beyond a little street payback with some brass knuckles. Now, all of a sudden, he takes out Sully in this dramatic fire. Why?"

"Maybe Sully had proof McLaughlin was involved in my father's death," said Georgia. "That's why he told Broph he was going to meet with the Feds."

"What proof? The case is nineteen years old," said Marenko. "The only proof was a witness, Cullen Thomas. And he's dead. Freezer killed *him* quick enough."

"How about the D.A.'s office?"

"They don't have any record of Cullen Thomas's interview," said Marenko. "I tried that route. It's gone. Nobody knows where it went."

Georgia's head felt like it was spinning. Her cheek throbbed. *Jamie Sullivan knew something about my father's case—something Cullen Thomas knew. Something Paul Brophy apparently didn't.* Marenko turned off the West Side Drive and into Hell's Kitchen. He slowly cruised the streets for a parking spot while Georgia tried to sort out this discrepancy. She looked across the street. The answer was staring her in the face.

"Stop, Mac."

"You see a parking space?"

"No. Something better. I just figured out what Cullen Thomas and Jamie Sullivan had in common."

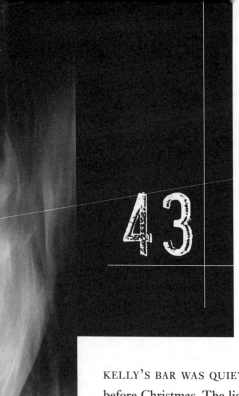

43

KELLY'S BAR WAS QUIET on a Monday night just a couple of weeks before Christmas. The lights glowed meekly from the one small window with a neon Killian's Red beer sign in it. The door looked like it had last been painted in 1963. Georgia wasn't even sure what color it was anymore—brown, rust—it was hard to tell. Marenko looked up at the sign, with a shamrock instead of an apostrophe in the name.

"I live two blocks from here and I've never been inside."

"Whatever you do, don't order the corned beef," Georgia warned.

Marenko frowned. "I don't get it," he said. "*Carter* comes here?"

"He's friends with Roberta Kelly, the owner," said Georgia. "He used to eat lunch here when the old Manhattan base was around the corner."

Marenko opened the door to the bar and Georgia followed him in. The men inside—and they were all men except for Roberta Kelly—looked as weather-beaten as the barstools. They did a double take when they saw them. Marenko might have been able to fit in with the evening crowd, but the bar was clearly a men-only kind of place.

There was very little noise inside the bar once they entered—only the clink of beer mugs and the white noise of a sports announcer discussing a Knicks game on the television. Even the two men playing pool at the beat-up table stopped and regarded them as if they'd walked into a private living room.

"Friendly crowd," muttered Marenko. "And these guys like *Carter?*"

"He probably never came here in the evenings," said Georgia.

"And he always carried his gun," Marenko added.

Bobby Kelly looked up from refilling a beer. As soon as she saw Georgia she slapped the beer down on the bar.

"I got nothing to say to you, love," she told Georgia.

"Mrs. Kelly, we just need to talk to you," said Marenko. "We can do that here. Or you can close down your bar, kick out all your patrons and have the same conversation in our squad room."

Bobby Kelly swung open the door to the kitchen and beckoned them inside. "What is it you want?"

"You know that Freezer set the fire that killed my father," said Georgia. "You told Sully that, didn't you?

Bobby frowned at Georgia. "What happened to your eye?"

"Never mind about my eye. Sully and your brother, Cullen, are dead because they knew something about my father's fire—something Sully's partner, Paul Brophy, doesn't know. What was it, Bobby? Their only connection was you. So if they knew, then you know. What do you know?"

Bobby turned her back to Georgia and bent over the sink. Her shoulders slumped. "I hate him," she managed to choke out. "I paid him and paid him all these years. Nearly went broke doing it. While he and those bastards sat around drinking in my back room."

"You mean Freezer?" asked Marenko.

Bobby palmed her eyes and turned to face them. "Yes, Freezer. And it's my fault Sully and Cullen are dead. It's all my fault."

"You couldn't know Freezer would kill them," said Georgia. "How could you know?"

"I'm the one who told Cullen about your father's fire in Astoria. My brother wasn't there. Lord knows where he was, but he wasn't there. I fed him all that stuff about Freezer. The date. The place. The time."

Georgia felt her limbs grow shaky. "How did *you* know?"

Bobby sneered in the direction of the bar's back room. "Freezer and all his cronies used to sit in there—in *my* bar. After charging me hundreds of dollars of protection money just so he wouldn't burn it down. He boasted about that fire—and other crimes, too. He wanted people to be afraid of him. I couldn't do anything. I had no proof. And besides, he'd have killed me, he would. Probably have burned my bar and made it look like a robbery."

"So you turned Cullen into a witness," said Marenko.

"My brother was in a bad place, he was. He needed information to trade on. And I wanted to get Freezer back for all the terrible things he'd done to me and other good people I knew all them years. It made sense at the time." She took a napkin and wiped her eyes. "I never told Carter it was me that fed Cullen the information. Never told the FBI man who came by after Cullen's death, neither. I was too scared."

"FBI man?" asked Georgia. She cut a look to Marenko.

"Yeah. He said he was FBI, anyway. He didn't much look it. But he showed me some I.D. He asked a few questions and left. I told Sully about it a few days ago when he came in for a pint. That's when I admitted to him that Cullen never saw Freezer set that fire. It was just talk I'd overheard." She dabbed her dirty white apron at her eyes. "Nothing I said was that terrible. Nothing to get a man killed over."

Georgia and Marenko looked at each other. Roberta Kelly was right. Michael McLaughlin had no direct witness to her father's fire. There was no reason for him to kill Jamie Sullivan over that. No reason for him to kill Cullen Thomas, either.

"I'm sorry about your father, love. I am," said Bobby Kelly now. "I'm sorry if I hurt you or brought harm to anyone. I never meant to. I can't even help you now."

Georgia squeezed her arm. "I think you just did."

Outside, the cold air burned their faces. Marenko wrapped an arm around her shoulder as they walked the two blocks to his apartment.

"Are you getting the same strange vibe I am?" asked Marenko.

"Yeah. Freezer had no reason to kill Thomas or Sully," said Georgia. "Yet the FBI was poking around in Thomas's affairs two years ago and it took over Sully's murder investigation now."

"What the hell are they protecting?" asked Marenko.

"Maybe the question is, who the hell are they protecting?" said Georgia. "I figured they took over Sully's case to protect Freezer. But why would they poke around on Cullen Thomas? His death was ruled a suicide."

"I think Sully figured out what was going on. That's why he made that appointment with the Feds. At the very least, he knew they were protecting McLaughlin. But maybe he knew a lot more."

"He didn't tell Paul Brophy," Georgia pointed out.

"Broph wasn't his partner anymore. He had a rep as a dirty cop. And he'd already taken a baseball bat to Freezer. Maybe Sully figured it was better to handle this one on his own."

"I thought Freezer killed Thomas and Sully because they had proof he'd murdered my father," said Georgia. "But they didn't. So what does that mean? That Freezer didn't murder my dad?"

"Maybe. Maybe not," said Marenko. "I'll bet Chuck Krause knows the answer. But the way things are going, no way is he going to tell us."

They stopped off at Marenko's car and he grabbed his clothes, tools and gear from the trunk where he had stashed them when he parked. Georgia carried his empty toolbelt over her shoulder. She liked the smell of the well-worn leather mixed with sawdust and sweat. The street was quiet and treeless. Lights glowed from hallways and flashing strands of Christmas decorations hung in windows.

Marenko's building was a brown-brick six-story walk-up with a fire escape running down the front. It was a hike to his apartment on the top floor. Inside, he didn't have a single Christmas decoration up. Not a tree. Not a wreath. Not a light. Georgia had bought him a little poinsettia, but it had withered and died on the windowsill.

"Scrooge had more Christmas cheer," said Georgia when they got inside.

"Scrooge wasn't divorced with two kids living thirty miles away." He threw his toolbox and work clothes in a heap by the door.

"Why don't you move back to Long Island, Mac," said Georgia. "You're always happier when you're around your family."

He walked into his galley kitchen and opened the door of his refrigerator. He stuck his head inside, as much to avoid her scrutiny as to retrieve a couple of beers. "I don't belong out there anymore," he mumbled.

"Sure you do," said Georgia. "Your parents are there. You're always hanging out with your brothers and their families."

"They're married. I'm not. I'd feel like a fifth wheel."

"That's easy to remedy."

He pulled out two cold green bottles of Heineken like he hadn't heard what she'd said and handed one to her. He clinked his bottle against hers. "Cheers. You want some ice for your face?"

"I don't think it will help—my face or our conversation."

He snapped off the cap on his bottle and gave her a look. "Don't start, Scout. Especially after tonight."

"I'm not pressuring, Mac. I'm just pointing out that you're not really cut out for the single lifestyle."

He tossed off a small laugh. "Thank you, Dr. Westheimer."

"All right. Be that way," said Georgia. "I'm trying to talk to you openly and honestly and you're getting defensive."

"I'm not getting defensive," said Marenko. "And I'm not getting married again. End of conversation."

Georgia put her beer down. "Maybe I should just go. You're tired and irritable tonight."

He straightened and put his own beer down on the counter. He took a step closer to her. Sometimes, she forgot how much bigger he was until he was right on top of her like that. "*I'm* tired and irritable? I'm working two jobs, Scout. I'm trying to give my kids something resembling a normal home life. And I still kept my promise to help Richie build that race car. You think being married to someone's a guarantee they'll be there? Do you think it would have changed your relationship with Rick? He'd still have left. Or just been absent in all the ways that mattered."

"You have a dim view of marriage."

"I have experience. You don't," he countered. "You think not marrying you is the same as abandoning you. I'm here, Scout. Maybe not every time you want me to be. But I'll be here when you need me." He pulled her toward him and snaked a firm hand down her back. He kissed her and she smiled.

"You're still not smoking," she whispered. "I like that."

"We'll see how long I can keep it up."

They made love in the bedroom as a wind rattled at the panes of glass behind the pulled-down shade. They both fell into a deep sleep that lasted until morning. Marenko had forgotten to set an alarm clock. They were awakened instead by the sound of a phone. Her cell phone. She stumbled out of bed and stubbed her toe on a chest of drawers while she rummaged for her bag. From a corner of window beyond the shade, she could make out the tepid light of an early winter morning. The red LED numbers on Marenko's alarm clock read 7:05 a.m. Had they slept any later, they would probably both have been late for work.

Marenko awoke and turned on a lamp beside his bed. Georgia had borrowed one of his flannel shirts to sleep in. It came down almost to her knees. His face was as pale and anxious as hers. They had to get up anyway, but a cell phone call at seven on a Tuesday morning had an aura of urgency about it.

"Yeah?" Georgia mumbled into the phone, expecting her mother calling to ask whether Richie had homework due or what he should have for lunch. Instead, the voice on the phone belonged to a man. It was tentative and hoarse.

"Georgia? I'm sorry to bother you, lass." *Seamus Hanlon.* A cold fist of bile gathered in Georgia's gut.

"What's wrong?"

"He's gone."

"What do you mean, gone?"

"Doug. Kerry said he went out for a run two hours ago and he didn't come home."

"Maybe he just took an extra-long run."

"No. It's more than that, Georgia. Kerry's dad, Ray? His gun is missing."

GEORGIA KNEW RIGHT AWAY where Doug Hanlon had gone: *Michael McLaughlin's house.* The address wouldn't have been that hard to scare up through friends in the police department. Georgia could have put in a call to dispatch and had half a dozen police cruisers at McLaughlin's place within minutes. But that wasn't why Seamus was calling her at seven a.m. and they both knew it.

"Love, please—he's my boy," said Seamus. "Maybe he's distraught. Maybe he needs psychiatric attention. But if you call the police, he'll go to jail—or worse."

"I'm not a hostage negotiator," said Georgia.

"He might not even be there. Maybe you can head him off. Maybe you can talk him out of it before . . ." They both knew what Doug Hanlon intended to do. Georgia wanted to do it herself. "I don't want to lose him now—not after all this," said Seamus.

"I'll try to find him," she said. "But I can't promise. You have to understand that."

Georgia clicked off the phone and turned to Marenko. She told him about Doug and the gun. Marenko let out a string of curses as he jumped into his pants.

"This is all on account of that friggin' tape ending up in the wrong hands. See what happens when you shoot your mouth off? You could be blamed for this, you know."

"I told you I didn't send Hanlon's father-in-law that tape," Georgia insisted.

"Doesn't matter. Brennan's right," said Marenko. "You're to blame for just putting the thought in some moron's head." He reached for his cell phone. "I swear, this thing just keeps feeding on itself."

"What are you doing? You can't call the cops," Georgia argued. "It would devastate Seamus. It would devastate the FDNY. People see firefighters, they think 'hero,' not 'lunatic-with-a-gun.' "

"You want to wait until Hanlon earns that distinction?"

"Can't we just *try* to find him first? I mean, what if he's not gunning for Freezer? What if he's just wandering around *thinking* about it? We'd be creating a publicity nightmare. At least if we find him first, we've got a chance to de-escalate this."

Marenko put down his cell phone and thought about it. Then he walked over to his duty holster, buckled it around his waist and checked his gun. "All right. We'll do it your way," he said finally. "We'll try to find him and stop him before he does something crazy. But you've got to understand, if the shit's already hit the fan, we don't have a choice. Innocent people could get hurt. We can't take the law into our own hands—not even for Doug Hanlon."

"Then let's find him before he gets that far."

It was two blocks to Michael McLaughlin's row house. Georgia and Marenko half-walked, half-ran the entire way. It was the longest two blocks of Georgia's life. They passed small grocers with their cellar hatches open on the sidewalk and newspaper vendors unbundling the morning's papers. Yellow cabs were just beginning to trickle back to the streets in force. At this hour, New York seemed almost like a small town as it flexed its sleep-addled muscles, waiting for the adrenaline to kick in. Georgia's adrenaline, however, was pumping full-force. She comforted herself with the fact that McLaughlin was not an early riser.

"Freezer's house is built like a fortress," Georgia offered up between gasps of air. "Doug will never break in."

"He may have cornered Freezer before he got a chance to get inside."

As they neared McLaughlin's building, they slowed their gait. Nothing looked out of place. His shades, always pulled down in front, looked unruffled. There was no sign of an obvious break-in. They walked across the street to the park. A few dog walkers milled about bundled up against the cold, but there was no sign of Doug. Just east of the Hudson River, along the West Side Drive, cars were inching forward on their commute into the city, but the street itself was quiet. Even the horses in the stables didn't stir, which surprised Georgia a little. Although it was cold—probably too cold to take them out, somebody should have been bustling around their stalls, cleaning them out at this hour.

"What do we do now?" she asked Marenko. They were both breathing heavily from the run, their breath misting in the morning air.

"We wake the bastard up, that's what," said Marenko. "We make sure he's breathing, then try to find Hanlon."

They crossed the street and rang his door buzzer. There was no answer. Marenko banged loudly on the door.

"Open up, McLaughlin. Believe me, you're gonna want to talk to us." Still no answer. Marenko walked down to the garage while Georgia moved to the other side of the building, next to the stables. She heard a quiet grunting and neighing inside. The horses were moving about. And yet, the big door in the center of the stable—once the garage door for the rigs—was closed. She was about to bang on the steel entrance door beside it when a small, grizzled man with a terrified expression ran out.

"He's got a gun!" he shouted breathlessly. "He's going to shoot."

"Who?" asked Georgia. "Who's got a gun?" But she already knew. In that sickening instant, she knew.

"A young man with blond hair. In a sweatsuit. He's going to shoot the man from next door."

45

GEORGIA PULLED OUT her radio and called for backup. She didn't wait for Marenko to join her. She unholstered her weapon, then aimed her foot at the steel door and gave it a swift kick. It swung open and she inched inside. Her nostrils stung with the smell of hay and horse manure.

"Doug?" she called out into the gloom. "It's Georgia Skeehan. Can you hear me?"

The only light trickled in from ancillary paths—through windows on the second floor, down the brick air shaft where the hoses used to be dried, in undefined shadows from the kitchen in back. It mixed with the dust and pollen off the hay until it had the weight of mist.

"Doug," she tried again. "Your dad sent me to find you. He's worried about you. He wants you to stop this and come home. I can take you home."

"I'm not going home," he shouted from inside one of the stalls. Georgia couldn't tell which one. She heard a couple of horses pacing behind their partitions.

Marenko was behind her now, easing his way silently into the doorway, gun in hand.

"Doug—" Georgia began, but Hanlon cut her off. His voice was tight and high, like he'd forgotten how to breathe.

"I've had enough of your bullshit. You lied to me. And you're lying to me now. You think I don't know what's going to happen? I'm going to die. And McLaughlin's gonna die right along with me."

"Let me come out into the open and talk to you," Georgia offered.

Marenko touched her on the arm and shook his head, but Georgia ignored him. "I trust you, Doug. You're your father's son. I know you wouldn't do anything to bring him pain."

She took several deliberate steps across the concrete floor. Marenko followed silently on her heels.

"Is McLaughlin all right?" she called out. She couldn't see either of them. Over the dividers, she could only glimpse the dark manes of the horses. Their eyes looked black and glassy in the diffuse light. She felt their nervous tension vibrate through her skin like a tuning fork. She stepped closer to the stalls. Marenko stayed just to her right, trying to scout the stalls for signs of them.

"Do you think this is what Tony Fuentes would have wanted?" asked Georgia. "For you to waste your life on scum like McLaughlin?"

"I kill him, he'll never kill another firefighter ever again." Hanlon's words rose up from the second to last stall on the right. Georgia walked slowly in that direction. She could feel the hay crunch beneath her feet and smell the sweat off the horses.

"That's not what people will remember," said Georgia. "All anyone will remember is that you took the law into your own hands."

"Fuck the law," yelled Hanlon. "Is the law going to put him in jail for the rest of his life? Is the law going to make sure he never hurts anyone ever again?"

Doug's words were punctuated by the squeal of sirens in the street. Inside the old brick firehouse with its 14-foot, pressed-tin ceilings, the sound had an eerie quality, like drowning cats. They told Doug what he already seemed to know. He was not walking out of this.

"I know what you're feeling," said Georgia. "That's why I'm here. Michael McLaughlin set a fire that killed my father nineteen years ago. I want to kill the sonofabitch as much as you do. But I can't. I'll always be a firefighter—just like you. I can't take a life—even a life as miserable as McLaughlin's."

"Then put your gun in front of the stall where I can see it."

Marenko reached out to stop Georgia, but her mind was made up. If she didn't try to calm Doug down, there was very little chance he'd walk out of here. She felt she owed it to Seamus to try. So she held her breath and gingerly stepped in front of the stall. She placed her weapon at her feet.

The stall was dark. It took a moment for her eyes to adjust. Doug Hanlon was crouched in a far corner of the empty stall with his left arm in a chokehold around McLaughlin. His right hand held a revolver—an old NYPD service weapon—pointed at McLaughlin's temple. At six-feet-three, Hanlon could match McLaughlin in size and weight. And twenty years McLaughlin's junior, he could probably outmuscle the former Westie if he had to. McLaughlin seemed to have calculated the same odds because he made no move to free himself. Yet he didn't appear afraid. Georgia suspected he'd had a gun put to his head many times before. He hadn't weakened then and he wasn't about to now.

Hanlon showed no such calm. Georgia had expected the young firefighter to relax a little when she gave up her gun, but he still seemed agitated.

"Get your partner out of here," he screamed. "Get him out now or I'll start shooting."

Georgia gave Hanlon a startled look. Marenko had made no noise trailing her into the stable. *How could Hanlon have known?* She had her answer when she looked up at a corner of the tin ceiling.

"You've got to leave, Mac," Georgia said as calmly as she could. "Doug can see you from a security mirror."

"I'm not leaving you in here alone," said Marenko.

"If he doesn't leave, I'll start shooting," Hanlon screamed. "I swear I will."

"Go, Mac. I'll be all right." She could see him in the security mirror, hesitating. "Please."

Marenko realized he had no choice. He retreated to the street. McLaughlin actually seemed to be enjoying the spectacle. "I see I'm not the only one this young punk got the drop on," he said calmly.

"Shut up," said Georgia. "I'm not interested in your bullshit. It's Doug I care about."

She thought her words might move Hanlon. But he had a cold, blank stare as he regarded Georgia. He made no move to harm her, but he didn't look like he cared much whether she lived or died, either. Though it was cool in the stables, he was sweating heavily. But he had a sure grip on the gun. She'd forgotten he'd been in the military. He was no stranger to weapons. He was capable of firing, and firing under pressure if he had to. Outside, she could hear police cars setting up. None of them was going to be able to walk out of here like nothing happened.

"You said you always wanted to be like your father," said Georgia. "But this isn't him. He wouldn't kill a man like this. You pull that trigger, you'll destroy him, too."

"It's too late," said Hanlon.

"No, it's not. There are people who can help you."

Hanlon tightened his chokehold on McLaughlin. He wasn't ready to give up.

"You want to kill me?" McLaughlin growled at Hanlon. "Kill me then. Get it over with."

"No, Doug," Georgia pleaded. "This isn't the way."

"Kill me," said McLaughlin again. "Go ahead, kill me, you stupid dumbass firefighter. You think you know everything about me? You don't know shit. And neither does the chick. Not about what I've done. Not about what I haven't done. Kill me and you'll see—dozens of people will die very soon."

Hanlon shoved the gun harder into the side of McLaughlin's skull. McLaughlin gritted his teeth, but his eyes stayed riveted on Georgia. He looked strangely calm. "Coyote," McLaughlin muttered. "I spoke to Coyote. I know what the Green Warriors are planning."

Hanlon looked confused. Georgia could read it in his eyes. The first signs of hesitation. The weakening of his resolve. McLaughlin, too, seemed to sense that chink in Hanlon's armor. He'd found a foothold and had begun to climb. "The Green Warriors are going to strike soon. I know the details. You kill me, you'll kill all those people."

"What's he talking about?" Hanlon demanded.

"Some very dangerous people," Georgia explained. "A lot of lives could be in danger. I don't want to take that risk. Do you?"

"He's lying," Hanlon insisted.

"I don't know," said Georgia. "But I know that if you kill him, we'll never know."

Hanlon swallowed. Georgia saw his Adam's apple bobbing in his throat. His eyes were bloodshot, his skin pale. He looked drawn, like he hadn't eaten or slept in days.

"I give up, it's like . . . it's like running all over again," Hanlon said softly.

"No. It's not. It's like saving dozens of innocent lives."

Hanlon stumbled to his feet and dragged McLaughlin into a standing position. Now, Georgia had a new worry. She sensed that Doug was beginning to waver, but that meant McLaughlin could sense it, too. A minute's hesitation could be all McLaughlin needed to turn the tables on both of them. She had to stay in control of the situation.

"Put the gun down, Doug," said Georgia firmly. "Put it down now and we can walk out of here."

"How do you know he's telling the truth?" asked Hanlon.

Georgia looked at Michael McLaughlin's calm, almost calculating expression. It hurt to look at him. He seemed so ordinary—so much like firemen she had known. The same broad build. The same lightly freckled face and strong chin. Her father had humped hoses and lifted beers with men like him.

"Several dozen people," McLaughlin said icily, "balanced against the lives of two firefighters."

"And my father," said Georgia.

"And if you're wrong?" McLaughlin asked her.

"I'm not wrong."

"Then kill me yourself, lass. Take the gun away from this loser and kill me yourself. If I was facing the man who murdered my father, that's what *I'd* do. Or are you too much of a coward?"

Georgia could see Hanlon's finger on the trigger. She saw the hatred in his eyes. And the pain. He wanted everything to end. He believed it would if he pulled the trigger. For a brief moment, Georgia could feel herself believing it, too. Her father deserved retribution. And so did Russo and Fuentes.

"Kill me," said McLaughlin again. He was playing head games with both of them now, gambling on who might crack first.

"Give me the gun," Georgia begged Hanlon. "It's just like being in a fire. You can't give in to your impulses. The enemy isn't outside you. It's inside. It's panic and desperation."

Hanlon loosened his grip for an instant. In a flash, McLaughlin was out of the chokehold. He lunged for Hanlon's gun, but instead of grabbing it, he only succeeded in causing it to fall from the firefighter's hands. Georgia dove for the weapon and her own. As she grabbed them, she heard a dull thud, followed by a release of air. When she got to her feet with both weapons, she saw that Hanlon had leveled a hard punch to McLaughlin's gut, which landed him directly into a pile of horse manure. He wasn't badly hurt. It was nearly impossible to seriously injure an old Westie like McLaughlin. But the fall into manure had stunned him just long enough for the police to enter the stable.

Hanlon stood against the opposite partition, rubbing his sore knuckles, waiting for the inevitable. He was going to be taken away in handcuffs. He knew that. But that didn't seem to be what was troubling him.

"I lost my nerve," he said softly, keeping his eyes on his swelling right hand. "I should've shot him."

Georgia shook her head. "No, Doug. You found it. Over time, you will realize that. Sometimes the hardest thing in the world to do is nothing."

"Is what you said about your father true?" he mumbled.

"I think so," said Georgia. "I'll never really know."

"Tell my family I'm sorry."

"You'll be able to tell them yourself," said Georgia, trying to sound more upbeat than she felt.

Police officers flooded into the stable. Marenko was with them. When he found her, his face seemed to flood with relief.

"That was a pretty stupid thing to do," he scolded her. "Are you okay?" She told him she was.

"Is Krause here?" asked Georgia.

"Outside. With Nelson and Reese. You want me to send him in?"

"Yeah. I've got to speak to him right away." She put a hand on his arm. "Mac? Can you stay with Doug for me? I may not be able to and I want someone with him I trust—"

"I won't leave his side."

"Thanks."

Marenko tracked down Krause while Georgia found McLaughlin in the firehouse bathroom, trying to scrape horse manure off his pleated silk pants.

"You finally look like the piece of shit you are," said Georgia. "Where's Coyote?"

McLaughlin regarded her in the mirror above the sink. His eyes were two cold little moss-covered rocks. "Ah, you'd like to know that, wouldn't you?"

"Listen, asshole. There are four dozen more men at Ladder Seventeen and Engine Twelve who'd like nothing better than to blow your fucking brains out. You think this is over? Wake up, Freezer. You're not a secret anymore. I don't have to keep my mouth shut about what you've done—to Russo and Fuentes, or to my father."

"You think you know about that, do you?"

"You killed him," she growled.

"I know how he died," said McLaughlin. His eyes sparkled like broken glass. He was enjoying her torment. "He died choking for air. Twenty minutes in that basement. Imagine, twenty minutes straining for a breath."

"You sonofabitch!" She went to slap him across the face, but he grabbed her hand before she could make contact.

"Ah-ah-ah, love. I wouldn't do that, for three reasons," said McLaughlin.

"First, because if you hit me, I'll hit back before any of these cops can come to your aid. And I can make that shiner look like a love pat by comparison. Second"—he forced her hand down—"because you need me to tell you about Coyote." McLaughlin squinted off into the middle distance. Georgia turned. Charles Krause was walking toward them now, with Scott Nelson by his side and Nathan Reese trailing behind.

"What's the third?" Georgia muttered.

"The third is, you are dead wrong about what happened to your father."

He held her gaze a moment. Georgia turned away, chilled by what she had seen—or rather, what she hadn't seen. His gray-green eyes were a void— blank and of unknown depth, like a stagnant pond. She couldn't read him. She had no idea whether he was telling the truth. And most chilling of all, she sensed he didn't care. To Michael McLaughlin, evil was as appropriate as any other course of action. He took no pride in its doing or not doing. It was all the same to him. Georgia was thankful to have somewhere else to turn her attention.

"McLaughlin knows who Coyote is," Georgia told Krause. "He said the Green Warriors are going to strike soon and dozens of civilians are at risk."

Krause looked at McLaughlin. "Is that true, Mike?"

McLaughlin shrugged. He didn't care.

Krause tried again. "If there's a Green Warrior hit and people die, the FBI can no longer protect you as an informant—do you understand? You want to retire on that nice bank account you keep offshore? The assets are frozen, Mike. And we can keep them that way until hell pretty much becomes the same temperature."

"Don't threaten me, my friend," said McLaughlin. "I'm holding all the cards here. More than you realize. Now, I can give you Coyote and tell you exactly where and when the Green Warriors are planning to hit. I can stop dozens of people from dying—make you all look like heroes."

"In return for what?" asked Krause.

"I retire. *With* my money. And, with a walk on the Café Treize fire."

"No," Georgia shouted. She turned to Krause. "Please don't do this, sir.

There must be some other way. Don't bargain away the lives of Russo and Fuentes like this."

"What's it gonna be?" asked McLaughlin. "The lives of two firefighters? Or the lives of dozens of civilians?"

"I'm sorry, Marshal," said Krause. "I have to consider the bigger picture." He turned to McLaughlin. "You've got your deal."

McLaughlin nodded. "The Green Warriors have sabotaged the Dalcor plant. When it goes on-line for a test run this morning, there will be a fireball inside."

Nobody had to be told the implications. The Dalcor plant opening was a major photo op for business and political leaders. The mayor would surely make an appearance. So would the city council president, several well-known community activists and plenty of press. But Krause looked personally pained by the news.

"My daughter," he choked out. "She's photographing the event. She's supposed to be there."

"Of course she's there," said McLaughlin with a slow smile. "In the Manolo Blahnik boots I bought her—to replace the ones Marshal Skeehan ruined. She's Coyote."

46

MCLAUGHLIN'S WORDS hadn't fully dawned yet on Charles Krause. But they had registered on Scott Nelson.

"We're toast," Nelson said to Reese. He was right, Georgia knew. Everyone in the New York office would be transferred and punished after a fiasco like this. And Krause would be ruined—in one fell swoop, he'd lose his daughter and his career. For at least three years, the Feds had thought they'd cultivated an inside line on the militant underbelly of the Green Warriors. And all along, it had been the other way around. McLaughlin was in bed—literally—with the enemy. And the enemy was closer than any of them had imagined.

Krause whipped out his cell phone. "This is bullshit, I'm calling my daughter."

"No," said Georgia, grabbing the phone away from him. "She can't be alerted. We don't know what she'll do." Georgia called over a police captain. "Please keep Mr. McLaughlin and Special Agent Krause under your close supervision. They cannot make any phone calls." Then she got on her handy talkie to Marenko. "Is Chief Brennan here?"

"Out front," said Marenko.

"Tell him we need units at the Dalcor plant, ASAP. We've got to stop the plant from going on-line—and evacuate everyone assembled. I'm coming out to explain."

As Georgia walked down the length of the stalls, Nathan Reese hustled over. He looked overwhelmed and confused. His boss and organization were going under, and there was nothing he could do to stop it.

"I want to help," he said to Georgia.

"Not now," she told him. She had no time for niceties.

"But I can help you," he insisted. "Most plants these days are run by computer. I *know* computers."

"Speak to my chief," she said. "If he says it's okay, it's okay by me."

Outside, the block was closed off to traffic. Dozens of emergency vehicles were clustered around the perimeter of the building. And it was all going to have to move about thirty blocks south. Georgia found Brennan. He looked ready for retirement after the last twenty-four hours. For the first time Georgia could ever recall, his shoes lacked their gleaming spit-polish shine, and his tie looked hastily knotted, with the result that his two chins became three.

"McLaughlin's full of shit," he said by way of greeting. "Once again, we've been had."

"What do you mean?" asked Georgia.

"The plant went on-line ten minutes ahead of schedule—at eight-fifty-one a.m. It's operating without a hitch. Everyone is being evacuated as a precaution. But the engineers and plant officials say it's a hoax. The mayor's embarrassed. And believe me, Skeehan, the mayor doesn't like to be embarrassed. Our next budget comes up, you better believe he's gonna remember this."

"How about Krause's daughter, Lauren?"

"No one can find her."

"She wasn't there?"

"She signed in, but since the evacuation announcement, no one's been able to find her. The PD's got cars out patrolling for her and waiting at her apartment in case she shows."

"It's possible McLaughlin made the whole thing up," said Reese. Brennan frowned at Reese like he was a homeless person trying to bum a cigarette.

"Who asked you?"

"You've met Agent Reese," Georgia reminded Brennan. "He's a computer expert for the FBI. He offered to check out the plant's computers and see if anything has been sabotaged inside the operating system."

"I'm sure the engineers are already doing that."

"It can't hurt to get another opinion," said Georgia.

Georgia could see Brennan wanted to argue, but he also wanted to get over to the plant and try to placate the mayor. He nodded to his Crown Victoria with a fire marshal at the wheel. "Get in. I'll decide what's necessary when we get there."

The marshal flipped the light bar and siren and sped thirty blocks south to the plant. Already, HazMat trucks and police cruisers were jockeying for space beside the limousines of important city officials, who could neither leave the site nor enter the building. If the mayor and his aides left, it might imply they didn't think the plant was safe. If they stayed, they were forced to huddle in groups or sit in their limos with no real time frame as to when they'd get to go back inside.

Georgia and Reese followed Brennan to a tight knot of men in hard hats and silk suits. Dalcor's senior management. The hard hats were all for show. They were being interrogated by operations chiefs in the FDNY and NYPD. A paunchy man wearing a hard hat was standing in the middle with some sort of intricate map of the plant spread out on the hood of a police cruiser. His thick, snowy eyebrows were knitted together behind black horn-rimmed glasses. He seemed bewildered and annoyed by the circus of emergency personnel before him.

"The plant went on-line at eight fifty-one this morning," the man explained. "It was operational for twenty-one minutes before we received the order to shut it down. There were no problems. The bomb squad has been through every inch of this facility and has been unable to locate any devices or abnormalities. If there was going to be a problem, it would have happened by now."

"Has everyone been evacuated?" asked Brennan.

"Yes," said the man with the snow-white eyebrows. "We evacuated them through the rear exit of the plant, as per our standard operating procedure."

Georgia focused on the glass-block building now. The whole plant was like a giant display window. Everything was visible. There was a front lobby area that appeared to be sealed off from the manufacturing portion of the plant. The manufacturing portion had two large emergency exit doors in front, immediately off the driveway, and an emergency exit in back, at the end of a long glass corridor with panoramic views of the Hudson River. There were a couple of forklifts and payloaders positioned along the driveway as well. They looked hastily parked, as if the construction workers had been here this morning, then evacuated with all the other civilian personnel. Like all construction jobs in New York City, the Dalcor plant was probably behind schedule.

"Why did you evacuate from the rear exit?" asked Georgia.

"That was the nearest exit," the man explained. "We were hosting our breakfast reception along the corridor. There's a viewing platform there, so people can see the storage tanks in the basement. We didn't want our guests walking through the manufacturing portion of the plant if there was a bomb."

"And you keep those doors open?"

"Once they've been activated, they can only be closed electronically from the main switchboard."

A stiff breeze blew off the Hudson River. Georgia turned up the collar of her coat. But it was more than the wind giving her a chill. She shoved her hands into her coat pockets and cursed softly. Nothing about the plant seemed out of the ordinary. Nothing. *Is this another one of McLaughlin's games?* she wondered. If so, then he'd succeeded brilliantly. He'd gotten himself out of a jam and helped further the Green Warriors' cause in the process. He could easily claim he was duped by the Green Warriors too. Georgia pictured him sitting down in some nice warm police station, quietly amused at the ruckus he'd created. She gritted her teeth. *Score another point for Freezer.*

THE MAN WITH the white eyebrows and the black-rimmed glasses was a Dalcor engineer. Georgia knew it the moment he began talking about applied flux and damping coefficients to the group of officials gathered at the front of the building. He agreed to take them on a tour of the plant's control room, in a sealed-off area overlooking the manufacturing floor, to demonstrate how efficiently the plant operated.

The room looked like the sound booth of a recording studio. It was filled with computers, gauges and digital equipment that meant nothing to Georgia. While Reese grilled the engineer, Georgia wandered about the room. The only window offered a view of conveyor belts stopped in midproduction and plastics cooling in injection molds. She recalled they were making computer casings.

She walked over to a stainless steel panel with three black dials on it. The needles on the first two dials were steady; the third was spinning erratically. Above the dial, a nameplate read *Storage Tank #3*.

"Where's storage tank number three?" asked Georgia. The engineer looked up from his conversation with Reese and the chiefs.

"There is no storage tank number three."

"But there's a dial for it here."

The engineer tilted his black-rimmed glasses and gave her a patronizing look beneath his snowy eyebrows. "There are two storage tanks inside the facility, Marshal. Butadiene from the holding tank outside the building is pumped into two storage tanks in the basement. Storage tank number three is merely a designation for a tank that Dalcor will build if it expands the plant."

"Oh."

The engineer went to return to his conversation, but Georgia again interrupted.

"If there's no storage tank three, wouldn't the dial read zero?"

"It would. And it does."

"Then why is it spinning?"

"Huh?" The engineer walked over and frowned at the gauge. "That's ridiculous. The entire plant's been shut down. We don't even have a third tank. There's no way we can have a . . ." His voice trailed off.

"A what?" asked Georgia.

The man didn't answer. He tapped some buttons on a keyboard. The basement storage tanks flashed on a grainy security monitor. None of them needed an engineering degree to see what the problem was. The return line that was supposed to direct overflow back to the holding tank outside had a valve on it—probably in anticipation of Dalcor eventually fitting it with a third storage tank. The valve was open and butadiene was pouring out of it and collecting in a depression on the basement's concrete floor.

"I thought you said the bomb squad went through this facility?" said Brennan.

"They did," said the engineer. "But it would've taken at least twenty minutes for the first two tanks to reach capacity. The return line is only for overflow."

Immediately, the engineer and the other officials from Dalcor began trying to redirect the flow of butadiene away from the return line. Brennan could see they were just in the way. He ushered Georgia and Reese out of the control room and into the driveway. There was nothing any of them could do until the leak was under control. Georgia walked the length of the driveway down to the pier. Reese followed.

"So much for my engineering knowledge." He shrugged. "A simple leak and I couldn't even pick it up."

"I don't know if it's such a simple leak," said Georgia.

Reese kicked at a loose piece of gravel and turned his face to the stiff breeze coming off the water. "Georgia, I'm really sorry about what happened to Doug Hanlon. I feel like it's all my fault. If I hadn't given you that tape . . ."

"You did nothing wrong," Georgia assured him. "Somebody else decided to take the law into their own hands. It's not your fault."

"I don't want to see any more firefighters die," he said wearily. "It seems like no matter how much good you try to do, it can never make up for the bad."

Georgia gave him a quizzical look. He seemed to want to tell her something, but in the end, he just reached into his coat pocket and pressed an envelope into her hand.

"What's this?" asked Georgia.

"The Café Treize tape," said Reese. "I had to break a few rules to get it, but I don't think Krause is in a position to string me up anymore. I want you to have it."

"Thanks," said Georgia, stuffing the tape into her bag. Suddenly, a bright white flash caught their eyes. Georgia and Reese turned toward the building. Inside, beside one of the conveyor belts, they could see a woman on fire. Her hair was in flames. Her skin was blackening and her right arm had been blown off at the elbow. Georgia thought all the civilians had been evacuated. Then she saw the remnants of a camera splayed out across a conveyor belt. She didn't need to see more to know that the figure was Lauren Krause.

Georgia heard voices over her handy talkie ordering companies to stretch hose lines and take the doors. One of them was Chief Broward, calling Ladder Seventeen to open the front emergency doors of the plant and evacuate the badly burned woman, while Engine Twelve hooked up the hose.

Georgia stood at the back of the building watching the woman writhe in agony. She was no longer on fire, but a box of computer casings was. The flames were consuming the cardboard and heating up the plastic. Noxious black smoke began to mushroom from the box and darken the windows. Even if the woman didn't die from her burns, she most certainly would die now from the smoke. Georgia watched the blaze with a sense of disbelief. Lauren Krause didn't seem like the kind of person who would blow herself up in a political protest. Had the bomb backfired? But McLaughlin was the Green Warriors' torch. Wouldn't he have rigged it? Surely he knew how to take down this whole building if he wanted to. But here was a small fire that had destroyed nothing except Lauren Krause and a few computer casings.

Maybe that was his intention, Georgia decided. After all, if McLaughlin really did want to get out of this racket, he wasn't the kind of man to leave loose ends. And Lauren Krause, his secret lover, was definitely a loose end. Still, the fire seemed nowhere near as deadly as the one that McLaughlin had promised.

A fireball. He'd called it a fireball. She had seen a fireball in Jamie Sullivan's apartment. She could still picture that long, narrow hallway and that persistent rush of air.

Georgia studied the open exit doors at the back end of the building. Air was rushing through them off the river, passing a viewing platform in the corridor. At the base of the viewing platform were the storage tanks—and the spill of butadiene. The entire mixture of air and petroleum fuel was being sucked in and funneled toward the small fire in the manufacturing end of the plant—the same area where firefighters were set to break down the emergency doors to put out the fire and rescue Lauren Krause. Georgia froze in realization of what was to come. By breaking the doors, firefighters would be unleashing a monster chain reaction of fuel, air and heat. And it would all be heading straight for them, just as it had for Jamie Sullivan.

"It's the same scenario," Georgia muttered. "It's the same goddamned scenario."

"What is?" asked Reese.

"Do you know about something called the Venturi effect?"

"Yeah, sure. It's a basic physics principle." He stared at the building for a moment, then caught her drift. "Shit. You think it's going to happen here?"

"I've got to stop Ladder Seventeen from taking those doors." Georgia got on her handy talkie to Brennan. "Chief. It's Skeehan. You've got to speak to Chief Broward. Tell him his men can't take those front doors. If they do, the fire will explode on them." Georgia started to explain, but Brennan cut her off.

"Are you kidding, Skeehan? You want me to tell a man with thirty years in fire operations that a rookie marshal is overriding his judgment? Stay out of this. It's not your call." Brennan clicked off.

"Can we close the back doors?" asked Reese.

"Negative," said Georgia. "They're mechanically activated. If the chiefs won't listen to me, then I've got to warn the men." As a fire marshal, she had no direct handy talkie contact with firefighters. The only way she could warn them was to physically put herself in front of them. She ran up the driveway to the front of the building, jumping over hose lines and past barricades to get to the men of Ladder Seventeen. Jack O'Dwyer was the first firefighter she saw. He was carrying a halligan, and when he spotted her, his expression turned grim. Obviously, Chief Brennan had already warned Broward and the men that Georgia might cause trouble.

"Get out of the way, girlie," growled O'Dwyer. "We've got a job to do. I'm old school and I don't want to hurt a woman, but if I have to physically push you aside, I will."

"Jack, listen to me, please. You open that door, there's gonna be a fireball behind it. I know what I'm talking about."

"We have our orders. Now be a good girl and get out of the way."

The younger men in Ladder Seventeen threw themselves behind O'Dwyer while the lieutenant radioed the chief about the situation.

"Skeehan," O'Dwyer pleaded, then cursed under his breath. "Broward will give you charges when he finds out about this. Hell, he'll give *me* charges for not moving you. Come on. Don't do this to me. I'm looking to retire next year."

He went to put his hand on the door. Georgia opened her mouth to argue, but she was stopped by a rumble of engine noise at the end of the driveway by the pier. She turned to see Nathan Reese in the driver's seat of a small payloader. The construction workers, in their haste to evacuate, had left the keys in their equipment. Reese was trying to shift the payloader into gear. It was making a terrible grinding noise and jerking back and forth. Georgia had no idea what he was doing. And then it suddenly dawned on her: he was going to try to ram the payloader into the glass corridor and vent the vapors.

"Nathan, you can't," Georgia screamed. "The payloader runs on diesel."

Reese gave her a knowing look. He seemed fully aware of what he was doing. He also seemed fully aware that it came down to a simple choice: him or the firefighters at the front doors. He pulled back on a hand lever and once again tried to get the rig in gear.

"I told you," he yelled back at her. "No more dead firefighters."

His words were drowned out by the sound of the drive train coming to life. The payloader began chugging straight for the corridor. There were a few stunned seconds before everyone else realized what the short, slight man in the spectacles was trying to do. Then the glass groaned and shifted like ice on a lake. It turned white and became shot through with crazed lines. But it didn't break. Reese stepped hard on the gas and switched into a lower, more powerful gear. Georgia had a sense that he understood what would happen to the man who broke the glass. *No more dead firefighters.*

She heard a buckle, then a crash as pellets of glass tumbled into the corridor. A hole the size of a car door opened in the hallway. Georgia smelled an overpowering fuel odor. For a second, nothing happened. But it was only a pause. A moment later, Georgia heard a whoosh of air push out of the building. As soon as it met up with the payloader, the colorless current of vapors exploded into a ball of orange flames. It flew across the payloader, instantly setting it alight along with Nathan Reese. Georgia watched the young FBI agent in horror as the flames engulfed him, driven by the force of the wind and the buildup of butadiene inside the building. Maybe it was an involuntary muscle contraction caused by the intense heat, but she swore she saw him turn to her and try to speak.

"Holy shit," said Jack O'Dwyer. "That dumb bastard." He and the other firefighters began running toward Reese. Engine Twelve scrambled over with the hose line.

It took less than a minute for the engine to douse the flames. As intense as it was, the fireball had flared out quickly once the leaked butadiene had burned off. But there was nothing pretty about the corpse left in its wake. Reese's body was black and hairless, his clothes reduced to charred tatters. The frames of his wire glasses had oxidized to a brownish red and the lenses were opaque with oil. But he had saved the firefighters. That, Georgia was sure of. When they opened the front doors to the plant, there was no fireball to greet them anymore. There was no one to save, either. Lauren Krause had died—before or after Nathan Reese, no one could be sure. As intense as the smoke was inside the plant, the engine was able to douse the flames within a matter of minutes. There was very little destruction.

Afterward, Jack O'Dwyer stumbled over to Georgia, clearly shaken. He took off his helmet and made the sign of the cross as technicians from the medical examiner's office took Reese's body away. "Bravest sonofabitch I've ever seen," he muttered hoarsely. "I don't even know his name, and he just saved my life and the lives of four other firefighters. He's a civilian, for crying out loud. Why did he do that?"

"I don't know," said Georgia. "I wish I'd known him well enough to answer that."

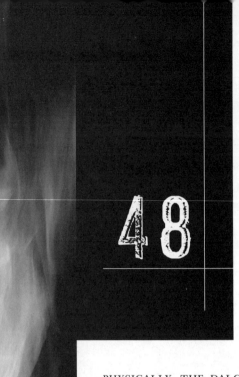

48

PHYSICALLY, THE DALCOR PLANT suffered only minimal damage. There was the usual destruction caused by smoke and water and the breakage of glass. Some of the conveyor equipment and wiring would have to be junked. But these were cosmetic rather than structural repairs, easily fixable within a matter of weeks. The death toll, which could have numbered several dozen, had been reduced to just two: Nathan Reese and Lauren Krause.

It was the psychological toll, Georgia suspected, that would be more difficult to repair. Although the butadiene leak had, thankfully, been small, Dalcor wouldn't easily be able to gloss over the fact that things could've been worse. Much, much worse. It would take months for officials from the EPA and the city's Department of Environmental Protection to come to any conclusions. Yet already, Georgia sensed civic leaders backing away from support of the plant. The Green Warriors had won the battle, thought Georgia. But perhaps they'd lost the war. Mainstream environmentalists were quick to distance themselves from the Green Warriors' philosophy and tactics. Money was bound to dry up after this. What might have been called "revolutionary" in the sixties was now called simply "terrorism." And nobody likes a terrorist.

It was early afternoon before Georgia was finished giving statements to the police, the EPA and her own guys at Manhattan base. Fire Marshal Sal Giordano offered Georgia a ride back to Lafayette Street. She accepted. She followed him and his partner through the police barricade and past a crowd of spectators and reporters. That's when she saw him. He was leaning on one of the barricades. He had the collar of his flannel-lined denim jacket up and his Yankees baseball cap pulled low across his face. He'd shaved. And changed clothes—not an easy feat for a man on the run. Then again, maybe he wasn't on the run anymore.

"On second thought," said Georgia to Giordano, "I may be a while. I'll meet you back at base."

She felt a small bubble of anticipation inside of her as she maneuvered through the crowd to meet him. She told herself she was just happy he was alive. But she knew it was more than that.

"Hiya, Gee Gee." His eyes traveled to the purple blotch on her cheek. "How's the face?"

"You hit me pretty hard."

"You asked me to, remember?"

"I don't believe it," said Georgia. "You're alive."

"I can't tell from your voice," said Rick. "Is that good or bad?"

"You could've called."

"Worried about me?"

Georgia let the question slide. "What happened with Buscanti?"

"I told him I was set up. I have no interest in playing informant. I'd like to live a long life. It didn't take long for him to realize I was telling the truth."

"Just like that? You told him and he believed you?"

"Sicilian handshake. Word of honor, all that shit. We're both Italian—believe me, that stuff counts. Besides, he knows I don't know enough to be of much use to the Feds anyway. And we both agreed we should keep it that way."

"Then it's over?"

"For me, it is. But not for Michael McLaughlin. Buscanti's very, very angry with McLaughlin for setting him up. I think you know what 'very, very angry' means in his circles."

"Does McLaughlin know this?"

"Not yet. But he will. Very soon." Rick squinted out across the Hudson. "I guess, being a cop and all, you'll have to tell your people and the FBI about the threat to McLaughlin's life."

"You *want* me to?"

"Absolutely. First thing tomorrow morning." Rick looked at his watch. "I mean, it's already almost three p.m. You're going home soon, right? It's been a tough day. *Tomorrow* would be a very good time to tell your chief."

Georgia and Rick locked eyes. She knew what he was saying. "I have a duty to uphold the law," she reminded him.

"The law didn't happen here, Gee Gee. You know that. The law, if it had worked at all, would've put McLaughlin in jail a long time ago for keeps. Cut everybody a break. Cut yourself one. Go home. Put the paperwork in tomorrow."

"That doesn't bother you?"

"You're asking the wrong guy."

"This isn't the way it's supposed to work."

"And if you handle this by the book, and two years from now, someone else dies, what good did you do?"

"I'll think about it," said Georgia.

"Sleep on it," said Rick. "You'll feel better in the morning."

"So what happens now?"

Rick shrugged. "I'm going back to my life in Toms River to try and get out of debt. If the Feds want to talk to me about the Green Warriors or Jamie Sullivan, they're welcome to. I don't know anything. I didn't do anything—that is, unless you want to charge me with assault?"

He was teasing, Georgia knew. But it irked her that he seemed so casual about all that had happened.

"And just like that, you go back to your life? After making a mess of mine?"

"You're not in trouble with the fire department, are you? I mean, that's why you asked me to hit you—so you wouldn't get in trouble."

"I wasn't talking professionally," said Georgia.

"You mean Richie? Gee Gee, I *want* to see Richie. The ball's in your court. Just tell me what you want me to do."

"That depends."

"On what?"

"On whether you're serious about being a part of his life. You can't float in and out of it at will, Rick."

"I'll do my best."

"That's what I'm afraid of." He gave her a hurt look, so she added, "Check back with me in a few days, okay? We'll try to work something out."

"No sweat." He leaned over and gave her a kiss on the cheek. "I'll call you." He began to walk away.

"You've said that before," she yelled after him, but he didn't seem to hear. He never turned back. Eight years had come and gone, and she still had that same pang watching him walk out of her life, not knowing if he'd ever walk back in.

She stood frozen to that spot on the sidewalk for a long time, oblivious to the spectators around her, to the official cars and rigs moving into and out of position. Finally, she forced her legs to walk in the direction of the subway. It was already after three. A light snow had begun to fall. At Fourteenth Street, she could catch the A train down to Spring Street, then walk the short distance to Manhattan base. Then again, she could catch the Uptown E train and just go home—leave Michael McLaughlin to the fate he deserved.

She walked east to Eighth Avenue. Crowds of shoppers lined the sidewalks, all of them, it seemed, carrying big bags filled with brightly wrapped packages. Sidewalk Santas in cheap red felt suits rang bells for the Salvation Army. In a clothing store's display window, miniature trains chugged through fake snow, and stuffed bears mechanically waved and smiled. Georgia stared into a window of a café with boughs of evergreens strung with white lights. Joe Russo and Tony Fuentes would never see this Christmas. Doug Hanlon might spend it in jail. Rachel Cross's family had known more than a dozen Christmases without her. And all those images paled against a deeper wound—the nineteen Christmases without her father.

"Dad, what do I do?" she whispered as the crowd of shoppers pressed in all around her. She tried to picture her father's face, his voice. But she couldn't. Sometimes that panicked her most of all. He'd become like a deer in the woods to her. When she least expected it, a fleeting image of him would flood her senses—the untamed, curly reddish-brown hair, the rugged good looks, the mischievous grin, the way he whistled—so loud and clear, you felt as if you'd be able hear him in Jersey. Always, he'd be in motion—throwing a ball, welding a pipe, grabbing his helmet and turnout gear. She had to stay very still to feel him, for if she moved, he would vanish. And she couldn't chase him or summon him back, no matter how hard she tried.

She reached in her bag for the brass key chain he'd given her shortly before he died—with his badge number replicated on a Maltese cross. She rubbed it like a talisman, hoping to conjure him now. She wanted to hear his voice. But nothing came. Only the honk of gridlocked cars and endless tinkle of Salvation Army bells. He wasn't here. This was one decision she'd have to make on her own.

At Fourteenth Street and Eighth Avenue, she took the stairs down to the subway. She ran her Metrocard through the turnstile. It was a big station. She could take the E to Queens and be roughly in the vicinity of home. She could take the A to Manhattan base. Her stomach churned. The minutes ticked by slowly. It was now three-thirty p.m. The FBI wasn't like the FDNY. They didn't work twenty-four-hour shifts. In another few hours, Scott Nelson and the others would be checking out for the day. Anything that happened after that would require a lot more effort.

She forced herself to remember the photographs of a disfigured Rachel Cross. She relived Joe Russo's wake and Tony Fuentes' funeral. She added

Nathan Reese's brave and selfless act to the list of deaths. *I'm not killing Michael McLaughlin if I wait until the morning*, she told herself. *I'm just not helping him live.* But the argument rang hollow. She knew what she was doing. When the E train came, she didn't get on. Instead, she walked down one flight to the A and took it downtown.

Randy Carter was at his desk in the squad room when she got to base. He seemed startled to see her. He rose.

"You okay?" he asked. "Giordano said you'd gone home. I was going to call you later."

"Any word from Mac about Doug?"

Carter nodded. "He's been transferred to a private hospital."

"The charges were dropped?"

"The D.A. has already declined to prosecute so long as the fire department gets him psychiatric help. If Doug gets his act together, the judge hinted that the department could reinstate him as early as next June."

"How's Seamus?" Georgia asked.

"A mess," said Carter. "But he's glad his son is alive and that he didn't kill anybody."

"Doug helped save a lot of lives today."

"Marenko told him that," said Carter. "It hasn't registered yet, but I think it will in time."

Georgia propped herself on the edge of her partner's desk. Unlike everyone else's at base, Carter's desk was meticulously neat. Papers were always bound in folders, the desk surface was visible and it was never sticky. "I need to talk to you about something," she said. "Privately."

Carter paled. He looked down at his hands. "I think I know what this is about."

"You do?"

He nodded. "Let's take a walk."

The snow had thickened by the time they got to the street, darkening the sky a little early—even for December. Carter walked briskly. Georgia sensed he had something he wanted to say. He didn't speak, however, until they had traveled north and west about ten minutes into Washington Square Park. The fountain was off, and the square was quiet this time of year. His voice sounded ragged when he finally broke the silence.

"My whole career—thirty-one years—I never once took the law into my own hands," he began. "I did everything by the book, girl. Everything. But— this is one time I couldn't." He turned to her. "I'm really sorry, Skeehan. I didn't know it would turn out this way."

Georgia stopped in her tracks and looked at him. "Randy, what are you talking about?"

"Marenko told you, didn't he?"

"I haven't spoken to him since this morning."

"I'm the one who sent that tape to Hanlon's father-in-law," said Carter. "I've already made a full confession to Chief Brennan and offered my resignation."

"What?" Georgia felt as if she'd just dived off the high board and someone had informed her there was no water in the pool.

"Michael McLaughlin's a cancer, girl. You can't just cover a cancer or take a few aspirin and hope it will go away. You've got to cut it out. I couldn't see any alternative."

"Then take charges, Randy. But don't resign. Why the hell would you resign?"

"Because it's the right thing to do. I breached my duties as a law enforcement officer. I put a lot of people's lives in danger today."

"You didn't know Hanlon would go off the deep end."

"I should have anticipated this," Carter admitted. "But I didn't. I figured Ray Connelly was a smart guy. He'd never let Doug hear that tape. He'd give it to his cronies in the PD. Once enough people in law enforcement heard it, the Feds would be forced to act."

Carter dusted off the snow on a park bench and sat down. He leaned his arms on his thighs and stared at his gloved hands. "Maybe the FDNY couldn't get Freezer. But for sure, the PD could take a shot at him. I couldn't let him get away. Not again. Not after what he did to all those innocent people." He shook his head. "Not after what he did to your *father*."

Georgia paced the walk in front of him. "So you're going to quit now—is that it? Run away?" She spoke the words like each had to be chiseled from a brand-new piece of stone. There was no template for anything like this in their relationship.

"I'm not running away," he bristled. "I'm taking my punishment like a man. I wanted to say something last night. But I couldn't in front of the Feds," he explained. "I would've embarrassed the department and basically admitted that you'd given me the tape, which would've hurt you more than helped you. That's why I didn't come forward then. But I accepted full responsibility for it to Brennan today."

"No, you haven't," said Georgia.

Carter gave her a confused look.

"You want to accept full responsibility? Then take charges, Randy. Apologize to Seamus and Doug and Ray Connelly. Let Brennan curse you out. But don't hand me this horseshit about quitting."

"It's the right thing to do."

"Fine." She threw up her hands. "You want to quit? Then quit. I came back to base this afternoon because I have a problem, and I needed help from the person I trust most on this job. I learned everything I know about being a marshal from him. Even when he makes a mistake, he makes it for the right reasons. But I can see that that man isn't here anymore. So I'm leaving."

Carter slumped further on the bench without answering.

"Freezer won, by the way," said Georgia.

He looked up at her. "What do you mean?"

"You told me yourself, he's a patient man. He wins by wearing down the opposition, finding the chink in his enemy's armor and burrowing in. Well, he beat you, Randy. He beat *us*. Because you're quitting, and the way I feel right now about a decision I've got to make, I'll probably end up quitting, too."

That got his attention. He straightened. "What's going on?"

Georgia told him about her conversation with Rick DeAngelo. "If I do nothing, there's a good chance Louie Buscanti will kill Freezer tonight."

Carter brightened for a moment, then his face clouded over as he worked through the implications. "You figure if you let Buscanti do the deed, then you'll end up feeling like I do—that you're no better than the criminals—is that it?"

"That's about the gist," said Georgia. "But telling's no good, either," she reasoned. "The Feds will put Freezer in the witness protection program. He'll get a new name, a new state, and a new chance to kill."

Carter rubbed his eyes and rose from the bench. They were both getting cold. "I was going to walk you over to Ladder Seventeen tonight," he admitted. "It just seemed like the right place to tell you. Now, I don't know where to go or what to do."

"I know what you can't do," said Georgia. "You can't quit. I need you on this."

"I don't have any answers," he said. "The only choice I made was to make that tape public. And it was the wrong one."

Georgia suddenly remembered the tape Nathan Reese gave her this morning. It was still in her handbag. She pulled it out and showed it to him.

"Before Reese died today, he gave me this. It's a copy of the Glickstein tape."

Carter's eyes widened. "I thought that was gone."

"I think Reese basically had to steal it off Krause to get it."

"That still won't do us any good," said Carter. "Look at all the trouble I got the department in making that other tape public."

"Maybe the problem was," said Georgia, "we didn't make it public enough." She turned to him. "You've got a lot of good contacts in the district attorney's office. Have you told any of them about the tape?"

"Negative," he said. "I didn't want to get anyone in trouble. That's why I sent it to Connelly, He could honestly say he didn't know who gave him the tape."

"What if you called a couple of your contacts in the D.A.'s office now and told them how the Feds and the U. S. Attorney have been playing fast and loose with McLaughlin?"

He shrugged. "They'd be ticked off. But not enough to go head-to-head with the Feds over it. McLaughlin would still probably end up under someone's protection."

"Would he? If the press knew what he'd done? If *The New York Times* and the *Post* and the *Daily News* heard the Glickstein tape, too? Wouldn't the political pressure on the D.A.'s office be overwhelming?"

"Everyone would know we did it," Carter argued.

"Knowing and proving are two different things, Randy. If Freezer taught me anything, he taught me that. Reese was an FBI agent and he gave me the tape, fair and square. There's no breach of security on our part by showing it to the D.A. As for the press, well, who's to say how a copy of it ended up in some reporter's hands?"

Carter nodded. He could see the logic. And the irony of it as well: Freezer might survive. But he'd be ruined by a chink in his own armor. He loved to show off, whether it was his John Constable oil painting, his lemon yellow Porsche, his affair with an FBI agent's daughter, or his ability to kill and get away with it. Now, his bragging would be his undoing.

"I got a friend in the D.A.'s organized crime unit," said Carter. "This would be right up his alley." Carter pulled out his cell phone. Georgia put a hand over his.

"You can't take this step and then quit, you know," she told him. "We're going to catch heat on this—maybe for months. You leave and—"

"I'll stay, girl," he promised her. "I'll take the charges and stay." He smiled. "I want to be in that courtroom as a marshal when Michael McLaughlin goes down."

49

MICHAEL MCLAUGHLIN WAS INDICTED on two counts of first-degree arson and two counts of felony murder in the deaths of Captain Joseph Russo and firefighter Tony Fuentes. That was all anyone could get him on, but it was enough.

The Feds, embarrassed by Krause's feckless policing of both his family and his informants, distanced themselves from McLaughlin. In court, he wore two-thousand-dollar Brioni suits, handpainted silk ties and a steady smirk, but it didn't sway public opinion. Daily, he was raked across the newspaper headlines as a thug who killed firefighters. Even the other inmates at Riker's, where he was being held without bail, treated him with contempt. Georgia had a sense he wasn't going to weasel out of prison this time. He must have begun to feel the same way, for as December wore on, she noticed that the smirk became less pronounced and he'd developed a noticeable twitch in his right eye.

Brennan knew Georgia and Carter were behind what had happened, but after the mayor praised the FDNY for its "excellent police work" in building a case against McLaughlin, even Brennan recognized that shining a spotlight on the leak would have been counterproductive. Neither Georgia nor Carter received any administrative charges.

"I had a feeling you'd do something like this," said Rick DeAngelo right after McLaughlin's arrest. He called her up one evening. She feigned ignorance.

"Come on, Gee Gee, I *know* you tipped off the press. And it's okay. That's just the way you are. You can't stay sore at people. Not even me."

"Want to bet?"

"Does that mean I can't come up and see Richie?"

"I'll get back to you," said Georgia. If Rick knew her, then she also knew him. His intentions were in the right place. Follow-through was another matter. "He'll visit Richie once," Margaret grumbled when she heard about Rick's request. "Once and never again." Her mother felt the entire visit would set Richie up for disappointment. Marenko, surprisingly, felt just the opposite.

"Now that he's out of trouble, I think the boy should see him."

"But what if my mother's right?"

"I think Richie needs to find that out for himself," said Marenko. "And I think you need to separate *your* anger from Richie's need to know his dad."

And so Rick came up the following Sunday. He and Richie went out for pizza. When Richie returned, he informed his mother that he'd invited Rick to take him to the Scouts' race-car derby the following Friday night. Behind the child's back, Margaret mouthed the word "Once." Georgia hoped her mother was wrong.

Doug Hanlon got out of the hospital a week before Christmas. The fire department assigned him to a desk job, which he hated, for the next six months. But Seamus was assured that if Doug showed himself to be psychologically fit, he could go back to full duty after that. Before Tony Fuentes' death, Tony had been building a bunk bed for his two oldest daughters. Doug vowed to finish the bed by Christmas. Seamus said that working on that bed had done more to restore Doug than anything else since the fire.

The men at Ladder Seventeen and Engine Twelve were eternally grateful to Nathan Reese for his selfless act that spared their lives. They asked Georgia to find out his parents' address. She got the address—in Bakersfield, California—from Scott Nelson. The firefighters wrote the parents a letter and sent FDNY T-shirts and an honorary helmet as a thank you. They received no reply. Georgia also sent a letter and got no reply. She wondered if the family was too grief-stricken to respond. At first, she thought about letting it go. But she had a phone number as well as an address. So one night she called. Nathan's sister answered. Her voice, initially so kind, took on a stiff tone when she heard Georgia's name.

"I'm sorry," said the woman. "My family appreciates your letter and the firefighters' tokens of appreciation. But they would rather you not contact them again."

Georgia was confused. "Did I say something wrong?"

"No, of course not," said the woman. "But . . . your father's death was a very upsetting chapter in their lives."

Georgia paused. She had no idea what the woman was talking about.

"You *are* George Skeehan's daughter, aren't you?" asked the woman.

"Yes, but how do you . . . ?"

"My brother told you, didn't he?"

"Told me what?"

"My family had a convenience store in Astoria, Queens, nineteen years ago," said the woman. "Nathan was just a little boy at the time. It was a terrible, terrible accident. He didn't mean any harm."

Georgia's heart felt like it had stopped beating. "Rysovsky," she murmured. "His name was Nathan Rysovsky,"

"My parents chose to Americanize it after they made a fresh start in California."

"But that fire . . ." Georgia stammered, ". . . my father's fire . . . a man named McLaughlin set it—not Nathan."

"My brother set the fire," said the woman. "I *saw* him do it. That man— he took money from my parents, yes. But he didn't set the fire. It was my brother. He was playing with matches. He didn't mean to burn anything. And it changed him forever. He was never the same. After that, he locked himself in his room all the time. Computers became his life. I don't think he ever lived down the guilt."

Reese's words echoed in Georgia's head: *No more dead firefighters.*

"We are very sorry for your loss," the sister continued. "Please understand that it is too painful for my family to say more."

"Thank you," said Georgia woodenly. The woman hung up the phone. She saw the words on Sully's phone pad now: *R @ 10:30 a.m.* She had thought McLaughlin had written those words. She had thought "R" was Rick. Maybe the "R" was for someone else—someone who knew about Rick DeAngelo and had scribbled his number on top of the note to throw off the trail.

THE NEXT DAY, on the Friday afternoon before Christmas, Georgia paid a visit to Riker's Island. Michael McLaughlin didn't seem the least surprised to see her. He seated himself on the other side of a Plexiglas partition and picked up the phone.

"I bet I know why you're here," he mumbled into the receiver. "And it's not to wish me Merry Christmas, either." The Irish lilt was gone. His voice had a sandpaper edge to it, despite his attempts at humor.

"Did you?" Georgia asked. They both knew what the question referred to. There was no need to elaborate.

"What makes you think I'd tell you if I did?"

She stared straight at him. "Because I saved your miserable life and you know it."

He tossed off a small laugh, but he couldn't hide the twitch in his eye. "You can't pin it on me, you know. There's no one who'll back up the story."

"I'm not looking for backup. This is you and me, Mike," said Georgia. "You can cop to it or not. Like you say, they can't pin it on you. And besides, you're going down for two murders, anyway. One way or another, this won't change things."

He stared at her, a slightly bemused expression on his face, but he didn't answer.

"Look," said Georgia. "When Doug Hanlon was holding a gun to your head that day in the stable, you said you didn't do it. Was that fear talking? Or was that the truth?"

"You won't believe me, whatever I say."

"Try me."

"I know who did it, and it wasn't me."

"It was Nathan Reese, wasn't it?"

He locked eyes with her from the other side of the glass. He said nothing, but he didn't need to. His expression said it all.

"Which means," said Georgia. "That you had no reason to kill Cullen Thomas. Or Jamie Sullivan. Neither of them could pin my father's murder on you."

McLaughlin still didn't answer. Georgia felt her stomach tighten. The implications began to fall into place. She wanted to close her eyes to them, but she couldn't. McLaughlin had boasted about a fire he'd never set—probably to score points with his underworld friends. Roberta Kelly had overheard the boast, believed it, and fed the information to her brother, Cullen, who regurgitated it to the D.A. in exchange for a lenient sentence on an unrelated assault charge. She could see the logic in that. Still, something didn't make sense.

"Nathan Reese was a six-year-old boy when he set that fire," said Georgia. "It was an accident—a mistake—just as Brophy and Sullivan originally stated in their report. Yet Cullen Thomas and Jamie Sullivan are dead."

"I got nothing to do with that," said McLaughlin.

"But you do," said Georgia. It was starting to fall into place. "You *knew* Nathan Reese was Rysovsky. You found out the same way Cullen Thomas found out. Once Cullen fingered you to Carter, the D.A. started looking into my father's death. And Rysovsky's name came up. You and Cullen both knew that if the FBI found out that Nathan Reese had set that fire, they'd dismiss him. It wouldn't matter that he'd only been a little kid at the time. A firefighter had died. So Cullen Thomas tried to blackmail Reese. But it backfired."

"Reese pushed Thomas out a window," said McLaughlin. "I had nothing to do with it. Knowing Reese, it was probably another stupid mistake."

"Perhaps," said Georgia. "But you knew you had Reese by the *cojones* after that, didn't you? You figured you could blackmail him for the rest of his life— if not for my father's death, then for Cullen Thomas's murder. Then when I started asking around about Brophy's assault on you, Jamie Sullivan started doing a little digging and found out about Nathan Reese. That's who he had the appointment with at the FBI: Reese. Nathan knew he couldn't get out of this without admitting he'd killed Cullen Thomas, so he killed Sully and set the fire to make it look like you did it—to get you off his back. And he scribbled Rick's phone number on Sully's notepad to get *me* off the case."

McLaughlin said nothing for a long moment. Then he smiled one of his blank-eyed smiles. "You see, lass? There are no sinners and saints. We're all one and the same. Good intentions, bad intentions—they don't mean shit in the end."

Georgia pressed a knuckle to her forehead. She didn't want to accept that. It was easier to accept that Freezer had murdered her father than to accept that all this violence stemmed from the desperation of an otherwise ordinary man. "At least Nathan Reese saved some people at the end of his life—at a fire I know you set," Georgia shot back. "Who have you ever saved, huh?"

"Myself," said McLaughlin with a shrug. "That's all we ever save, lass— ourselves. The rest is an illusion."

"I hope you rot in prison," said Georgia.

"It's not over yet," said McLaughlin. But the confidence was gone from his voice. As Georgia got up to leave, she saw his eye twitch and the smirk disappear as he was led away. She had a sense that even Michael McLaughlin knew it was, indeed, over.

And yet his words haunted her as she drove back over the Hazen Street causeway from Riker's Island into Queens. She had hoped that putting

Michael McLaughlin away would help her make peace with some of the anger and heartache over the loss of her father. She wanted closure. But in the end, there had been none. Nathan Reese had made a horrible childhood mistake that haunted him for the rest of his life and cost the lives of two other men. He was not a bad man, but he had done some bad things. McLaughlin, Georgia realized, was at least partly right. Life was never clean and simple. It was always a negotiation between the best and worst impulses inside us. She had to learn to accept that—in Nathan Reese, in Rick DeAngelo and in herself. She had to move on.

For a brief moment, as she pondered this, she had the sense that her father was sitting beside her in the car. She swore she could smell his Old Spice aftershave and hear the tune he always whistled. The lyrics came back to her now. It was an old song from a group called The Flying Machine. It was popular when her parents first met, around 1969: "Smile a little smile for me, Rosemarie." Marie was her middle name. She always loved when he whistled it.

It was getting dark by the time Georgia arrived back home. Tonight was Richie's race-car derby. Georgia searched the block for the beat-up Ford Econoline van Rick had driven up in a week and a half ago. It had his name and business on the side. It would be easy to spot. But she didn't see it.

Her stomach began a slow somersault. She wondered if her mother would greet her with an "I-told-you-so." She worried that Richie would be in tears. Instead, she heard commotion from the kitchen when she opened the front door. Richie was in his Cub Scout uniform, putting the final touches on his race car. Margaret was pouring soda. And someone else was in the kitchen as well. Georgia walked in to find Marenko seated at the kitchen table, wolfing down a chicken sandwich her mother had made for him. He was wearing a white shirt that he'd unbuttoned at the neck. A striped tie had been discarded on the table beside him. He looked like he'd just come from work. Georgia gave the three of them a puzzled look.

"Where's Rick?" she asked.

"Car trouble," said Margaret, tossing out the words in that disgusted tone that suggested the only thing wrong with Rick's car was the man driving it.

"He's driving up tomorrow," said Richie with a shrug. He didn't seem too disappointed. Georgia had Marenko to thank for that and she gave him a grateful look.

"I thought you couldn't take him," she said. "I thought you had to work."

"I asked Rudy to cover for me for a few hours," said Marenko. Rudy Hoaglund was another supervising fire marshal at Manhattan base. "I'll pay him back Sunday night by coming in early." He chucked Richie on the shoulder. "We'll just have to make this short and sweet, right, Sport? 'Cause I gotta go right back to work when this is over."

"I'm ready," said the boy.

"You're not upset?" Georgia asked Richie.

He shook his head. "I'll see him tomorrow."

Georgia stared at her son with fascination. He seemed able to accept the men in his life on their own terms. If a ten-year-old could manage that feat, then Georgia had to start trying to do the same. For Richie's sake, she had to let go of her anger and bitterness at Rick. She had to forgive, forget and move on.

"Thank you," Georgia told Marenko. She gave him and Richie each a kiss as they headed out the door. "I can't tell you what this means to him— and to me."

"It's no big deal." Marenko shrugged.

"Maybe," said Georgia. "But it's the 'no big deals' that count."